A Time After the Apocalypse

Aaron Bennett

Published by Aaron Bennett, 2022.

A TIME AFTER THE APOCALYPSE

First edition. August 21, 2022.

Copyright © 2022 Aaron Bennett.

ISBN: 979-8218061227

Written by Aaron Bennett.

PROLOGUE

Seen from afar in the cold, silent vacuum of space, the planet could almost have been slumbering peacefully as it turned calmly in the void. High in geostationary orbit above the deceptively placid blue-green orb, a massive artificial satellite floated serenely. The station's central mass formed a thick disc, flattened at both ends and extending a number of comparably stubby spokes along its circumference. Encircling the five mild wide satellite, and completely dwarfing it, was an array of solar power collectors sufficient to power an entire word. These collectors were not providing energy to the homes and cities they cast a country size shadow upon, instead their purpose was to power something far more vital to the planet.

The central power relay station was active, performing its imperative function with hard planned efficiency, gathering solar radiation into colossal capacitors before shunting it onward. huge green energy beams ten feet in diameter projected from the blunt spokes, lancing arrow straight to smaller relay satellites chaining together into a loose net of power lines around the planet. At the last satellite in each relay chain, narrower energy beams were directed downward to the planet surface, supplying the monumental power required at the transition sites.

Simultaneously, a fleet of spacecraft far grander than any attempted in this world's history, or possibly that of any single planet, protectively surrounded the sphere. Incredible though the fleet already was, more ships rose from the surface to join the peerless force currently in orbit. Imposing capital ships, some as much as a mile in length, were interspersed amid a vast host of one and two man fighter and bomber craft as numerous as snowflakes in a blizzard. Many of the larger ships were of a simple utilitarian design, more giant crate than sleek aerospace vessel. A simplicity of form accounted for by the frenzied rush to mass produce them. Some of the smaller craft, by necessity of the requirement of atmospheric reentry, were of a smoother, more appealing shape due to aerodynamic considerations carriers. Command ships, and other big extra-planetary vessels, were boxy and less aesthetically appealing than the fighters.

A shuttlecraft broke away from one of the big command ships, a tiny spot of light speeding toward nearest relay satellite before following its energy beam down. Descending into the atmosphere on glowing heat shields, the shuttle reached the beam's terminus in moments, a enormous cube of solid green energy. Military personnel and vehicles covered the ground around the transition site, looking not unlike a busy anthill when viewed from above. As at every critical site on the surface, troops were in place and ready for the invasion. As ready as they could be.

Far from any of the transition sites, military posts, or population centers, and nestled securely in a small valley within a somewhat remote mountain range near the eastern seaboard of a major country, stood a modest cutting edge military complex. EMF Invasion Command was alive with activity, both biological and electronic. Personnel inside the base walked or jogged everywhere, making reports and checking systems to verify that all functionality was optimal. No one wanted to be responsible for a mistake that could lose the coming engagement.

Inside the command center the atmosphere was thick with anxiety, and tense with anticipation. If the enemy delayed only a little longer, transition would be accomplished, and the XRs would fail even should the EMF lose the fight. Technicians at their stations called out reports almost too quickly for any single person to follow.

"Squadron eighty-two has reached position in orbit:"

"Platoons twenty through twenty-six ready to defend population zone B-four."

"Orbital defense platforms read green on all systems."

"Fleet Com reports ready to engage."

Sitting ramrod straight and resolute in the command chain centered on the rear wall was EMF chief military officer general John F. Samson. A dignified man with slate gray hair and a sharp gaze, the sixty-three year old career army officer had served with distinction in the previous intercontinental war, a conflict that ended three decades ago. When it came time for the OWG to select a man to lead the invasion defense, Samson was approved with minimal grumbling from the politicians.

"Are the Omegas in position?" Samson asked in his carefully cultivated baritone. The reply was crisp and instantaneous. Only the best the EMF had to offer were posted here.

"Yes sir. All Omega corps troops here reached designated deployment areas."

Despite his precisely regulated outward appearance of calm strength, Samson was as anxious as any green recruit. *Has it already been a year since we discovered the XR fleet*? He thought remembering the events of these twelve turbulent months. This time last year, the world's foremost scientific mind, a man known by most as the Professor, had informed the world's governments that a tremendous force of extra-terrestrial robots was soon to invade. The Professor had decrypted communications signals intercepted by a deep space listening probe. Once decoded and understood, the enemy force was concluded to be comprised entirely of intelligent machines later designated Xeno Robots or XRs. The intercepted messages spoke of an invasion of our world, with the intent of taking from us the recently created transfer technology, and the related pinpoint data. No reason for this was communicated

When the veracity of the intercepts was officially confirmed and accepted, a deplorably slow and tedious process involving useless bureaucrats in endless debates, the date that the invasion would be launched was determined to be less than a year away. Nations across the planet sprang into action, forming the One World Government, and establishing the EMF virtually overnight. It was impressive how quickly everyone came together to get things done. Nothing like an impending apocalypse to unite people behind a common banner. Samson was brought in practically on day one to oversee the manufacture of weapons, and the training of troops, formulating and coordinating defenses on a global scale. Much of the world's economy was redirected to building and training a military force that could counter the XR threat, resources and manpower were volunteered with surprising selflessness in most cases.

There were inevitably those who tried to profit from the situation, but it took few examples of confiscating everything a person owned under the wartime powers act and placing then in a combat unit, to dissuade most forms of outright profiteering. And now, a year after the first warning, the invaders were expected to arrive within the hour. The problem was, that no one, not even the Professor, know exactly when it would kick off. Would transition complete in time?

"Time to transition?" Samson asked, mostly to give himself something to do, the number was displayed prominently on one of his screens.

"Thirty-four minutes sir."

"Contact the temporal lab, ask the Professor if the last, package is away."

In a sterile lab below the command center, the pace was more measured, if no less anxious. The technicians and scientists present in the computer saturated space, checked and reviewed every figure and calculation, determined to get each number perfect to the last decimal. If a mistake was made now, there was no time left for second chances. There were no more packages to send, no backups available. Even if there were, it was too late to send another, it took too long to generate the transference field. If someone messed up and a package ended up at the wrong coordinates they would never find out. The technology had been outlawed decades before and was now devoid of any means to monitor an arrival.

Dominating the entire front wall of the room, was a large machine of recent manufacture, and plain of appearance. Its core was an enclosed cube of a compartment six feet across covered by a transparent door, and it was the undeniable center of attention for all present. Strong technicians placed a vibrantly colored capsule five feet in height into the compartment, positioning it exactingly in the precise center of the space, before closing the door to seal it inside.

At a control panel on the left side of the compartment, a technician was entering commands under the watchful eyes of an elderly man in a ubiquitous white lab coat. The man was thin of build and average in stature, his white hair frazzled in a way that said he did not care enough to properly tame it. His eyes, however, were clear, and focused intensely on the task at hand, his posture stooped and head bent to the screen.

A voice from the intercom disrupted the proceedings, and unwelcome intrusion into their critical work. "Command room to temporal lab. General Samson requests status of final package."

Pressing a button on the intercom, the elderly man responded, not masking the irritation in his voice. "This is the Professor. The final package in the chamber and will be delivered in seven minutes." It was closer to six minutes and forty seconds, but he was aware that too much precision only served to annoy military types.

"Thank you Professor, command out."

He watched as the last instructions were entered and confirmed, not missing a digit during the interruption. He was pleased by the proficiency of the technicians. At his nod the system was engaged. The compartment began a resonant hum and vibration with the final buildup of the transference field, the interior glowing brightly and arcing with blue-white electricity. The light flickered rapidly in a now familiar pattern, and the capsule slowly faded to vanish a minute later. With this final delivery complete, the Professor quietly removed a data card from the panel, and covertly dropped it into a pocket. Entering a last command into the terminal, one that no one would detect, he slipped silently from the room. The lab technicians were too busy celebrating their success to notice his departure, which he was immensely glad of, having no interest in long farewells for people he would never are again.

An alarm sounded in the command center, and red lights flashed on walls and consoles, temporarily interrupting the endless litany of reports and announcements.

One technician was quick to recognize the alert's meaning. "Sensors show a massive disruption in space at the edge of far orbit. Something is exiting fold space, a lot of something."

"I want a full tactical analysis of the enemy fleet the second they enter real space. Relay the data to all EMF commands." Ordered Samson with a calm he did not feel. "All initial combat elements are to proceed to intercept positions, and engage the XR fleet when in range."

The spatial distortion, was an area far larger than the planet itself. Light bent and rippled strangely across the vast field reentry point, as if a pebble the size of a moon was tossed into the galaxy's biggest pond. When the fold event's visual anomalies faded, the XR fleet came plainly into view. Some of the XR ships were truly gargantuan in scale, dwarfing even the largest EMF ships. Astoundingly, the XR fleet with its thousands of ships was composed almost entirely of capital class vessels. This led some among the EMF defenders, to mistakenly wonder if the fight would be easier than they had anticipated. Moments later those fleeting hopes were dashed, as the XR carriers began to disgorge innumerable fighter craft and dropships.

The intercept forces and XR fleet raced to meet each other, neither side wasting a moment to start the engagement. The opposing fleets opened fire on one another at the earliest opportunity, pinpoints of red and green light spearing out in search of targets. The neat, orderly pre-battle formations broke apart in a ballet of interwoven chaos, ships maneuvering to avoid the deadly lightshow. Many ships dodged past the incoming laser fire, primarily the smaller, more agile fighter craft. Others were not so fortunate, disappearing in unceremonious clouds of debris. A barrage of intense bursts from an XR battle ship, pounded into the hull of an EMF destroyer, until it exploded in a brilliant flash of light when its missile stones were compromised.

Comm chatter filled the cockpits, and bridges of EMF craft, their pilots and captains struggling to gain a tactical advantage over the closest enemy vessels.

Alpha squadron leader barked terse orders to his pilots. "Alpha two, move up to cover delta four. Alpha six, you have an XF on your four o'clock low. Alpha three, stay on my wing."

On the bridge of EMF command ship Event Horizon, admiral Victor Horace studied his tactical screens, deploying ships to counter the XR fleet maneuvers in his sector. "Bring up fighter attack wings, one, five, and eight to combat enemy force in grid C-six. Send green squadron to concentrate on keeping those XFs off of the Dakota."

One man EMF fighter Blue-four, who's pilot had already taken out six XFs, deftly juked around the shattered husk of an enemy dropship using it as a shield against laser fire from behind. The pilot spun his fighter three hundred sixty degrees on its y-axis, unleashing a burst of fire at the twin XFs that chased him. One XF spiraled away out of control, the second broke apart. The little triangular XFs were lightly armored and not particularly well flown, making them easy targets to pick off individually. He dodged a pair of loser bursts from two o'clock high. They may not be good pilots, but they were dangerously plentiful.

Most of the intercept forces were quickly destroyed by the far superior XF numbers, sending the Event Horizon retreating at full speed, firing every laser battery and missile in its arsenal in a desperate attempt to avoid destruction. Three XFs made it past the screen of fire, to come in on a suicide run at the command ship's bridge. The triple impact and resulting explosion, ignited a great plume of flame as atmosphere vented from the mortally wounded ship. A series of secondary detonations tore jagged sections of hull plating from the Event Horizon, as it disintegrated in a bull of fire and molten debris.

Fifteen minutes into the battle the XR fleet was fully dispersed around the planet, engaging the defenders in a close combat, and dispatching drop ships escorted by XFs to descend to the surface. EMF orbital defense platforms armed with anti-ship lasers and half mile long magrail cannons, thinned down the XR capital ships far too slowly. Losses were mounting fast for the significantly outnumbered EMF forces, a rate impossible to maintain for long. And while the XR fleet lost ships faster, they were also pressing the attack.

Both EMF fighters and surface mounted anti-aircraft laser and kinetic projectile artillery destroyed many of the XR drop ships before they could touch down. Sadly there were simply too many of them coming for the overtaxed defenses, and they landed to disgorge charged of deadly XR ground units. There were three types of XR unit, the machines were not big on pointless diversity, lacking as they were in organic creativity. Infiltrators were the common grunt, roughly human in shape and size, under six feet tall, lightly armored, and brandishing hand lasers. The next step up were the XR shock troops designated heavy combat XRs. The HCs were larger than infiltrators, and more heavily armed, carrying laser rifles and equipped with a multi-rocket launcher on one shoulder. Last were the mobile artillery platforms designated tanks, essentially a laser and missile turret riding on armored tank treads. Immune to fire from small hand lasers, the tanks were formidable weapons.

General Samson listened to reports from his comm techs, and studied the tactical displays, directing his forces when needed and seeking an exploitable weakness in the enemy. The XRs did not so much employ a specific strategy as overwhelm his people with superior numbers and machine-like coordination.

"Enemy dropships touching down in population centers and transitions sites in greater numbers. EMF troops are engaging."

"Transition site beta is under heavy assault."

Samson absorbed the information, and issued the only orders possible in an impossible situation. "All Omegas are to repel the enemy at transition sites, they must be protected at all cost." He pressed a button on his console, and entered an authorization code into the prompt. "Inform the computer center to initiate sequence Endgame." He looked at the fleet ship counts, the battle was not going well. "Time to transition?"

"Seventeen minutes to transition sir."

"Heaven help us if that fleet breaks through before transition." Came a gravelly voice from behind.

He glanced over his shoulder at his second in command and close personal friend, colonel Peter Bremington. Bremington, a stocky man of middle years with brown hair and hazel eyes, had served under Samson during the war, and the two remained friends over the intervening decades.

"The last two administrations have seen peace, I am not about to let the world end on my watch. I plan to retire an old man, and live quietly on a ranch somewhere."

"Whatever you say old man, you'd die of boredom in six months"

Samson held up the first two fingers of his right hand "More like two." Throughout this exchange Samson's eyes never strayed from his displays, most of his attention trained on the battle. A pattern of behavior was emerging. "Have you noticed the synchronized, I would say swarm-like, movements of the XR fleet?"

Bremington leaned toward the display. "Now that you mention it, they do seem to work in groups, rather than individually like we do. What's percolating in that gray head of yours?"

Samson circled an area on the interactive screen with a finger, isolating a small portion of the battle. "I suspect that all of the ships in each zone are being controlled remotely by a ship borne computer, an artificial intelligence. If I'm right, this could be the break we need to win this thing."

Bremington tapped the communications signal readout. "If we can trace all of their comm signals, we could theoretically locate your AI." Samson raised his voice to give the order. "I want the comm traffic between the XR vessels analyzed. I want to know if any of those ships is sending or receiving more transmissions than the others.". Then softly to Bremington. "If we can find this AI, we could halt their momentum, or even go on the offensive.

Omega corps lieutenant Anne Peterson, was commanding the force tasked with defending transition site delta, watching more XR ground forces close on her position on the tactical display of her armor's visor, she wondered how much longer her embattled troops could continue to held off the enemy. The first wave of XRs wiped out nearly a third of her contingent of regular army troops, and two of the five Omegas assigned to her. The second wave was coming on fast, would be on top of them in moments. The regular troops in standard issue combat armor were an impressive slight, but in Omega power armor she was a walking tank. Unlike the drab olive of standard issue EMF gear, her elite unit was encouraged to paint their armor unique colors. She chose flat violet, through it was more the gray of laser scorching at this point.

Given the choice she would have preferred to fight alongside more of her fellow Omegas. Men and women she had trained side by side with for months, but that was never the plan. The one hundred and three expensive super-soldiers were always intended to be dispatched to various strategic locations for the invasion. She was concerned that no one in the corps had seen Omega commander Zachary Mason in more than two weeks, not since he had gone in for one last enhancement, one that none of the other Omegas received or knew the nature of.

Pushing the question of Zack's whereabouts to the back of her mind, she blasted an XR that came charging out from behind a hill. A scream prompted a glance at her HUD, in time to see a green 'friendly' dot wink out on her tactical radar, signifying the death of yet another one of her men. "Keep to cover as much as you can, and pick your targets." She admonished sharply on tac comm. "I don't care if you grunts are offed, but I won't have you screwing up the mission." She only wished she knew what it was they were giving their lives to protect here.

The second wave arrived in force, creating a deafening symphony of laser fire and explosions. White and black smoke rose to mix in the air, filling it with a gray haze that obscured the scrap and corpse littered ground. It was hard enough keeping trained soldiers alive, she would hate to be responsible for defending a civilian population center.

Infiltrators were quick on their feet as XRs went, but relatively easy to kill, going down after only one or two hits from an ordinary hand laser. The HCs were encased in moderate armor, rendering them slightly harder to destroy, but still nothing a decent laser could not handle. The XR tanks were proving to be more of a problem, it was the tanks that killed the last two Omegas. At ten to one not even an Omega could come out of a fight with artillery turrets unscathed. If the machines came at them one on one, the men and women of the EMF could take them out without a challenge. Even at three or four to one the XRs would be flattened. But in these numbers the things were deadly. They were slowly wearing down her troops.

She concentrated on destroying the tanks with her Omega weapon at maximum output, entrusting the smaller XRs to the capable regular troops. Rolling to the left to dodge a missile from a tank, she hit her attacker with a burst from her laser. Catching a moment's breath, she lobbed a grenade into a cluster of HCs harassing a pair of EMF troops. The explosion rained scrap on the relieved men.

Another missile hit feet to her right, sending rock ships pinging off her armor. Break time was over. Power dashing between two tanks faster than their turrets could track her, she shot them point blank, destroying both before they had a chance to attack. After taking down a third tank, she saw two less green dots on the radar. This could not get on much longer, she did not have the troops for it.

"Tell command we need reinforcements, we're being overrun." She ordered her comm tech, who was hunkered down in a secure location nearby.

One minute and two kills later a reply came. "Command says no dice, we got to protect the glowy cube with what we've got."

It was the answer she expected, if not the one she needed. Knowing that the EMF was pressed this hard everywhere, did not make her feel any better about it. If something did not change soon, they would be killed and the site lost.

The civilian population had been evacuated to hardened shelters for their protection, large cities emptied days in advance in an effort to prevent death and injury in a panicked last minute rush. Large, well armed contingents of EMF troops were deployed to protect each shelter, or group of shelters. Tasked with the defense at one large city sector, was an EME army battalion led by major James Davis. Davis was given two objectives by his section commander, to protect the civilian shelters, and to limit to the extent possible, damage to the city infrastructure.

This sector was mostly quiet so far, experiencing only small enemy incursions that were easily stopped. The XRs were not all that interested in attacking cities yet. That was not to say population centers were left entirely unmolested, only that the XRs were focusing their strikes on military bases and transition sites. Davis and his troops faced minor attacks by XRs that resulted in the destruction of something in the neighborhood of a hundred machines, and statistically acceptable troop losses. Davis knew this pattern could not hold for much longer, it was only a matter of time before the machines arrived in greater numbers.

The XRs primarily stuck to the wide city streets, and while they did not adhere to the traffic signs and signals, they did not exceed the sedate twenty-five mile-per-hour downtown speed limit. They had no reason to deviate from the paved streets and blaze a new trail, when such convenient pathways were provided for them. The upshot to this for the defenders was that the machines came on in straight lines like a shooting gallery, making them easy to pick off from distant cover or rooftop sniper positions. The streets around them were slowly cluttering with the twisted remnants of broken XRs, forcing the not so nimble machines to climb and stumble over their fallen companions, proving that these robots could not charitably be deemed graceful.

The booming roar of a supersonic craft, echoed indeterminately along the steel and glass walls of the city's man made canyons. Davis craned his neck skyward to search for the decelerating dropship he knew was coming, locating it to the south where it was moving toward them fast. "Artillery, blow that thing out of the sky."

Either the artillery guys were preparing to fire anyway, or had impressive response time to his order. No sooner had the order left his mouth, than heavy blasts impacted the dropship. In seconds the acre long, book-shaped vessel was falling from the sky trailing smoke. Its momentum carried it forward at hundreds of miles-per-hour, until it hit the pavement with a tremendous, ground-shaking crash. The slightly pancaked craft slid to a grinding stop inside the EMF defensive perimeter, killing several solders in the process. Worse XRs not violently disabled in the impact and terminal deceleration, exited the broken ship.

Adapting to the changing circumstances, Davis issued orders without hesitation. "Units Charlie and Epsilon, intercept and destroy those XRs. Do not let them reach a shelter."

For sixty long seconds the XRs were allowed to advance from their scrap metal cave unimpeded, firing on anything their software designated as a target. The EMF troops soon moved in, running up to attack the XRs from both sides. Stray shots hit windows and walls, raining glass and polycarbonate into the street. The air grew murky with smoke from fires caused by the crash and firefight, thickening with the stench of burnt flesh and scorched alloy. Caught inescapably in the open between two groups of EMF troops, the XRs were swiftly torn apart.

The EMF troops were poised to finish off the latest XR threat unscathed, none of the XRs managing to kill a single soldier, or to reach cover within the thirty story office tower the dropship was illegally parked next to. No further XRs were coming out of the ship, and the defenders were returning to their posts, when the street was rocked by a large shockwave.

The dropship vanished in a huge explosion, spraying shrapnel everywhere and throwing parked cars like baseballs. Ducking below an armor clad fender for cover until the crashing stopped, Davis looked to where the dropship had rested, and was stunned by what he found in its stead. A crater was scooped out of the road, and much of the office tower's lower levels were simply gone, ripped away to be deposited as bits of small and large debris up and down the street. Some of it was embedded in the very truck that protected him. There was a deep groan of overstressed steel, like the roar of some prehistoric animal come back to life, it reverberated in his chest and rattled the fragmented glass on the truck's hood. The wounded tower shifted and began to topple, a tree felled by a gargantuan axe.

Not knowing what else to do, Davis shouted into the comm. "Everyone get back, the tower is coming down." He stared in shock as windows bent and shattered in distorted frames, creating a non-stop hail of glass shards, joined by furniture and facade. The building tilted slowly over, its great bulk falling far more rapidly than it appeared. Unable to tear his gaze from the horrific spectacle, a dread of realization penetrated his stunned mind, and he sought confirmation from one of his men. "What's in the path of that tower?"

The man tapped a command into his rugged, army issue portable terminal, he spoke with a tremor in his voice. "Sir, shelter Bravo is directly below that tower ."

There was nothing to be done, no evacuation to be enacted, no aid to be rendered. They could only watch helplessly as tens of thousands of pounds of concrete and steel, toppled in seeming slow motion to the ground. It took what felt like hours, for the towering man-made mountain to smash into the street and the smaller buildings in its path, crushing all in its inexorable descent. The huge steel skeleton collapsed in on itself on impact, throwing twisted girders through the air, and annihilating whatever happened to be in their trajectory. The flying beams smashed and impaled human and XR alike, utterly uncaring who or what stood in their way. One soldier was cut in half when a huge pane of glass sheered through him like a knife through a ripe pear. The street shook wildly from the titanic force of impact, knocking soldiers from their feet and setting off car alarms for blocks. A heavy cloud of dust billowed out from the wreckage, making it impossible to see more than a few feet away.

"Status report!" Barked Davis slapping a filter on his face, and attempting to mask the horror in his voice.

"We've lost all contact with the shelter, not even the emergency beacon is transmitting. The XR advance faltered, but more of them are on the way."

"There were two hundred thousand people in that shelter." Came a hollow voice from the right.

The first man continued his toneless report. "Sixteen EMF troops were lost in the tower's destruction, number of wounded unknown."

Forcing down the surge of bile rising in his throat, Davis marshaled his people. "Okay men, the XRs got one shelter, it sucks, but there are more of them here to defend. Keep your stuff together, and do your jobs."

A block up the street from Davis' command post, the air was clogged and nearly unbreathable with the artificial, and probably toxic fog, making it difficult to find targets through burning lungs and watery eyes. The EMF targeting system utilized a combination of electronic signals, motion detection, and triangulation of enemy fire to display target information on soldiers' HUD's. Infrared was ineffective on XRs, and visual scanning was reduced to almost zero in the fog.

"You'll pay for that skyscraper!" Growled EMF private Morgan firing into the cloud.

"I hope the insurance on that building covers exploding alien space ship damage." Joked corporal Bowers in an attempt to lighten the mood.

"I'd hate to see their new premium."

"We all know this will be declared a disaster area, and the government will foot the bill" commented a third man.

"Alright, cut the chatter and scrap some bots." Admonished sergeant Brent Iverson.

A grizzled man in his early thirties, Iverson spent much of his adult life in the army. He was a gruff and dedicated man who took grief from no one, and believed firmly in the idea that training and brains trumped heroes in combat.

"How am I supposed to know if I'm hitting anything in this soup?" Grumbled Morgan.

"Shoot at what your HUD tells you to, until it doesn't." Iverson suited actions to words, unloading a barrage of laser bursts on a red dot his HUD indicated was an XR, until the dot winked out.

Following Iverson's example, his squad fired into the fog at the unseen enemy. The machines did not seem to be as impaired by the dust cloud as the EMF troops obviously were. Their shots still missed, but not as often or by as much. They must rely on other tracking systems.

A soldier was hit in the chest and dropped, a black hole melted through his body armor. "Keep your heads down and fire from cover, show me you're good for more than looking ugly in chow line," shouted Iverson. He snapped off shots with one hand, while dragging the dead soldier behind cover. He set a marker on his HUD for the man's location, he would be retrieved after the battle. "Wait here for a bit kid, I'll be back for you later."

A series of explosions shook the area, raining rock and scrap down on them.

"Sarge, we've got eleven tanks coming our way from the east." Announced Bowers.

Pulling a heavy laser rifle from the magnetic clips on his back, Iverson clicked off the safety and checked the radar for the stated tanks. "Spread out and use your big guns, these things don't go down easy. Jansen, take two men and circle around to their left flank. Tell me when you're in place." He pointed at two soldiers "You, and you come with me, we're going to the right flank. Keep your heads down, and stay close."

Iverson led his men forward at a trot, as stealthily as large men moving in full combat armor could go. Staying in a jogging crouch, he kept what cover he could between his men and the tanks. He darted from behind an abandoned truck to a concrete barrier, then to the low wall of a subway entrance. Two-hundred yards from the incoming enemy, he hunted for a good spot to effectively ambush the XRs from, while staying behind any object that might protect them from the artillery. It took him a short time to find a suitable location and second after he settled in Jansen signaled that his men were also ready. He needed to remind himself to put Jansen in for a promotion when this was over.

Iverson watched from behind a concrete and rebar traffic barrier, as the tanks rolled noisily by on clattering metal treads, the steady noise proclaiming that stealth was not high on their list of priorities. The instant that tank number eleven was past, he gave the order. "Open fire, take them out fast. Don't give them time to return fire."

Popping up from behind the barrier, he sighted on the first tank in line, firing long bursts at maximum output. Green energy punched holes into the couch size turret, showering sparks and dark lubricants around it. The tank shuddered to a stop, creating a roadblock to box in the tanks that followed. His men scrapped four more before their turrets swiveled to fire back. The concentrated fire from the tanks began to reduce the barrier to rubble, spraying the men with concrete chips. Iverson took a graze on the shoulder, and another one of his men went down, while four more of the tanks were reduced to slag. He lost one more man as the final two tanks were disabled.

Taking advantage of the momentary calm, Iverson set markers for his downed men, and called his tactical man over the comm. "Status update, what's happening out there?"

"XRs in your immediate area are down, but another large group of reinforcements is coming in from the north."

Slapping a med patch on the stinging burn on his shoulder, Iverson hiked to Janson. "We got more XRs coming, patch yourselves up, and find something solid to hide behind for an ambush." *This fight better not take much longer*, he thought, *or I may not have to worry about retirement after all.*

A pair of E-31, single man atmospheric fighter planes roared through a tight bank, their powerful ram scoop engines howling as they came around to find new targets. The human pilots in these particular war planes had racked up more kills than either of them cared to count, destroying dozens of dropships and countless EXs over the course of the battle. There was no end to the XRs, like flies at a trash heap.

The roughly wedge shaped XFs were half the length of an E-31, or approximately the mass of a big pickup track. The two craft had comparable weapon payloads, and a similar layer of armor plating. When it came to maneuverability the E-31 had the edge in this environment, primarily because it was specifically designed for intra-atmospheric combat, where the blunt nosed and chubby XFs did not so much slice through the air, as shove it aside by brute force. XFs tended to operate in groups of three or more, rather than singly or in pairs like the EMF planes. An XF's surface was a random, mottled grayish color, as if they were manufactured quickly and without any consideration for appearance. E-31 pilot call sign Hawk and his wing man Rake, had been in the air since the XR fleet left foldspace. He was experiencing an eerie sense of deja vu, as if he was flying in a training simulator, instead of in a real plane in actual combat. XFs flew in repetitive patterns the same as computer controlled simulations. Exhibiting algorithmic flying with a total lack of creativity or initiative. They followed what he would describe as a predetermined program, making them predictable and easy to kill.

He and Rake bore down on a cluster of four XFs in precise formation, the closest red dots on his tactical radar. Firing his lasers in short, rapid, machinegun-like bursts at the lead XF, the first volley flew wide of the target, a slight misjudgment of relative velocity. Gently adjusting his aim by easing the flight stick over, he fired again, this time punching a line of holes across the enemy fighter. The XF broke apart, the pieces falling uselessly from the sky and making him glad everyone was evacuated to shelters, and no one would be killed by the debris he was raining down. The other three XFs separated in a standard evasive pattern, one that he was well familiar with. Following the center XF, he checked his HUD to verify that the XFs were still running the same evasive routine. He pushed his plans into a series of rote high-G maneuvers, firing on the XFs whenever his cross hairs went green for target lock, or when his instincts told him he had a shot. In under ten seconds, the XF tumbled from sight unpowered. XFs three and four were no longer nearby, ordered away on some other pressing task, possibly the same one he so rudely interrupted. XFs liked to make things more difficult by attacking in swarms of up to ten, and those were bad odds no matter how stupid an opponent was. Of course, as had just happened, they were prone to fleeing from a fight for no obvious reason.

"Delta three, there are three XR dropships entering the atmosphere in your sector. Break off your current engagement and eliminated them," ordered AirCom.

Three red dots changed to red Xs his radar, designating the dropships as priority targets. Selecting a target on his display gave him more detailed information, distance, elevation; velocity, and specifications on vehicle type when they were available. Highlighting one of the dropships revealed that it was miles from him and descending fast. Banking his plane around on an intercept course, and hauling the throttles to their stops, he was pressed into the seat at several times normal gravity. He estimated that it would take nearly a minute to reach the dropships, and at their speed they could land shortly after that. He would have to shoot the ships down in record time, the men on the ground could ill afford to face more enemy reinforcements. There were over a hundred XRs on each dropship, an exact count had yet to be communicated to him, and every ship he destroyed could save countless lives below.

Fifteen seconds out from the dropships, two XFs strafed him, scorching one of his wings. "Evasive Charlie two." He called to Rake.

Smacking the throttles to low, he extended the flaps to slow his plane precipitously. The XFs, poor at adapting to unfamiliar tactics, rocketed past him. He slammed the throttles to full, firing on the XFs before they could think to evade. The first was destroyed in Hawk's initial valley, the second by that of his wing man.

He reoriented on the dropships, flying fast to make up for lost time. The XRs had descended to an altitude of under five thousand feet, and were moving at what he believed to be their top air speed. The XF distraction, only seconds in duration, had cost them valuable time. They would be hard pressed to destroy the dropships before they could land.

Linings up his crosshairs on the rearmost of the three ships, Hawk opened fire, peppering the enemy with laser bursts. After a few seconds of aftermarket ventilation, the ship exploded in a cloud of fire and smoke. Rake matched him to similar result. With no time to spare, Hawk pushed his plane recklessly through the fire, looking for the final dropship as he emerged on the other side. The target was not where he expected it to be, searching his tactical radar, he found it diving fast for the ground. The dropship was practically falling from the sky in a possibly suicidal attempt to unload its deadly cargo.

Dropping his plane into an almost vertical dive, one he might not be able to recover from, Hawk noted that they were over a forest, but the sparkling glass towers of a city rose above it not far ahead. With his throttles locked at full, he desperately tried to line up a shot on his target. "Come on, move." He growled through clenched teeth, fighting to retain consciousness as the blood was forced from his head. His plane screamed past two thousand feet. "Faster, you worthless hunk of junk". He urged his overtaxed plane.

"Pull up Hawk!" Shouted Rake in his ear. "It's already gone." Tuning out the worried cry of his wingman Hawk kept his shuddering plane pointed resolutely just ahead of the dropship, willing his crosshairs to turn green with target lock. When they did, he unleashed a protracted burst of laser fire on the boxy enemy ship, stitching it with a line of glowing holes, long seconds later, the dropship started to break up as they passed six hundred feet. At three hundred it exploded, raining hot scrap on the trees. He hoped there were emergency crows to put out any fires. His plane rocked as it was pelted by shrapnel on its way through the debris cloud that was formerly an enemy ship. He wrestled the flight stick back between his knees, the proximity alarm blaring at him, canopy filled with an adrenaline spiking sea of green.

"Pull up!" Screamed Rake.

Hawk's E-31 leveled off two-dozen feet above the treetops, its engines whining in protest, then it began to climb. "That was too close." He muttered, sweat pouring down his flight suit.

"You alright?" Relief was evident in Rake's voice.

"Plane's going to need paint, but I'm..." Hawk's voice cut off when his Plane erupted into a fireball, a million pieces of hot alloy flinging over the forest.

"No!" shouted Rake disbelievingly, "You couldn't let it go, could you? Always have to play the hero. Burn you." Rake banked his fighter away from the city his friend died protecting, and looked for a new target. "Delta four to AirCom, Delta three is down, returning to combat zone." He reported as his jet roared back to the fight alone.

· · · ·

HIGH ABOVE THE PLANET the conflict was going no better. The XR invaders had the EMF defenders completely surrounded, and still badly outnumbered, even with the greater losses on the XR side. The battle was not likely to go on too much longer. The twisted remains of a vast battleship superstructure drifted aimlessly, momentum carrying it along its last powered vector, a timeless celestial voyage that would only end when the ship was dragged into or collided with a larger heavenly body. Small fighter craft played a deadly game of hide and seek around the derelict, uncaring of its ultimate fate. Broken fragments of structure from the orbital defense platforms, floated uselessly in the void alongside countless hulls of ships both small and large, cluttering space sufficiently to make maneuvering extremely hazardous and growing more so by the minute. Even the sprawling, orbital shipyards had taken a severe beating, still clinging to the unfinished skeletons of vessels under construction. Completion dates would have to be pushed back. Beams from energy weapons flew everywhere like a glowing swarm of hyperspeed enraged insects, adding to the chaos of flying through the mad house of bottle.

EMF command ship Bane of Cerberus with its small fleet, remained on station above the central power relay satellite it was tasked with defending, the huge ship hardly a pale dot against the solar array that was its backdrop. Commanding the Cerberus in its desperate struggle, was admiral Genma Hoshi. Hoshi was allocated thirty-two capital ships to complete his objective. Only fourteen of that original force were still in the fight, and for some of them that status was debatable. He had eight battleships, two fighter carriers, two destroyers, and two missile carriers. He was down to his last sixty-three fighter craft, fifty of which were fighters, and the rest bombers woefully low on missiles. Fortunately, the majority of the enemy's big attack ships were engaged further out, kept busy by the primary defense elements of the fleet. But enough XR ships were reaching him, to cause his shrinking battle group serious damage. On or two more big incursions, and the satellite would start taking hits.

Watching his complex array of tactical displays, Hoshi directed the overall defense as needed, relying on the captains and pilots of his individual ships to make moment to moment combat decisions.

"Orbital defense platform Beta-twelve is offline." Reported a technician.

Damage reports and status updates continues to flood in fast, an endless litany of negative information.

"Column of Fall taking heavy damage."

"Carrier Zeus' lightning down to ten percent missile capacity."

"Terrashield has launched the last of her fighters."

This is it, thought Hoshi, *everything is on the table. If we can't repel the XRs now, we lose the planet.* Hoshi looked at the main display. *At least the enemy fleet seems to have fully committed itself as well, we still have a chance of winning, slight thought it is.*

Enemy battle group has broken through the outer defenses, and is approaching our position.

"What is their strength?"

"Enemy force consists of four battleships, ten dropships, one carrier, and twenty-one fighters."

"Leave three battleships and twenty fighters with the Cerberus to defend the satellite, all other ships are to intercept the enemy."

On his screen the ships deployed as ordered, moving toward the enemy group. His missile carriers unloaded their tubes first, launching salvos of powerful warheads at the XR battleships. The rest of Hoshi's fleet narrowed the gap with the enemy, firing on targets when in range. The XR ships returned fire in kind, taking out many of the incoming missiles before they could impact, the warheads vanishing in blazing flashes of light visible from thousands of miles distant. Inevitably, some of the EMF missiles struck home, exploding on XR hulls. One battleship went dark, set adrift before the groups came together.

The two fleets traded blows, battleships on both sides drilling heavy laser blasts into each other with relentless fury. Glowing sections of armored hull plating twisted off to cool in space, exposing vulnerable circuits and systems to attacks. The XR dropships did not stick around for the fight, trying to sneak past the defenders to deposit their cargoes on the surface. Their mission did not include pointless annihilation at the cannons of EMF warships. Dropships were equipped with relatively light weapons that were no threat to the big attack cruisers, but they fired at anything that came within range regardless. EMF bombers hit the dropships with missiles and lasers, destroying three in quick succession before XFs swooped in for their defense. EMF fighters came in next, rushing in to take on the XFs, but not until after several bombers were lost to enemy fire. A violent explosion sent a shockwave of shrapnel through space, an EMF battleship destroyed.

Hoshi watched this unfold from the bridge of the Cerberus.

"Battleship firestorm destroyed." Reported a technician seconds before the shock wave rattled the ship.

The Firestorm vanished from his tactical display. *I'm losing ships too fast, the satellite must survive until transition.*

"Two XR dropships have entered the atmosphere."

"Inform AirCom of the threat." Ordered Hoshi.

"The last XR battleship has been destroyed, no enemy ships in our zone."

"Order all ships to retrieve life pods, and return to standby positions." Said Hoshi automatically, his attention already back on the larger conflict. *Command had better find a weakness in the XR fleet soon, or there won't be anything left down there to return to.*

From the air, the EMF Invasion command base looked deceptively calm, few personnel moved between buildings in the emergency lockdown, and a mere handful of vehicles plied its smoothly paved streets. Inside the overloaded communications building, technicians were hard at work, frantically checking and maintaining equipment taxed beyond what it was rated for, or ever expected to handle. Some of the technicians checked comm frequencies, verifying that transmissions were properly routed, other technicians relayed orders between battle groups and commands, in an endless stream of voices drowning out all other sounds in the room. Encryption codes were verified, confirming identification and authorization. Inquiries were made, mostly for more troops or ships, and answers were given, primarily denials for reinforcements that did not exist. Perhaps most important were the unsung heroes of the tech world, the men and women who physically monitored the equipment itself, replacing burned out or broken components on primary and backup systems in turn, ensuring that no unit was ever down completely. In battle this was the most important facility in the base. If communications were to break down, there would be no way to coordinate the overall conflict. Every system in the building had multiple backups and redundancies, in fact, there was an entice backup communications facility located ten miles from the base in a hidden bunker in case of the catastrophic failure of this primary comm building.

Under normal operations, the command center located in the heart of the base, was an open, easily accessible structure. At four stories it was the tallest building in the complex, and was covered with windows to give important personnel a view of the surrounding mountains from their offices on the top two floors. But during an emergency lockdown as it was now, the windows were automatically covered by thick armored shutters, and concrete barriers had risen from the side walk at ground level. The command room on the top floor was encased in a vault of hardened alloy, protecting it from all but the most determined or destructive attack. Laser turrets were mounted on base root tops to repel airborne foes, and subterranean escape tunnels ran into the mountainside for miles.

The level of activity in the command room had diminished not an iota in the passing minutes of battle, if anything the pace was faster than ever. Endless reports were made and orders given, voices overlapping without pause.

"Orbital fleet strength reduced to thirty-nine percent."

"Central command to FleetCom all reserve forces are to be moved to relay satellite defense."

"Major population centers suffering significant damage. Twenty-six evacuation shelters have been destroyed, ten more are structurally compromised."

"XR dropships reaching the surface in greater numbers."

"XR fleet strength at forty-six percent."

"General Harding requests reinforcements"

"Command to general Harding, all reserve forces are already committed, you must hold your position with current forces."

A technician walked over to Samson. "I sent the communications signal report you requested to your terminal sir."

Samson nodded acknowledgement and dismissal. There was a file labeled XR Comms in his received documents box. He opened and scanned the file quickly, going over the signal numbers in descending orders of magnitude. He compared the top signalers with the historic battle data. "Have you noticed that these large, round XR ships have stayed completely out of the fight?" He highlighted one of them on the screen. "Not one of them has fired a single shot since the XRs arrived and from the comm analysis I was given, there are far more transmissions to and from these ships, than from the rest of their fleet combined." He brought up an overall map of the battle on his terminal, the planet reduced in size so that it did not dominate the image entirely. He enhanced the round ships around the planet. If you look at where these ships are deployed, you will see that they are equidistant to each other, and as a group have full coverage of the planet. Exactly what I would do if I were to run a coordinated assault on an enemy world. I believe that these ships must serve as a communications and control system for the XR fleet. At the very least these comm ships are coordinating the XR forces, and perhaps directly controlling them. If I am right, the entire XR fleet is being controlled by a centralized artificial intelligence, possibly in one of those massive command ships. Their tactics are far too uniform and precise for me to think otherwise."

Bremington rubbed his chin thoughtfully. "So if we were to destroy these comm ships, we might be able to disrupt the XRs enough to rally our forces for a counter offensive?"

Samson nodded. It was time to take the offensive. "Order all orbital battle groups to break off current engagements, and redeploy to destroy the XR comm ships immediately." He selected all of the comm ships on the display, sending the coordinates and data to the main tactical screen on the front wall. The numbers would update automatically if the ships moved. "Tell them to hold nothing back, that this is the XRs' Achilles heel, and their destruction will devastate the enemy. Only the relay and power station defense groups are to remain on station." Samson looked at Bremington and spoke softly. "Now we sit back and wait to see if my gamble pays off, or if we lose it all." He leaned back and listened to his orders being relayed to the fleet.

Bremington's reply was just as quiet. "Whether this works or not, there won't be much left of our fleet."

On the opposite side of the planet, and thousands of miles beyond its atmosphere, the half mile long rectangular bulk of EMF battleship equalizer pounded away at one of the smaller XR Battleships. The XR ship had fewer heavy weapons than its EMF counterpart, but its more thickly armored hull plating would usually make a direct contest between the behemoths a relatively even match. In this particular instance, however, the EMF ship was accompanied by a support group of twenty bombers, and thirty-one fighters. After a brief lopsided exchange, the XR ship stopped firing and split apart amidst electrical discharges and explosions.

On the bridge of the equalizer, captain James Carter stood with feet planted wide on the metal deck, steadying himself against the shockwaves rocking his ship. He was studying the tactical displays, hunting for his next target. A comm technician called out to him with unexpected yet welcome news from command.

"Captain, we have received new orders from Invasion Command, and they include target coordinates. The orders state that all EMF ships not assigned to defend the energy relay satellites, are to immediately disengage from current firefighter."

"Lucky were not in one right now." Muttered Carter.

The technician continued without pause. "And they are to destroy XR vessels designated as comm ships with all haste." Tactical information and coordinates for the comm ships was routed to Carter's terminal, along with the orders.

Carter examined the main tactical display to locate the nearest comm ship, one was reasonably close, only two hundred miles from the Equalizer. He sent the coordinates to his helmsman. "Helm, take us to these coordinates. I want to move at maximum sublight speed and to avoid XR ships when possible. Now punch it. Tactical, tell all gunners to fire on XR ships that come within range, but that the comm ships are the priority. Relay that to our fighter escort."

It's about time the eggheads down there figured something out. I hope there comm ships prove to be the critical enemy weakness command claims they are, if not, this fight is over. We don't have the ships left to try anything else.

EMF ships over the entire orbital sphere changed course without warning, moving at full speed to intercept the comm ships, redeploying in near unison to execute their new orders. The unexpected and systematic alteration of tactics caught the XRs completely by surprise, their limited algorithmic thinking unable to adapt with any alacrity to a sudden change in enemy behavior. The XR AI entered a temporary logic loop without an exit parameter, in other words, the computer was stumped. This brief XR indecision gave the newly aggressive EMF forces persons time to reach their objectives, leaving the XR fleet to ponder whether this move was an actual threat. Some EMF ships were nearly in firing range of the comm ships, before the XR fleet understood the situation and began to marshal a defense. The race was on, EMF ships dashing to destroy the comm ships with every weapon they had left, and the XR fleet flying to protect the mission critical vessels.

Both sides kept up running fire fight, blasting each other whenever they were close enough for a lock. For a minute fleet wide tactical displays were a picture of absolute chaos, ships moving in every direction at once without the slightest hint of order. Then the situation clarified, the XR fleet moving to intercept the EMF ships en route, or to take up station near the comm ships for their direct defense.

The XR comm ships numbered twelve in total, and were dispersed evenly in orbit around the planet. The comm ships were rounded in a vaguely disc like shape two thousand feet in diameter, they bristled with innumerable antennas, laser transmitters, and other communications equipment. They were armed with only light ship to ship lasers for defense, and their armor was thin for their size. These were ships purpose built to handle fleet communications from behind battle lines, they were not intended or designed to fight.

With more than half of the XR fleet out of action, there were gaping holes in their carefully ordered formations, holes large enough to park a small moon in. The first group of EMF attackers to reach a comm ship, did so unmolested, making short work of its requisite allotment of then XF defenders. The battleship devastator with its escort of fighters and bombers arrived with weapons blazing, blasting the comm ship with everything in their arsenals. Dozens of missiles and countless laser bolts raced to the XR ship, impacting unimpeded on the unshielded vessel. Large tracts of hull were burned away, and craters appeared along the doomed ship's long axis. Less than ninety seconds from when the order was given, the first comm ship was annihilated.

Recorded data on the comm ship's weapons and armor were immediately transmitted to the rest of the EMF fleet, aiding in the destruction of the other eleven ships. The next three comm ships were eliminated moments after the first, all of them dying quietly as they possessed no munitions to explode or atmosphere to ignite. Comm ships five through eight were somewhat better defended, their protectors inflicting moderate losses on the EMF attackers before they too were destroyed.

The removal of two thirds of the XR communications network, caused an obvious and substantial change in the behavior of their fleet, particularly in the sectors around the destroyed comm ships. Their synchronization rate plummeted, in most cases their behavior becoming totally erratic. Some of the smaller craft, primarily XFs and dropships, flew into open space without a change in speed or direction.

On the surface of the planet the change was even more pronounced, with XR forces turning unpredictable. Many simply stopped moving altogether, arms dropping limply and head dropping as if they had run out of power. Others wandered away with no evident destination in mind. A few began to attack fellow XRs, turning to fire on each other without provocation, much to the amusement of EMF troops. Those that did continue to fight were markedly less effective than before, but still had numbers sufficient to pose a significant danger to the decimated EMF defenses.

Before EMF ships in orbit could reach the final four comm ships, the XRs were able to get a working defense in place. Positioning battleships and XFs to protect the last of the critical assets.

On the bridge of the Equalizer, captain Carter watched the constantly updating tactical displays with barely concealed annoyance. His next target was now protected by three XR battleships, two dozen or so XFs, and one of the enormous XR command ships. The ships, designated as command ships for no better reason than sheer size, were three times bigger than an EMF battleship. According to sensor data the command ships had thick hull armor and substantial armaments. And there was a big indentation on the forward hull that no one could identify the purpose of. Joining the Equalizer were three missile carriers and two more battleships, each with an escort of fighters and bombers.

The missile carriers, with their long-range warheads, were the first to fire, their deadly salvos racing toward the XR ships. Seconds later the rest of the EMF and XR ships opened up with all batteries, filling the blackness of space with streaks of light. EMF fighters and enemy XFs packed the top of the kill list, vanishing in brief explosions that lit space like fireworks at a ballpark when the home team wins. Power crystals and atmosphere ignited to disintegrate pilots and circuits, alike EMF missiles, payloads measured in the low megatons, homed in on their targets. Many were destroyed by defensive fire from the XR ships, the rest hit their marks in violent explosions, causing considerable structural damage. EMF bombers came in next, launching their loads of smaller missiles as effectively as any pilot could in the heat of battle. In moments an XR battleship was destroyed, rocked by secondary explosions when its power core was hit. The EMF battleships entered the fight, trading weaponized energy with XR ships like bruisers trading punches in street brawl. The battleship leopard, practically held together by this time by chewing gum and ingenuity, went up in a mighty blast that left a trail of bright red debris along its last powered vector. The Equalizer pummeled an XR battleship, claiming the second capital ship of the group, but not until after that same ship blew away a missile carrier. The third battleship lasted moments longer under the combined battering from two of its counterparts, going dark as it lost power.

The XR command ship, already heavily engaged at that time by missile carriers and the EMF bombers, was now targeted by the EMF battleships. The combined firepower of so many capital ships was more than any one vessel could withstand for long, no matter how prodigious its dimensions and capabilities. Great segments of armored hull were dislodged from the XR behemoth, the heated alloy left to drift away without note. The command ship was able to destroy one more missile carrier as the last few XFs were mopped up, leaving it the sole defender of the comm ship. A line of missiles made it past the cruiser's weakening defenses, impacting the huge ship in direct succession, burrowing a tunnel nearly to the far side of the superstructure. Anti-climactically for its grand size, the command ship's death was not an event to tell tales of to future generations. It made no grand explosion to reward the EMF forces for their hard work and losses, did not break apart at the seams to entertain onlookers. All power readings simply dropped to zero, and the huge ship drifted with no further signs of activity.

That final missile carrier survived intact, but in exchange for killing one of the enemy's most powerful weapons, it was out of missiles and out of the fight. With nothing to stand in its way, the Equalizer quickly destroyed the comm ship.

Carter searched his display for another comm ship, only to learn that they were destroyed while he was busy with this one. The XR forces were in total disarray, but in accomplishing this feat, the EMF fleet had been all but eradicated.

As Samson predicted, the elimination of the XR's communications network was a decisive blow against the machines, who obviously had little to no autonomy in individual units. The majority of the XR fleet, along with all of their ground forces, had lost all cohesion, no longer working together and in many instances attacking each other.

Watching his displays for any residual threats that might be posed by the invaders, Samson issued new orders. "Redeploy all remaining ships, they are to take up station around the power relay satellites. Defend the transition system, only attack those XRs come to you, if any are capable of doing anything." If there were no more attacks, then his forces could regroup and mop up the XRs strays. For a moment he wanted to take a breather, let his blood pressure return to normal after being elevated for so long.

"The second XR command ship is approaching the main power relay satellite with a battle group." Came the worst possible announcement from a technician.

Samson winced. "Time to transition?"

"Four minutes, thirteen seconds."

"Alert admiral Hoshi of the threat, and send any ships that are in the sector to reinforce him."

"The nearest battle group is in sector A-twelve."

"They won't get there in time." Said Bremington.

Samson nodded. "It's all up to Hoshi now. Don't let us down."

Hoshi watched silently while his ships efficiently cleaned a way the last few XFs from the latest XR incursion, a short task given the enemy's current lack of initiative or self preservation. When his ships were all back in their standby positions, he looked over the wider tactical displays wearily, not really expecting anything from the debilitated XR fleet.

A technician called out sharply. "A XR battle group is heading our way, led by the command ship."

Checking the updated data on the displays, Hoshi saw that with the command ship, there were three battleships and an escort of thirty-four XFs. All of them vectored directly to the power relay satellite, and his little fleet was all that stood in their path. The three battleships moved around and slightly in front of the command ship, forming a protective barrier between it and the EMF ships.

"Call all nearby ships for reinforcements, tell them to get here fast." Ordered Hoshi. In addition to his own command ship, half the size of the XR equivalent, he had only three battleships and one nearly depleted missile carrier under his command. His escorts were down to twenty-two fighters, and eleven bombers. He hoped they could hold out enough for more ships to arrive, otherwise it was an uncomfortably even fight, possibly weighted in favor of the XRs.

The loss of communications that so crippled the rest of the XR fleet, appeared to have no particular effect on this command ship and its escorts, indicating that the enemy AI was housed within, or at least a computer capable of controlling other XR ships that were close to it. The oncoming XR ships showed none of the erratic behavior evidenced by the rest of their fleet, pushing toward him in perfect formation. Examining the command ship growing larger in his displays, Hoshi noticed something unusual. The large concave disc on the front of the vessel's superstructure, a depression of at least fifty feet in diameter, was now sporting a perimeter of pyramidal nodes.

The instant ships were in range weapons fire erupted in space, lighting the blackness with multi-hued energy beams and brief flashes from missile detonations. The EMF attack slowed the XR ships, but did not stop their determined advance. Battleships on both sides closed on each other, the XR cruisers breaking formation to engage the EMF ships directly, keeping them away from the massive XR command ship. The XFs did the same duty with the EMF fighters and bombers. While the other XR ships were busy with their own battles, the command ship continued to move unimpeded toward the relay satellite without slowing its approach, the nodes on the command ship began to glow, deepening to a bright red as energy concentrated around the disc.

Someone on the bridge cried out in alarm, drawing a sharp glare from Hoshi at the breach in discipline. One that quickly faded as the words sunk in. "Detecting a massive buildup of energy from the XR Command ship!"

Hoshi zoomed his display in on the disc, realizing with mounting dread what it was. "Order all ships to attack the XR command ship now, concentrate fire on that forward disc!" He shouted, not caring that he was now the one breaching protocol, fearing that he was already too late.

The EMF ships blasted all cannons at the Command ship, but the power buildup was already reaching its peak. Beams shot out from every node point simultaneously, converging eighty feet above the exact center of the disc. The combined energy streams formed a huge, angry red beam, a four foot wide laser that lanced out directly at the power relay satellite. The colossal laser eradicated and vaporized everything in its path, incinerating an EMF fighter and melting a hole clean through a battleship. It hit the satellite without immediate effect, and for one glorious moment it looked like nothing was going to happen. The satellite's power output was unchanged, a fact that lulled some into a painful state of premature relief. But the malevolent red energy interfered with the precisely calibrated frequency of the satellite's green flow. The pleasant emerald energy emitted by the satellite since the lengthy transition process was initiated, morphed to a dark, sickly orange color. The orange energy moved down the relay chain oscillating nauseatingly, proceeding all the way to the transaction sites on the planet surface.

The XRs had not mounted a serious attack for several minutes, and with only seconds left on the transition clock, lieutenant Peterson believed they had succeeded, that the EMF had won. She leaned on the side of a newly battered truck, breathing a sigh of relief when the clock on her HUD ticked down to zero. She watched the enormous green cube slowly fader exactly as they explained it in the mission briefing. It looked like the transition was working.

Then it all went inexplicably wrong. Without warning, the energy beam from orbit with its steady comforting glow changed, and a sickly citrus energy slammed into the translucent cube with what locked like a physical blow. The nearly transparent green surface fluctuated to orange and rippled like a flag in a breeze, sending vibrations through the ground felt for miles. Peterson watched helplessly as the slow fading stopped, and the cube vanished with a tremendous clap, like that of a gigantic crash of thunder.

"I'm sorry Zack, I failed," she whispered as the shockwave rolled over her.

The chain reaction resulting from the mixing of incompatible energies, was nothing short of cataclysmic, a life ending event beyond imagining. The energy, intensified by the abbreviated transition, reversed course. It surged upward through the relay satellites, destroying each of them in turn. The capacitor laden satellites exploded with such unmatched fury, that all EMF and XR ships nearby were obliterated in the blasts, Ironically, the surge ended its path of uncontrolled devastation, by annihilating the odious command ship that originally spawned it.

With nowhere else to go, the undiminished destructive energy mingled with the shockwaves from the former relay satellites, radiating outward in every direction at once. Fragmented energy beams and concussive force from ship and satellite explosions, bombarded the planet from every point on its surface simultaneously. Absorbing this as well as it could without tearing apart completely, the planet was rocked by huge quakes beyond the measure of any scale. Tremors pushed outward from the transition sites, spreading with incredible speed, and triggering natural fault lines and volcanoes including the enormous calderas on multiple continents. Cities were shaken by forces that utterly overwhelmed structural supports, reducing them to rubble. Entire countries were covered in seas of molten rock, and burned in pyroclastic firestorms. New mountains thrust up where there were previously open plains, old mountains crumbled, and large tracts of land tumbled and sank into the ocean. Turbulent seas swept far inland in titanic tsunamis, leveling all in their path. When it seemed that no further destruction could be visited upon the wounded planet, the debris created by the broken fleets and satellites rained down to smash into the dirt and water. Not even the moon was left untouched, energy discharges scorching its surface.

The normally blue-green gem was now obscured by an enormous gray cloud of ash that blotted out the sun, broken only by pockets of reddish fire and magma, as the seemingly lifeless orb burned.

CHAPTER 1

150 years later...

Dawn had come and gone without fanfare an hour previously, the sun on its way up the eastern sky already warming the barren, rocky dirt under its gaze, a sample of the furnace like summer afternoon to come. Only the palest ghost of a breeze caressed the land, still calm from the night's relative cool. The dry, dusty ground was cast in the drab browns and grays of dirt and rock, marred occasionally by a sparse growth of scraggly green plants, stunted by too much sun and too little rain. The gentle wind passed close to the ground, rustling dry leaves and stirring up puffs of dust and grit that swirled and eddied before settling again. Here and there small furry rodents and leathery skinned reptiles, dashed and scurried between hiding places looking for food in their arid ecosystem.

Visible from miles away in this flat empty desert, a narrow billowing cloud of dust and dirt was kicked up from the valley floor, generated by the rapid passage of four tall, knobby black tires over the ground. The tires belonged to a somewhat unusual truck-like vehicle. It was twenty-four feet in length, and ten in height. It rode fifteen inches off the ground, to traverse any obstacle its driver chose to pass. The front cab section was built from a frame of tubular metal, and housed four seats bolted to the solid floor pan. Behind the cab was a boxy rear compartment comprising two-thirds of the vehicle's overall length. The entire construct looked cobbled together from spare parts, that nonetheless was well made. It was tinted a deep green, and generated a mild electrical hum as it moved.

Driving the curious vehicle, was a fairly average young man of no more than twenty years of age. His slightly shaggy green hair fluttered in the wind of the open air cab, and his dark blue eyes shined with intelligence. His clothing was clean and neat, if non-descript, consisting of dark gray shirt, pants, and a similarly gray jacket. All of it accented in green at the cuffs, collar, and waist. A pair of rugged black boots protected his feet.

Standing on the seat to his right, without regard to personal safety, was a young woman of the same age. She wore a sleeveless athletic top and shorts in purple, with wide pink stripes down the sides, and boots of the same design as the man's. On top of her clothes, she was also adorned with unobtrusive pieces of metallic armor in the same purple as her clothing. The armor parts were attached to her limbs and torso from head to foot, with a wide circlet across her forehead. Her black hair whipped around wildly in the wind, the central streak of purple dancing merrily. Her black-furred catlike ears were pointed slightly backward, and her tail was held low behind her. The features were a normal trait for Grymals, one of the alien races still on the planet after the Devastation. Grymals all had ears and tails similar to local animals, some were covered in full body hair or fur.

She gripped the window frame laughing happily. "Come on Mark, drive faster."

"We're going plenty fast already, Kat." Replied Mark in amused exasperation. "And would you please sit down? If we hit a rock or something, you are going to fall out."

"No way, I won't fall, I'll fly."

"Actually," interrupted the AI housed in the computer Mark had strapped to his forearm, and hidden beneath the sleeve of his jacket. "It is far more probable that you would fall. In the event that you were forcibly ejected from the Truck at this velocity, you would be unlikely to have sufficient time to reorient your body and activate your armor's flight pack. The resultant high-speed impact with the rocky terrain, would most certainly result in significant physical damage."

Kat dropped sullenly into the seat, her ears twitching irritably. "Yeah, yeah fine Sky, I'm sitting. Happy now?"

"My emotional state is not at issue here, but rather your continued physical wellbeing. Relative to which, it is advisable to keep extraneous noise to a minimum, so as not to attract unwanted attention."

"I know that, but it's no fun to be quiet and slow all the time." Sulked Kat staring at the desert. "How much longer before we get to the scrapward?"

"Not too much, we should see the hills soon."

"I hope we run into robots, I want to have a little fun."

"We are going there to gather scrap for raw materials to turn into goods we can trade

for food, not to fight robots and play around."

"You just want to make boring stuff like hammers and pots." She grumbled.

He sighed, this was a well worn argument, for which he had an automatic reply. "I have to make things that people want and need, they won't trade valuable food for something silly, like a toy dog." He picked a toy dog at random, trying to think of an item useless enough to make his point and end the discussion. He should have known better.

She smiled mischievously. "What about a fire breathing toy dog? That would be wizzer."

"How best to put this," said Sky. "So that even you will understand. No one, other than an individual with equally disturbed mental faculties, would ever conceive of such a thing as a fire breathing toy dog."

"I wasn't talking to you Blinky. Stay out of it or I'll have my dog melt you."

Sky was indignant, or performed a good emulation of the emotion. "I am a sophisticated computer and artificial intelligence. My name is Sky, not 'Blinky.'"

"Okay you two, play nice." Mark glanced at Kat, who was trying not to laugh. "Anyway Kat, I know you like to explore the scrapwards looking for data cards."

Kat stared ahead as if seeing something beyond the horizon. "Do you really think people used to live in the scrapwards? The old video games and videos are one thing, showing safe, clean cities with lots of people, but all we've seen in real life are broken, old ruins."

"Actually, what you saw in those videos and games, is a reasonably accurate representation of what the scrapwards ones were." As usual, Sky spoke as if he had been there, which might be true, they had no idea exactly how old the AI was. "They were vast cities prior to the devastation, sprawling for miles over developed land. Millions of people used to live, work, and recreate in some of the largest cities. There were enormous towers hundreds of feet tall often referred to as skyscrapers, that were capable of holding thousands of people at once. Between the buildings ran smoothly pared roads crowded with automobiles, carrying the inhabitants to their destinations."

Kat rolled her eyes extravagantly in disbelief, a motion that included a wide arching of her head. Clearly she thought this to be a fairy tale concocted by Sky for an undisclosed purpose, or may be an extreme exaggeration. "Come on Sky, I'm not stupid. There are not millions of people in the whole world. If there were, there's no way you could feed them all. Can you imagine how many sheep, and chickens, and fish they would eat. It's ridiculous."

Mark cut into stave off another argument. "You've seen the images and videos Kat, you know the cities existed."

"Yeah, okay, there were huge cities. But I still say there's no such thing as millions of people."

The tips of the Jagged Hills for which this scrapward was named, peeked above the horizon ahead, growing smoothly larger to fill the Truck's windshield as they approached. Now that he could see the hills, it would only take another hour for them to reach the scrapward. In his experience, scrapwards were typically named for some prominent geographical feature nearby, a landmark that made them easy to find and identify.

It was his hope they could avoid encountering robots or bandits in or around the scrapward, no matter how much Kat wanted to. His preference was to avoid a fight, but he know that Kat enjoyed brawling, to the point that he constantly worried for her safety. Kat was an undeniably skilled fighter, both with and without weapons of all kinds, but she had a bad habit of rushing in without thought, and attacking anyone or anything that looked to her as if they might be a bad guy.

Soon the scrapward itself was in sight. It was situated below a series of knife edged, rocky ridged hills maybe two hundred feet tall at their highest point, and mostly devoid of vegetation. The scrapward was three miles across, and formed an irregular squarish shape. Outside the readily identifiable boundary of the scrapward, was flat, empty land holding only hints of pavement, or building foundations to show that more structures once existed there. Inside the unmarked perimeter of the scrapward, the ground was littered with a variety of fallen and shattered buildings, and smaller random debris. Large chunks of concrete in unpredictable shapes and sizes lay everywhere, lengths of bent and rusted rebar poking out of them like a balding head of hair. Huge steel beams rose twisted and torn from abbreviated buildings to sit in heaps, the stripped skeletons of enormous, desiccated beasts. The countless husks of what were once land vehicles, cluttered packed and pitted roadways. The scrapward was primarily dull shades of gray, or brownish rust with only rare splashes of somewhat brighter color, or patches of green where desert plants grew through cracks in the old pavement and concrete. The hot noon sunlight sparkled and shimmered in the scrapward, where it reflected off of fragmented and cracked glass, or the rare bit of shiny metal.

The reason this old city, and others like it, were called scrapwards, was because scrappers and scavengers came here from far and wide to salvage anything they could use or trade. Scrappers would find tools, raw materials, books, and other items of value at a scrapward, then trade those finds at towns and farms for food or other needed supplies. Some of the more advanced scrappers like Mark and Kat, would use the raw materials to make their own trade goods. The various towns and settlements were always hungry for more tools and cook ware.

As they neared the scrapward, Mark sought out a good place to hide the Truck while they were away from it. The still erect walls of a roofless building less than a mile from the ward fit his needs. Driving into the structure by way of a partially missing wall, the wheel bounced on the rubble of an old floor as he pulled the Truck fully inside. Turning off the Truck, he and Kat got down from the high cab, and he activated the security system to alert them if the vehicle was tampered with. They had learned the hard way that people would steal anything they could, and maliciously break what they could not. One of the first upgrades he made to the Truck, using tools he conveniently found in the back after they ironically stole it from some thieves, was to install a rudimentary anti-theft system. A system that now involved self-tracking lasers, and high voltage discharges.

Mark pulled a motorized folding cart out of a side compartment on the Truck. He would use the cart to carry the collected scrap back when they were done. Kat meanwhile, grabbed a collapsible platform that she wore like a backpack, which she would use to haul whatever scrap she chose to find. Mark and Kat each put on a device they called a heads-up-display, named after a similar tool Kat saw in a video. The HUDs were data and communications devices. They clamped behind a user's ear, with a thin arm extending to place a foldaway screen in front of one eye. The HUDs included sensors to detect materials and useful substances for when they scavenged, and also to find and track robots, bandits, or any other known threats. They were capable of displaying maps, videos, and other information as required. Mark had programmed the HUDs with a locater beacon, so that he and Kat could always find one another. They were voice activated and controlled, responding only to a registered user.

"Display list of needed materials." The data scrolled onto Mark's HUD screen, where he scanned it for a minute. It was the usual staff, metals, plastic, glass, rubber if it could be found, and other miscellaneous materials at progressively lesser priorities.

"I'm going to look for data cards. I'd like to find some new games and videos." Kat held up her media and game player for emphasis. "If I'm lucky, I might even find some music." The MGP was by far Kat's favorite toy. It could play music, videos, and games in many different formats, either on its own small screen, or by wirelessly connecting to other devices like the HUDs. She had found the thing years ago in a scrapward, and to his amazement, when the power crystal was replaced and charged, it worked. He offered to make her a new one with the swarm to replace the scratched and faded original, but she adamantly refused to part with it, carrying it wherever she went.

Mark smiled at the declaration of her intention to play around. "Okay, go have fun. But make sure you bring back some good scrap when the day is over."

"I will." She turned to run into the scrapward, the octagonal silver eye tattooed on her calf flashing in the sun.

"And stay out of trouble!" He shouted after her, entirely certain that she would define trouble differently than he did.

She waved at him, but did not look back or slow her pace, focused entirely on discovering imagined treasures.

"I consider the probability low, that Kat will return with much of any real value," offered Sky.

"May be not, but at least she will have a good time doing it."

"So long as she does not create or attract unnecessary problems for us, I will withhold complaints upon her return."

"That's reassuring." Mark secured his tool pack on the cart, turned on the motor, and walked it toward the old city. He pushed the cart to a good speed, needing the motor assist only a little when it was unloaded. He moved fast, knowing how dangerous it was to be in the open this close to a scrapward, he wanted to get into the relative shelter of the buildings quickly. Once inside the perimeter he activated the scanning program on his HUD, using it to locate a good concentration of the materials they needed. The HUD displayed a grid overlay of the scrapward map, which he had made with a drone on a previous visit. Material locations were marked on the grid relative to his own, with distances included. Each location showed a list of the materials present, along with the quantity of individual resources.

During past explorations of scrapwards, Mark had found many pieces of old technology or software code, and he recorded the blue prints or source code in memory storage. He could later retrieve the data to recreate or modify the discoveries to suit their needs. The value of any given find was unpredictable, one day's trash could turn out to be the next day's, unexpected necessity.

Going over the HUD's scan results, he saw a promising concentration of materials two thousand feet ahead and to the left, and started off in that direction. Because there were so many scrap wards in the world, and material was plentiful within them, it was not hard to obtain basic resources for crafting trade goods. Scavenging could be harder for those who did not have the ability to construct tools out of scrap metal, it could be downright hazardous for those who encountered predatory scavengers. There were thieves who, instead of doing the work of scavenging themselves, would watch for people leaving a scrapward with a full load. If these people looked weak or vulnerable, they could be attacked or killed for their scrap. For this reason, most scavengers carried weapons to protect themselves and their finds from predation, he and Kat were no exception.

Mark made his way slowly over the wreckage of the old city, caution being wiser than haste now that he was no longer in the open. If he was not careful in a place like this, it was all too possible to step on something that could puncture or slice open a foot, or put his weight on a weak spot of pavement that would drop him into a sewer or subway. Even if he was not injured in such a fall, the stink of waste left to stagnate for a hundred and fifty years was not an experience he would wish on anyone. He glanced at his HUD regularly, staying alert for movement or heat signatures that might be people or robots. Sky would warn him of the presence of either, but it made him feel safer to confirm it himself.

The broad, paved roads, called streets that divided scrap wards into somewhat irregular sections, were littered with junk, most of it derelict vehicles abandoned or ownerless after the Devastation. They were frequently partially stripped by earlier scavengers and occasionally there would be a little faded paint visible on their decaying, rust riddled carcasses. Large segments of old buildings lay collapsed along the streets, leaving whole stretches of concrete and steel worn and pitted from exposure to wind and rain to block his way forward. The potholed and cracked street was littered with glittering shards of glass, bits of old furniture, and other random detritus, not all of it pleasant to look at or smell.

What was life like for the ancient people? He wondered while breaking down the remains of a plastic chair, loading the sun-bleached pieces on to the cart. He thought about the lives of the city dwellers, of what it would be like to stay in such enormous buildings with so many other people. Did they love together peacefully, or did they fight and prey upon one another? Did they eat and sleep communally or avoid interaction? He had difficulty picturing the scrap ward as it must have looked when it was a city. The people who lived now, did not build anything nearly as big as the ruined structures that surrounded him. The majority of these buildings were badly damaged, seldom reaching more than twenty or thirty feet in height.

Some of the signs on buildings and poles was still legible, and he made a mental exercise out of trying to decipher their time obscured meanings. Each street he passed had its own name and there were even different names for streets. There were avenues, parkways, boulevards, and roads. Why did the past people feel such a strong need to come up with so many names for the exact same thing? After all, it would be far simpler, and less confusing to number them in a basic grid based system. With a grid everyone could be given a set of numeric coordinates, and they would know exactly where to go. But they were intent on making it more troublesome and confounding to find their way around. There was no point in him worrying over it, the people of the old world were long dead, and he accepted that there were parts of their world he would never understand.

Following the indicator on his HUD, he reached a large flat paved area covered in old land vehicles, all lined up in more or less neat rows. There was a faded sign above what he took to be the entrance, since it was the only part free of vehicles. The writing on the sign was mostly visible, STADIUM PARKING ONLY. All others will be towed at owner's expense. Having no idea what the message meant, he ignored it and examined the vehicles. Although they were worn by age, damaged, and partially salvaged in some cases, there was still a great deal of useable material to be had here.

"Alright Sky, time to work. Mark approached a derelict and set out his tools. Most of the time the only thing he needed was a multi-purpose cutting laser to chop the scrap into manageably small pieces. He also had hammers, prybars, shears, and other hand tools in his pack. Once it was broken apart, he would load the material onto the cart for the trip out of the scrap ward. When his tools were prepared, he activated the cutter and set to dissecting the first vehicle of the day.

Kat liked to make a workout and a game out of her scavenging time, especially when she was on her own. If a thing was worth doing, she may as well have fun doing it. Jogging into the scrapward, she set her wrist lower to its lowest, non-damaging output, the one she used for target practice, so that it would emit only harmless beams of colored light. It was a useful setting for training and target practice, or for pointing to things in the distance.

The area became her own personal gymnasium and shooting gallery, a playground of obstacles and imaginary enemies. She ran through open, flat spaces, vaulted and flipped acrobatically over cars and boulders in her path, swung on poles and ledges, and rolled or slid under low hanging beams. Relying on the automatic alarms of her HUD to warn her of potential danger, she leaped and romped her way into the ruins of the old city. She pretended to be surrounded by robots on all sides, imagining the killer machines moving in to attack her. She took aim at small objects, the mirror on the side of the husk of a vehicle, a doorknob hanging loosely from a busted door. She drilled laser fire into the nonexistent enemies, while ducking under pretend lasers in return.

When she was happy with the improvised target practice, she altered the settings of her antigrav flight pack, reversing the output to actually make herself heavier. She then loaded a hand to hand combat simulation into her HUD. The tool could display any kind of image or animation the user desired. In this instance, she had it show the first of a series of martial arts opponents that she had programmed into memory with Sky's help. The images shown were seamlessly superimposed over what she actually saw around her, the HUD then incorporated objects from the environment into the simulation.

Getting into the fake fight, Kat punched, kicked, and blocked phantom attacks from her digital foes, fighting with every ounce of speed and ferocity she could muster under the increased weight generated by the flight pack. In minutes she worked up a good sweat, and with the defeat of her tenth straight adversary she was breathing hard, signaling an end to training.

Deactivating the fighting simulation, she loaded a music playlist to listen to on her hunt, and reduced the gravity on her flightpack to normal. Today's music selection was heavy on fast paced songs her MGP identified as rock, the high tempo perfect to keep her moving quickly in her limited exploration time. A while ago she used the HUD's built in sensors to comprehensively scan a data card, determining its exact composition of plastic, silicon, and copper. This allowed her to create a custom sensor template she saved for future searches. So far it had served her well.

She felt light without the heavying of her flight pack, down to her normal hundred and twenty pound weight. She adjusted the position of the platform on her back, as it had shifted with all her running and jumping. It was important to bring scrap back at the end of the day, unless she wanted to endure another long lecture from Mark and Sky. But there were hours to go before she needed to worry about it, and not until after she collected a bunch of new data cards. She could even find something fun to play with, like when she discovered the MGP. If she was really lucky, some robots would turn up for her to destroy, that would be a good day.

According to her HUD, there was a very promising concentration of what should be data cards to the north. It could be the largest cache of them she had found to date. The reading was a mile from her, and while there were closer spots to look at, most of them were much too small to waste her time with on this trip.

Starting out for the deposit, conveniently marked on her HUD with a green X, she looked with curiosity at everything she passed, hoping to spot something amazing. The scrapward was partially cooperative with her wish, except when it came to color. The streets and buildings were almost uniformly gray, with bits of black or brown thrown in for variety. Every so often an old vehicle or sign would show a hint of color, but most vehicles were covered in a thick patina of reddish-brown rust, or at the least, were so faded as to make their original color indeterminate. She wondered if the people in these cities preferred everything to be so dull, or if they had laws of rules that only their vehicles could be different colors. She would try to ask Sky about it sometime. And on the topic of vehicles, there were always tons of them in the scrapwards, could every person have had more than one? Perhaps each person had several of them, and they were painted a specific color for each intended task. For instance, they might have had a blue one to fetch water in, a green one for food, best of all a pink one just for fun. Kat had yet to see a pink vehicle, but believed there must have been a lot of them. If you could paint your vehicle any color you wanted, why choose a color other than pink?

She passed the remnants of a big square building with an ugly hole torn from one side, and she could picture a ginormous animal wandering the city to take bites out of buildings, a concretosaur. Some of the building's windows had the occasional pane of intact glass in place, too dirty to see through clearly. Here and there along the street were whole doors interspersed among the broken or missing ones. The complete doors were mostly made of metal.

In spots bits of text were clear enough for her to read. The writing on doors rarely made sense to her, which probably meant she knew too little of the past to understand it. Confusing or not, she liked to read them. Some of what she read was, 'Brontin Business Tower,' 'Fresh Doughnuts,' whatever a doughnut was 'Open Late,' and 'Jaywalking prohibited,' which was more confusing than most. She knew that a jay was a type of bird, but could think of no reason they would not be allowed to walk here, or hop, or whatever it was birds did on the ground. Some things about the old world would always be incomprehensible.

She reached the green X on her HUD, a location that turned out to be a small collapsed building. Hanging crookedly from the front of the structure by a single rusted bolt, was part of a broken sign saying 'Movies, Music, and Games.' What was most likely the name of the store, was almost completely missing above the remaining text. According to her HUD, there was a large quantity of data cards buried somewhere under the rubble. All she could do was cut her way into the structure, and hope that when she reached the interior, a few of the cards were intact and functional. Climbing to the peak of the seven foot tall mound of rubble that was a store, she centered herself directly over the highest concentration of data cards.

"Please let there be some working cards under this stuff." She intoned as if making a sincere plea, or perhaps a small prayer.

Altering the output of her wrist laser to a medium intensity cutting beam, she slowly sliced out a section of outer roof, and tossed it over the side of the mound. Underneath was more of the ruined structure. She repeated the cutting procedure one layer at a time, sort of like removing all the leaves from an ear of corn. Why was corn called an ear? It did not look like any ear she had ever seen. She spent an hour carefully clearing a path to the cards, humming along with her music, and all the while daydreaming of the amazing things she would find on them.

When the last piece of roof finally came away from the hole, she found what she took to be crushed wire shelves on the floor of the shop. Scattered between and around the shelves was a shining treasure trove of flattened and mangled media boxes, radiating a plethora of vibrant colors and imaginative titles where they lay newly exposed to daylight. Because they were shielded all this time from the harmful ultraviolet rays of the sun, the labels and covers were clear and sharp. The collapsed building may have smashed most of the data cards into tiny, unreadable fragments, but it also protected them from the ravages of the elements.

Eyes alight with uncontained excitement, she picked up each box, read its title and examined the cover art, before opening it to retrieve the data card from its crushed cardboard depths. There were movies and videos with titles like Vampire Apocalypse, and a Time for Rain. Games with names such as Galactic Death Ring, and Stories from Fantasia. And a variety of music albums and collections. Unsurprisingly, if disappointingly, most of the data cards were busted, many smashed to little bits, some, obviously cracked to unusability. A few, however, appeared physically sound. She placed the whole cards into a pile to be tested later on. She carefully expanded the hole as needed, and felt around or crawled through open pockets until she got her hands on every last box. When she was certain that nothing had escaped her, that not a single potentially functional card was lost, she placed the intact cards into a pouch tied to her waist, and climbed out of the building.

Now that she was no longer crawling around a darkened hole, the sun's declining position told her that it was becoming late. That meant she had to hurry and gather scrap, then heal it back to the Truck. And more importantly, the faster she was done working, the sooner she could test the new data cards.

Glancing half heartedly at the day's material list confirmed what she expected, that it was more of the same old scrap they always wanted, no special request searches this trip. Sometimes special requests could be fun, but not when she had better things to do. Vehicles were perfect for quick scavenging, they contained most of the materials Mark made stuff out of. Steel, glass, plastic, and tire rubber were all plentiful in vehicles, in addition to copper, cloth, and silicon in smaller amounts. She walked to a cluster of four vehicles, and unfolded her platform on a flat spot of pavement. Checking that her laser was still on the right setting, she started by cutting off a roof, then removed windows and severed body panels. She put each part on the platform as she worked tossing it on with minimal concern for organizing or balancing the load. Steel was the top priority since it was always in demand. Mark used it to make tools, cookware, and sometimes vehicles or buildings. Next came the plastic parts and rubber tires, although what was left of the tires was prone to crumbling when lifted which could be very annoying. Sometimes a vehicle would have old synthetic cloth that was salvageable. The cloth could be turned into harnesses or clothing, typically for her and Mark.

Some materials, the super strong alloy her armor was made of for example, were very rare and much harder to find. What they did possess of that metal, they took from the armor plated vehicles of an abandoned military convoy they stumbled upon. What they did not use for her armor or the armor plating on the Truck, was broken down into bricks for storage. Along with the armor alloy, they kept a supply of rare and not so rare materials on hand. Metals like gold and palladium, crystals and gems, like diamond. They also had stores of some common but useful substances like silicon for circuits, graphite for lubrication and fabrication and a variety of plastics. Mark strongly believed in being prepared for anything, and his habit of hoarding supplies had saved them from trouble more than once.

Three hours of dissecting later, the sun was falling low on the horizon and the platform was stacked with a respectable amount of scrap. She considered it to be a productive day of scavenging all around. She secured the hefty load, lashing it down firmly with straps built into the platform. She unclipped the platform's control unit from its storage slot, uncoiling the tether that connected the two together and served as a towing cable. She activated the platform's antigrav, making it lighter until it floated five feet above the ground. The platform was designed by Mark to be towed by Kat while she was flying. Its weight and elevation could be altered as needed via the controller. She activated her flight pack, rising into the air with a firm grip on the tether

When her flightpack was in use, two small ovoid antigrav units on the back of her armor, between her shoulder blades, extended four inches from the center of the pack. They made a light humming sound while she flew, too soft to hear from more than a few feet away. The return trip to the Truck would take far less time in the air, than it had coming in on foot. She was so excited to start checking the data cards that it felt to her like it was taking a lot longer. "I'm going to play a new game tonight." She smiled in anticipation; and flew faster.

Mark's day was at least a productive at Kat's, he had every reason to believe it was more so since he adhered to the list. He had filled the cart almost to its two thousand pound capacity, a slightly arbitrary number based on the known strengths of its component materials. But unlike Kat's grab everything in sight method of gathering, he was for more selective of the type and quality of the scrap he collected. It was long and tiring work, and he was more than ready to return to the Truck.

"Kat has arrived at the Truck." Reported Sky.

Mark placed one last bundle of wires on the cart. "I hope she brought decent load of scrap with her."

"Sensors on the platform indicate that it has been filled to two hundred and sixteen pounds beyond capacity."

"That's good." Mark arched his back to ease sore muscles, then smiled. "And if I know Kat, she has data cards too."

"Her heads-up display reports the successful acquisition of data cards. The quantity suggests a high probability that some of them will be functional."

When the final bit of scrap was loaded onto the cart, Mark verified that everything was evenly distributed for balance and strapped securely in place. That done, he grabbed his tool bag and gave the area casual once over to be sure that he left nothing important behind. "I wouldn't mind playing a new game or two myself." He checked his HUD for any kind of movement between him and the Truck. "Sky, do you detect people or robots? "

"At present I am unable to detect the presence of mechanical or biological entities in the area,

"We should head back then. Turning on the cart, Mark began the slow, rugged trek through the scrapward. It was a good thing the cart was here to do the hard work for him, he was much too tired to push and shove the heavy load without the motor. The cart made a crunching sound as its knobby tires rolled across the rocky concrete rubble of the old city. Bits of stone kicked up here and there by the cart's passage, ticking and pinging off of whatever hard surface they happened to hit. The compact electric motor generated high torque for moving heavy loads, but was nearly silent most of the time, only making a significant whine when it had to push itself up a steep hill or over a larger obstacle

Mark tried to always leave a place by a different route, than the one he used to enter it. That way it was harder for anything or anyone to set an ambush for him. for the same reason, he scavenged at a different scrapward each time they went out. Traps were harder if he was unpredictable

In a curious mood now that his work was done, Mark had questions about the past, and Sky was the closest thing he had to an expert. "Can you tell me what this strap ward was like before the Devastation?

"Certainly," began Sky in his information dispensing voice. "As you know, the landscape was dramatically altered by the cataclysmic event known colloquially as the Devastation. Valley's became mountains, islands were absorbed into the sea, forests turned into barren desserts, and more that I will refrain from itemizing of this time. Because of these unparalleled geographic alterations, and the reality that cities were damaged beyond the possibility of recognition. The specific identification of this, on any other city is exceedingly problematic if not impossible. I am, however, able to provide you with generalized information that would be applicable to a city of this size, if you so desire."

"Yes please."

There was a brief pause while Sky parsed and collated data. "A vast number of people by your standards, would have lived and worked here. Even more people would have commuted here from the surrounding a suburban area to work or recreate within the city. Many people lived their entire lives in the city, leaving it only infrequently, if ever. Jobs available to people in a city included clerical or office work, sanitation such as refuse collection, or service related positions, most typically in food preparation or distribution. Recreation, entertainment, or leisure activities on offer in these urban centers were plentiful and diverse, One popular spectator event was a form of ritualized combat. The warriors were very large males dressed in brightly colored shorts, and little else. Before combat was allowed to commence the warriors were required to demean and insult each other for several minutes. Combat was performed on a roped off square platform that was incongruously called a ring. The ring boundaries did not stop warriors from venturing into the audience, to retrieve a chair from a spectator for use as a weapon.

Despite having asked, Mark tuned out much of what Sky was saying, he was not sure that all of Sky's data regarding the old world was entirely accurate. Many times what Sky told him was incredibly bizarre, making it sound as if the people of long ago were all insane. Once Sky told him that people wrapped the dried leaves of plants in paper, then lit the paper on fire to inhale the smoke. Even more ridiculous, was that they supposedly did this to help them relax. He had a hard time making sense of such strange tales. Were they really true? He suspected that Kat preferred the odd stories, probably finding them funny. Who knows, she might even believe them. He chose not to tell Sky of his lack of belief, there was no sense in offending the AI, if that was even possible.

At the edge of the scrapward he looked consideringly at a building, briefly wondering what it was used for when this was a city full of people. He paused for a moment to scan for potential threats, before stepping out to cross the open space between the scrapward and the hidden Truck. Walking swiftly over the rocky ground, and feeling like a target the whole way, he covered the distance in four minutes. He was relieved when the Truck came in to view, particularly when he spotted Kat on the ground alone and unharmed. Kat already had her scrap stowed, and her platform put away.

Seated cross-legged on the dirty floor with her MGP in hand, Kat was completely engrossed in what she was doing. Her eyes stared intensely at the little screen, giving it her full concentration. In front of her rested two short piles of data cards, with more of them strewn randomly around her. The MGP made its annoying error noise and Kat removed a data card from the device with a frustrated growl, demonstrating why there were scattered cards by tossing it. Gently, almost reverently, picking up another card from the taller stack, she brought her hands together and softly chanted.

"Please work for me little card, I'll take really good care of your from now on if you work."

When she was done, the card was inserted into the MGP and tested is for readable data seconds later the error noise sounded to report a negative read. She growled loudly and flung the offending card away with the other failures. Not stopping as Mark approached, she slid the next card from the stack, and repeated her little ritual

He directed the cart to the Truck. "Found any working cards yet."

"Some." Came the terse reply

Thinking it beneficial to his health not to bother her for a while, he left her to it, and opened the rear doors on the Truck. Unstrapping the scrap, he took care to load it evenly into the main storage area, He knew from near disastrous past mistakes that a shifting load could be dangerous when he was driving fast, particularly as speed almost invariably meant they were running from something. Although running was not the concern these days that it once was. When he was satisfied that everything would stay put, he closed and locked the doors, collapsed the cart into storage configuration, and shoved it into its storage compartment locking the door on it.

The last of his work finished, Mark pulled off his gloves, brushed the dust from his clothes, and sat with Kat. But not too closely. He waited quietly for her to check the cards

He first met Kat when they were both very young, around five years old at best guess. He had just lost everything and everyone he knew, and she came stumbling, out of the woods behind him, her stomach rumbling. A filthy, starving girl in badly torn and stained clothing, and a look

of object fear in her purple eyes. Just about the sorriest thing he had ever seen, and at that moment the most beautiful, a ray of light in the darkness. They became family to each other that day and were totally inseparable ever since, no matter what adversity came their way. Kat was happy and outgoing, able to see the upside of any situation, always finding a way to have a good time. It was as if she saw the world as her own personal playground. On the downside, she could be impatient and quickly frustrated at times. She was even known to have a violent temper when provoked, but she did not stay angry for long, and never hold a grudge.

Kat woke him from his reverie with a boisterous whoop. "I got another game!" she carefully removed the valuable card from the MGP, which had already made a full copy of its data, and set it down on the stack of working cards, pulled on a soft cloth laid out to protect them. Smiling with victory, she picked up another card to test, resuming her ritual. In the end, she found one more video, and a card full of music. This was a good day, many times she came away with no working cards at all. But then again, looking at all the cards scattered on the floor, this was an unusually large haul. After checking the last card, to a negative result, she copied the new data to recently made data cards, then placed the new and old cards into a hard metal case that she stored all of her data cards in to protect and store them.

She stood and stretched with a wide yawn, raising her arms above her head with wrists crossed. Her joints popped loudly from sitting in the same position for so long. She smiled broadly at him. "Thanks for waiting for me to finish, we can go now. You drive while I try a new game."

He grinned as she helped him to his feet, and they walked together to the Truck. The dead cards were left where they lay, forlorn, and again forgotten. He opened the driver's door, the security system having already been deactivated by Kat, and climbed into the seat behind the wheel. Once they were both strapped in, he pressed his thumb to the biometric scanner, and pushed the power button to turn on the Truck. The Truck used electric motors, and only needed to be turned on to be driven, but the biometric security helped ensure that only he or Kat could do so. It was a sensible precaution, considering how they got the Truck in the first place

The Truck was their home, their transportation, and their lifeline. It contained all of their most important possessions, their food and water, everything they needed in order to survive. It was their only vehicle, what allowed them to travel from place to place and what offered them rapid escape from danger. They rarely slept inside the Truck, frequently spending their nights in caves or the towns they traded with. There were two, fold-down bunks in the back of the Truck, but they were small and seldom used. If a night was pleasant enough, they could sleep on cots under the stars or beneath a retractable canopy. Leaving Sky to watch for bandits, robots, or the occasional dangerous animal.

They were currently staying in a secluded cave not too far distant from the Jagged hills scrapward and it was to this cave that Mark would return them. It was pushing early evening the sun a hand width above the horizon, but the day was still warm and bright. The quiet calm of the drive was interrupted only by the crunch of tires on the rocky ground, and the digital music and gunfire on the game Kat played on her MGP.

The terrain was not entirely consistent, at times relatively flat and free of major obstacles, but it could also be pock marked with holes, or interrupted by large rocks or boulders. The Truck's tires were three feet tall and fifteen inches wide, contributing greatly to the vehicle's high ground clearance, and its ability to be driven practically anywhere.

The Truck's exterior was covered by a layer of highly efficient photo voltaic cells, coated in a protective skin of super tough transparent memory polymer tinted a dark green. Mark had to practically fight Kat to make the Truck green, as she demanded pink. The electricity collected by the cells, was stored in a pair of high-density synthetic power crystals. The crystals were a pre-Devastation technology and had a very large storage capacity for their size. Two medium sized power crystals could run the Truck at normal output for several days on a single charge, more than they had ever needed. The synthetic crystals were a technology they could not replicate, the reason for their value as trade items when found the bigger the better. Thankfully they were quite difficult to damage.

Almost directly in their path ahead was an odd heap of rock and metal. It was more than likely nothing more than a harmless collapsed building, but it was a formation he did not remember being here, and that alone made it worth avoiding. He steered wide of it to be safe. Right before they passed the rubble, an alarm sounded in the cab loud enough to be obnoxious over the wind flowing through his window. A second later the entire mound shifted, rising rapidly from the ground.

As the mass lifted higher, rock sloughed from it to clatter loudly on the ground. In seconds an unknown mechanical monster materialized from the mound, to charge right at them. It was a huge robot startlingly reminiscent of a massive metal crab, with a rounded central body and small stubby head. Four legs sprouted from either side of the flat topped carapace, and a pair of long three-digit manipulator arms mounted in the front. It was constructed of a bluish alloy, and clad in thick armor plating on limbs and body, shooting upright on the multi-jointed legs, the robot's body stood fifteen feet in height, and twenty wide from leg to leg. The crab's long legs gave it impressive speed, and it soon started to close the gap between them. Mark stomped on the accelerator pedal, Kicking up rocks and dust while steering away from their pursuer.

Losing all interest in her game, Kat stared at the robot in awe and shouted. "All right, it's a super robot attack crab! Now we can have fun!"

He spared her an exasperated glance, one that was utterly ignored by the enraptured Grymal. She was smiling wide eyed at the monster chasing them, practically jumping out of her seat in excitement over her unbelievably good luck. "This is not a good thing Kat. That thing could seriously hurt us, or at the least badly damage the truck." He hoped his stern tone would help her understand the seriousness of the situation, but knew it was a wasted effort.

Still grinning but trying not to look too thrilled, which meant she only appeared to be having the second best day of her life, she spoke in a more subdued tone. One that sounded like she was only mildly amused by the prospect of facing a huge robot. "I didn't say I was happy we're being attacked by an awesome giant crab bot. But since we are, I may as well enjoy it."

Mark bit back a caustic reply.

A minute later Sky offered an evaluation of their attempt to escape. "I do not believe the Truck is capable of outrunning this robot. It has an overland velocity at least equal to our own."

"I guess we can blow it up then." Kat sounded as if nothing in the world would please her more, than to fight an unfamiliar giant robot that could probably crush her armor without trying, which was likely true. She stood on her seat, activated her flight pack, and leaped into the air to valiantly plunge headfirst into battle with their immense foe. Or in simple terms, she was in a rush to play with a new toy.

Mark rolled his eyes in frustrated resignation, and activated the Truck's weapon systems with the press of a button. "Sky, target that robot and hit it with our big turrets."

A pair of identical laser turrets rose from their storage positions on the back of the Truck, turning to target the oncoming crab. Kat flew around the crab pelting it with blasts from her forearm lasers. The weapons were having little discernible effect on the bluish armor of the robot. Larger beams from the turrets joined Kat's smaller bursts in hitting the carapace, scorching streaks onto the alloy, but causing it no damage.

Sky vocalized the obvious in case they missed it. "Our lasers do not appear sufficiently powerful to damage this robot, I recommend employing an alternative strategy."

"I'm open to suggestions."

The crab, unfazed by their attacks and undeterred in its pursuit, was gradually closing on the Truck. Without slowing, it picked up a man sized rock, and hurled it with ease at the truck. The boulder hit the ground far too close for comfort, shattering on impact and spraying the Truck with shards of stone.

Mark's heartrate jumped in alarm, thumping wildly in his chest. "Sky, target those rocks with our lasers, don't let them hit us."

"Compliance."

"Kat, try shooting that thing with a missile."

The crab lobbed more rocks at the Truck, and at Kat who was a hummingbird flitting around above it. Kat had no trouble dodging the clumsy attacks, while Sky expertly shot rocks out of the air before they came close to striking the Truck.

Kat's armament included four small but potent concussive missiles. The weapons were rarely used, her lasers being more than sufficient to blast the robots they usually fought. Arming a missile, she aimed it at the crab's body and launched it. The weapon raced through the air trailing a white streamer of propellant, impacting on the armor with a sizeable explosion. When smoke from the blast cleared, the armor was scuffed and blackened, but otherwise undamaged.

"The missile only scratched the crab, I don't think we have enough of them to stop it. We would need like a thousand more." The joy had left her voice, as the reality of an indestructible foe sunk in.

The crab closed on the Truck unwaveringly, their lead becoming distressingly small, and the rocks much too close.

"Do you have any ideas?" Kat dodged another rock and maintained a steady it useless, stream of laser fire. "We can't keep this up all day."

"I have detected a deep ravine approximately two miles to the northwest of our position. If we jump the Truck over it, the robot may be unable to follow us".

Mark swerved right to head for Sky's ravine, the location already marked on his HUD, and saw a flash of something else on the map far from them. "Works for me. Kat, you heard Sky, we have to reach that ravine. Keep shooting the crab to distract it.

She took him a bit literally, "Distraction huh? No problem, I know what to do." she replied calmly. She shouted at the crab while maintaining her attack. "Come on you big, ugly, worthless excuse for a crab. Your mamma was a snow blower."

"I do not anticipate any alteration in the robot's behavior, from the act of insulting its non-existent parentage."

Mack said nothing as be completed the sharp turn to point the Truck at the ravine. The crab lost ground to them as it made the turn more slowly, skittering over the rocky terrain on its long, less nimble legs and smallish feet.

"Show me a scan of the ravine, Sky."

"Displaying three-dimensional topographic image."

A detailed small-scale projection of the ravine appeared to his right. The foot long hologram rotated slowly in front of the windshield, listing the segment's actual length at one mile. Dividing his attention between driving and examining the image, he saw what looked to be the skeletal remnants of a wide bridge. The base support structure was partially intact on either side of the ravine, leaving most of the fifty foot gap empty. The rest of the erstwhile bridge must have fallen into the deep gash. Large steel girders stuck out from the support randomly, like the fingers of a giant twisted. hand.

"Kat, when I start to jump over the marine, I need you to shoot the ground in front of the crab with all your weapons really kick up the dirt.

"Tell me when."

Mark flipped a switch on the console, routing power to the antigrav jump system he had built into the Truck. He almost never used the system, it was hard on the suspension and tires, but he was glad to have it when needed. "Sky, please calculate the settings we need for the jump, then map it to the button for me. I don't want any mistakes when we jump.

A second later the calculations were complete. "Antigrav is set at forty-two percent power, and jump duration is at six point three seconds."

He could see the ravine now a dark slash across the landscape. The supports of the bridge extended high above the ground. Pedal jammed to the floorboard, he drove full speed for the old bridge. He could see the far side clearly, and pointed the Truck straight at the jutting girders on the opposite wall of the canyon. He anxiously watched the edge of the drop off race to meet him, hammering down the jump button at the last moment.

"Kat, now!" He shouted as the Truck lurched off of the ground to soar over the gap.

Kat fired lasers and missiles into the dirt twenty feet in front of the charging crab, rock fragments, dirt, and smoke filled the air in the crab's path, completely obscuring it in the Truck's side mirror. Without hesitation the crab ran directly into the cloud, and leaped after its prey. The Truck came down on the far side of the ravine with a mighty bounce on its big tires, fishtailing in a slide to the right, before Mark spun the wheel to straighten it out and regain control. Kat pelted the crab with laser fire on its unaided flight. For one, gut churning, moment, he was certain the crab would land successfully behind him, but rather than touch down feet first on the ground, the crab's mighty carapace struck a girder dead on with a wrenching clang. The momentum of the jump, combined with the crab's sheer mass, impaled its large body on the rusty beam, firmly lodging the robot halfway down its length.

The crab struggled violently to free itself, its legs thrashing wildly in the air like a beetle flipped on to its back. Electricity arced across the steel and jumped between the robot's Legs

"Oh look, a crab on a stick." Kat launched her last missile at the base of the girder, snapping it off with a loud crack. It fell, crab and all, into the dark abyss below. Two seconds later a shattering crash issued from the depths. The fight had served to work up Kat's appetite. "Can we have crab kebabs for dinner?"

CHAPTER 2

Kat woke damp and stiff, a shaft of golden sunlight lancing through a break in the branches to shine in her eyes. She shivered in the cool dawn breeze, shifting on her perch to extract her arms from the tangle of narrow tree limbs she was slumped over. Her skin was raw and red, the rough bark leaving ugly marks and angry scratches all over her exposed arms, her threadbare and torn clothing offering scarcely any protection to the skin it sort of covered. At least she was mostly dry this morning, rain was not uncommon in recent nights, and it was many a morning she came awake drenched and miserable. She looked out at the forest, her view only partially hampered by the thinning screen of leaves on the trees. The summer green of leaves was slowly giving way to brighter red, oranges and yellows as trees went dormant with the onset of fall. The pretty changing colors of the foliage was what she liked about this time of year, a welcome diversion from the endless palette of green on offer over the heated months of summer.

The temperature was on a steady decline over the last few weeks, but the welcome breath of cooler air brought with it a regular drenching of torrential rain. Bracing her feet on the thin branches to keep from accidentally falling, she raised her arms upward to encourage fresh circulation in her sleep weakened muscles, feeling the unpleasant stickiness of humidity mixed with a dirty grittiness, she peeled the shirt from the skin of her neck. A good washing was in order the next time they encountered a stream.

Hunger was a constant, unwelcome companion for her, food being hard to come by on their own in the woods. Most days they ate insects, or if they were lucky, a small animal or bird. Mark's talkative computer Sky sometimes identified roots and mushrooms they could eat, but his memory held only limited information on edible plants. Her stomach rarely grumbled anymore, the only indication of her great hunger, was the deep, yawning emptiness that reached from her naval to her spine.

A soft intake of breath brought her gaze to Mark, he was nestled snugly in the crook of a branch, with his arms around several more. They slept high in trees most night by necessity, it was a lot safer than sleeping on the ground, where wondering robots or bandits could find them. Few people, or robots, thought to look up. She shifted to rub her thigh where a branch was pressed into it. Trees might be safer, but were never comfortable.

She was reluctant to wake her dozing friend, the oblivion of sleep was frequently preferable to the reality of hunger and pain, doubly so it he was having a pleasant dream. Staring at his exposed arms and hand, she was disturbed by how skinny they were. His skin looked stretched thinly over mere bone and sinew, that she knew her own body was no prettier was not a comfort. They really needed to find a reliable source of food, if things continued as they were they may not survive much longer. They knew the locations of several villages and farms where food could be found, but it was never free for the taking. Most people were not unsympathetic to a pair of starving kids, but they did not have such a surplus of food that it could be given away for nothing, some form of trade had to be worked out for the literal fruits of their hard labor. People were consistently in need of good tools and workable metal, things to that could be located by searching scrapwards. The problem was that two small, weak, children, were easy prey for the thieves and bandits who prowled the wards. More than once she and Mark had barely escaped such an encounter with their lives, and several times they came away badly injured.

It was a little over three years since the day she had met Mark, or as she thought of it, the day he rescued her. It was in a forest a lot like this one, but far from here or maybe not so far, everything here was forest for miles and miles, so it could all be the same vast expanse of trees. A tree ocean. And it might not have been that far, distances were much greater when she was five years old. She grunted at that, neither of them knew for sure how old they were. They had no memory of their parents, and it was no more than a guess that they were both about eight now, Sky agreed with the estimate and she trusted his judgment because he was really smart. Today she was determined to find them food, it was her duty as Mark's self-appointed protector to keep him healthy and safe. She was never going to be alone again.

She wrapped her legs firmly around the branches beneath her, bracing to catch Mark if he started to fall, then gently shook his arm to wake him.

"Mark, time to get up." There was probably no one nearby to hear her, but she spoke softly just in case.

Mark groaned softly as consciousness slowly resurfaced. He raised his head." Morning?" He mumbled.

"We need to climb down and look for food." They each carried plastic bottles with screw on lids for water, something they found in a partially collapsed building in a scrapward. There were lots of the bottles there in different colors. Mark chose green, and her's was pink. They ate well after that find. Most of the best stuff in scrap wards was hidden in partially or fully collapsed buildings, those that normal people were too scared to enter.

She unscrewed the cap from her bottle, tipping it back to drizzle what was left into her mouth, she shook the empty bottle meaningfully in Mark's face. "And water too." She shoved the bottle into her bag, then dropped it and her stick spear to the ground, hearing them clatter on branches as they fell.

"Yeah."

She climbed downward from their twenty foot perch, selecting her footing with care and staying under Mark to catch him if he slipped. She was sore from falling during a bad climb a week ago, and had no wish to add to her injuries. The branches got thicker and farther apart the lower she went, with the bottom most branch a good seven feet from the leafy ground. She lowered herself to dangle by her hands for a second before dropping the last few feet, where she hit the layer of crackling leaves with a jolt absorbed by her lean legs. A mild twinge of pain in her knees told her the landing was too hard, it faded quickly.

Mark came down moments later with somewhat less coordination, and a bit more noise. Grunting as his butt hit the ground when his legs buckled under his weight. He grinned at her sheepishly. "Oof."

Grinning in return, she pulled him up and helped brush the leaves free his pants. "Bug hunt."

The problem with bug hunts was not that they were hard to find, in fact there were insects all over the place, tons of them. The real issue was that they were mostly so small, that it was hard to eat enough of them to fill her stomach. Ants for instance, could take hours to pick up a few at a time and stuff into her mouth, and all the while the big ones would bite her all over.

Other insects had to be avoided altogether, bees and wasps stung and bit a lot, and spiders could make her very sick. Worms were one of the best, there was no way for them to hurt her, and they were so big she did not have to eat that many for a decent meal. Worms were easiest to find after it rained, when they wriggled to the surface all on their own. Plus the water made it easier to dig.

The ground this morning was damp and muddy, leaves and muck clung to her shoes with every step, seeping through holes and tears in the thin material. Soon her shoes were packed with gritty goo, and walking in them was scratchy and unpleasant. She tried to ignore the thick paste squishing between her toes, searching the ground and plants for food. Every once in a while they were able to kill and cook a larger animal like a rabbit or a raccoon, but that was rare. They were too quick and crafty to easily catch, disappearing into the bushes or up a tree before she or Mark could shoot or spear them. She and Mark each carried a hand laser taken from a robot. The weapons were big for their hands, but useable two handed. The energy charge in them was low, giving them few shots to waste, shots that had to be saved to fight off robots or bandits. Also, the lasers tended to char small animals to inedibility, or incinerate them altogether. Throwing rocks or stabbing with her stick spear were better options, she kept some good rocks in her pockets for that purpose.

They hunted for an hour, crunching down on whatever bugs they encountered, when Mark brought up something important. "It will be winter again soon, and this year. I want to have enough food to last us until spring. It's too hard to find food and scrap in the snow."

She knew he was right. When it was really cold and snow covered everything, the bugs and animals hid in holes in the ground or in trees, sometimes not coming out for months. They would have to find a steady source of food soon, or they might be in real trouble. They had barely scraped by the last two winters, scavenging in the forest while trying not to freeze to death, and trading what little scrap they found for food at villages. Even trading scrap could be dangerous, they were both so small that some people would take their scrap and give them nothing in return. If they were extra unlucky, the villagers would hit or attack them to steal their scrap. Lasers were only a limited deterrent for thieves, who were bigger, more numerous, and better armed. Another problem was that pulling a weapon on some people only made things worse, people did not like to be threatened, it made them angry, and angry people beat them harder.

"The only way I can think of to get that much food is to trade with a village, and that means a long walk carrying heavy scrap."

Mark lifted a chunk of rotting wood with a grunt, turning it over so the bottom was now the top. A writhing mass at scuttling critters was revealed underneath. He scooped a handful into his mouth. "We may not have any choice. We need food, and I don't want a repeat of last winter."

Kat nodded, crunching wriggling bugs that poked into the soft flesh of her mouth and tongue with hard shells and pincers. She thought back on last winter, how bad it was. They used an unoccupied cave for shelter and warmth, but bugs were scarce around it, and small animals non-existent. To make matters worse, the snow was really bad, too deep and cold to attempt going to a scrapward, not without freezing solid in the attempt. As it was, even brief forays outside left them with numb skin and painfully icy toes. It was not an experience she cared to repeat.

"When do you want to go?"

"It will take us at least three days to get there, plus we need time to search for good scrap, a day or two more. I say we finish eating and leave in an hour."

An optimistic estimate when it came to eating bugs, but it was not like they had anything, better to do, and the days were not getting any warmer. "Okay."

For Mark's hour they filled their stomachs as much as they could on insects, the log bugs turning out to be the largest meal of the morning. The sun was now well above the eastern horizon, warming the air sufficiently so that she no longer shivered. Now that it was time to go, they asked Sky to use his sensors to find water to fill their bottles with, clean water if they were lucky. Sky's sensors had a limited scanning range, he could detect things accurately for one or two hundred feet, unless they were shielded in some way, such as being blocked by concrete or rubble. Even the trees of the forest acted as a damper on his readings. They trudged through the mud following Sky's directions, their feet making squishing sounds as the damp ground sucked greedily at their shoes.

When they reached water, Kat found it less than appealing. Sky had brought them to a small pond of cloudy water topped by a film of scummy dirt and detritus floating on its surface. It was nothing more than a shallow depression between two trees, where rainwater had accumulated in yesterday's downpour. Kat harbored no expectation of a pleasing taste, but it would hydrate them, if it did not make them sick.

Mark unscrewed the cap from one of his dark green plastic bottles, then dunked it into the pond, filling it to the brim with brownish water. It came away a sickly color.

Lifting her second bottle from the pond, Kat took a deep swig of the water. It tasted heavily of dirt, but was not as bad as she feared. Topping off the bottle again, she screwed the cap on tightly and rose to her feet, ignoring the wet mud that clung to her skin through the threadbare knees of her pants.

"Show us the way to the scrapward, Sky."

Sky was smart enough to know what Mark wanted, and projected a holographic map in front of them. The map showed their current location with a green dot labeled 'us,' and a red square some distance away with the word scrapward written beneath it. An arrow above their dot showed the direction they were currently facing, the arrow turned when they did, telling them where to go. It was a system of navigation they used frequently, and it worked well. With Sky around to guide them, they would never get lost.

They started out at a speed that could be maintained for hours. She usually let Mark take the lead and set their pace, knowing she could move faster and go for longer. She learned early on that Mark was not her equal in strength or speed, and without a better explanation, she assumed it was because she was a Grymal and he was a human, or because she was a girl. She had not been around other people enough to reach a different conclusion.

Every few hours they stopped for a short rest, looking for spots with large rocks or logs where insects were likely to hide might as well combine resting with eating, she reasoned. Kat carried a three foot long stick spear as big around as her wrist, she had made it by stripping the bark and branches from a fallen tree limb, and sharpening one end to a point. If a stick broke after a particularly vigorous use, she searched out a new branch on the forest floor. In the event they were attacked, the stick could be used a weapon, not that it was all that helpful against lasers. The stick's main purpose was for hunting animals for food, and she was getting pretty good at throwing it like a spear.

Sky's sensors were decent when it came to do detecting the movement or body heat of people or large animals, or the electromagnetic signatures of robots, but they had limitations. They were not sensitive enough to find small animals like rodents at any kind of distance, and even for large targets his range was not great, dropping to no better than a few yards in places like forests where trees interfered with his scans. Which was why she felt no surprise when a squirrel sprinted out from behind a tree, and Sky failed to alert them to its presence. She let Mark continue walking to draw its attention while she held perfectly still. The squirrel froze, its eyes on Mark, giving her time to raise the stick over her shoulder and throw it. She scored a direct hit, impaling it through the side. It was thrashing on the stick and screeching when she reached it. She quickly snapped its neck to end the suffering.

"Squirrel dinner." She announced, tying the body to a line at her waist. If they were lucky, she would kill two or three more little animals, and tonight they would feast.

Mark hurried to praise her for the bleeding furball. "Way to go."

This close to winter the animals started to put on weight, fattening themselves to survive the lean months of dormant cold. This plump little guy was no exception, she estimated him to be a solid two pounds, a lot of meat for a small rodent.

As the day wore on the temperature rose, and with it, unfortunately, so did the humidity. Already thick enough in late morning to cause sweat to soak her stained grayish shirt, by midafternoon evaporation from the sodden ground turned the air into a stifling soup of cloying wetness. Her shirt, worn thin to near transparency, clung to her like a grimy second skin. The air was dead calm among the trees, not a whisper of wind at hand to rustle leaves or relieve hot bodies.

Over the course of the day's trudging walk Kat speared two more animals, a little gray mouse, and a bird the size of one of her torn up shoes.

It was a vast relief to her when shortly before sunset, noticeable by the changing color of sunlight above the trees, Sky announced the detection of a stream. The thought of cooling off and washing the sweat and grime from her body, gave Kat renewed energy. Following Sky's holographic map, which was updated to show the stream, she grabbed Mark's hand and dragged him to the water. She heard the faint gurgle of moving water, well before the small stream came into view. It was not quite her height across, and only inches deep, but in her eyes it was a super water playland.

Pausing only to untie the animal line at her waist and drop her pack and stick, she splashed into the stream, submerging herself as best she could, clothes and all in the lethargic current, she closed her eyes, luxuriating in the cool flow washing over her, taking with it her heat and sweat. A pair of quiet splashes told her that Mark had stepped into the water. Grinning wickedly at a sudden impulse, she sat up and thrust water at him with both arms, drenching him from head to foot

He looked at her with raised eyebrows. "Good thing I took Sky off before getting in the water."

That was an odd thing to say, Sky was what he called waterproof, why would it matter if the computer get wet? The question distracted her sufficiently, that she was not ready when Mark kicked water at her as payback for splashing him. In her seated position the water rushed up her nose and filled her open mouth. She rolled to her knees spluttering and coughing as if she was drowning. It took her a moment to recover, and when she did Mark was grinning at her, pleased by the success of his sneak attack. Clearing her nose with a blast of air from her lungs, she pulled her arms back and thrust them forward, palms cupped, spraying Mark with water in retaliation. The battle was on.

Mark lobbed water at her using a two-handed scooping gesture, shoveling it as fast as his arms could move, she improvised a windmilling motion with her forearms, tossing water at him with alternating hands. It was hard to say how long they went at it, but when it was over, they were out of breath and panting from the exertion, and dripping wet.

She slogged onto the bank, mud sucking at her shoes and the feeling of grit between her toes. "I'm going to wash now, since I'm already wet".

"Uh huh," Mark agreed, skinning out of his shirt.

Rinsing out her shoes, she was surprised by how much mud came out of them, tinging the water brown as the dirt was carried downstream. When she dunked her head in the water to clean her hair, she ran her fingers through it repeatedly, pulling apart the tangles by force and wincing with each sharp tug on her scalp. Neither of them had a change of clothing and had to put the sodden cloth bock on when cleanup was done to let it dry. Despite being wet and shivering from the cool water, it was good to be clean.

"I'm going to start a fire, while you prep dinner." Mark began picking up sticks for the fire.

Kat untied the animals from her line, took the small knife from her bag, and went to the stream to strip and gut her kills. By the time she had them skinned, plucked and mounted to sticks for cooking, Mark had a decent fire going in a little dirt hollow surrounded by rocks to prevent it from spreading. she collected some large rocks, using them to prop the sticks over the fire, and positioning the meat close enough to the heat to cook it, without scorching it in direct flame. With the meat roasting, she sat by the fire to warm herself and speed the drying of her clothes.

They watched the meat cook over the dancing tongues of yellow orange flame, hearing the sizzle and pop of hot fat and juices. Every two or three minutes she rotated the sticks to heat the flesh evenly. On the fourth turn a faint but not distant sound reached her pointed cat ears, a snap like a branch breaking under a heavy foot. She gazed into the dark forest, her night vision shot from staring at the fire, her ears twitching, back and forth in search of another sound.

"Sky," Kat pitched her voice low, so she would not miss more snaps. It was too late to prevent someone from knowing their location, not with the beacon of firelight to follow. "Can you see anything on your sensors? I heard a branch break."

The reply was instantaneous, and it was irksomely dismissive, though the volume was modulated to match her. "Had I detected anything classifiable as a treat within sensor range, I would have informed you immediately. Although my range is admittedly limited within this dense growth."

Mark watched her with concern in his eyes, pulling his bag closer and taking out his laser.

Hearing no further unusual sounds for several minutes, she was ready to accept Sky's word that nothing was there, and reached over to rotate the meat again.

No sooner had her fingers touched the first stick, than Sky shouted a terse warning. "Robots coming from the south-west."

Kat spun in a crouch, zeroing in on the now audible running footfalls of robots with her sharp ears. The night was a splotchy glowing blur to her fire dulled eyes, but the grind and creak of unlubricated mechanical joints was unmistakable.

Mark was on his feet tugging insistently at her arm, his bag and laser in hand. "Run!"

She leaped up, snatching her own bag, and stumbling blindly into the trees after Mark. Upon seeing two fleeing biologicals, the robots opened fire. Red beams from three or more lasers zipped past them, impacting on random trees in a shower of sparks and bark. As was common with the antiquated machines, their aim was off, sometimes way off. Which was to be expected from one hundred and fifty years without calibration of their targeting systems. But even bad shots hit the bullseye sometimes. Mark and Kat sprinted wildly onward, risking broken bones from tripping over roots or rocks in the near total darkness. Neither of them attempted to shoot back at their pursuers, it would be a pointless waste of their low laser charges. Even if they could see the robots well enough to hit one, it would not deter the others from chasing them. Machines did not feel fear or intimidation.

Lucky for them, these robots were slow and had short attention spans, quickly losing interest in targets that were no longer in sight, and in minutes the crashing footsteps faded behind them. Mark, taking note of the lack of rampaging robots, slowed his pace to a more sustainable jog. She followed his lead, searching the forest around them, now that her normally excellent night vision was returning.

They stayed on the move for some time before Mark decided they were safe enough to call a halt to their flight, staring up into the branches of a thick trunked tree. "We should sleep in the trees again." He panted lightly, catching his breath, but sounded more resigned than tired.

"Right. But how about we eat these first?" She held up the sticks, three cooked animals still stuck on them, only a little dirty after their forest escape.

He shook with suppressed laughter, a big grin spreading on his face. "I can always count on you to remember the food."

She passed him the stick with the fat squirrel, only a bit leaner from being cooked. "Someone has to think of the important stuff."

She polished off the two smaller animals, picking the bones clean and licking all of the grease from her knobby fingers. After eating they climbed upward until the branches were bowing under their weight, and settled in for the night. Exhaustion quickly claimed them after the run.

In the morning they woke to the pink light of dawn, ate what insects were readily available, and resumed their slow trek to the scrapward.

Their journey dragged on without change or surprise for another two days, a long, humid walk under a canopy of dry falling leaves.

When the scrapward peeked out through the trees on the third day, the muddy ground was mostly dry from the last rain. Puffy white clouds fought with clear sky to block the sun, but more precipitation did not seem imminent. As scrapwards went, this one was on the small side, its main concentration of toppled and broken buildings two miles across at the widest point. A razed span of old city continued on for another mile or so from that central area, the buildings there mostly removed by scavengers or reclaimed by nature, with a boundary marked by the sparseness of trees within.

This flat, open borderland was the most dangerous part of approaching the scrapward. There was almost nothing to hide behind, leaving them utterly exposed to any who were watching, and this was a place that never lacked for predators, not all of them walking on four legs.

She and Mark were crouched behind some leafy bushes at the boundary, looking out over the area for anything that might be remotely dangerous.

Mark broke the silence. "See anything?"

She was about to answer in the negative, but spotted a neat little set problems. "There are six or seven robots over by that dead tree." She pointed to where the machines stood inert by a leafless tree.

The robots were clustered together motionless and hunched over, heads turned down to expose the solar panels on their backs. Normally the solar cells were hidden under a protective plate of alloy, that slide out of the way when their power crystal ran low. According to Sky, these solar cells became less effective over time, taking longer and longer to charge as they aged. Which was why robots spent so much of their time standing helplessly in the sun.

What they were deciding now was whether she and Mark should take a chance on attacking the robots where they stood, in the hope they were low on power and therefore easier to destroy, or leave them as a threat that may have to be dealt with later. Her vote was to fight now, it was better than waiting to see what happened. Fighting was more fun too.

Mark came to a different conclusion. "I think we should leave them alone, go around the long way." He gestured to the right, well away from the robots.

So much for fun. "Okay."

They moved stealthily from tree to tree, slinking along out of sight from any who might observe them from the scrapward, but would be visible to people hiding in the forest. Her gaze was trained primarily on the buildings that grew ever larger with their approach, while Mark continuously glanced at the robots in apprehension. Mark had then walking well past the line of broken buildings denoting the start of the scrapward, pushing on until the bulk of several large structures stood between them and the sunbathing robots. He stopped behind a low hanging branch, his head swiveling right to left in search of threats.

"Anything out there, Sky?"

"I detect no heat signatures or movement within sensor range."

"Okay, come on." Mark left the trees, knowing she would be with him. He walked swiftly in a low crouch toward the nearest building, trying to remain hidden behind various bits of rubble.

They paused at what was left of a crumbling wall, looking for anything larger than a rodent that was moving. For the moment the place appeared empty, which was not the same as saying it was safe. Having done this before they knew what was valuable, and had a fair notion of where to find it. The scrapwards were old, so old that it was hard for Kat to imagine such a long passage of time. Due to that great age, much of the treasure they once held was picked clean by scavengers many years past. What remained of value, would be located inside one of the decaying structures. Hazardous places to explore, filled with shifting rubble and walls prone to collapse at the slightest provocation. But if they were to find objects of sufficient worth to trade for winter long food, inside was precisely where they much go. The worse a building looked from the outside, the more likely it was to have what they needed.

Wending a precarious path over the unstable heaps of concrete, iron, and unpleasantly, squishy leavings best not identified, they moved with slow caution into the crowded ruin of tumbled buildings. They tried to make their passage a silent one, but every object and surface conspired to announce their presence to the world. Loose debris shifting on surfaces slicked by rain moistened waste, did not aid their stealthy goal. Every clack and clatter of falling artificial stone, was cause for cringing and quiet curses, accompanied by hiding to watch for any drawn to the sounds.

After an eternity of softly creeping into the ward, Mark raised an arm to point to the right. "That one looks good."

Good was not exactly how she would have chosen to describe the indicated structure, but it was definitely a promising candidate for scavenging. The building was at most three stories tall, with rubble mounded on and around it that had certainly been additional floors in the past. Any street level entrances that once existed were buried under tons of ragged concrete, an opening higher up the uneven concrete walls revealed an interior clogged with more collapsed material from former walls and ceiling. It was as dangerous and unappealing an edifice as she could envision, promising certain crushing death to any dumb enough to plumb its decrepit depths. In other words, it was perfect.

She nodded and moved toward the building, trying to find a way inside as they got closer. She saw a small, seemingly unobstructed hole on the second floor wall, a dark void no more than two feet wide in the dirty gray surface. They made a complete circuit of the building, finding no larger gaps from ground level standing beneath the hole, she craned her neck back, running her eyes over the wall to find a way to reach the opening. She scaled the wall slowly, wedging her fingers and shoes into gaps and crevices in the concrete cliff. The thought that her fingers and toes might be crushed by an unexpected shift in the rubble did not much concern her, most of these buildings were fairly stable on the outside, having done their major shifting decades age. It was the smaller chunks of relatively undisturbed debris inside that she was worried about.

Hanging from the second story wall, she stared into the hole, trying to make out something, anything, of what may await them, but only a depthless blackness returned her sun dulled gaze. Her skin itched from being so exposed high on a gray wall in afternoon sunlight wearing contrasting colors, it was an open invitation for trouble. She squirmed into the hole, blindly groping at unseen surfaces to guide her. Nothing shifted or fell on her right off, and she helped Mark climb in after her. She crawled forward on hands and knees, reaching out to feel for obstructions ahead or holes below. A few yards in, the way opened up until she could no longer touch the walls or ceiling around her. The building might not be as broken as it looked from the exterior.

Very little light penetrated this far in, they would need more in order to explore for trade goods. "Would you give us some light, Sky?"

Normally the little light on the front of Sky blinked a soft blue color, but it could be made to shine more brightly, enough to illuminate a small area when it was dark. She averted her eyes from the light, only watching it wave as Mack scrambled out of the hole. The darkness was held at bay by no more than ten feet, what lay beyond that remained cloaked in impenetrable murk, save for the odd glint off of a reflective surface. They were in a mostly intact room with doors on two walls leading deeper into the derelict structure. Three plastic chairs and a rectangular box taller than she was were the only objects present, the furniture was too large to take out with them, but plastic might be worth breaking apart if nothing more valuable presented itself. She forced open the locked drawers of the box, and was rewarded with dust for her effort. Choosing a door at random, she pushed further into the ruin. Dust rose into the air with each step, lifting bits of dancing gray to define the sharp edges of Sky's light, where it cut a cone across the dark. Cracks were prominent in the walls and doorframes, leaving her hesitant to open closed doors for fear of bringing the roof down. Any given door could be all that stood between them and imminent collapse. A stairway led down to the lower floor, the stairs leading up ended in uneven rubble that may or may not be passable. Her gut said not.

"I say we go down." She whispered. The chances of being heard in here were slim, but experience bred caution.

"Why not?"

Mark stayed behind her, holding the light so that it pointed ahead, feeling safer with her in the lead. The second floor, gray and unappealing, was left gladly behind. The stairs emptied into a big room that continued past the reach of Sky's light, and was filled with tables and chairs. On the tables that were still standing, and scattered across the floor amid other debris, were endless plates, bowls, and utensils.

"Do you see this?" She cried joyfully, caution a faded memory amid such treasure. She rushed over to collect spoons, forks, and knives. If was the single most stupendous trove she ever laid eyes on, bigger almost than she could have dreamed. They would stay fed all winter, for several winters.

She looked over at the sound of clinking metal, a smiling Mark was stuffing valuable utensils into his bag. Good metal tools and cooking implements were among the most sought after trade goods. Forks were not worth as much as say a saw or a hammer, but two or three dozen of them could be traded for a whole sheep, and only a few far a chicken. Thinking about roasted sheep had her mouth watering.

They both had their bags full to bursting, when a thought burst into her head. "If this is a room where lots of people sit to eat, then there must be a huge kitchen here too."

Mark's smile widened in the ghostly blue light. "And kitchens have pots and big knives." He finished her thought.

Leaving her how heavy bag where it lay, she ran to the closest open door, one of a pair of double doors with little round windows in them. It was too dark in the next room to see anything, forcing her to wait impatiently for Mark to bring Sky. "Come on, hurry."

The room came into view with frustrating slowness, as Sky's dim light shoved weakly against the dark at Mark's approach. Cooking implements of every conceivable kind littered the floor and counters, hung from hooks on the walls, and rested on metal racks. There were bowls, untouched for countless years and caked in gritty dust, some so big she could hide in them. Knives, spoons, and utensils she did not recognize dangled from overhead, while unusual machines small and large sat dormant, plugged into outlets that would never power them again. In one corner was the crown of a pale white dome. Bones were not an altogether foreign sight in a scrapward, but most were hauled off by predators or buried by survivors long ago.

Ignoring the ancient skull, she moved through the kitchen looking for good knives. Knives in general were highly prized, the most valuable blades were the jagged edged ones Sky called serrated. Modern metal workers had a hard time replicating them. She had a small pile of them collected, when Mark came over with a medium sized pot partially filled with more. She dumped her finds into the wide pot. Their handles mostly reaching no higher than the lip of the deep container. There was room for more in the pot, but it was already close to too heavy, and they would have to carry it a long distance.

Mark dropped the pot with a satisfying rattling thud. "I think we have all we can take this trip."

Kat lifted the pot to verify its weight, it was not too heavy for her now, but a few hours of toting it would be tiring. Many rest breaks were in her near future. "You're right. We should go."

In the eating room she slipped the straps of her bag over her shoulders, feeling weighed down by all the metal, and followed Mark up the stairs. On the second floor she shoved the pot along the narrow passage to the hole they came in through, the bright daylight blinding her going out, as the darkness had coming in. At the edge she looked down the outside of the wall, trying to figure out how she would get the pot to the ground without dropping it, which could damage the valuable knives.

"Any ideas?"

"Mark opened his bag and thrust his hand inside, the utensils clinking as he rummaged around. "Ah." His hand withdrew clutching a long coil of rope. He looped it around the handles on either side of the pot, and knotted it at the top to form a triangle. "I will climb down first, then you can lower it to me." He mined letting the rope out hand under hand.

She gave him a thumb up. "Got it."

He shifted his bag and snaked out of the hole feet first, his knuckles turning white where they gripped the edge, his head soon disappearing from sight as he descended.

Walking on her knees, her back slightly hunched in the confined space, she awkwardly hauled the pot to the wall with both hands. After another swift survey of the area below, she watched Mark climb down. The muscles in his arms and neck stood out with the effort of holding a bag that weighed half again as much as he did. She worried that the strain might prove too much for his weaker arms, and he would fall and hurt himself. But the descent was short, and soon his feet were touching the ground. He set his bag down and gestured for her to send him the pot. She lifted it into the air and slowly let out the rope, holding it away from the wall to the best of her ability, only a few inches with such a heavy load. Hard as she tried to steady it, the pot still picked up a small swing, scraping the wall more than once on the way down. The noise was not loud, but even small sounds carried in a scrapward.

When it was in his reach, Mark grabbed the bottom of the pot and eased it to the ground. She tossed the rope down to pool at Mark's feet, and followed after it. The climb down left her arms sore and her fingers raw, but she would be fine for the trek out. Mark had already untied the rope, and was spooling it on his arm when she joined him.

He stuffed the rope into his bag. "Ready to go?"

In answer she picked up the pot and stepped away from the building.

A gruff voice spoke to them. "Not just yet kid."

Kat nearly jumped out of her skin, the knives rattling metallically in the pot. Standing not twenty feet in front of them, was a tall human male holding a hand laser pointed right at her. Her head darted around, searching wildly for an escape route, but more men were rising from behind rubble on all sides. She silently cursed herself for not looking harder from above, she should have seen these men. They must have watched her and Mark enter the building, and prepared this ambush while they were inside.

The man recognized her desire to bolt. "You got nowhere to run girl, and if you try, you'll make me mad, then I'll have to shoot you." He gestured menacingly with the laser. Now put everything down and get on your knees facing the wall."

She nodded reassuringly to Mark, trying to lend him comfort she did not herself feel, then obligingly set the pot and her bag on the ground. Turning away from the thieves, she dropped to her knees on the hard rubble, and waited for whatever came next. The minutes dragged on in a torment of fearful anticipation, listening to every sound behind her and imagining the worst. She heard footsteps draw near, and the tinkle of metal as the thieves went through their bags, them the faint rasp of a knife cutting something soft.

"Hands behind your backs." Commanded a low voice, different from the man she identified as the leader.

She complied instantly, feeling calloused hands tie her wrists together with rope, and understood that it was the rope she heard being cut. They were tying her with her own rope! With her wrists immobilized at the small of her back, her feet were yanked up without warning, damping her face first, painfully, onto the concrete. Her ankles were tied together as her wrists had been. She would not be running any time soon. Trussed up, she was heaved helplessly into the air and dumped stomach first over a thick shoulder, her chin poking into the man's back. Her transport started walking, bouncing her around as he crossed the uneven terrain. No one spoke, knowing better than to make too much noise, lest the ambushers become the ambushed, or in her and Marks' case, fall into possibly worse hands. These, at last, hand not killed them yet. From her inconvenient perch, Kat could not see where they were being taken, could only stare at the scenery passing by to her right. Comfortingly, Mark was unharmed and close to her. She could bide her time and find a way to escape later.

Time wore on in the near silent march, the soft slap of shod feet on hard concrete, and the gentle rustle of clothing, were all that distracted her from the regular thumping of her chin on the thief's back. She and Mark were ungagged, their captor's justifiably unconcerned that they would call for help. They knew as she did that there was no one to call to, and shouting might attract the attention of robots, something no sane person desired.

By the time her abductors stopped, a short distance into the forest outside the scrapward, her stomach ached from where the man's shoulder was digging into it. It came as some relief when the world spun around her dizzyingly and she was lowered to the ground, not entirely gently, and Mark was deposited next to her. With a firm admonition to be quiet, they were left alone.

She counted eleven men in the band, humans and Grymals wearing simple shirts in faded grays that would blend in with the concrete heavy backdrop of the scrap ward. They carried a nose wrinkling scent that implied washing was not high on their list of priorities. Most bad beards or thick stubble, poor grooming was also a thing. The men who were left to tend camp had dinner roasting over a log fire, two dog-size animals of some kind. Cloth or hide was strung up between trees, canopies for the men to sleep under out of the rain. The smoke wafting to her was laden with the tantalizing smell of cooked meat, rousing her hunger, but food was not important right now, or maybe less important. None of the men paid their captives much attention, sparing no more than the odd glance to be sure they were behaving, they were focused on the loot.

Kat wriggled and wrenched her wrists, pulling at the ropes that bound her, loosening them to free her hands. While she worked, her eyes roved the camp, hunting for something useful to their predicament, before locking onto a sight so awesome that the thought of escaping abandoned her. Parked right behind her was a pair of functional vehicles, or she assumed they worked from their condition. Both were free of rust or significant dents, and every tire she could see was devoid of cracks and major wear. The closer of the two was a simple five-seater not unlike many that could be found in a scrapward, with a squarish body and good ground clearance suitable for most terrain. The second, larger vehicle was something completely new to her. It was long and wide, with a tubular frame and big bumpy tires. There were four seats in the front, and two benches running the length of the open, framed-in back.

Working vehicles with good tires were so rare and amazing, that she had trouble thinking of anything else, retaining only the sense to speak softly. "This truck is totally radical." She learned the phrase from an old sign during a recent scavenging trip, adding it to her fun list of old things to say "Do you think we might ride in one of these?"

Mark matched her volume, if not her enthusiasm. "This is not the time for that." He paused as an idea hit him. "Sky, scan these vehicles. I want to know how to drive them, and if we can even turn them on."

In seconds an animated diagram, complete with text instructions, was projected onto the leafy dirt between them. It sat dimly in the shadow of Mark's body, where it could not be seen by the thieves. "The larger vehicle is ready to drive with the push of an on button located to the right of the steering wheel. The smaller vehicle however, requires a key that is not present. Operation of the vehicle is exceedingly basic, designed for use by slow thinking biologicals. Turn it on, place the automatic transmission into drive, and depress the accelerator pedal. The left pedal actuates the braking system to slow and stop the vehicle, and the steering wheel allows it to turn to the left or right."

Mark studied the diagram briefly, then nodded. "You can turn off the hologram." The projection faded. "We wait until they go to sleep, then we jump into the truck and drive away fast. What do you think Kat?"

She smiled, imagining all of the fun they would have with the truck. "I like it.".

"The tricky part will be freeing ourselves from these ropes. Do you think you can untie me if we sit back to back?"

She gave an experimental tag with her right arm, testing her progress on loosening the rope. Happily her hand nearly pulled clear out. "I almost have my hands free already. Tell me when you want to go, and I'll untie us."

Mark was impressed. "Good work. Now we wait for these guys to start snoring."

The thieves eventually tired of cataloging their ill gotten haul, and tore ravenously into the roasted meat, the animals hard to identify without heads or skin. The meat was consumed rapidly amidst much talking and laughter, the naked bones discarded into the fire. Neither food nor drink was offered to the captives, who were left alone and hungry in the dark. Hours later the men had mostly drifted off to the canopies to sleep, and the quiet of night enshrouded the camp.

Despite her exertions over the day, Kat felt energized, pumped up in anticipation of their imminent escape. The last man lay down to sleep, his snores joining the disharmonious, grinding chorus of his fellows. These guys were overconfident or really stupid, they left not a

single man to keep watch while they slept. The waiting wore on her nerves, surely the thieves

were sound asleep by now. Her muscles were twitching with impatience by the time Mark spoke.

"Now Kat. Untie us and get into the truck."

Her hand slipped out of the loosened binding with no resistance, and she immediately worked the knot at her ankles. Seconds later she tossed the rope away, and undid the knot a holding Mark's wrists. "Do your feet and start the truck, I'll be right there ."

Ignoring Mark's confusion, she hauled off without letting him speak. She picked her way silently to their bags on the balls of her feet, they worked hard to find that stuff, and she was not going to let these stupid thieves keep it. She lifted the bags slowly one at a time, her breath catching when the utensils clinked together inside, but none of the men stirred. With a heavy bag on each shoulder, and the pot of knives in her hands, she was forced to arch her back and waddle, her feet spread wide apart under a weight heavier than her own. Mark stared past her fearfully from the driver's seat of the truck, his thumb poised over a button near the steering wheel.

Then the night went crazy.

"Robots approaching the camp from the south." Announced Sky.

Glowing beams of red lit the night, shattering tree bark and striking the ground by the fire, the robots targeting the heat source. Kat ran, sort of. Sky's sensors again proved to be useful almost after the fact. Shouts rose from the startled thieves, who scrambled to their feet in confusion. Some of them snatched weapons, firing blindly into the dark. A man stumbled into the fire pit scattering smoldering logs and burning ash, before tumbling to the dirt screaming curses, some of them quite inventive. Several men ran for the vehicles

Mark stabbed the on button. "Get in."

Kat tossed her burdens into the back with a surge of adrenaline fueled strength, grabbed the frame to vault into the seat, and was spun around to slam into the vehicle

"Where do you think you're going?" A bearded man snarled in her face, his breath so bad it could wilt leaves.

There was no time for a proper fight, they had to escape right now. She rammed the heel of her hand into the man's elbow, hearing a deep crack as the Joint gave. He stepped back with disbelief clouding his eyes, giving her room to deliver a spinning jump kick to his temple that dropped him. She bounded into the seat beside Mark, rapid acceleration pushing her back.

The thieves shouted anew at the theft of their vehicle, lasers flashing by as they sought to dissuade the young hijackers. Bright lights flared to life on the truck, in time for Mark to swerve hard to avoid plowing into a tree. Kat guessed the attacking robots to be part of the group of sunbathers they saw earlier that day, or was that officially yesterday now. She was glad Mark chose not to destroy them. It would not take the thieves long to destroy the robots and give chase. Sure enough in less than a minute the lights of the second vehicle came on, bouncing over the ground in pursuit

"Get the lasers from our bags Kat, I think we need them." Shouted Mark over the rushing wind. He did not slow or take his eyes from the illuminated patch forest rushing at them.

She stood in the rocking truck, holding onto the seat one handed to stop herself from falling. The bags were lodged against a large metal box behind the rear seats. She had them open in seconds, the utensils spilling to clatter around the truck. With one laser in hand and the other on the seat, she looked to see where the thieves were. A red bar of energy zipped past the truck to her right answering the question more effectively than the blinding head lights could.

When a second beam scored a hit on the tubular frame by her head, Kat fired back, knocking out one of their lights in a pretty rain of yellow sparks, that disappeared too quickly for her to properly enjoy. The effect was so nice that she repeated it, blasting three more lights in rapid succession. She aimed for the fifth of the vehicle's six lights, ignoring the less accurate shots from the thieves. Right as she was pulling the trigger, they swerved hard right. Too late to stop her finger on adjust her aim, the beam lanced out to hit the vehicle somewhere on the side, she heard a deep whoomph, a sudden release of trapped air, and the last two lights spiraled violently to her left. There were shouts of fear, screams of pain, and a series of bangs and crunching metal. The lights vanished well before the sounds stopped.

"Are they still chasing us, Sky?" The answer seemed self-evident, but she wanted confirmation.

"The vehicle has undergone precipitous deceleration in conjunction with rapid uncontrolled course alteration on multiple axis."

"Does that mean they crashed?"

"Correct."

Mark let off of the accelerator, slowing the vehicle to a more reasonable speed for driving through a dark forest. Not that any speed was appropriate in these conditions. "I can't believe we got a way, and with all our stuff."

"Don't forget this wicked cool truck."

Mark's smile was visible in the reflected light from the front of the vehicle. "What do you think we should call it?"

Kat could think of nothing really interesting to name the large vehicle, at least nothing Mark would not immediately overrule. When in doubt keep it simple, it always worked for her. "Why not call it Truck?"

"Truck it is then. And I have some ideas for upgrades. This can be our own wandering home."

Kat leaned back in the seat. They had a vehicle, and trade goods to make it through winter, things were starting to look up.

CHAPTER 3

Mark opened his eyes early in the morning, laying on a padded mat on the floor of the cave they used as a home for the last two weeks. After their encounter with the big crab robot at Jagged Hills, he continued driving to the cave to rest for the night, drained physically from fear and adrenaline. This cave was one of several they lived in regularly, depending on where they were. This one was located in a secluded stretch of small hills, with an entrance not easily seen from a distance when open. It was warm, dry, and relatively comfortable. The interior was a rounded shape twenty feet in diameter, with a ceiling more than a foot above their heads when standing. They had space to sleep in, with plenty of room left over to work and cook. There were enough hills and trees outside, that hiding the Truck was not difficult. And in all of the times they had stayed here, they never encountered anyone or anything near the cave. Not that it could be seen with the door closed.

Because of their unanticipated fight with the robot, they arrived late the previous night, the sun long set. They were too tired to cook a hot meal, eating cold food from their supplies with no crab meat to Kat's disappointment. Afterward they unrolled their sleeping mats and went to sleep.

Rising from the thinly padded mat, Mark gathered fresh clothes from his bag and got into the sonic scrubber to clean himself. One of the pieces of old technology they found schematics for, the scrubber used pulses of focused sound to break up and remove dirt and grime, all without the need for soap and water. This scrubber had a metal rod frame connected to it, with a privacy curtain for showering. They also had racks and rods for cleaning dishes, laundry, and other items. Another advantage to the scrubber, was that it took only five to ten minutes to complete a cycle, depending on the settings used.

Dressing in the fresh clothes, he put the dirty ones in to be cleaned, and set himself to making a hot breakfast. They had electric cooktops to heat and cook food on, and a variety of pans and utensils to prepare it with. He had built a refrigeration unit and a freezer to preserve food, from which he now removed a section of roasted sheep. Letting Kat sleep longer, he quietly placed a pot of water on a Cooktop to boil, before adding ground corn to make a simple porridge.

Sky possessed a seemingly limitless data storage capacity, and had a large catalog of schematics and templates in his memory. Mark could recreate or modify tools and machines from the ever expanding database, using their collected scrap as building materials. Sometimes when they were scavenging, he would find new bits of old technology and Sky would scan them in detail to add to his database. When they found readable data cards, or computers that contained schematic designs, or programs, the information could be added directly to Sky's memory.

He and Kat brought their created tools and devices to trade for supplies, going to farms and towns to acquire the food, water, and sometimes cloth that they needed. Any other raw materials they required, could be gathered on scavenging trips.

No sooner had Mark finished cooking, than the smell of hot food roused Kat from sleep. She threw aside her blanket carelessly, yawned hugely, and stretched from her pointed ears to the tip of her furred tail. Groggy and none to steady on her feet, she stumbled to the small table, drawn. by the scent of porridge and meat permeating the cave. She dropped unceremoniously into the chair across from him.

Mark slid a big bowl of steaming cornmeal and a plate of sliced meat to her, followed by a fork, knife, and spoon. He watched her shove meat into her mouth bare handed. "Would you please use the fork, and try to take smaller bites?

"Mff, mfum." Mumbled Kat around a mouthful of food. She stuffed more into her mouth, making no move to pick up the fork. At least she would have to use the spoon for the cornmeal, it would be quite a feat to scoop it out of the bowl effectively with her fingers.

"It is considered impolite in most cultures to speak with your mouth full." Said Sky. "And it renders you completely incomprehensible, sadly not a far step from your normal state of semi-intelligibility."

She took another bite "Hm."

Mark ate his own meal more politely, with utensils. Not for the first time he wondered how Kat was able to eat so much when she was so small, she stood five feet seven inches tall, and weighed around one hundred and twenty pounds. She was slim and athletic of build, and very active. All of the exercise she got might account for some of the calories.

"Thanks for breakfast." Kat gathered the dirty dishes, loading them onto a rack for the scrubber, and activating a cleaning cycle. For someone who loved food so much, Kat was a remarkably bad cook, she usually left the cooking to him, opting instead to clean after they ate. A good arrangement for everyone.

Leaving, Kat to her morning activities, he passed through the open mouth of the cave, which Sky would have closed automatically if he detected any danger. Blinking his eyes against the bright morning sunlight in front of him, he surveyed the area. It was much greener here than at the Jagged Hills scrapward. The ground was populated by a small number of short trees and plants, and the dirt was not so hard and compacted beneath has booted feet though still rocky and dry.

He strolled the short distance to the Truck, deactivated the security system with his thumbprint and code on the door's locking device, then put on a HUD. "Display list of trade goods to be made today." The list scrolled onto the HUD screen, mostly simple items, pots, cooking implements, farm tools, hammers, and so on. It was the kind of items that were always in demand, but that not everyone could make for themselves, at least not of the same quality that he and Kat could produce.

When he was done reviewing the list, he started taking the necessary scrap out of the Truck's storage space. He removed several large bars of steel, rubber and plastic for hand grips and handles, and copper for wires and electrical components. With a sizeable pile of raw materials prepared, he opened a locked compartment on the side of the Truck, to pull out a large, black metal case. The nearly three foot wide case was secured by two locking mechanism as was the Truck, a biometric scanner and numeric keypad. The case rattled as its contents shifted.

He entered the unlocking code, and pressed a thumb to the scanner lifting the lid when the lock clicked. Inside were tiny bits of shiny metal. Each of the little objects was a mere two millimeters across, and at a glance could be mistaken for ball bearings. Held in a pouch under the case's lid, was a slim, rectangular, touch screen control unit six inches wide. He slid out the controller and turned it on, waiting for it to boot and run a startup diagnostic sequence. The silver beads in the case rose into the air to form a well-defined cube, their movement creating a buzzing

sound not unlike a swarm of metalic bees. After a moment they settled gently into the case with a mild clicking noise, the buzzing subsiding as thousands of miniature antigrav units switched off. A chime sounded on the controller as the last touched down and message on the screen stated, "Nanomachine diagnostic complete, swarm operating at full capacity."

The controller contained a regularly updated copy of Sky's object and schematic databases stored in the form of nanomachine creation templates for direct implementation by the swarm. The user interface was programmed with an easy to navigate menu. The creation menu divided objects by type, size, and function, allowing quick navigation for the user to find and select what they wanted to make. It also included a text search engine, if they knew what an item was called in part or whole. The nanomachines were self replicating if any of them broke or deactivated, the others would replace them without prompting. There was no project too large or complex for the swarm, so long as it was provided sufficient materials to complete it.

Kitchen implements were at the top of the day's build list, he would start the swarm on making pans. He scrolled down the creation tree beginning at cooking tools, then pots and pans and finally he chose the specific pans he wanted to create. With ten general use steel pans entered into the build queue, he outlined the location where raw materials were to be taken from. That last was a critical step in the process, involving three separate confirmation prompts. The swarm was programmed so that it would not function unless a well defined location was specified. If the swarm was to operate without a clear place to take materials from, it could the theoretically break down anything nearby to construct new objects, including what it already finished making.

Once the parameters were set, he activated the creation program. The nanomachines rose from their case in a narrow line, buzzing over to the scrap he had readied for them, and began to deconstruct it. Each tiny mechanical worker was equipped with an antigrav unit for flight, capable of carrying material several times its mass, or generating a field of heavier gravity to compress created items. They had a laser for cutting, heating or welding, and four, multi articulated manipulator arms. Because the nanomachines could repair or replace each other when damaged or destroyed, nothing short of the complete catastrophic obliteration of the swarm, could disable or diminish it.

In a precisely choreographed ballet of tightly controlled motion, the nanomachines each removed a tiny piece of material from a steel bar, adding it to the new object bit, by miniscule bit. They formed a steady, rounded loop of indefatigable mechanical workers floating above the ground, moving so fast that they could be a solid bar to an onlooker. A bar that sparkled and shimmered with reflected sunlight. With the swarm building at such a small, precise scale and with incredible attention to detail, the finished products were superior to those made by more traditional methods.

The quality of nanomachine-built objects was limited by two primary factors. First, the nanomachines could not alter the molecular makeup of an existing substance, could not convert iron into gold or manipulate the composition of a chemical. But they were capable of manipulating those materials that were present. Impurities such as rust could be removed or worked around. The second limitation was that a created item was only as good as the template used to make it.

Mark and Kat had found the swarm during a scavenging expedition several years ago, undeniably one of the luckiest acquisitions they ever made. Before then they were only able to trade things they discovered in scrapwards for food, a very literal feast or famine situation entirely dependent upon what they came away from the ruins with. There had been times in the past, far too frequent for him to care to dwell on, when they had nearly died of starvation for lack of something worth trading for food. Due to the extreme importance of the swarm, he made several backup swarms, and squirreled them away in carefully secured locations. If anything were to happen to the primary swarm, they would not be left without one. He would never let Kat starve again, ever.

Mark enjoyed watching the tiny robots at their work, it was sort of like seeing an object being magically poured into existence from an invisible pitcher.

By the time Kat emerged from the cave wearing her armor, the smarm had finished constructing several pans of different sizes and types. she stomped over to him, her eyes on the collection of cookware a look of bored resignation painting her face. "I knew you were just going to make pans."

"Don't forget spoons and hammers too." He said reasonably.

"You really should make a fire breathing dog toy. People will want it, especially if it's pink."

Not this again. "No one will want a fire breathing toy, it could burn down their home or maybe hurt someone."

"They could use it to protect their crops." she argued.

Sky pointed out the obvious flaw in this notion. "There is, in reality, a high probability that your mechanical fire starter would ignite and burn the very crops you suggest that it should protect."

"Ugh, fine." Kat threw her hands upward in exasperation. "But one day you'll regret not making the dog."

"Unlikely."

Giving up, she stalked away muttering in annoyance. She was off to explore, or exercise, or otherwise entertain herself while he was busy. She would be back in a while, most likely when she was hungry, which in his experience would be no more than a few hours. She was serious about most things, but was rarely truly angry. She will have forgotten her irritation before she returned.

In three hours he had a large collection of trade goods stacked neatly next to the Truck, and a completed list. Along with the usual pans and tools, were a number of more specialized items. For example, there was a small water pump with solar cells and a hose, it was specifically requested by someone in one of the villages they traded with regularly. The village recently dug a well, and wanted a pump and some watering cans and buckets to facilitate retrieving and using the water. The cans he made from stainless steel to prevent rusting.

Placing the latest completed item with the rest, a large, serrated knife with a curved tip, he returned to the cave for a short lunch. They had a number of food storage and preparation devices on hand, that he made using the swarm. There was a machine that sealed food into metal cans for preservation, from which they kept a supply of canned foods in the Truck, but those were reserved for when they ran short of fresh or frozen food, like in the middle of winter. There was also a bread making machine that let them eat fresh bread with their meals.

He ate an apple and some bread and decided it was a good time for target practice at their little range. He tried to practice with his laser at least twice per week and after their encounter with the strong crab robot last night, he had a strong desire to be prepared in case of another attack.

He and Kat set up the target range a short walk from the cave mouth. It was Kat's idea to prepare a place where they could practice with real lasers, and he agreed without reservation, he also ended up doing most of the work. He selected several holographic targets, belted on his laser, and left the cave. It was a hike of four minutes down the rocky path curving around the hill to the shooting range. The practice area was an open, flat space cleared of rocks and plants. At one end they placed a row of large, flat-topped rocks on which to set the targets, and a shallow groove was cut into the ground at the other end, a literal firing line.

He put the targets one at a time on the rocks, and had them run a random practice cycle. He retreated to the firing line and verified that his laser was set to emit a weak beam of light for the practice. The targets were black, two inches tall and five wide, and they were pentagonal in shape. They could display anything from a simple two dimensional bulls eye, to a more complex three dimensional animated image, a robot or a fictional monster for example. When an image was hit, sensors in the target displayed the point of simulated impact, and calculated an overall score for the session.

He flipped the HUD screen away from his eye to clear his field of vision, and to avoid relying on its targeting enhancement. "Run practice program." A nondescript humanoid robot appeared above one of the targets, its laser moving to shoot him. He shifted aim to the robot and hit it in the torso. It dissolved in an elaborate dispersal of photons. Another target materialized, a filthy, one-eyed bandit with missing teeth in a scowling face, his hands held a dirty old gun. Mark's first two shots connected with the bandit, his third missed, but by then it was already vanishing. The last target conjured a large snarling beast out of a fantasy nightmare, its rounded body supported by thick tentacles that thrashed wildly, and drool poured from a mouth lined with razor sharp, dagger like teeth. Flinching instinctively from the monster's audible roar, Mark missed it abysmally with his first blast, but nailed it with the following two.

He paused the session, his racing heart had him gasping for breath. Kat had a nasty habit of programming strange creatures from games and videos into the targets, anything that struck her as fun or amusing. Now that his heartrate had slowed to where he could think, he recognized this particular monster from one of their favorite fantasy games, it was an unimportant but ugly beast called a malbo. He wondered when Kat had added the creature to the target database.

He resumed the session, resolved not to be startled again, and continued for an entire hour before turning off the targets, He checked his score, concluding that while he would never come close to Kat in accuracy, he could hold his own in a firefight. Between Kat's superior reflexes, and the fact that she practiced almost daily, it was not a fair comparison for him to make.

With his practice over for the day, he collected the targets and started back to the cave. Hiking upward on the dry path, Mark wondered again why Kat was so much faster and stronger than he was. He knew that Grymals were physically superior to humans, but Kat seemed to be significantly stronger than she should be. Maybe Sky had an answer rattling around in his circuits "There is something. I've been curious about for a while now, Sky. Why is it that Kat is so much stronger and faster than other Grymals we've met?" If only she was that much smarter too.

"I have been monitoring and analyzing her physical condition for some time, as I do for you and the Truck for diagnostic purposes. I find myself in agreement with your assessment of Kat's heightened abilities. It is my estimation, based upon cumulative data, that Kat is twenty-five percent physically superior to a normal Grymal of equal size and fitness. Her strength, speed, and reflexes are all measurably greater than should be expected by statistical variance."

Mark was not sure how he felt about being lumped together with the Truck for diagnostic monitoring, but did not comment. "Do you have any workable explanation for her abilities? Could she simply be that much more athletic than normal people? Or is it some kind of disorder that might turn out to be harmful to her in the future?"

"So far as I am able to determine from my limited medical database, her enhanced physical attributes are genetic. They appear to be an integral component of her DNA. That is to say, they are a fundamental aspect of her base physical makeup. However, such a high degree of variability from documented norms is improbable, and unlikely to occur naturally. As to Kat's long term health, I have concluded from my observation and analysis that she is not at risk for negative side effects. I will continue to monitor her health as best I am able without a dedicated medical database, but there is no reason to believe that she will develop any problems."

"That's a great Sky, thanks. Since I don't have to worry about her health, I can just be happy that she is so strong."

He was beside the Truck now, standing in front of the pile of extra scrap from his earlier work, which he started to gather. Opening the back doors, he loaded the scrap into the storage area.

While he was busy with the cleanup, Sky continued. "It is not Kat's health that should concern us, but rather we should consider her thoughtless penchant for landing as in unnecessary trouble. And her uncanny ability to find dangerous situations. I am amazed that she has not caused us all to be killed or offlined, or at the very least severely injured. She is a purple haired menace."

Unexpectedly, Kat popped up from behind the Truck's hood, where she must have been resting or waiting for dinner, and she did not look amused. She stalked toward him with her long canines bared. "A purple haired menace, am I?"

"Now Kat." Mark raised his hands and backed nervously away. "There's no need to be angry. I'm sure Sky didn't mean it, isn't that right, Sky?"

Kat advanced a few steps coming around the Truck and lifting her hand, fingers curved into claws. She was a cat ready to pounce on prey.

"Um, Sky? would you please tell our good friend Kat, that you don't really think she's a menace?"

"I absolutely meant every word that I spoke, my vocalization was precisely what I intended to convey. Kat is a magnet for trouble of all varieties. Many of the hazardous situations that we have experienced, are as a direct result of her poorly considered actions. By way of mitigation, I do not believe she endangers us intentionally."

"Thanks Sky, that helped a lot." He muttered.

"You have some scrap to break down. Let me help you with it." She lunged at his left arm.

Mark barely dodged Kat's outstretched hands, moving his left arm behind his back,

farther from Kat. His right arm was held in front of him to ward her off. It was hard to say how serious she was about this, she and Sky argued semi-frequently, but she had never tried to actually damage him.

She circled him slowly, trying to reach Sky. "You can't keep Sky from me for long."

Knowing she was right, he switched to subterfuge. He opened his eyes wide in feigned surprise. "Kat, there's some kind of big bat robot flying this way." He pointed at the sky behind her to sell the trick.

Instantly smiling, she spun around looking for the robot, searching the sky for the phantom machine. she turned back to Mark. "I don't see..."

When Kat's eyes left him, Mark took off full blast in the opposite direction to escape her wrath. By the time he heard her speak, he was several yards away and running fast. She growled loudly in frustration and gave chase, her footsteps closing at an alarming rate.

"That was so mean. You know how much I like strange robots. I really wanted to see a giant flying bat robot. It could even have been pink." She shouted across the rapidly dwindling gap between them.

He pumped his legs for everything they were worth, but a few strides later, it sounded like she was running right on his heels. He did not dare glance back to see how close she was He sprinted down the narrow sloping path to the shooting range, and was almost there when he heard a grunt of effort from Kat. A second later she slammed into him, driving them both to the hard ground. They struggled for a minute, rolling back and forth on the rocky dirt, then he was pinned down with a grinning Grymal sitting on him.

She yanked Sky's computer body off of Mark's forearm, the straps giving way painfully. She held it above her head triumphantly. "I have you now."

"Wait!" Wailed Sky in an uncharacteristic display of simulated emotion. "I apologize profusely for giving offense. I was wrong to call you a menace, no matter how warranted the appellation may be. You are very helpful, and a diligent worker. I do not know how we could have survived all of these years without you here to protect us."

Kat solemnly placed Sky on the ground. "Thank you, Sky, that was very nice of you to say. I'm glad you recognize how important I am." Then, unable to hold it in any longer, she slid off of Mark and laughed loudly.

Mark flopped onto his back and joined in the laughter. After a moment Kat stood to look wistfully at the sky.

"I really would love to see a fantastic flying bat robot, its grant pink wings flapping as it soars on the wind." She sighed and held out an arm to him. Grasping, her wrist, he rose his feet, and they dusted themselves off. She smiled at him. "We are really dirty now, and there's a hole in your shirt." She poked him in the back through the hole, helpfully demonstrating where it was.

He flinched. "We know who's fault that is, don't we Kat?"

"Yeah we do. Thanks a lot, Sky."

"What a perfectly rational conclusion to reach for a biological. We should all blame the artificial intelligence for dirtying two corporeal entities. After all, it is not as if I were a collection of advanced rode housed inside a computer, and therefore inherently incapable of direct interaction with the physical world."

Kat was laughing again as he picked up Sky, tightening the straps on his forearm. It was a tricky thing to do one handed, but he did have a lot of experience at it. The setting sun was touching the top of the hills, its dying light bathing the land in red and gold. "We should head to the cave and eat dinner. I'll cook while you clean yourself and change. And don't forget to wash your dirty clothes when you're done."

"Sounds good to me." Said Kat walking up the slope." And I always clean my clothes."

Mark hid a smile. "Is that why I find purple clothes sitting in a pile by the scrubber so often?"

"I didn't say I cleaned them right away." She asserted defensively. "Only that I always clean they, eventually."

He chose to let it go at that, she might actually believe when she found her clothes cleaned in the morning that she had done the work herself and did not remember.

Stumbling blindly into the unlit care, he fumbled around for the table to turn on a light, reminding himself for probably the hundredth time to put one by the door. He opened the refrigerator unit to retrieve food for dinner, while Kat went to the scrubber for a shower, dropping her clothing into a pile. After her shower, he was amused to notice that she immediately picked up her dirty clothes and put them into the scrubber.

Merk filled two plates with bread, meat, and vegetables, piling a lot more on Kat's plate than on his own. Kat could easily eat twice what he could, and tended to do so twice as fast. It was as if she feared the food would somehow vanish if she took her time.

Kat sat across from him at the table, nodding gratefully at the plate he placed before her, with a fork stuck prominently into the meat. She rapidly stuffed bread and meat into her mouth, ignoring the fork once she dropped it to the table. He worried that she might choke on her meal.

"You do know that don't have to inhale your food? No one is going to take it from you."

She cleared her mouth with a big swallow, her throat expanding with the unusually polite gesture. "No one will take it from me, not that I would let them if they tried. But if I eat all this food slowly, it will get cold before I can finish." She shoved another hunk of bread into her mouth.

Spearing the last bite of meat with his fork, he finished it and left the dishes to Kat while he gathered clean clothes for a shower. He pulled Kat's clothes from the rod they hung on in the scrubber, and neatly folded them on the table next to it. He removed his boots and stepped inside the privacy screen. When it was on, the scrubber made only a faint noise akin to a waterfall heard from far off. The pulsing sound waves imparted a gentle tingling sensation on his skin, reminding him of a breeze ruffling the short hairs of his arm.

After showering, he dressed and examined the hole torn in his shirt from wrestling with Kat. *I'll have to fix this tomorrow*, he thought hanging his clothes in the scrubber and turning it on.

While he was showering, Kat had loaded their dishes onto a cleaning rack, and placed it next to the scrubber. Kat herself was sitting cross legged on her sleeping mat, happily playing a game on her MGP. Even with it kept considerably low, he could hear lasers and explosions from the device as she was no doubt saving the world from impending doom. A little digital mayhem would be fun later, and unlike when fighting real robots, blasting their virtual relatives was safe entertainment.

Mark waited by the scrubber for his clothes to be cleaned. When the cycle ended he removed his clothes from the machine, put the dish rack in, and started a new cycle. He folded his clothes, placing them in his bag with the torn shirt on top, a reminder to himself to mend it in the morning.

He sat at the dinner table and had sky open a holographic display, loading up the sensor data from their one-sided fight with the crab robot. He remembered seeing a split-second flash of something registering on a sensor scan, something that could be important if he was right about what it was. At the time it appeared, he was too busy trying to get away from the crazed robot to worry about it, but now he could look into it.

"Sky, I want you to analyze our fight with the crab. I'm not expecting much, but see if you can determine a weakness for us to exploit. We need a way to destroy these things, there will be more of them out there. We can't impale them all on bridge supports."

"Understood. I will inform you of my conclusions."

"Good. There is one more thing. I want you to check the sensor logs we collected yesterday, for the area we drove through when we were running from the crab. Look for any unusual readings, no matter how faint."

"Is there something specific that you would like for me to find in the sensor data?"

"I thought I saw a quick reading on the screen when we were busy with the crab. It was gone so fast I might have imagined it, but I want to be sure if it was there, and if you agree with me on what it was."

"Am I to conclude from your circumspect manner of speech, that you do not intend to inform me of the nature of your theory, until after I have completed an analysis?"

"You wouldn't want me to make it too easy, would you?"

"Oh, certainly not. Everything must always be unnecessarily difficult for the AI."

Mark laughed. "Seriously though, I really just don't want to influence your results."

"Very well, I estimate completion in ten point six-two minutes."

"Thanks Sky, I'll look at your results in the morning. Right now I'm going to play a game for an hour or two before sleeping."

He fished a game controller out of his bag. The controller wirelessly interfaced with his HUD, it was a design he customized from templates they had for similar devices. There were buttons and controls on it to allow him to play most of the games in their database. On his HUD he loaded the game he was playing for the last week, a personal favorite of his called the Last Dream VI. A while back Kat found a compilation of all twenty-four games in the long running series. Out of the two dozen games in the series he liked six the best, while Kat's preference was for number four, which he also really enjoyed. He sat at the table to play, settling into the chair for an extended session. He was about to attend the evil emperor's banquet, and he wanted to be sharp to answer all of the emperor's questions.

Two hours on Kat's gentle snoring reached him, inducing him to yawn deeply. He saved his progress in the game prior to turning it off, having been double crossed by the villain, who was betrayed in turn himself. He walked to Kat and turned off her MGP, her character had died and respawned after she fell asleep, and was waiting tirelessly for renewed input. Mark draped a blanket over Kat and laid down on his own mat. Pulling on a blanket to ward off the night's chill, he quickly descended into sleep, his dreams dominated by evil emperors and angry magical creatures.

He awoke in the morning to the red light of dawn reflecting warmly from the cave wall, shining in a narrow shaft through the cave mouth. Sitting up, he could bear light snoring from Kat. She was sprawled gracelessly on her mat, the blanket bunched up around her torso. She tended to move a lot in her sleep, sometimes violently. The biggest reason why Mark kept his mat several feet from her.

Mark stretched and yawned as he rose to his feet, restoring oxygen and blood to sleep deprived muscles. The blanket he folded and dropped onto the mat. Taking out the food for their breakfast, he catalogued their supplies. There was plenty of food to last then several days without opening any cans, but they would have to trade for more soon.

He prepared a hot breakfast, warming bread and grilling meat in a shallow pan. The savory smell of hot meat roused Kat like magic from her sleep. She rose clumsily to her feet rubbing her eye. She wobbled to the table, flopping into a chair with more force than was appropriate for the tortured piece of furniture. They ate quietly, and cleaned up when they were done.

Mark snatched his torn shirt from the bag, and left the cave. He walked to the Truck. "Okay Sky, what did you learn from your analysis?" He removed the nanomachine case from its compartment and opened it.

"The design of the crab robot is consistent with other pre-Devastation built robots that we have encountered. However, there are no robots of its size or form in my database. I believe it was created by the same entity responsible for constructing the other known robots. I surmise based upon the robot's overall design that it was intended to function as an all-terrain cargo and utility transport. As you may have noted, the crab possessed no visible armament, it could only hurl rocks at us, or attack directly with its manipulator arms. The crab was covered in an indeterminant alloy armor, sufficiently strong to render our current weapons incapable of inflicting quantifiable damage to it. Until such time as we are able to upgrade our weapons to destroy the crab, it is my considered recommendation that we avoid future encounters with them. I have taken the precaution of programming our sensors to monitor for the crabs specifically, in the unfortunate event that we were to stumble upon another one. There is a problem related to our sensors and the crab. The sensor may not be sensitive enough to detect a crab in time for us to evade it."

Mark set the swarm to repair his shirt, and initiated it. "While I have no desire to fight another crab, or any robot for that matter, Kat I'm sure, thought it was great fun to find an unstoppable killing machine bent on our destruction. We should quietly steer clear of crabs, and neglect to tell her we did."

"I am entirely in agreement."

"Now that we have that settled. Did you learn anything interesting from the sensor data?"

"In the course of our flight from the crab robot, we picked up a very faint sensor reading at extreme range. Normally we would not have detected the location at all from such a distance. I can only theorize that atmospheric conditions were a contributing factor, or that somehow our proximity to the crab robot boosted their effective range. Whatever the reason, the recorded data indicates that there is some at least partially functional pre-Devastation technology in the region. The power signature suggests that it is not generated by a robot. I detect none of them near the reading. That said, I cannot guarantee the absence of robots or other dangers."

The nanomachines finished with his shirt and returned to the case. He examined the shirt critically, but there was no trace of the tear. He closed the swarm case and locked it. "Would you display a map with this cave and the technology site on it, please? Then overlay it with the closest of our trade locations."

A holographic map appeared before him, it showed various towns and farms including names and information on each one, and distance to them relative to this cave. Their current location and the site of the technology reading were displayed most prominently, the cave in green and the site in red. They had traveled and explored this region extensively over the years, and with their semiregular visits to most of the listed destinations, there was little they did not know of within a month or two. Not listed on this map were those locations hostile to them. Many hostile locales were bandit camps, and places occupied by abnormal robots. Thieves and bandits by nature moved frequently, making them hard to pin down.

A normal robot was essentially predictable, it attacked people and sometimes animals on sight, either singly or in a group. Abnormals were different, they almost always worked in groups. But rather than attack indiscriminately and wander aimlessly, they stayed in a confined location for reasons unknown, and attacked only those stupid enough to violate their territory.

A perusal of the map had him smiling. "White Sheep village is not too far from that technology site. I think we should trade with them for food, and at the same time we can visit with our friends. Then we investigate the site."

He returned the swarm case to its compartment and locked the door, then loaded yesterday's trade goods into the Truck. He put them into large plastic crates, sorting by type, and stacked them in the rear cargo space.

When everything was securely stowed, he returned to the cave. Inside Kat had finished cleaning from breakfast, and was in the middle of manually putting on her armor. In standby mode, her armor was a collection of unobtrusive purple and pink metal parts that she wore all over her body, each retracted into small enough pieces, that they did not restrict her movement. Her helmet shrunk into a wide circlet resting on her brow, and the forearm segments were not unlike metal bracers. When changed to combat mode, the individual parts extended toward each other to form a completely enveloping second skin, protecting her from most direct laser hits and moderate explosives. Although Mark had upgraded the armor over the years, he did not originally design it. The base schematic came from an unusual data cylinder Kat carried with her, one he had only ever seen two of in his life. Sky was able to identify the cylinder as a data storage device and read it.

Mark slid into a seat at the table, patiently waiting for kat to finish latching the last segment of armor in place. "When we fought the crab, our sensors detected what we believe is some pre-Devastation technology. And it could be partially active. I want to investigate the site, try to find something we can use, like a weapon that can destroy a crab."

Kat sat in front of him smiling wide in excitement, then looked upward in though, one finger tapping her chin. "Ooh, I really hope we find something good, like Killer scorpion robots that fight in a death match, or a giant pink submarine shaped like an octopus that spits acid ink."

He started mutely at Kat for a while to compose his reply. "You and I have very different notions of what would be good to find."

Her eyes met his in puzzlement. "Huh?"

"Pink octo morph submersibles aside. We may discover technology of a practical application. Possible device or data that would improve your lives, a medical database for our health scanner for example. Even you have to agree that such a database would be infinitely preferable to animal shaped aquatic vehicles, or fighting arachnid robots."

Kat departed the table and started aggressively packing, jamming items forcefully into her bag while muttering to herself. "An octosub would be a practical application if we need to dissolve stuff under water."

Mark smiled, joining her in packing, and tried to improve her mood. "Before we go to the technology site, I want to stop at White Sheep village. We can trade for food, and catch up with our friends." His ploy worked, as he knew it would.

Happy again, Kat smiled at him. "That will be a lot of fun. I can't wait to tell Mika and Tula about the super crab robot. I bet Mika will cook for us."

Uh oh, this could be bad. He had to stop her from saying the wrong thing to their friends. "Um, Kat? Maybe you shouldn't tell them about the crab, you know Mika worries about us."

"Of course she worries, the same as we do about her, we're all friends. What does that have to do with the crab robot?"

Logic was not going to be effective here, he had to keep it simple and hope she understood. "Please try not to say anything that would upset her, like now much danger we were in, okay?"

She shrugged and returned to packing.

Mark folded the scrubber's privacy curtain and collapsed the rods that supported it, then carried them to the Truck. When they traveled for more than a day or two, they took any important items with them. The swarm could easily recreate simple objects like tables and chairs, so those were left behind to conserve the limited space available in the Truck. There were several caves like this one where they stayed from time to time, depending on where they were. Each cave was partially furnished for future use.

Mark loaded the scrubber with its curtain and rods into a compartment, then returned to the cave for more. He passed Kat along the way, a load of stuff in her arms. He collected his bedding and bag, then looked for what else they would take on the trip. Consolidating everything on a table, all that was left were the cooking appliances and food. He would have Kat grab those while he put the bedding into the Truck.

Kat was at the cave entrance as he was leaving. "I have what we're taking with us on the table, grab that and seal the cave when you're done, alright?"

"Sure, no problem."

Mark had used the swarm to build a two foot thick stone slab door for the cave. The door was opened and closed by two, powerful electric motors. When sealed it was difficult to tell the cave was there, the lines on the door and hill fit to together tightly, with the door matching the contours of the surrounding rock. On the outside, it could only be opened by operating a skillfully hidden switch.

He packed everything into the Truck, shoving at the blankets and mats to cram them into their allotted space. When Kat arrived with the final load, he stowed it all and locked the compartments. He opened the driver's door, and heaved himself into the cab. He left the removable top latched in place for now, knowing the day would be warm and sunny, and they would be glad of the shade before it was done. The top was made of the same super tough alloy as the rest of the Truck's shell and Kat's armor, and could be removed if they wanted to drive with the sun on their heads and the wind blowing in their hair.

Kat, with MGP in hand, was programming a music list to play during their trip. "I can't wait to see our friends, I bet Tula will love my new games and videos."

Mark pushed the on button and checked his HUD for signs of danger, then put the transmission in drive and rolled forward. "I hope you chose some good music. It's going to be a long drive to White Sheep."

"I have three hundred of my favorite songs lined up, and I added the music from Jagged Hills. All of that together will last for hours. Plus if I get bored, I have my new games to play. I fell asleep last night in the middle of the mute mapper level. There are a lot more ugly alien zealots to blast."

Driving north-east following the marker on his HUD map, Mark watched the scenery slowly change. The dry, rocky ground dotted with somewhat sparse trees and bushes, gave way to softer dirt and more trees, although they were still on the stunted side. The sun rose in the sky to their right, becoming obscured by the roof at mid morning. When he stopped for lunch, the noontime yellow orb was at its apex above them. Wind no longer blowing through the window to cool him, sweat prickled his skin.

The day was hotter than he realized. The Truck was parked near a short tree, perhaps eight feet tall, but leafy enough to provide them with spotty shade. The meal consisted of simple cheese sandwiches, which they ate sitting beneath the branches, enjoying a light breeze that stirred the wide leaves, causing shadows to dance over them.

"Do you think things have changed in White Sheep?" Asked Kat after swallowing the last bite of her third sandwich.

Mark polished off his own bread and cheese before answering. "We were there only a few months ago, I don't expect things to be much different than we left them. And not a lot ever changes in a small village like White Sheep. Their most pressing concern is probably the health of their sheep."

"I don't want them to be bored, maybe we can bring some excitement to them." She said cheerfully.

He held no illusions of what the villagers would think of Kat's brand of excitement, but he might be able to convince her to tone it down. "Like the time you blasted a hole in the village wall, when I was installing a laser turret?"

"I only wanted to be sure it was working, I really thought it was pointed somewhere else."

"Then there was the time you almost burned down an entire field of corn." Added Sky catching on to Mark's plan, or perhaps taking the opportunity to be vindictive.

"There were crows eating the corn, I didn't know you're not supposed to shoot them with lasers." She replied defensively.

"Or when you nearly destroyed the pavilion by stomping through a support beam in your armor?"

"Hey, that's not fair. There was a big spider crawling across the floor, it could have bit someone. I didn't mean to stomp that hard." She complained.

Mark tried hard not to laugh, she had been tormented enough. "I'm sure they will be happy to see you again. If you can refrain from breaking everything in sight." Maybe almost enough. "They're always eager to trade for our tools."

Face red, Kat looked like she wanted to run and hide. "I think we should go now, the sooner we leave, the sooner we will arrive." She marched stiffly, to the Truck.

He allowed himself a small grin and followed her.

Three more hours of bouncing over the rugged terrain saw them nearly to White Sheep village. The land on which the village was situated, was far greener than where he and Kat had come from, with more plants, taller trees, and some late summer flowers in bloom. They were much farther north, where it was comparatively cooler and wetter.

The land was more or less flat, the only things on the horizon for miles in any direction were trees, which was why the fifteen foot high perimeter wall of the village was already visible from three miles away. He could make out the upper curve of one of white sheep's large water tanks where it stood next to a field of crops. Among other things in lesser quantities, the village grew corn. While rain was sufficient for the local vegetation, a field of thirsty cultivated plants required a dedicated water supply. Villages like this one could trade goods they produced, food and clothing, for water at the water plant on the coast. The need for supplemental water was not great, and the trades were fair, leaving few with any shortages or reason to complain, too loudly.

CHAPTER 4

Nearing the village, Mark became aware of a herd of sheep not far from the village wall, lazily nipping at the grass even as their keepers tried to move them. A healthy carpet of sheep-trimmed grass covered the uncultivated ground surrounding the village. Trees and bushes grew in abundance farther away. The field of crops whose water tank he had seen an approach, stood next to the wall on the west side. The tassels on every ear of corn were brown, announcing the ripeness of the golden treasure hidden within. A handful of brown tile roofs poked out over the protective wall.

The day was waning, the sun's reddening rays slanting low in the western sky. The villagers herded their sheep toward the gate assertively, determined to get the recalcitrant animals into pens for the night. More importantly, they were eager to reach kitchen tables for well earned dinners, after a sweaty day of labor. The village wall, which he knew to be six feet thick, was constructed from layers of expertly grouted and stacked mud bricks, one of the finely crafted products produced by White Sheep. On previous visits Mark provided the village with solid steel brick molds made to their specifications. The molds gave them the ability to turn out large quantities of bricks fast, and in uniform sizes.

On brick towers jutting above the wall at regular intervals, stood sentries keeping watch over the countryside around the village. Each tower held one of the big laser turrets he helped to install, slightly larger and more powerful than those on the Truck's roof. One of those turrets was the one Kat accidentally blasted the wall with. Korta was not amused that day. Some of the closer sentries pointed at the Truck, calling down to people in the village. A pair of Oriths launched from the towers, soaring out from the village for a closer look, though they would already know who's vehicle this was. The Oriths circled overhead for a minute, then the smaller one with black feathers waved down to the Truck, and they wheeled around to return to the village to report what they had seen.

Oriths were essentially identical to short humans, standing an average of four and a half feet tall, and slim of build to the point of appearing malnourished by human standards. Their most obvious physical difference from human, was the large pair of functional wings growing from their backs, allowing them to fly like the birds from which they descended.

A small group of people emerged from the main village gate, a ten foot wide log construct almost as tall as the brick wall. Mark stopped the Truck thirty feet from the people and turned it off, no reason for anyone to worry that he might run them over. He and Kat exited the cab, and watched the four villagers walk over to meet them. Leading the men was an intimidating wolf pared Grymal. He stood more than six feet in height, bulged with dense muscle, and his bared canines lent his face a fierce mien. Behind their imposing leader, was a dark haired dog Grymal, and two average but strong humans. Their clothing was plain wool in blues and browns, and they were weathered and hardy in the manner of shepherds and laborers.

Mark and Kat stood side by side at the Truck's front bumper guard, waiting for the wolf to stride purposefully to them, his face stern and his shoulder length hair flowing in the breeze of his passage. Upon reaching them he could hold the facade no longer, and the wolf's face split into a huge smile exposing rows of white teeth. He lifted the two of them together in a crushing bear hug.

"Mark, Kat!" Boomed the big man. "Good it is to see you."

"Good to see you too Korta." Mark gasped out, rubbing his arm to regain circulation when he was released.

"Hi Korta, how are Mika and the kids?" Asked a grinning Kat, not at all fazed by the hug.

"They are very well little Kat, and glad will they be that you are here. Come, let us go to my home. We will talk of what you have been doing these last months. Trade may wait until the morning." Korta turned to reenter the village.

They followed in Korta's wake, taking two strides for every one of his. People had gathered in front of the villager during Korta's greeting, they parted for him as he passed through the big gate. A small, one room guardhouse was situated inside the gate, the man on duty stared out at a narrow window at them. Mounted to the wall where the gate closed, was a wide metal bar on a vertical pivot, that would be lowered into hooks on the gate to lock it at night or in emergencies.

Along the inner side of the perimeter wall, were the watch towers. They were less than ten feet wide, and reached over the top of the wall. A wood rung ladder ran up the side of a tower to a covered platform enclosed in a short wall, acting as both a handrail and a barrier against enemy fire. Bolted to the beam floor of the platforms, were the laser turrets, sitting high enough to hit targets close to the wall. Oriths were frequently tasked with lookout duty for two reasons. Because they had better vision than dull sighted humans. And because they could fly, an ideal trait for looking more closely at approaching strangers.

The houses and buildings in the village conformed to no specific plan in layout or design, although they were structurally similar. They were placed haphazardly along twisting roads, and faced no set direction. Did the roads come first? Or did the buildings go up, and the roads then try to squeeze in where there was room? Two adjacent buildings might be pointed the same way, or back to back. One pair sat corner to corner diagonally. Every structure was built around a log frame with plank floors and brick walls, and was protected by roofs of mud brick tiles. The buildings were one or sometimes two stories tall, and many of them had covered porches.

Korta led them down the hard packed dirt streets snaking through the village organically, like the veins in his arm, presenting Mark a picture of daily life in White Sheep. Children ran and played in yards or between houses, wearing sturdy wool clothing and leather shoes made from sheep hide, much of it a bit dirty from a long day of work and play. A group of screaming kids kicked a yellow ball, shoving and jostling for position as they tried to strike a board serving as a goal. Another child stood in front of the board to defend it. All of the youngsters laughed and shouted, oblivious to the world around them. A bulky man in a leather apron passed them, pushing a cart laden with mud bricks that must have weighed twice what he did. A youth beat a thick wool rug with a stick where it hung from a pole. He struck it more vigorously than seemed necessary for cleaning, which probably had something to do with the two girls who watched him and giggled. Through the open window of a larger building, women were seated at rows of machines spinning thread from wool. The finished spools were piled into baskets to be taken to dyers for coloring, before moving on to the weavers where they would be transformed into clothing and rugs.

The village market, a short street lined on both sides by shops and stalls, was shutting down for the evening. Shopkeepers pulled racks and boxes of goods inside, locked doors and lowered boards over displays. Many of the shops were already closed, the attendants and owners gone home for dinner. One shop keeper was hauling an armload of colorful cloth bolts inside as they passed, the dark haired man nodded at Korta absently. Like most people he saw, the man's interest was in the visitors, who were the recipients of friendly smiles and earnest greetings. A short woman stopped to ask Korta a question about the market opening in the morning, there was apparently some uncertainty as to whether they were working or not due to trading. No one wanted to miss a chance at acquiring new stuff, and no traders brought better stuff than he and Kat.

Mark knew from past visits that Korta's home was situated at the fur edge of the village square, as mayor he had a prime location and a house larger than most. It was a moderate two story structure with rooms for each of his two children, a guest room, and a large office that saw use for council meetings and other official gatherings.

They rounded the bend at the end of market street, and entered the village square. The open, grassy space may have been dubbed a square, but it was more of a vaguely rounded shape outlined by curves and flat spans dependent on the buildings or streets comprising its uneven border. At one end of the square, close to Korta's house, was a large, low wooden platform. The platform was used by the mayor and village officials as a seating area during important events, or for ceremonies and to give speeches or announcements.

The square was a beehive of activity this day, people moving every which way to prepare for a gathering of some kind. Mark knew from experience, that villages like this one would use any excuse they could find to have a celebration. His arrival with Kat, was sufficient reason for a day off from work. News of the traders had spread like fire through the village, and these preparations must have started before he set foot inside the gate.

They were halfway to the platform, threading their way past people carrying tables and other heavy burdens, when an excited voice shrieked his and Kat's names. His head snapped up to see a pair of young, wolf eared Grymals running over the well-tended grass at them. The two youths shared the same wolf ears and tail with Korta, and were no older than twelve or thirteen. The boy slowed to a walk as he came close to them and grinned boyishly. In contrast, the girl ran full speed into Kat, wrapping her in a hug that nearly knocked them both from their feet.

Mark shook the boy's hand as his sister started talking in a rapid string of uninterrupted speech. "Kat, I'm so happy you're back. You were gone too long again, and I was beginning to worry that something happened to you. Riss was on watch duty with her father at the wall today, and she saw your truck driving in. She flew to my house to tell me you were here, and I ran fast as I could to find you. But here you already are almost to my house, so I didn't have to run very far. You have to show me more moves, I've practiced what you taught me every day, and I'm getting good. You know Malaka had her baby? He's a boy and he's so cute, you're going to love him. He sleeps a lot."

Turning away from the relentless verbal torrent, Mark spoke to the boy. "Hello Raag, how is your mother? Have you and Tula been behaving yourselves?"

"Of course we have." Said Raag indignantly, then gave the lie to his words by glancing sideways at his father. "Mostly."

Korta boomed a laugh. "Speaking of mostly. Did the two of you leave your mother alone to prepare for our guests' arrival, while you ran to talk to your friends?"

Tula's unstoppable monologue came to a grinding halt, and Raag went red in the face, looking like kids caught with a handful of cookies before dinner. They spun on their heels as one, and ran to their home as fast as they had from it.

Korta laughed harder at their retreat.

"I'm going to help Mika too, see you later." Kat ran after the kids.

"Ah, it is good to be young, is it not?" Korta slapped him heartily on the back, making him stumble.

Mark rubbed his shoulder wincing. "So Korta, it looks like the village is doing well since I was last here."

Korta stopped at the platform, staring seriously at the villagers hard at work placing chairs on the smooth wooden deck. He sat on the edge of the platform, waving for Mark to do the same while gathering his thoughts. "You are right in this, times in truth have favored us here. There are many healthy sheep, the water flows freely, and the corn grows tall and strong. There have been no attacks on our trading groups, nor raids on the village by bandits. Look at my people." Korta gestured grandly at the square before them. "They are happy, they are prosperous, and because of this they are complacent. It is hard to stay vigilant, when it is has been many months since we were raided by thieves or bandits. Longer since last any have seen robot. It lets people think that perhaps they no longer exist. For all this peace and calm should I be happy, I wish nothing more than for the wellbeing of my villages. And yet I find I am deeply worried instead. I worry that this very lack of trouble may itself foreshadow some even greater problem. That those who would do us harm, have not gone as it appears, but rather are preparing for a far more deadly attack. An attack that would harm not only a few people and sheep, but would devastate our entire existence here."

Korta sighed expansively, pushing air from his lungs in a forceful gust of wind, and shaking his large, shaggy head. "Bah, you must forgive may dark ramblings friend, I fear I become cynical as I grew older. I have prosperity, and all I see are krumpins in the shadows, come. "Korta rose to his feet, his mood restored. "Let us go to my home, and see what my lovely wife has made us for tonight's meal." Winking conspiratorially, he added. "And perhaps we can prevent fried Kat form eating it all before it reaches the table."

Mark laughed with Korta, walking beside him to the Grymal's house, almost directly behind the platform. There was a wood slat fence framing a small yard, and smoke rose from the brick chimney. Korta guided him to the front door, which faced away from the square. From the voices he heard upon stepping inside, he knew that everyone was gathered in the kitchen. Mika was an excellent cook, and never tired of preparing food for friends and family.

The front room was furnished simply, several polished wooden chairs with high backs were positioned along the walls for guests. The plank floor was covered by one of the thick rugs the villagers wove, geometrically patterned with triangles and squares in red, blue, and orange. Resting on the rug was a low table, and a glossy, tree limb bookcase resided in a corner, holding a somewhat random selection of books. Due to the rarity of printed works, the library was Korta's most prized possession. Because of the presence of books here, and in other homes, the people of White Sheep were considerably more literate than those in most towns and villages. Using the swarm, Mark could, and often did, make books for people. Korta's collection held several of these, but his preference was for originals when he could get them. This random collection method explained some of the more curious titles on the shelves. Ridman's Guide to Real Estate, Blubber to Burly in Six Weeks, Agnostics for the Uncertain.

Moving past the hearth, made of stones in a variety of sizes and types, they entered the kitchen. Mark inhaled deeply the smell of cooked food permeating the house, making him realize how hungry he was. Laughter and light hearted conversation grew louder on entering the kitchen. A pretty wolf Grymal tended the oven, removing a loaf of bread with a thick towel, her long gray hair fastened behind her head with a black clasp in the shape of a bird in flight. Her plain shirt and pants were the deep blue of sapphire, and her face hold a motherly smile. Sliding the bread from its pan with an expert flip of here wrist, she left it to cool on a board, and stirred a large pot of mutton stew simmering on the stove top. The aroma of meat, vegetables, and bread was enticing.

The conversation, such as it was, continued to be dominated by Tula relating local events she thought significant. "... so Raven kept flying out of her reach, shouting 'You can't catch me, you're stuck on the ground without wings.' And she kept flying and laughing while Salana chased her around jumping and trying to catch her, but Raven only flew away and yelled more. After a few minutes Salana sat and ignored Raven, like she was giving up. Raven got curious and came down to see what was going on, and Salana turned real fast and threw a bunch of mud at Raven. Hit her right in the face. Raven screamed and fell flat on her butt. She sat there spitting and coughing, and trying to wipe the mud off. Me and everyone were laughing because she looked so funny with all the mud." Throughout her recitation Tula went on setting the table for dinner, her story never slowing or pausing.

Kat sat in a chair at the table, laughing along with her friend. Raag, helped with the table setting in silence, uninterested in his sister's tale, which he had likely heard more than one.

March smiled in greeting at the woman making dinner. "Hello Mika, the food smells wonderful as always."

Mika nodded at his compliment. "Thank you Mark, now wash up and have a seat. We are nearly ready to eat." She picked up the plate of bread she just finished slicing. "Put this on the table for me Tula." Passing off the bread, she started filling bowls with stew. "And you can help with the stew Raag." The boy carried steaming bowls one at time to the table.

Mark dutifully washed his hands in the sink with water drawn from storage tanks by electric pumps he brought on a previous visit. He dried his hands on a towel hanging by the sink, then sat across from Kat.

A small metal bowl on the table held fresh creamy butter, and when everyone was seated, he spread some of it on a slice of bread, watching the pale yellow butter melt into the soft steaming surface. He bit into it eagerly, savoring the taste of fresh bread and butter, something he rarely had the chance to enjoy. Butter was not readily available away from villages and farms, and Mika backed fantastic bread. He always ate at least two of three slices when they were here.

As usual Kat raced through her food like her tail was on fire, squishing whole slices of bread into her mouth, and practically drinking her stew, hardly seeming to notice the chunks of meat and vegetable. Korta was amused by Kat's customary haste, while Tula and Raag watched the spectacle with fascination.

After waiting in vain for a minute for Kat to moderate her intake speed, Mika gently intervened. "You can slow down Kat, the food is not going anywhere. And please close your mouth while you chew."

Embarrassed, Kat obediently slowed her frantic pace.

Korta started a conversation. "My friends, how have you been these past several months? You look to be in fine health." He glanced at Kat. "You certainly have healthy appetites."

Kat kept her eyes on the bowl before her, concentrating on eating with a measure of decorum. A strenuous endeavor.

Marked answered for them. "We've been fine, no serious problems to speak of. For the most part we stay to ourselves and out of trouble. We go out to scrapwards to scavenge when we need to, then make trade goods from the scrap. We rarely encounter bandits or robots, and when we do, they can't outrun the Truck." He was careful not to mention the crab, he did not want to upset Korta or Mika with their narrow escape. He shot Kat a long, meaningful look, shaking his head slightly when she met his eyes.

Unfortunately, Kat either completely misinterpreted his meaning or was intentionally ignoring it. Her notion was what was appropriate to tell their hosts, was a bit different than his. "It hasn't been all boring. For one thing, I found new games to play on my MGP, and more videos to watch. There are still working data cards hidden in the scrapwards, and one day I will find them all. Also, I wanted to make a fire breathing dog for trade, but Mark and Sky don't think anyone would want one for some reason. You guys think people would want a fire breathing dog, right?" She paused, looking from face to face for agreement. When no one came to her support she went on. "Anyway, on our way back from the scrap ward a couple of days ago, something really amazing happened."

Mark coughed and shook his head, trying to stop her, she went on unheeding.

"We were driving away from the scrapward with a full load of scrap and games, when this incredible super crab robot appeared right in front of us. It stood up in our path, and started chasing us for no reason, other than crabbiness. It was fifteen feet tall and clacked loudly as its big metal feet hit the ground. Clack, clack, clack! "She tapped her spoon hard on the table to demonstrate. "It had huge hands on its long arms, and started throwing big rocks at us. I flew out of the Truck and shot it with my lasers. They didn't hurt it at all. Mark blasted it with the Truck's bigger lasers too, but nothing did any damage or slowed it down, not even a little. The crab was faster than us, so we couldn't run away. Then Sky found this deep ravine, and we drove right for it. The crab was behind us, getting really close to the Truck, still flinging rock at us. Mark reached the edge of the ravine and jumped the Truck over it. I blasted the ground in front of the crab to blind it with dirt, but it jumped through the dirt cloud. The Truck landed safely on the other side with a bounce, but the crab didn't make it, it was skewered on a big metal beam sticking out of the ground. It was stuck on the beam, wiggling is legs to get free. It hung there for a bit, sparks shooting between the legs. Then I shot the beam and it fell out of sight, and exploded when it hit the bottom. Bang!" She slammed a first on the table to punctuate her story, making Tula and Raag jump in their seats.

Mark cringed, turning away from a grinning Kat to look at their hosts. The kids were wide eyed with wistful astonishment, the eagerness of youth longing for adventure. Mika was concerned, while Korta stared at Kat blankly. Kat seemed to realize something was wrong, her grin fading in the silence.

Finally Korta spoke. "I am sure that our friend Kat is exaggerating her incredible story in a misguided attempt to entertain us, and they were never in any real danger. Is this not true friend Kat?" Kat opened her mouth to speak, but Korta cut her off sharply. "Is this not true?"

Kat closed her mouth and nodded firmly.

Korta fixed Mack with a steely gaze. "We will speak no more of this for now." His tone promised a lengthy discussion later.

With Kat chastised for inappropriate dinner conversation, the rest of the meal passed without incident, or excitement. When the food was gone, Kat ensuring that it was, Korta invited Mark to sit with him on the porch. Kat and the kids were left to clean the kitchen, under Mika's supervision. Korta sat with his back to the railing, staring silently into the night, considering what to say.

Coming to the conclusion that the big Grymal was angry about Kat's story, Mark dove right into an apology. "I'm sorry for not telling you about the crab. I didn't want to worry Mika."

Karta shook his head, his loose hart waving gently from side to side. "No my friend, you were correct in not telling Mika of your crab, and I expect nothing less from Kat than to boast of fighting such a monster. No, I have deeper concerns than a distressing dinner. Korta's visage turned grim, and he addressed what truly preoccupied him. "This great crab robot only adds another layer to my worries that something larger is waiting to happen. I do not like this new robot, one that none have seen before, not even you who travels the land. A robot far larger and stronger than any I have heard of."

"I understand what you're telling me. But as you said, I drive around most of the region every few months. And in all our recent travels, I have seen nothing to suggest a large gathering of bandits or robots, unusual activity of any kind, or other signs of a probable attack. In fact, I have noticed the same decline in raids and attacks that you have."

Korta raised his head, a thought occurring to him. "Tell me, how was this crab able to surprise you? Should not your computer Sky have seen this beast before it was upon you?"

Mark frowned, the same question had troubled him for days. "I have thought about that, but I have no answer for why it did not register on our sensors sooner. Do you have an idea, Sky?"

"I am not certain of the specific cause of the detection anomaly. The crab did not trigger an alert an our sensors, until it was at a distance of one hundred and eighty-two feet from the Truck, and then it may only have been the motion sensors that pinged off of it. I have run a comprehensive diagnostic on the sensors themselves and on our detection algorithms, but I can find no discernible fault in our systems. In an effort to prevent this situation from recurring, I have increased the sensitivity of the detection algorithms, this should provide us with a small improvement in warning time for future encounters. More will have to be done if other robots display similar properties."

"Properties?" This was the first Mark was hearing that there was something special about the crab, aside from its size. He felt a stab of irritation that Sky had not shared this information when they talked before. But it faded quickly, Sky could be frustratingly literal, and he had not actually asked." What properties are those? Are the crabs unusual in some way. Do they have something we have not seen in normal robots?" That should be specific enough to get the AI talking.

"I have little specific data relating to the crab, primarily due to the fact that our sensors were so ineffective on it. The crab returned only superficial readings, and only at a very limited distance. I surmise that the crab possessed a previously unknown form of sensor shielding. There is a possibility that it was equipped with a kind of active stealth technology, one that is not in my database, perhaps an inverse wave signal to cancel out our scan frequencies."

"Is this stealth technology completely new, or is it something only these robots are equipped with?"

"I have no historic data on a robot with stealth capabilities that would compare with what we observed on the crab. It is my conjecture that this is an entirely new adaptation, and on exceedingly recent one at that. I have never detected anything in the past that would suggest the prior existence of a system comparable to this. More disconcerting is that my data suggest the crab itself to be of recent manufacture, most probably in the last thirty days."

"I don't like that at all. From what we know of the robots, they have changed little, if at all, in the decades they have been here. What would make them change now? Did something happen that we are not aware of? Is there some new controlling force updating and rebuilding them? I'm starting to talk myself into sharing your concern Korta, maybe there is a perilous new threat out there. I can only hope not, hope that it is all a big coincidence."

"As do I friend Mark, as do I." Said Korta softly.

Mark was provided with a bed in Korta's guest room for the night, while Kat shared a room with Tula. He was glad the two of them were in a different room, they would have kept him awake all night in endless chatter. As it was he lay in bed for some time unable to sleep, his thoughts repeatedly circling back to his conversation with Korta, when he finally did drift off, it was a troubled slumber filled with distressing dreams of an invisible robot army.

He awoke late in the morning to the smell of meat drifting into the room. Morning sunlight was shining through the window, helping to dispel the night's lingering shadows, refreshing him for the new day. Rising from the bed, he stretched, listening to voices and laughter outside the window as he dressed in clean clothes from his bag. He left the room, hungrily anticipating Mika's cooking.

In the kitchen Raag was finishing his breakfast. The day was earlier than he thought.

A smiling Mika placed a plate of food on the counter, and slid it to him. "Good morning Mark, did you sleep well?"

"I did, thank you." He carried the plate to the table.

"Kat and Tula have gone to play around for the morning, and Korta is in the square preparing for the trading and tonight's festivities. He wants you to join him when you are ready."

Raag finished eating, washed off his plate and fork, and made straight for the door.

"Be sure to help your father in the square." She said to the closing door.

"I will." Came Raag's muffled reply.

Mika watched him eat for a few minutes, seeing past his outer calm to read what he was really feeling. It was something she was uncannily good at, maybe it was a mother thing. "You look a little tired, are you sure you slept well?"

He forced an energetic smile. "I slept fine Mika."

She started at him for a moment, cracking his facade. "Alright, you slept fine. Then would you tell me what's bothering you? I know Korta is worried over a possible attack on the village, is that what has you upset?"

In an attempt to buy himself time to think, Mark stuffed a slice of meat into his mouth. He had no wish to worry Mika, especially when there was no real evidence that something was going on. He also did not want to talk to Mika behind Korta's back, particularly at the risk of telling her things that Korta might not want her to know. When his mouth was clear, he said. "As I told Korta, I have not seen anything out there to indicate any attack is coming. In fact, I have seen no activity at all from robots or bandits." He smiled at her again.

She nodded, not entirely sincerely. "I shall take your word on it for now, it is nice of you to try and reassure me, if misguided." She smiled to move the conversation forward. "You and Kat really should visit us more often, everyone likes having you here, and Tula admires Kat. I love you both as if you were my own children, so please be more careful. No more fighting giant robots, alright?"

He felt tears threaten to fall at the sentiment. "We'll do our best to avoid them, or I will anyway. And I will try to keep Kat out of trouble too."

Mika laughed softly, a pleasing, musical sound he never tired of hearing. He was deeply touched by her words, Mika and Korta had become like parents to them over the years. Parents they only saw four or five times a year, a major contributing factor in what kept them on such good terms. Neither he nor Kat remembered much of their lives from before they met at about five years of age, and had no knowledge of their parents. Korta and Mika were the best, friendliest people he knew, and he liked to think that his real parents would have been like them.

Mika glided to his side, placing a warm hand on his shoulder. "Mark, Korta and I have been planning to ask you this for a while. If you are willing, we would like for you and Kat to live here in White Sheep with us. We would help you build your own house, with a workshop for you, and an exercise space for Kat. We have not told Tula and Raag of this, and if you say no, I would prefer they not know. You don't have to decide right away. Talk to Kat, and take a few days to think it over. Let us know you answer when you're ready."

Mark was completely taken out of the blue by the offer, living in only one place was not a thing he spent time contemplating. It had him feeling strangely warm inside, as though a piece of his life was magically falling into place, one he had not known was missing. Home, a place with friends\ and family where he belonged, a thing he never expected to have for himself. "Thank you Mika, this means a lot to me. I will talk it over with Kat, but I think we would enjoy living here. Having a home here."

Mika squeezed his shoulder. "You go and take care of your trading, the whole village will be there to see what you brought us. Korta will have tables for you in the square, don't keep them waiting. I need to cook some things for tonight's celebration, I will see you later." She took his empty dishes to the sink.

Mark nodded, a smile glued to his face he had no desire to ever be rid of. He left through the front door, making his way around the house to the square, deep in thought as he floated to the main village gate where the Truck was parked. He saw Tula and Kat run by laughing and smiling, they waved merrily at him and he returned the gesturer. He had to admit that he always enjoyed being here, their trading visits to White Sheep were among his fondest memories. To live here, for this to be their permanent home, was like the best dream he could imagine. Just thinking the word home was almost magical. A home was one of those things other people had, people with parents and normal, loving families, not strange outcastes like the two of them. But now it would be theirs too.

Before he knew it, he was standing by the Truck, only vaguely aware of how he came to be there. Concentrating on his work, he loaded the crates of White Sheep trade goods onto the cart. Once the crates were secured and the Truck locked, he pushed the cart into the village. People began to surround him almost the moment he passed the gate, the laden cart an open invitation to ask what he had brought and to try to get a jump on the trading. He let each of them know in friendly, but firm terms, that no trading would be conducted until he was properly set up in the square. By the time he reached the grassy line that marked the square boundary, there was a small parade of villagers following him, talking amongst themselves in speculation of what was on the cart, and anticipation of what they wanted.

The ground of the square sprouted more people now than grass, packed most tightly around the platform where he always conducted trading. Mika was right, it really did look like the whole village had come, or so close to it as to make no difference. Korta was standing by several tables on the front edge of the platform. The big Grymal saw him and bellowed for people to clear a path. A bubble reluctantly opened before him, the villagers trying to keep or take spots closest to the trading.

At the tables Korta lifted the cart, goods and all, onto the platform and clapped Mark on the back. "As you can see friend Mark, the village has readied itself to claim your tools. Please set out what you will, and we can begin."

Mark was an organized person by nature. The crates were filled with like item, and he emptied one crate per table to maintain that order. Pots, pans, and cooking utensils went on one table, saws, hammers, and hand tools on another. Everything was placed neatly on an open spot, where people could see and examine them; he wanted everyone to know exactly what they were trading for. White Sheep was one of the better places to trade. The villagers generally made fair offers for his goods, and trading was calm and orderly. Part of the reason for that good behavior, was because

Korta stood behind him during trading to monitor the proceedings. Few people wanted to upset the big wolf.

There was little that he and Kat genuinely needed from people, and that came down to food and sometimes water. The water they could gather on their own from streams and lakes, or collect when it rained or snowed. Food was more complicated, they could hunt for animals and forage for leaves, roots, and nuts, but those were the kind of tedious tasks even he had no patience for. It reminded him too much of the past, which meant that farming was absolutely out of the question. At White Sheep he traded for mutton, corn, and a number of other vegetables and fruits. Water and wool could be had here, but they rarely needed them. The village produced clothing, furniture, and rugs, all things the swarm could make when or if needed.

At the end of trading the tables were empty of goods, and the crates were full of mutton, vegetables, wool thread, and water. He was at it for three hours, finishing a bit short of mid-day. Most people were happy with their acquisitions, but a few wanted more. He made a list of their personal requests promising to bring those items on his next visit.

He loaded his refilled crates onto the upper shelf of the cart, and removed a pair of boxes from the lower one. The first he passed to Korta. "This is for the village, it's another set of solar panels and a power crystal to help charge the turrets. I figured it would be useful, the laser turrets eat a lot of power."

Korta lifted the box with one hand as if testing its weight, holding it at eye level. "I thank you for this thoughtful gift, as usual you bring precisely what is needed.

Mark held out the second box. "This one is for Mika, I know how much she loves to cook for people, so we thought she might like these. Kat helped choose the pattern on them."

Korta opened the lid with his free hand to peer inside. The box contained a set of stoneware plates and bowls packed with strips of cloth to prevent breaking or scratching. They were a vibrant white with a pattern of green corn stalks along the outer edge, and the dark blue outline of grazing sheep in the center.

"Ah my friend, you have again chosen the perfect gift. Mika will truly cherish these lovely dishes." He closed the lid. "Now let us take your new supplies to your truck."

Korta left both boxes on the platform, utterly unafraid of having them stolen, and hefted the cart to the ground, muscles bulging beneath his shirt. They proceeded in silence to the main gate, people hurrying by with burdens for the celebration that lifted spirits, more than they wearied muscles. There was an atmosphere of expectation in the air, and a smile on every face, including the men standing watch at the gate.

Mark unlocked the Truck to pack away the supplies, feeling tempted to munch on a bright red apple sitting at the top of a crate, but held back to save his appetite for the lunch Mika would have waiting for him.

"Mark, this morning Mika will have spoken to you of coming to live here in White Sheep with us. I want you to know that I have spoken to the village council, and we all would like for you and Kat to call this your home. Tell Kat that if there is anything you require, you need only to ask, and I shall do what I can to help."

Mark loaded the Truck while they talked, it helped to hide the emotion on his face. "Thanks Korta. I can't say for certain what we will decide, but we do think of White Sheep as a kind of second home. I am a little worried that Kat may not be the most appropriate role model for Tula, who knows what mischief they might cause."

Korta's laugh rang off of the Truck, he did not do anything quietly. "Yes, I fear that Tula will soon be begging you for a fire breathing dog, or some equally dangerous construct." Korta's tone became semi-stern. "Do not of course give her any such thing."

Mark laughed with him. "I can't believe she actually told you about that. She wanted me to make one and bring it along for trade, and she wanted it to be pink! She couldn't understand why I did not want to make one."

When their laughter subsided, Mark finished stowing the supplied and the cart. More out of habit than from any read need here, he activated the security system. Together they returned to the square, retrieved the boxes from where they waited, untouched on the platform, and entered Korta's small yard. It always seemed a marvel to him, that a place could exist where he could leave something out in the open and come back later to find it still there, undamaged. How novel would it be to live in such a place. He almost stopped in his tracks at the thought, he was already thinking of what life would be like here. Somehow he knew that his mind was made up, this was going to be his home. It felt good.

Korta deposited the solar panel box on the ground behind his house "I shall install these sometime tomorrow, they will prove very useful in the days to come I think. As you have seen, there will be a celebration this evening for your visit. There will be food, music, and merriment. I expect everyone to attend, and no work to be done this day."

"I don't mean to cause trouble for you, I hope no one is too inconvenienced."

"No my friend, do not be concerned. Such festivity is good for the village, it keeps people happy and productive, a welcome intrusion into their lives. Now go and give Mika your gift, she will be in the kitchen cooking for tonight. I am needed in the square to oversee the preparations." Korta administered a parting slap on the back and left him.

Mark shifted the box to one arm, and fumbled the door open almost dropping the dishes, pushing his way inside with a muffled rattle. Mika looked over from her cooking when the kitchen door slammed against the wall. "Sorry." He apologized. Raag was helping his mother, Kat and Tula were not present.

Mika saw him and smiled. "Hello Mark, I take it trading is over for the day. How did it go?"

"Yes, all done, and it went well. I got enough supplies to feed us for a while."

"Not too long I hope. You really should visit us more often, if you do nothing more." She glanced at Raag and changed the subject. "What is it you have brought into my kitchen?"

"This is something we made for you Mika. It is a present from Kat and I, I hope you like it." He pulled a chair away from the table, put the box on it, and opened the lid.

Wiping her hands off on a towel hanging from the waist of her pants, Mika came over to see what was inside, a glowing smile crossed her face. "These are lovely Mark, thank you." Raag's frown said he did not agree.

"I now have the nicest dishes in the village." She unpacked the bowls and plates, stacking them on the table. "I have to confess that Kat spoiled the surprise a little. Before she and Tula went out, she told me that you were giving me some boring plates, instead of something fun like a pink flying bat. Thank you for the plates Mark."

"You're very welcome. And speaking of Kat, has she been back yet?"

"She has not returned since leaving with Tula and her friends. I don't expect her back until later. Feel free to rest, or to have a look at what is happening in the square."

"Tula gets to play around with friends, while I'm stuck here cooking." Muttered Raag irritably as he stirred a pot on the stove.

Mika gave Mark a wink behind Raag's back. "Yes, and tomorrow Tula will be busy cleaning, while you spend time with your friends."

Mark downed a slice of bread from a plate on the counter, then left Mika to her work. A nap was a good idea, he wanted to stay up late for the celebration, and sleep now was exactly how he would do it. He went to the guest room, took off his boots, and laid on the blanket covered bed. A feeling of contentment pervaded him, as he slipped into a light slumber.

CHAPTER 5

It was dinner time when Mark entered the kitchen of his family's home. He smiled at his father and siblings already seated at the table, and at his mother who was setting down a platter of sliced meat. He assumed his place between his sisters, accepting a plate from Kat that was a bit full for him, and participating in the happy conversation. He was not at all clear on what was being said, but found that it did not bother him. All that mattered was the feeling of belonging, of having people he cared for, who cared for him in return. All was right with the world, this was how things were here, and how they always would be. He had the vaguest sensation that this was something he had longed for, even if he was unaware of the need until this moment, this carefree sliver of reality. And it was something he would fight to keep, would die for if necessary.

A voice called his name, distant and urgent. The faces of his family obscured, turning him cold with fear that this voice would take them from him. If he followed the voice, his home and family would be ripped away and lost.

"Mark!"

The voice came louder, pervading his whole being and filling his mind with its need. The world around him blurred, washing away like dirt in a deluge, and shaking violently as it faded to a void of indistinct light. A cold hand clamped onto his shoulder, dragging him harshly from his chair and from his happy home.

"Come on, wake up."

Mark's eyes jolted open, trying to focus on the quaking, wood colored world. His foggy brain caught up with him, slowly piecing together the situation. He was on a guest bed in Korta's house, and Kat was standing over him trying to homogenize his insides. Her fingers dug into his shoulder, shaking him vigorously, snapping his head side to side painfully. Somehow managing to catch her wrist with his hand, he croaked out a shaky admonition.

"Kat, stop! I'm awake." He sat up, gingerly rubbing her abused neck. "You almost shook my head right off my body."

She freed her wrist and straightened, staring at him contemplatively. "No, I don't think that's possible, heads can't pop off from a little shaking." She thought a bit more. "I wonder how far it would fly if it did pop off."

Not wanting to dwell on the notion of flying heads, particularly his own, he hastily changed the subject. "I need you to listen to me for a minute, there's something important I have to tell you. This morning Mika and Korta talked to me about the village. They invited us to come live here in White Sheep with them. I told them that I would discuss it with you, and we would think it over before giving them an answer. We would build our own house, with a workshop for me and a training area for you. We would still need to go to scrapwards to scavenge, but if we live here we will have to contribute to the village. Some of our trade goods will be used to get water from the water plant for example. And we would be expected to help the other villagers when needed, like rebuilding a house if it's damaged in a storm." He watched for her reaction.

Kat clasped her hands above her tail where it poked out from the back of her shorts, and started pacing the length of the room, her head tilted forward and eyes staring at the floor. "We would have a home like in the videos, and here in White Sheep with our friends. It will be a lot of fun living here. Mika and Korta are already like our parents, and I could spend more time with Tula and Riss and all their friends. I could paint my room pink, and have a second bed for Tula when she visits. There would be a little room for the fire breathing dog, it could be a guard dog to protect the house. Mika might start teaching me now to cook, not that I want to cook all the time, but it would be nice to know how. Then we could..."

Kat ramped up into full creative insanity mode, speaking faster and more animatedly the longer she went on, and her ideas becoming more and more fantastic. Mark could only stare in bemused astonishment as she paced the room and talked. After many non-stop minutes she wound down, running out of ideas for the time being, but her excitement was clearly undiminished.

"...And around the castle we'll have a huge pink wall topped with big laser turrets firing pink beams. And the pink fire dogs will roam along the wall hunting for bad guys to roast."

Sky spoke into the ensuing silence before it could drag on too long, though with a distinct lack of tact. "Kat, I believe that I can speak with relative certainty for the citizens of White Sheep village when I tell you this. I do not think that a single villager has any desire to have their entire community transformed around them, least of all into a bizarre, candy colored, medieval fantasy city. As to your remaining delusions, with hard work you may eventually accomplished a small number of them."

Kat was somehow surprised, and clearly disheartened, by Sky's revelation. "But the people in my Candy World games look so happy. Why wouldn't the villagers want to live in a candy city?"

"Consider the fact that the residents of Candy World are dressed entirely in confectionery, and are named after food items. In reality a cupcake hat is neither a pleasant nor practical thing to wear."

Mark stifled a laugh. "I take it you like the idea of living here with our friends?"

Kat's smile returned full force, her candy city ideas shelved for now, but not likely forgotten. "Yes, I think it would be wonderful to live here." Her ears lowered uncertainly. "But to be clear, we still get to fight robots sometimes, right?

"Yes Kat, we will still fight robots when we inevitably run into them." He did not add that he would actively try to avoid such encounters. Kat would always be Kat. She sometimes saw the world as if it was one of her games, in which she was unquestionably the hero. She wanted to save the day, and expected everyone to live happily ever after. And although it was his preference to avoid a fight, he knew that Kat liked to destroy robots. He would not be the one to deny her some fun, and he kept his opinion to himself. Mostly.

She jumped up and down in glee, her boots slapping loudly on the floorboards. "I'm going to find Tula and tell her the good news." She paused with a hand on the doorknob, remembering her reason for waking him in the first place. "The party is starting, see you there."

She was out the door and down the hall before he could respond. He pulled on and laced his boots, then went to the kitchen. It looked as though everyone had already left for the party. He might as well head for the square to join them in the fun.

The moment he opened the kitchen door, the sounds of music and merriment, a low thrum in the background until then, pushed at him like a strong summer wind. Laughter, song, and conversation from hundreds of mouths filled the air, a joyous cacophony imbuing the evening with sense that all was right in the world.

The square was crowded with people, so many that they were backed all the way to Korta's fence, leaning against the slats and posts in relaxed conversation. To avoid disturbing those who blocked the rear gate, he cut through the house and took the long way to the square via the road. What greeted him there momentarily overwhelmed him with its intensity. Food and drink, filled his nostrils with new smells at every shift of the mild breeze, shouts, laughter, and music ebbed and flowed in his ears. And a gathering of people far larger than he was accustomed to, moved in a writing mass, running, dancing, and walking in every direction. A smile spread on his face unbidden, it was days like this that made life worth the effort.

Winding his way through the crowd, with only minor jostling, his eyes were drawn to the platform, where a group of villagers performed music using a number of simple instruments. A carved wooden flute whistled high, clear notes. Taut strings thrummed on hollow boxes. And tones high and low were tapped onto sheepskin drums. A woman in a wide, red skirt stood at the fore, singing energetically in time with the beat.

Tables lined up in a double row were set along one side of the square, laden with elaborately presented food. Next to these were yet more tables, with dozens of chairs where people could sit to eat or rest. The sight, and wonderful smell, of so many different dishes, triggered a twinge of hunger in his stomach, and a gush of saliva in his mouth, drawing him to the platters and bowls so generously heaped with culinary delights. He was stopped along the way by several of the younger villagers, thanking him for the day off of work for a celebration.

He lifted an empty plate from a stack of them at the end of a table, and proceeded to fill it with food. There was meat cooked in every conceivable manner, roasted in glazes, sautéed with vegetables, breaded and fried, and ground into seasoned balls. He saw corn boiled on the cob, whole grilled mushrooms, and cold salads with colorful flowers and leaves. There were breads, muffins, and cakes both sweet and savory stacked high, loaded with meat, cheese, nuts, and fruits. It was all very tempting, and far too much for any one person to try everything. And while Kat was sure to gorge herself in the attempt, he limited himself to only marginally more than he believed he could finish.

He sat with his feast, savoring every scrumptious bite of food, tasting flavors he had not experienced before. He might have to ask some of the villagers to share their recipes with him. He might have to ask some of the villagers to share their recipes with him. He found Korta and Mika sitting at the head table, closest to the platform, engaged in lively conversation over their dinners. Raag danced with a pretty human girl, the pair smiling and swaying to the music. He polished off his plate with difficulty, the last few tidbits a serious struggle, but he was determined not to insult the cooks by discarding a single morsel.

After depositing his empty plate on a pile of dirty dishes to be taken away and cleaned, he wandered the perimeter of the activity feeling several pounds heavier. There was an area marked off for games, some requiring a degree of skill. Throwing darts at a target, or tossing a ring around a post. One involved rolling a heavy all into rows of wooden boards painted with images of robots. There were games of luck using dice or cards. Games of physical strength, such as the ever popular arm wrestling. And a game where two people were tied together with a rope on one ankle, the object being to drag the other person off of their feet, while trying to remain upright.

The gaming zone was, unsurprisingly, where he discovered Kat. She was sitting at a table preparing to arm wrestle a much larger Grymal. Her opponent was tall and muscular, with striped yellow and white cat ears and tail. A young Grymal woman stood behind him, cheering him on. Tula, a brown haired human girl he recalled as being named Salana, and black feathered Orith he recognized as Riss, were on Kat's side of the table. The human judge running the contest asked if everyone was ready, counted to three, and shouted go.

Kat's trio of friends cheered her on loudly, arms waving and fists pumping. Kat's arms slowly descended as if she was losing, but Mark was not deceived, there was a tiny smirk on her face. She was toying with the man. The Grymal smiled prematurely at the presumed ease of his victory, his lady friend cheering him happily. When Kat's arm was halfway down she grinned, then slowly pushed her astonished opponent's arm in an arc all the way to the table.

The poor fellow was stunned, not believing what had happened, his friend patting his arm in consolation. Kat's friends rushed in to congratulate her, more excited by Kat's win than she was.

The judge officially declared Kat the winner, and asked the contestants to shake hands. Kat shook the man's hand solemnly, then sat to wait for her next match.

Tula spotted Mark and dragged Salana over to him, leaving Riss with Kat. "Mark." She grinned. "Kat wanted to come play the games and found out there were prizes for the winners. We told her she could play an easy game like ring toss to win a good prize, but she saw the cakes near the arm wrestling table, and said she would win one. We couldn't convince her she didn't have to arm wrestle to win a cake." Salana nodded confirmation. "Some of the guys here are really big and strong, so I didn't think she could beat them all, but so far she has beat everyone she's wrestled. Mother said Kat would want to win the cake she made because it's pink, but I didn't believe she would arm wrestle all these big, strong men for it. She only has to win twice more to get the cake. Oh, hold on a second, she's about to go again, we have to cheer her on." She hauled Salana back to Kat.

Mark stayed where he was to watch Kat arm wrestle, far enough away to avoid being hit by overexcited spectators accidentally. He assessed Kat's three remaining competitors. They were all very large men, likely some of the strongest in the village. The judge called out the pairings for the semi-finals. Across from Kat sat a big human not much older than she was, but he was taller and had thick, bulging muscles.

The judge started this match as he had the previous. "Is everyone ready? One, two, three. Go!"

This time Kat opted not to play with her challenger, taking his size more seriously than the last man, she simply pushed his arm slowly down. Halfway to the table she struggled briefly, her arm shaking with strain. It appeared that this human was somewhere close to her in strength close, but not equal.

"Kat is the winner." Announced the judge when the loser's hand touched the table. Anything else he might have said was drowned out by Tula's exuberant scream. Mark wondered if the poor guy would suffer permanent hearing loss thanks to the hyper girl.

"Kat and Mallo will face off in the final round." Stated the judge when the noise subsided.

Kat again shook the hand of her vanquished foe, this one not as shocked by his loss as the last, but no more pleased. When Kat sat, she covertly rubbed her biceps as if her arm hurt. No one else noticed the action, but it was clear to him that she was wearing down from too many consecutive matches. His gaze shifted to the second winner. Mallo was a large Grymal with graying black hair, and the tip of one of his catlike ears missing. He was clothed in a pair of black pants and matching sleeveless shirt, revealing arms corded with muscle and crisscrossed by old scars. His six foot height and scars would have made him imposing, or even frightening, were it not for the warm smile and easy laugh that softened his features.

Tula and friends were at his side again, with Tula chattering away. "Mallo is the best hunter in the village. He's super strong, even stranger than my dad, but not as tall. I think he's the handsomest man too, but Salana thinks he's too old." She shot a small glower at her friend, Salana shrugged indifferently and started at Kat. "But I think he's great, don't you? Mother says he had a wife before he came here, but I guess she was killed by robots a long time ago. I want Kat to win, but I don't think she's strong enough to beat Mallo. They're starting, everyone pay attention."

Salana caught Mark's eyes, and rolled her's at Tula grinning. How did Tula talk for so long without taking a breath? Maybe she had found a way to continue speaking on the inhale, doubling the time she could go on.

The judge started the final match. "We are down to out last two arm wrestlers." He gestured grandly at Kat, really getting into the job. "It's everyone's favorite wandering trader in purple, Kat!" The crowd cheered loudly, led by Tula. "And she's up against that toughest man in White Sheep, the great hunter Mallo." The cheering was at least as strong for Mallo as it was for Kat, maybe a little more so. "Are you all ready?"

"Yes!" Yelled the crowd.

"Kat, Mallo. Are you ready?" They nodded to the judge and grasped hands over the table. "One, two, three. Go!"

For several drawn out seconds it looked like nothing was happening, that perhaps they had ignored the command to start. Their arms shook slightly with the strain of two evenly matched people of great strength testing each other's might, their hands swaying back and forth under a force that could bend an iron rod. The villages cheered on their favored wrestler, exhorting him or her to push just a little harder, as if they had a personal stake in the outcome. Both Kat and Mallo were breathing hard, gulping air between mighty heaves of solid muscle, neither giving an inch of ground. Then it happened, Kat's arm dipped, her face red from a supreme effort.

Seeing Kat on the brink of losing, and knowing how upset that would make her, Mark had a sudden flash of inspiration. "Cake! Cake! Cake!" He chanted at the top of his lungs. He poked Tula in the arm as he continued to shout. Tula picked it up, perhaps understanding its purpose, and soon more in the crowd joint them in the strange chant. Most would have no idea what it meant, but were too caught up in the moment to care.

The reminder of what she was doing this for did the trick. Kat's expression changed from one of worry, to one of determination. Kat uttered a guttural growl, and with a giant, grunting heave her arm came up, and Mallo's hand hit the table with a slap heard over the roaring of the crowd.

"Kat wins!" The judge did his best to be heard above the frenzied onlookers, who were all shouting, even those who had rooted for Mallo before Kat's victory.

Kat leaped to her feet, knocking over her chair, and hopping up and down laughing. Tula screamed and hugged him so hard he thought she might crack a rib, then ran over to do the same with Kat.

Kat extricated herself from Tula's hug, exchanged a few words with Mallo while shaking his hand, and headed to the prize table. Mallo openly rubbed his hand looking thoughtfully at Kat. Mark came to Kat as the judge instructed her to select her prize. She raised the pink cake for everyone to see.

When she tore her gaze from the cake, she noticed him standing there. "Mark look, I won a whole cake just for me, and it's totally pink."

"I see that, good for you."

"I already ate so much food that I'm all stuffed. I can't eat any cake now, but later some time I'll cut into it. I'll give a piece to you, and Tula and maybe Riss and Salana can have a little too." Her enthusiasm waned as she mentally divided the cake. "I bet it's the most wonderful cake ever, and I might not have won it if it wasn't for everyone shouting cake. I heard that, and I thought about the pink cake, and I had to win. Could you take may cake back to Mika's house for me? Tula and I want to play more games and dance."

He accepted the cake from her. "Sure, I will put it on the kitchen table, you have fun." Holding the plate with both hands, he smiled as Kat skipped away with her friends.

He walked to the nearest edge of the square where there were fewer people and less activity, following the perimeter around to the street by Korta's house. *I think it will be good for Kat to live here, she could use more friends to spend time with, and a mother to help mellow her a little.* Life would not always be parties and games, but a stable, predictable, environment would do a lot to ground her. He wondered what daily life would actually be like for them in White Sheep. They would have to help with the day to day running of the village, and contribute to its protection. He expected to have less free time, but he would never have to worry about having enough food or water, or want for companionship with over two hundred people around.

If possible, he wanted to elevate the level of technology in the village, such as ensuring that every home had electric lights and refrigeration. It was something that he would need to discuss with Korta before acting on, but he was sure that there were many things here he could change for the better, things no one would reasonably turn down.

He went in through Korta's front door, his unlocked front door, his footsteps loud in the empty house as he walked to the kitchen and set the cake on the table for Kat. He suspected that Mika had made the cake specifically for Kat, knowing that Kat liked pink and was likely to win one of the contests for it. But she probably would not have guessed that Kat would win the arm wrestling contest. He left the house to return to the partly, closing the lockless door, and contemplating the level of trust that required.

The street was bathed in the warm red light of the setting sun, giving gentle voice to the lateness of the evening. In another hour it would be dark. The air was warm, but not unpleasantly so, perfect weather for staying up late to enjoy a celebration. There were solar powered electric lights in place around the square and along the streets, another technology he brought to them on previous visits. They would come on when darkness fell.

At the end of the street Mallo leaned casually on a post, his arms folded. The scared Grymal watched the square, head nodding to the music. Mark had not spent much time in Mallo's presence, could barely remember even speaking with him, but saw that Mallo possessed a relaxed confidence, as if he feared nothing. The Grymal was soft spoken and friendly, but was not overly interested in socializing. Mallo faced away from Mark, his ears pointed at the square, and gave no indication of noticing his approach.

When Mark was five feet away, Mallo spoke without turning from the square to look at him. "Hello Mark, you and your companion Kat look to be happy and healthy. It brings warmth to my heart to see young people like you living your lives without anger or pain. I can see in your eyes that you have experienced much suffering and sadness, but have not allowed it to defeat or control you. You must possess great inner strength."

What was this about all of a sudden? Inner strength? Him? That was not how he saw things, he did what he must to survive. "I don't consider myself all that strong. Kat's the one who's strong, without her I would have given up long ago."

Mallo nodded, motioning to Kat who was dancing with her friends in the square. "Yes, she is strong, and she moves like a fighter. Would you tell me who has taught her to fight?"

Another question out of nowhere, this was the first time in all his years with Kat, that anyone asked him who trained her to fight. He honestly had no answer to give. "I don't know who taught her, of if anyone actually did. I have known her almost my entire life, and while she trains constantly. I know of no one who actually taught her to fight. I don't think Kat could tell you either, not if it was before we met."

Mallo accepted his vague non-answer equitably, rather than being irritated by the lack of explanation, he smiled. "It's not important, I was merely curious. Perhaps I can persuade Kat to honor me with some friendly sparring before you leave." Mallo fluidly straightened to a standing posture, his grace speaking of long hours of physical training.

Mark watched the Grymal stride powerfully away, wondering why any sane person would want to fight Kat, he certainly knew better than to try. It must be a thing with fighters, it was not, to the best of his knowledge, a Grymal thing. He knew that Kat incessantly challenged herself, training endlessly with VR fighting simulations, or battling actual robots whenever possible.

Turning from Mallo's receding back, he continued on into the square. It was time to join in the fun, and at the top of his list of things to do was play some of the games. At the gaming area, located on the opposite side of the square from Korta's house, he singled out the ring toss as a starting point. The games were free to play for anyone, but prizes were only presented to contest winners, all others played for fun or bragging rights, or to practice for the next contest. There were lines in front of the individual games, but none of them was longer than five or six people. At the ring toss he was provided with three metal rings, each three inches wide, and placed behind a line five feet from narrow wooden posts. His hand eye coordination was not this best trait, he considered himself to be average. It was no surprise when his first two rings bounced uselessly off of the posts, and his third missed altogether. Finding a single attempt sufficiently humiliating, he moved on to the next game. This was the ball rolling game with the robot boards. As before he had three tries at it. What was it was with everything being in threes, was there an unspoken universal law? What was wrong with four of five? The smooth balls were five inches in diameter, and painted a vibrant yellow that was rapidly scuffing from repeatedly hitting the boards. His performance was much less embarrassing here, with him knocking down one board each on his first and last rolls, but hitting only the curved wooden backstop on the second.

He tried luck based games like dice rolling, which involved groups of four people vying to out roll each other. He spent a solid twenty minutes playing the games, the time passing quickly. These kinds of games were a fun diversion, but they could not reach the entertainment value of a good video game. He decided to skip the strength games entirely. Apart from knowing he did not have the strength to win one of them, he had no desire to hurt himself, a likely outcome of any serious attempt. Having played all the games he cared to for the time being, he wandered over to watch the dancing, from the safety of the side lines. Men and women, youths and children, all dressed in fancy, colorful clothing reserved for special occasions like this, moved to the rhythm of the music, not all of them moving smoothly. Turning and swaying gently to the slower songs, bouncing and stomping when the tempo picked up. Smiling faces came and went in the throng, mixing and weaving in some unpracticed choreography, rarely staying in one place for more than a few seconds. He stared at the ever-changing sea of motion for a while, wondering if he dared participate. Kat was good at dancing, as she was at any physical activity she cared to try, which made him a little self-conscious at times like this. Everyone he saw was enjoying themselves, and not all of them were particularly graceful, lending him the confidence to step into the crowd. He initially felt clumsy and awkward, believing that everyone must be watching and judging him. But the faces around him were happy and guileless, and his unease slipped away to where he could relax and enjoy himself, moving his body to the beat of the music. Over time new faces entered the dance, and tired bodies left it to rest.

A burning sensation built in his legs from the constant motion, and he left the dance area to seek a place to get off of his feet. A pair of Oriths intercepted him, their short stature making them seem to appear out of nowhere. At several inches over four feet in height, they were average for their species, barely reaching his chest. Like most Oriths, they were slim of build and avian in appearance, with fine boned, narrow faces and wide hawkish noses. They otherwise looked human, except that in the place of hair on their heads, they were crowned with fine feathers. Their most striking features, were the two, large feathered wings sprouting from their backs near the shoulder blades.

The taller of the two, with shimmering black plumage on his wings and head, addressed Mark while tilting his head slightly to the side. "Mark, I am

Falto, and I am pleased to meet you. This is my friend Fees." Falto dipped his head to his red-brown companion.

"Hi there." Mark shook each of their hands. "How can I help you?"

"We are told that you can make trade items for special requests, in this true?"

"'I can, yes."

"Then we request that you make a visual magnification device to help us see longer distances. Something similar to binoculars, if you know what those are, that we can wear while flying, and can easily adjust with one hand. These would help us with scouting, and aid in protecting the village. We will take as many of them as you are able to build, fourteen to twenty would be perfect. We are willing to trade two whole sheep for them. Do you think this is something you can do, or is it too complex?" They watched him consider their request with hopeful eyes.

Ignoring their child like voices, which were normal for adult Oriths, he pictured a general outline of what they wanted in his mind. "I think I can come up with something that will work. I should have them ready by my next visit."

They offered him profuse thanks, and were smiling happily when they left him.

"Sky, please make a note of the Oriths' request, and remind me of it in a day or two."

"Done."

Resuming his trek to an empty chair, he successfully arrived this time, and sat down to relax for a while. *I'm really going to like living here,* he thought. *Kat is happy, the villagers are friendly, and there's plenty of meaningful work to keep me busy. I've never had a home before, or ever expected to have one. Never had people other than Kat to call family. I think this will be a good home for us, and with a few additions to its defenses, we can protect White Sheep from robots and bandits.*

Mark slouched in the chair, staring at the sky as the last orange and red light faded to night. Automatic photo sensors in the small but bright solar powered lights, turned them on as it grew dark, bathing the village in soft white luminance. The lights were a fine addition to the village, exactly the sort of thing he liked to do for people, a little gesture to improve their lives.

Some time later he still stared at the stars, happily contemplating the future. He tapped his foot in time with a song he had heard twice so far, a happy, upbeat tune about a curious sheep getting into various bits of trouble. Kat looked at him and broke away from the group of people she was talking to. She walked over with a bounce in her step, and sat next to him smiling.

"You're missing the fun sitting here all by yourself, you should come and dance with us."

"I danced earlier, it was fun, and now I'm listening to the music and resting. I also ate some food and played a few games. I may eat more in a minute."

"I really like it here. Everyone is nice, and I've been having a lot of fun since we came. It's great."

Mark straightened in the chair, looking Kat in the eyes. "You know that when we live here it won't be a party all the time, and you won't always get along with everyone."

She laughed as if what he said was obvious. "Oh, I know that, and I know I will have to help with work around the village. But I think it will be fun here most of the time."

Knowing Kat so well, there was a question he had to ask. "And 'fun' includes fighting robots I take it?"

Kat nodded enthusiastically. "Of course it does, preferably at least once per week. Hopefully big, tough, cool looking ones with many arms and big lasers. Wings might be fun too."

Shaking his head ruefully, Mark chose a diplomatic reply. "We don't want life to be boring, do we?"

She slapped his arm playfully. "That's the spirit. I think it's time for more food, and more games."

Mark smiled, everything was going right for a change. Maybe the old books were right, and there really could be a 'happily ever after.'

CHAPTER 6

Kat sprang to her feet, intent on stuffing herself with every morsel she could force down. She made it three steps, when the peace of the night was irreparably rent by a harsh, blaring alarm. Chaos erupted around them, villagers running in every direction at once.

Angry shouts and anxious voices cried out for answers or orders, fear and uncertainty supplanting festive happiness.

"What's happening, Sky?" Demanded Mark more aggressively than he intended, fear prickling his skin with sweat. This had to be a mistake, there was no way the village was being attacked, not now. He took a deep breath, forcing himself to stay calm. Robots never came in groups larger than four to twelve. And between the Truck and the village defenses, they could repel any number of bandits.

"The village perimeter sensors are detecting a substantial contingent of robots closing on our location from all directions simultaneously. The robots are currently at a distance of one point three miles from the perimeter wall. At present velocity they will be in range of the wall turrets in three minutes and seventeen seconds. Scans indicate that they are equipped with the same stealth technology that the crab was. They were undetectable until microseconds prior to the alarm sounding. I apologize, but it was impossible for me to have alerted you earlier." Reported Sky at a high volume to be heard over the alarm and shouting.

People raced all over preparing the defense of the village, everyone knowing what to do in an emergency, but it looked to him like half panicked disorder. Ignoring the villagers, who he could not really help directly anyway, he tried to learn more information on their attackers. "Launch the drone Sky, I want to know exactly what is out there."

"Drone launched, visual contact in twenty-seven seconds."

Mark looked at Kat. "Put on your armor in battle mode, now. You need to be ready to fight. But try to stay out of trouble, if there are more crabs out there, you won't be able to stop them."

Kat nodded, whether in acceptance or just to shut him up was hard to say. "Right." She tapped a sequence into the wristpad she was thankfully wearing, then stared skyward toward the main village gate where her armor had been left in the Truck. Seconds later a blur of pink light shot out of the darkness, flying right at them. Spreading her arms outward from her body, Kat jumped, when the armor reached them. The light split apart, the dark purple armor, illuminated by soft pink lines of energy, separating into a humanish shape. The individual pieces attached themselves to Kat, each part precisely latching onto her body one by one in a rapid fire sequence almost too fast for the eye to follow. The flightpack locked on last, and Kat landed smoothly on her feet. She tapped another code into her wrist pad, activating combat mode. The armor parts extended toward each other, until she was completely covered by articulated allow plates. The visor dropped across her eyes to complete the transformation from Grymal girl to metal knight.

"I have acquired a visual feed from the drone, it is of the robot force directly east of White Sheep Village. Displaying now."

A holographic screen projected in front of them, and Mark almost wished it had not. What he saw chilled him to the core. There were dozens of the normal, human sized robots carrying hand lasers, and possibly more weapons unseen. He had never heard tell in even the wildest rumors of a robot force so large. There were enough robots on the screen to destroy White Sheep, and that was only a small part of what must be an army of hundreds. Even worse for the village, there were four of the giant crab robots, which might as well be invincible for all that he and Kat could hurt them. Each crab had a cage-like metal construct on its back, made of thick silver bars. But there was something else very disconcerting about the robots he was looking at, something he had no explanation for. Every single machine appeared to be brand new, as if it had been built in the last month. To his knowledge no one had ever seen a new robot, they were without exception old and broken. Could someone out there be building new robots? Or perhaps more distressing, could the robots themselves be replicating?

Kat's face plate was open as she stared bloodlessly at the display, he looked at her eyes in that pale face, gauging her reaction. For once she was not happy or excited at the prospect of fighting robots. Her face held an aspect of grim determination, as if she was trying to find a solution to an unsolvable puzzle, and would not give up until she did. For reasons he could not quite name, it scared him.

"Kat?" He spoke loudly to draw here back from the abyss her mind was falling into, she reluctantly looked away from the projection. "There's no time to evacuate all of these people from the village, and if we tried, the robots would kill them before they made it very far. But we may be able to keep the robots busy long enough for most of them to reach the shelter. Here's what we will do. You fly me to the Truck, then go to the opposite side of the village to fight. I will use the Truck to destroy as many robots as I can on my side you do the same on yours. Don't get any closer to the robots than you have to, your armor can only take so many hits before you start getting hurt. And when I say we're leaving, you fly right back to me, okay?"

The visor on Kat's armor closed, sealing her off from the world. "I understand, let's go." Her voice was slightly artificial coming from the external speaker, but even so it was unnaturally flat and emotionless. She tapped a button on her wrist pad, activating the propulsion and antigrav pods on her armor, which extended outward four inches on either side of her back. She held out her hands to him, and he took hold of her wrists, grasping them firmly as she lifted off from the ground.

From fifty feet in the air he saw that many of the villagers, starting with women an small children, were already filing into the shelter. They entered by way of an innocuous storage shed on the edge of the square. The adults were climbing and flying to the towers along the wall to man the laser turrets, preparing a futile effort to repel the machines. Passing the wall, he looked outward into the forbidding dark. The advancing robots, visible by the glowing red dots of their photoreceptors floating like vengeful fireflies in the night, were nearly in range of the wall turrets.

Then he was on the ground releasing Kat's wrists. "Remember, don't do anything dangerous, I don't want you hurt."

"It's time to kill robots." She replied flatly before rocketing toward the far side of the village.

With every second critical, he had no time to dwell on Kat's odd behavior. He deactivated the Truck's security system, stubbed his toes when he jumped into the cab to turn the vehicle on. He quickly pressed buttons to switch on night vision mode for the windshield, and to power up the weapons system. The moment the green of night vision allowed him to see the world clearly, he floored the accelerator pedal, tearing up dirt and grass as the Truck struggled for traction. He drove right at the nearest group of robots, pushing the Truck hard.

"Sky, I need you to take control of the roof turrets, destroy as many robots as you can. I will concentrate on driving and trying to avoid their lasers."

"Understood. Lasers active, targeting system online. I will focus fire on the humanoid robots, there is no point in depleting our energy reserves by targeting the crabs."

The Truck's heavy laser turrets rose from standby positions with a motorized hum, and began firing on the robots. The more powerful stationary turrets on the village towers were already firing, the smaller robots that took hits were instantly out of action, nearly vaporizing in the thick streamers of green light. But there were hundreds more of them advancing, and the power crystals in those turrets had a finite charge, it would not last.

Sky's accuracy was impressive, not quite at Kat's level, but superior to most people, including himself. He fired rapidly, taking down machine after machine. The robots attacked the Truck and the wall in equal measure, and equal dispassion. Their lasers were strong enough to cause the Truck damage, but sufficiently weak that it would take some time for them to wear down the vehicle's armor. When a robot fell, the one behind it stepped over the chassis and maintained the attack. Robots did not become demoralized by the loss of a companion.

"The robots' weapons do not at this juncture pose a threat to the structural integrity of the Truck. However, I must caution that a prolonged engagement would prove dangerous.

"Tell me something I don't know." Mark snapped.

"Is there a specific topic you would like to be enlightened on." Returned Sky in a close approximation of sarcasm.

"Sorry, never mind." Mark swerved to evade a barrage of concentrated laser fire, a speedless collection of red pinpricks in the veil of night. He glanced at the wall, large chunks of brick were missing along its length, it would not hold for much longer. Sickeningly wet shapes lay below the wall, where villagers had been hit and fallen from the top. They lay in motionless heaps he averted his eyes from.

He turned the Truck toward the wall, hoping to give himself more room to maneuver. Only then did he realize how close the village really was. The robots were boxing him in. "We need to find a way to get behind the robots. In a minute they will push us against the wall and destroy the Truck. Focus the turrets on blasting us a hole through the robots."

"Compliance."

Checking the targeting radar on his HUD, he found the lowest concentration of marching robots, and drove the Truck to it. There were only four humanoid robots between him and the open territory behind the enemy force. The truck bounced hard over the rough ground, jarring his teeth as he accelerated. The roof turrets fired incessantly, loosing blinding streaks of light over the cab as they barreled down on the group. The robots were not unresisting targets. They fired back, their shots leaving tracks of blackened alloy and burnt polymer in their path. The first robot was hit in the chestplate, falling in a sparking heap. The one to its left was nearly cut in half at the waist, its torso twisting over like an opening hinge. One of its arms flailed wildly to stay upright, the other tracked the Truck ineffectually with its laser. It was a showcase of the mindless tenacity of robots, following their programming until rendered utterly unable to dose.

Mark steered the Truck at robots three and four. The left front tire bounced over the bifurcated bot, causing Sky to miss. A second shot went wide, but Sky quickly adjusted aim and destroyed the third robot. The fourth robot lost an arm in a last frantic shot from Sky. Mark slammed down the accelerator, shouting wordlessly, and the Truck crashed into the smaller pieces, electricity sparking across them. Then it was gone and they were behind the robot formation. Sky adeptly shifted to other robots, and Mark drove along the back of the oncoming army.

Kat was scared, no, make that terrified. She was out of her mind with fear, unable to think coherently. She had never been scared like the before, never experienced true fear, not known what it felt like. Oh she had been nervous, a little afraid at times. She had even occasionally worried that she or Mark would be badly hurt. But she had never come close to feeling this kind of gut-wrenching, mind-numbing terror. In the past she had known that no matter how bad things were, no matter how tough an enemy they faced, they would always be alright. They would always defeat their enemy, or if it was too much find a way to escape.

But it was different this time, this time she was fighting an enemy she could not defeat no matter what she did, and from which she could not run. There was a whole village she had to protect, and if she ran they would all die. Her friends were in horrible danger, people she knew and cared for could be killed, were being killed, people almost as important to her as Mark. But what was worse, what ate at her until it felt like she was tearing apart inside. Was the terrible certainty that even if she died, if she gave her very life attempting to protect them, she would still not save her friends. No matter what she did, how hard she fought, the robots absolutely would not stop until everyone was dead. She felt utterly helpless and alone, there was no plan, she was too scared to think of anything useful. The only thing she could do was fight, to keep destroying robots until this ended, one way or another.

Her speed was unmatched, pushing herself faster and faster, beyond anything she had ever done. She swooped between groups of robots, firing with both arms in an endless barrage of destructive pink energy, silencing many before they could move to return fire. She landed hard, shooting a nearby robot. She ducked an arm blow from the robot next to her, grabbing its leg to swing the machine like a freakish club into two more. They crashed together with a crumpling clang, and she released the bent leg. A robot trained its weapon on her. She rolled toward it, the alloy claws on her forearms extending on her way up. She slashed through its vaguely skeletal torso, cutting armor and circuits like they were firm cardboard. She was airborne again while the last robot was falling to the trampled grass.

She had lost track of how long the battle raged, it may only have been minutes, but it felt to her like hours had gruelingly passed. She had no idea how many robots lay broken by her hands, knew only that it was not enough, not anywhere close. There were too many robots, hundreds of them, they were already at the wall and blasting a hole through it. Bricks and shards of bricks tore from the wall with explosive force, shattering on armor plating and unfeeling metal limbs. Soon robots would be walking the village streets, hunting people in cold, remorseless determination. For all she knew they already were. She was peripherally aware that people had died, in the same way she knew that robots were broken. But did not allow herself to dwell on it, could not let her mind fully grasp what it meant, not and keep fighting. All she knew right now was that she must save the village, had to save Tula and Mika and their friends and families. There was no other choice, no one else would come to help them.

The crabs worried her mort, occupying every spare thought in her head. Even if every last one of the smaller robots could miraculously be destroyed, she had no clue what could be done about the crabs, she wondered, not for the first time, why the crabs held what she thought of as huge baskets on their backs. What would the crabs need baskets for? What could there be in White Sheep that robots wanted to take? What did robots want at all? They did not eat, did not sleep, felt no discomfort or pain. She only knew that they attacked people, indiscriminately and without cause. Sky said that they had done so for the last hundred and fifty years. But why did they attack people at all? If she could only figure that out, she might be able to stop the attacks and keep everyone safe.

She shook her head violently to clear it, now was not the time for idle thoughts, she had to concentrate on what was going on around her. Thinking could wait for another day, if there was one.

A crab was almost to the wall, pelted by a constant rain of lasers from the heavy turrets. The turrets caused minor damage to the crab's armor, forming small glowing divots where the beams made contact. But that did not stop it, the crab moved inexorably forward. Nothing short of annihilation would dissuade the crab from its programmed task. The crab stopped at the wall, raised its huge manipulator arms high, and brought them crashing down on the mud brick. The crab smashed the wall like an angry child pummeling a sandcastle. Mud brick shattered and flew everywhere, raining in a brown hail. The crab's big, three digit hands, pulled brick from its newly created hole, tossing it like so much garbage. When the gap was sufficiently wide, robots began to enter the village, swarming over the crumpled wall.

She raced desperately to stop them, a fresh wave of sharp terror washing over her. Her only thought was of protecting her friends. "Mark! Robots are inside the village! They broke the wall, and they are going inside! I can't let them do this, I have to stop them?" She shouted into the comlink, not noticing the panicked shriek in her voice.

"I have to stop them!" Mark heard Kat's terrified scream in the cab. He was trying to prevent the Truck from being melted by so many lasers, while at the same time maneuvering into a good attack position. Kat's message drove all thoughts from his head. He had never heard a tone like that from Kat, she sounded scared. No, it was worse than that, she sounded out of her mind with fear. Kat was never afraid.

He was suddenly filled with worry for her. "Kat." He spoke into the audio pickup on his HUD. "Can you hear me Kat? Are you alright? Be careful Kat, don't do anything dangerous." There was no reply.

Driven by an unaccustomed fear for Kat, he yanked the steering wheel hard over, skidding the Truck to face the village, nearly overturning it in his haste to reach her. Kat under normal circumstances was unpredictable, but she never did anything too stupid, nothing that would get herself killed. But Kat scared and unthinking, there was no telling what she might be capable of. He saw the wall clearly for the first time in several minutes. The crabs had torn it apart, and robots crowded into the village. If he was lucky, most of the villagers were locked safely in the shelter.

Sky was shooting at the invaders, but his firing rate had reduced dramatically, the shots coming more and more infrequently as the battle dragged on. "Mark," began Sky almost hesitantly, not a normal behavior for the AI. "There are far more robots than we have the capability of destroying, we are running dangerously low on power. I estimate that we will be completely unable to fire the lasers in another five minutes and twenty-eight seconds."

Mark refused to contemplate the implication of Sky's words, angry more at the fact that the AI was right, than at the words themselves. He knew what the answer to his next question would be without asking, but he did not want to believe it, there had to be another choice. "What's your point Sky? In case you haven't noticed, I'm a little busy right now." He hated the anger and fear in his voice, but could not stop it.

Sky spoke gently. "We cannot save the villagers from an assault of this magnitude. We have done all that we can for them. I must recommend that we retreat to a safe location now, while we still retain the capacity to flee."

There was a sick churning in Mark's stomach, bringing him close to losing the food he ate at the celebration. He knew that Sky was right, that they had to leave now if they wanted to survive, but it was so hard to think of abandoning the villagers to the robots. "Our friends are in there." His voice was disgustingly whiny, it was all he could do not to cry. "This was going to be our home. How can I run away and let the robots kill them?"

"You know that I am right Mark, there is no other option, we must collect Kat and leave while we have the power reserves to escape you know that she will not want to go."

Mark slumped dejectedly in his seat, the last of his resistance evaporating with his hope. He looked at Kat's locator dot on his HUD, and turned the Truck to drive full speed for the other side of the village. He had to reach Kat fast, before she got herself hurt. And he had to think of a way to convince her to leave.

Then, to his immense horror, he saw what the cages were for. The crabs were grabbing people and dropping them into the cages. For some incomprehensible reason, the robots were taking people. He tried to slow his breathing, to think rationally. As bad as this was, it at least returned to him a sliver of hope. He may not be able to save the villagers now, but perhaps they could be rescued later.

He was focused on reaching Kat, his eyes scarcely leaving her beacon on his HUD, and willing the truck to go faster. "Can you hear me Kat? Please answer me. I'm coming for you, please meet me at the Truck." Her silence scared him. He drove faster.

Kat was numb, physically exhausted and mentally drained. Her weapons were almost gone, her power crystal hovering at the brink of total discharge. Yet she could not relent, fighting on as if possessed by some feral demon. Robot parts covered the ground in a rough blanket of sparking scrap. She knew what the basket were for now, had seen villagers dumped into them like potatoes into a sack at harvest, and the crabs continued to pluck their terrible crop.

She was deathly tired, her body aching. It felt as though her leg must collapse beneath her at every step. There were too many robots, when she killed one, it was like two more rose to take its place. Exactly like a hydra, her crazed mind supplied. She smacked her helmet with the back of a hand. Keep it together Kat, stay alert.

Not long after the crabs had broken the wall, she saw Tula chasing a stupid sheep that got free from its pen. She screamed at the idiot girl to forget the worthless animal, and get to the shelter. She had not seen Tula since them, and hoped the girl did as she was told. Many villagers took lasers from fallen robots, and were fighting the machines with their own weapons. Kat herself relied on lasers from robots, trying to extend her severely depleted reserves. Too many people with scorched clothing lay inert on the ground, or were dropped into one of the horrid crab baskets.

She alternated slashing nearby robots with her claws, and blasting those farther anyway with the purloined hand lasers. Her whole body throbbed with pain, every movement she made sending renewed waves of agony through her limbs. Crabs were tearing open buildings to find more victims for their catch. She hoped they would not discover the emergency shelter, there was every reason for her to believe that it was safe. The shelter gave off no detectable heat signature, or energy readings, and it was shielded from sensor scans. She told herself that the robots could not see it.

She fought her way to the village square, where she kicked and clawed the shelter entrance shed until it was nothing but flat rubble covering the armored door ten feet below. It was the best she could come up with in the time available to her before the crabs arrived. With the shelter as hidden as she could make it, she slowly worked her way to the wall, trying to draw robots away from the square.

She was thirty feet from the wall, slashing the head off of a robot, when she saw Mika only twenty feet away. The motherly Grymal was pressed to the side of a building, her head and hand poking around the corner to shoot, her targets being a pair of robots climbing the wall rubble. Mika was so focused on keeping robots out of the village, that she failed to notice a robot several feet behind her, aiming its weapon for a kill shot.

Kat's blood chilled to ice. "No!" She breathed launching herself straight for Mika. "Mika! Behind you! Duck!" She shouted at the top of her lungs. She lifted her laser to shoot the robot, saw Mika cast a curious glance in her direction. Mika's questioning expression morphed into a grimace of agony as the robot shot her, burning a gruesome hole through her chest.

Kat's laser melted the robot's head a heartbeat too late, and Mika collapsed face first to the dirt. Kat slid to a stop over Mika, blasting the robots Mika was attacking. Kat fell to her knees beside Mika uncaring of the pain it caused her tortured legs. She gingerly lifted her friend's body into her arms, hugging Mika close, heedless of the warm blood flowing onto her armor. Kat tore her helmet off, the metal joints, ripping free of her chin. She barely noticed a burning tingle in her right calf.

Her eyes welled with tears. "You have to be alright, you have to. You can't leave us, Tula and Raag need you. I need you. Please, please don't go. Me and Mark were going to live here, you were gonna be our family. You were gonna by my mother." Her voice dropped almost to a whisper, the strength to speak escaping her, her vision badly blurred by tears.

Mika coughed harshly, covering Kat with a frightening spray of blood. "Kat, sweet Kat." She rasped weakly. "They took Tula in one of those awful cages. You have to get out of here, get away." Kat opened her mouth to protest, but Mika gave her no chance to speak, "Don't argue, the village is lost, you know it is. There's nothing more you can do to help. If you go now, you might still help, Tula ...Later..." Mika's voice was slow and hoarse, the words barely audible. "I love you, tell Mark..." she coughed again, the merest rasp on the back of her throat, let out one last wet, sighing breath, and lay still.

Kat hugged Mika tightly, holding her mother's head to her cheek and rocking back and forth. She was empty, a deep void opening inside of her that would never be filled. It was over, everything was over, it had all been taken from her. "No, no, no." She mumbled in his belief. "Mika can't be dead, this was going to be our home, you were going to be our mother." Her voice grew louder with each word. "THEY DID THIS !" She roared at the broken robot. "The robots did this! They killed Mika! MIKA'S DEAD! MIKAAA!" Every light on Kat's armor blazed a brilliant red, as if physically manifesting her blinding rage. Her eyes were aflame, burning with hatred beyond imagining, beyond all sense and reason. She turned that fiery gaze on the wall, and on the invading machines.

Everywhere Mark looked the perimeter wall was a flattened mess, partially crushed chunks of mud brick lay strewn on the grass. The obliteration of the once protective barrier becoming a symbol of the destruction within. Bodies of villagers lay contorted in stomach twisting poses by the wall, broken and trampled, their dark blood reflecting light from fires raging in the village. He thought life had already shown him the worst it could offer, but nothing could have prepared him for this. The smell of burning wood, and of charged meat he did not want to imagine the origin of, made him stick. It was all he could do not to spray the Truck's interior with the food he ate at the celebration, an event that felt a lifetime ago.

He was dismayed by what he saw inside the wall, crabs wandered freely, tearing apart every structure without opposition, their cages maddeningly full of people. He heard shouts and screams over the sounds of destruction, expressing pain and anguish at the unbearable. Few robots still roamed outside the village.

A new alarm sounded in the cab, startling and shrill in the enclosed space. A display flashed an urgent warning in red, Sky shut off the alarm to tell him what it meant. "Kat's vital signs have spiked precipitously. Her heartrate is one hundred and eighty beats per minute, her blood pressure and internal temperature are similarly elevated. All readings are dangerously high. Her helmet has been removed, severing all communication with her. The energy output of her armor is beyond the measurable range of its sensors, far beyond the capacity of its existing power crystal. But her power reserves report a reading of near depletion. I can offer no explanation for any of this."

Mark glanced at Kat's location on his HUD, the beacon thankfully still active. "we're almost there Sky, just a few more..."

The Truck rounded a bend in the shortened wall while he was talking, bringing a heart stopping spectacle into view. He was having trouble mentally processing the nightmare confronting him, becoming light headed as his brain struggled for oxygen. Ahead of him, a crab, its cage strangely empty, was being forced back from the village under a relentless barrage of heavy laser fire. The fire was generated by two of the laser turrets from the village wall towers. These turrets, each weighing over two hundred pounds, were wielded by Kat, one in each of her slim hands. It was impossible, there was no other word for it, and yet he could not deny the evidence of his eyes.

Kat herself was demonic. Her armor, normally exhibiting a cheerful pink glow, now shined a deep, terrifying crimson. Adding to the macabre effect, she dripped with fresh blood. Her helmet was gone as Sky said, and her blood smeared face was contorted into rictus of unspeakable rage. Her eyes were opened unnaturally wide, her lips peeled back in an ugly snarl that exposed her pronounced canines. Her catlike ears were pointed backward and held low to her head, and her tail lashed the air violently.

She stalked at the crab in hateful determination, discharging the turrets with all the speed her fingers could employ on the triggering mechanisms, which in Kat's case was only limited by the weapon itself. There were no functional humanoid robots here, only melted and dismantled scrap littering the ground. The crab's manipulator arms were raised like a shield, a desperate attempt to protect itself from the furious onslaught.

Mark stopped the Truck two dozen yards from Kat, staying out of the path of insanity, watching the scene in stunned disbelief. One of the turrets ran out of power, Kat shook it a couple of times in annoyance, and tossed it with no more effort than she would a wad of crumpled paper. She moved forward, step after indomitable step, firing relentlessly with the remaining turret. But in seconds it too was out of energy, and was discarded much as the first.

The crab, mistakenly concluding its attacker to be helpless without the big lasers, began to advance on Kat. She howled in undaunted fury, and kept walking. The crab swung a manipulator arm at her, intending perhaps to crush or capture her. She leaped into the air, landing on the monstrous hand. Before the crab could process the inexplicable behavior of this small biological, she took hold of the hand and jumped off, twisting the arm sharply as she fell. There was a tremendous crack, and inconceivably, the arm tore loose at the elbow joint. Kat lifted the arm at the joint end, hefting it in the manner of an enormous, weightless spear, the pointed fingers forming the spear head. A slow learner, the crab swung its other arm with a crash that shook the ground and vibrated the Truck. Kat handily dodged the attack, the crab crude and clumsy compared to her nimble speed. She ran up the grounded arm faster than the crab could raise it. When she reached the crab's wide, cage topped carapace, she leaped high into the air pointing the spear straight down, and thrust it with all her might. With a horrendous, ear rupturing screech, the arm drove into its host until the blunted fingertips emerged underneath. The crab twitched and its legs gave out, dropping the carapace to the grassy dirt where the speartip was buried. The force of the impact rocked the stationary Truck, bouncing it on its suspension like a boat rocked by a wave. Kat jumped from the crab before it hit the ground, landing on flexed knees facing the Truck.

Acting on instinct, and no small degree of desperation, Mark opened the door and tumbled clumsily from the cab to run to Kat. His headlong sprint stopped five feet from her, when the claws on her right forearm extended, her armor bathing everything in blood red light.

"Are you alright?" He asked, hesitantly talking another step forward. She said nothing, her slumped shoulders rising and falling with each heavy breath.

"Kat? It's me, Mark. Can you hear me?" There was no trace of recognition in her lifeless eyes, nothing at all in that steady gaze. She stared blankly in his direction, not focusing on him, or on anything at all. A knot formed in his gut, pulling almost painfully at his insides. What was wrong with her? It was as if her mind was vacant somehow. Looking her over, he could find no obvious injuries, the blood was not hers. But that left the question of who the blood did belong to, he was not so sure he wanted an answer to that. Robots did not bleed. What he did want to know, was why she was not talking, everything else could wait.

Swallowing his fear, he walked slowly forward, taking baby steps while holding out his empty hands to her. He spoke softly, as if approaching a wild animal. "Kat, it's alright now, you can stop fighting. We're going to leave. I will take you someplace safe. You'll be okay. Come on, be good Kat."

She blinked, a tiny flutter of her eyelids, and her eyes tried to focus, her brows drawing together unsteadily. Her claws retracted to a faint rasping. He reached out to her with agonizing slowness, touching her arm tentatively. Tears sprang from her eyes as if a faucet had cranked on, flowing down her ash darkened cheeks.

She struggled to speak, her mind returning from wherever it had gone. "Mark? Mikas's... Mika... They..."

Her eyes rolled up into her head, and the lights on her armor extinguished. She collapsed bonelessly, and he barely caught her arm before her head hit the ground.

"Kat! What's wrong?" He shouted in panic.

"Mark." Said Sky calmly, restoring a measure of his own. "Kat's vital signs have returned to normal. Sensors indicate that she has entered a state of deep sleep. I am detecting robots approaching our location from the village, investigating the destruction of this crab I expect. I recommend immediate evacuation."

Mark pushed back the panic, and fought to drag Kat's body to the Truck, heaving her limp form backward a few feet at a time. He shoved her into the seat, fastening the harness around her waist, then climbed into the driver's seat. He allowed one last lingering look at the smoldering ruin that was almost home, blinking at the tears obscuring his vision. He turned the Truck away from the village, and fled into the black night.

CHAPTER 7

The cave is on the small side, Mark thought tiredly. It was perhaps eleven feet on a side, and somewhat inconveniently shaped, narrower at the back than the front. The ceiling was uneven, nearly scraping his head in one spot, and composed of very rough stone. It was not as clean as he would have preferred either. The floor was dusted with a thin layer of dry dirt, bits of naked rock peeking through. The dusty skeleton of an indeterminate animal inhabited a back corner, its eyeless sockets silently reprimanding him for disturbing its tomb. The air was still and musty, the bones were not the only things to have rotted here, and the wind did not find a way inside to clear the smell. Though the morning sun had long since risen, the cave stubbornly remained dark, as if the sun was reluctant to shine into its thin mouth, an opening of three by four feet.

Mark noted and pondered all of this only peripherally, his mind so muddled with fatigue and worry, that he could scarcely command a coherent thought. In fact, he had only a fuzzy idea of now they came to be here in the first place. He remembered a blur of darkness as he fled from the robots, having no real thought of where he was going, or what he would do when he got there. For hours his desperation pushed him to run for away from the robots, to find a safe place where they would not be discovered. For a time that need drowned out his sorrow over the destruction of White Sheep. As the adrenaline faded and fatigue set in, all he could think of was helping Kat, she was the only thing left that mattered. He was in no condition to make decisions, or even to so much as think, and he was aware enough to know it. Which is how he knew it must have been Sky who guided them to this cave. He could not say how long it took them to get here, or how long it was since they did. Try as he might, he could only conjure brief flashes of incomplete memory to explain their arrival.

Judging by what he did remember, he must have caused Sky no end of annoyance asking after Kat's health every five minutes. But each time he asked, the AI calmly replied that her condition was unchanged, that her vitals were normal, and that she was sleeping peacefully.

With Kat's armor completely drained of energy, it had been beyond difficult for him to haul her limp, armor clad body into the cave. Twin grooves in the dirt of the floor traced a wobbly path from the entrance to where she lay, where her heels had dragged on the ground. It frustrated him that her armor could not be removed without first recharging it, but it could not retract with no power. He retrieved a charging station from the Truck, along with his tools just in case. But when he connected a cable from the station to her armor, nothing happened, it would not take a charge. Since he knew the charger to be functional, he opened a small access panel below the flightpack on her armor, grateful that rolling her ever did not wake her. He was astonished by what was inside, the crystal powering her armor was cracked.

The synthetic crystals they used for a power source, were virtually indestructible. They were a pre-Devastation technology, one that could not be replicated, something to do with the specific crystalline matrix according to Sky. This was the first broken crystal he had seen, he did not know they could even be scratched. He installed a fresh crystal from their stores, and ran a charging cycle. This was the only drawback to using the crystals, they could only hold a charge when installed in a device. This made them extremely safe to handle and store, but it also rendered them inconvenient in an emergency, since they could not be swapped. With the crystal charging, the sat and stared at Kat. She was a mess, her armor spotted and smeared with dried blood, giving it a sort of rusty veneer. Her face and hair were similarly crusted in blood, some of it having flaked off when he moved her into the cave. Her normally clear, pale face, was mottled with spots like a brown and white cheetah, if such animals existed.

He brought several more practical items into the cave, including light, food, and water. He wet a cloth with water, and gently wiped Kat's face and hair with it, being careful not to scrub so hard it woke her. She badly needed the rest, maybe more than he did.

What happened to you out there? What was that terrifying transformation? You were out of power, fighting a robot you can barely scratch with a full charge, and you destroyed it easily. Your armor flooded with so much power that the crystal broke. Where did the energy come from? I don't understand it. What you did was impossible. How did it happen? He rubbed his forehead hard between his thumb and forefinger, trying to order his cluttered thoughts. It did nothing to help.

When Kat's face and hair were cleanish, he set aside the bloody cloth, and dumped the water outside, too tired to worry about wild animals being attracted by the smell. He checked the power level of her armor, with remote help from Sky since the helmet was missing, it was high enough for basic functionality. He entered a code into her wristpad, causing the armor to retract into its standby configuration, the clatter surprisingly loud in the cramped, silent cave. He removed her armor piece by piece, confident that if the rippling and clacking of moments age did not rouse her, then taking it off was unlikely to. When he was done, he placed her on a sleeping mat, and draped a blanked over her. She stunk of sweat and smoke, but a shower could wait. Her armor on the other hand, could be cleaned right away.

There was no scrubber in the cave. He stumbled through the cave mouth in exhaustion. He was surprised by how late it was, the light, already so dim in the cave, was fading with the onset of late evening. The sun would be down in less than an hour, telling him how terribly distorted his time sense was. He surveyed the area distractedly, a grassy place populated by trees and plants. He could not be bothered to learn more. The Truck was parked behind a stand of leafy trees. He at least had the sense to hide it, or Sky had. This cave was part of a line of smallish hills, none of them more than a hundred feet tall. To the left and right, all the way to the horizon, there was nothing to tell him where this was, but neither was there anything strange or imminently threatening. *How far did I drive last night? Has it even been only a single night, or did I drive all day too? I'll have to figure it out with Sky later. And more importantly, we have to decide what to do now.* His mouth opened in a tremendous, jaw cracking yawn. *But first I better sleep for a day or two.*

Removing the scrubber from the Truck, he remembered to lock the door and reactivate the security system. Carrying the unusually heavy scrubber to the cave was a chore. It was difficult for him to walk a straight line, or to stay on his feet at all. It was all he could do to haul the thing inside, without dropping it or tripping over his own feet. He put up the curtain, quietly loaded Kat's armor onto a rack he placed in the scrubber, and ran a basic cleaning cycle. Laying on a mat next to Kat, he pulled on a blanket, and swiftly surrendered to a deep, and mercifully dreamless sleep.

Her world was a dark, indistinct blur. Smoke choked the air, filled it with thick motes of ash that floated and swirled, obscuring anything more than six feet distant. Kat was in a town or village somewhere, she could tell that much from the houses and buildings peeking through the gray and red haze. The buildings were engulfed in raging flames, the heat pulsing at her in blistering waves that sucked the sweat from her pores. The night was alive with flashes of dancing flame. And over the crackle of burning wood, came the tortured screams of those injured or near death. People were dying, bodies littered the ground she walked on, their blood turning the dirt beneath her feet to dark red mud. Her lungs ached, coughing on the acrid smoke and recoiling at the stench of charred flesh.

She glimpsed hideous shapes in the smoke, there to fade only a heartbeat later, vanishing like some ghastly apparition. Strange, evil things twisted in rage, and thirsting for blood. They stalked her, yearned to torment her, hungered to rend the flesh from her bones. But they would not kill her yet, not until they had taken from her everything and everyone she cared for. She wanted to stop them, to fight and destroy them, but she was so weak she could barely stay on her feet. She stumbled onward, forcing one foot in front of the other in the sucking muck. She could not give in to fatigue or fear, she had to help her friends, had to stop the phantoms before everyone was gone. She looked closely at every face on the bodies she passed, they were familiar faces, faces of people she knew and cared for, people she loved, their expressions warped and frozen in the agony of a tortured death. There was little Riss who loved to fly, clumps of feathers missing from her crushed wings. She passed Korta, his great strength useless in death. She nearly collapsed in despair when she saw Mika, a black hole burned through her chest, her vacant eyes a silent accusation. Swallowing a hard lump of grief and shame, she walked painfully on. There was still someone left, one more person she must save, even if it killed her. The one person who was always there for her, who had taken care of her for as long as she could remember, the one who mattered most to her in the world. He was her family.

The wet squish of rapid footsteps spun her to the right, poised to fight. He materialized out of the smoke like a ghost, running toward her, vast relief at finding her etched into the tight skin around his eyes. When they were only feet apart his mouth opened to speak, but whatever words he may have uttered were lost to the night. One of the cruel phantoms rose up behind him from the haze. It had blazing red eyes and trailed fiery streamers of light as it moved, its narrow black torso was cracked and oozing a viscous red substance that glowed like lava. Thin, crooked arms like withered tree limbs extended from its sides, each knobby hand ending in a pair of long vicious claws. "Haaate." It whispered in a drawn out rasp, as of wind escaping a furnace. It impaled Mark through the heart, lifting him off the ground on its claws, and spraying Kat with a geyser of blood. He made a wet, gurgling sound, his eyes unnaturally wide with untold torment. His body slid from the claws, blood dripping over his lips, and fell to the mud out of her reach.

"Maaark!" she screamed from the depths of her being.

Kat lurched to a sitting position, a sharp pain shooting along her spine. She was confused and disoriented, struggling with a blanket that was tangled in her arms. She was drenched in sweat, but felt chilled to the bone. She could still smell the rotting corpses, the cloying stench of decay that coated her lungs and made her want to retch. She looked around the dimly lit space in terrified panic, until she found Mark sleeping peacefully nearby. She panted in relief, tears filling her eyes as her racing heart threatened to burst from her chest. *It was a dream, a horrible, ugly nightmare,* she told herself gaining gradual control of her emotions. Breathing normally again, she took stock of her surroundings. They were in a small, unknown cave, a skeleton in the corner explained the rotting smell.

Where are we? She had no idea of how they ended up here, or of where here was at all. She remembered the celebration in White Sheep, recalled winning a cake in the arm wrestling contest. And then, a blank. A deep emptiness rolled over her as it came back to her in a crushing avalanche. Robots attacked the village, they killed people or took them away in baskets. There was no White Sheep anymore, it was burned and the people were gone, the robots had stolen their home. She crushed the grief, no good could come of drowning in tears of self pity and sorrow, she must be strong to rescue Tula and the other surviving villagers. They were what was important now, besides Mark they were all that mattered. But now could she save them? The crabs were unkillable, and she did not know where to start searching for them. Details were irrelevant, she had Mark for that, he always knew that do to.

Kat took a deep breath, and coughed, wrinkling her nose in distaste. *I really stink, time for a shower*. Pushing to her feet, she winced in pain from every muscle, they throbbed deeply as if she had exercised too hard the previous day. She lifted her arms overhead in a stretch intended to loosen her stiff body, and scraped her hands on the rough rock of the ceiling, the cave was a bit low. Pulling open the curtain on the scrubber, which was conveniently prepped for her use, she found her clean armor inside. She set the rattling tray of parts on her sleeping mat, and stepped into the machine. Since there was no change of clothes for her in the cave, she hung what she was wearing from a rod to be cleaned with her. The sonic pulses soothed her abused muscles, unknotting them and encouraging fresh blood flow through her body. It was so relaxing that she ran two more cycles. By the time she was clean and dressed, her body was much less stiff, but still quite sore.

Despite her shower, the stink of sweat lingered in the cave, more obvious now that she was clean. She hung her blanket in the scrubber, and stepped on a wet cloth on the floor, she snatched it up, and was alarmed by the scent of blood that came with it. Instantly fearing for Mark, she rushed to yank the blanket off of him, looking over his body for serious injuries. Flipping him gently over, twice, she concluded that the blood was not his. She sighed out her relief, dropped the blanket on him, and put the bloody cloth into the scrubber.

She explored the little cave while waiting for the cleaning cycle. There was not a lot to see. The place was small, dark, and almost uniformly gray and boring. The only even remotely interesting thing was the old skeleton. She was sort of curious about what kind of animal it came from, but unless it was fuzzy and pink with big claws and sharp teeth, it was not worth figuring out.

The boredom was interrupted a few minutes later, when the steady drone of the scrubber clicked off. She folded the blanket and put it on her sleeping mat, and with nothing better to do with the cloth, she dropped it onto the blanket. She went to the low cave entrance and ducked her way outside. It was early morning, the bright orange ball of the sun rising in the sky. She greedily inhaled the cool morning air, all the sweeter after the musty cave. The scent of freshly blossoming flowers carried on the breeze. She gradually stretched the sore muscles across her body to test them, and winced. *I'm not hurt too badly, I should be ready to fight robots in a day or two.*She roved the landscape with her eyes. *Two days will give me time to look around.*

The gloom and dread imparted to her by the nightmare was mostly gone. The loss of White Sheep was no less upsetting, but the villagers would be rescued, their homes rebuilt, and the villainous robots punished. Languishing in sadness would not help anyone, something she knew all too well.

A drawn-out grumble from her empty stomach told her that it was time for breakfast. Seeing the Truck behind some trees, she walked over and turned off the security system. Opening the door, she rummaged in their supplies. "I wonder what happened to my cake. We must have forgotten it in the battle. Someday I'll get another one." She felt an acute sadness at the thought, but determinedly squished it. It was only a cake, she could ask Mark to make another one whenever she wanted. The thought did not help.

Perfectly aware of how bad her cooking was, she had to do something simple. She took out bread, butter, and honey for the meal followed by a cooktop, knife, spatula, and an iron skillet. Supplies in hand, or more accurately in plastic crate, she returned to the cave and dumped it by a table Mark brought in earlier. Only then did she remember plates. She started the skillet heating on the cooktop, and jogged stiffly to the Truck. When she returned with plates, the skillet was hot. She sliced the bread and placed the slices in the hot skillet, toasting them until lightly browned on both sides. She stacked the toasted bread on a plate, turning off the cooktop after the last slice was done. She spread butter and honey on the bread, taking a big bite out of the final slice. She closed her eyes, sighing with pleasure. She was a lot hungrier than she thought, and that was saying something. She better wake Mark before taking another bite, or there might not be any left for him.

Bread in hand she walked to Mark, tearing another bite from the slice. "Mark." She called loudly around a mouthful of sticky bread. When he failed to rouse, she shook him gently. "It's time to wake up, I made breakfast." She was proud of herself, not only for cooking them a meal, but also because it was really good.

With a little slightly rougher shaking, Mark opened his eyes and blinked sleepily. "Kat?"

"Come on." She urged with a cheerfulness the food was beginning to restore. "Get up, I made breakfast." She grabbed his hand to pull him unsteadily to his feet.

"Slow down Kat." He protested, stumbling forward and nearly falling. At the table he squinted at the plates, and understanding of what she said dawned on him. "Wait, you made breakfast? Should I be worried?"

Kat frowned petulantly, pretending to be hurt. "I go to the trouble of cooking us a hot meal, and you make fun of me? That's really mean." Her frown pulled up into a grin, and soon he was grinning too.

She split the bread onto two plates, and passed the smaller stack to Mark. She watched him take a bite, his eyebrows rose in surprise, and the corners of his mouth twisted upward.

He finished the first slice with a full smile. "Okay, you did good. I like the toasted honey bread so much, that I will clean up after we eat."

She downed another slice, pleased by the compliment. She looked to the cave entrance, where a thin sliver of sunlight poked through the opening. "Do you know where we are? I was outside earlier to get stuff for breakfast, but nothing is familiar."

Mark swallowed to clear his mouth. "I really have no clue. When we left White Sheep, I was driving fast with no destination in mind, trying to get away from the robots. I was planning to ask Sky about it after I slept. Can you tell us where we are, Sky?"

"We have traveled one hundred and twenty-two point three-four miles in a direct line from White Sheep Village." Sky projected a holographic map into the air to her left. On the image was a white dot with the legend 'White Sheep Village.' From there a red line showing their twisting escape route extended to a green dot stating 'we are here.' "In distance actually traveled, the journey required on additional twenty-eight point one-two miles."

Mark had an idea of what they should do now, as she know he would. "Please display the location of the technology reading from our battle with the first crab."

A blue dot appeared on the map to the north-east of the cave, 'Technology Site' was printed above it. "The origin of the technology reading, according to our initial scan, is one hundred and fifty-two point four miles from our present location. Based upon my data, it is centered within a small valley, which in turn is sheltered in a mountain range. This cave is on the southern edge of that range."

Mark stared intensely at the map for a long time, his eyes seeing through it to something for away. Her patience was running low when he finally spoke. "Right now we have no way to destroy those crabs, their armor is too thick for our weapons. I think we should rest here for a day or two to recover our strength, then head to the technology site, try to find a weapon capable of destroying the crabs."

She looked at the map, staring hard at the square that represented White Sheep. The thought of destroying crabs appealed strongly to her, she burned to get revenge for her friends. Her teeth clenched and her vision narrowed at the edges, she rubbed at a stinging in her right calf. Going to the technology site would take time, time in which the crabs got farther away. But if it gave them a means of fighting the crabs, then it would be worth the delay.

"Okay, let's do it. When you're ready, we will go look for a new weapon." She was so worked up over the need for revenge, that she had to do something physical, violent, whether she was sore or not. "I'm going outside, I'll be back later." She stood, collected her armor, and started for the cave entrance.

"Kat." Mark's voice was worried, having picked up on something in her tore. "Don't push yourself too hard, I don't want you hurting yourself. Especially after what happened at White Sheep."

She smiled to reassure him, not fully understanding what he was saying, but appreciating his concern. "I'm alright. And besides, what's out there that can hurt me?" She hooked a thumb at the entrance to end the discussion.

Outside she shoved around her armor on the tray, picking out her wristpad to strap it on. She would start the morning with exploration, see if there was anything interesting here. She would start the morning with exploration, see if there was anything interesting here. Tapping a code into the wrist pad, she stood with her arms outstretched and her ankles two feet apart. The armor parts, linked by tracking ships, antigrav, and wireless energy transference, rose into the air and affixed themselves to her body. The sequence ended with her armor attached. She bent and twisted to be sure of full mobility. Satisfied, she made her way down the gentle, grassy slope from the cave, wondering where her helmet was. She did not remember losing it, but if not it should have been in the tray. She would have to ask Mark later, maybe it was packed in the Truck.

She stopped at the Truck to retrieve her MGP and a VR HUD, without bothering to search for her helmet. Because she would be exercising, she also collected a container for water to stay hydrated, the bottle was pink. Gear in hand, she continued to move away from the cave heading south-ish, looking at the scenery as she walked. Nothing caught her attention, mostly small bushes and flowers, interspersed with the short grass that covered the landscape. There were more of the leafy trees that hid the Truck, standing three feet higher than the roof turrets, and roughly spherical in foliage. The vegetation was green and healthy, not yet withering or changing color with the onset of all. Birds flitted between the trees, or landed in the grass in search of bugs or seeds to eat. It was pretty obvious even without the HUD radar, that there were no robots nearby, birds did not stick around for the machines. Unfortunately, for her, there was nothing particularly fun either.

She cast about for a good spot to do some training. After a few minutes she found what she was looking for, a wide, flat space free of major obstacles that should do the tricks. It was sufficiently large for a training session, plenty of room to run without tripping on anything. She took the time to clear larger rocks and plants from the area, then moved to the center of the clearing.

She lowered the VR HUD over her head, adjusting the straps for comfort. The virtual reality HUD consisted of noise canceling earphones to block out unwanted sounds from the environment, and a lightweight set of blackout goggles with surround vision display screens. It isolated users from all aural and optical inputs, to immense them in a virtual environment. It displayed fully interactive images that included full peripheral vision. External sensors on the unit detected all body movement, accurately incorporating user gestures into the simulations. Sensors also scanned the surrounding area, and detected obstacles and objects were added to the program, enhancing interaction and preventing accidental injury. As a safety feature, simulations would automatically pause when a moving object came close, the distance of the pause dependent on the velocity of approach. The system was tied into their communications gear, allowing the user to receive incoming messages or warnings.

She shook her head to make sure the VR HUD was secure, losing it in the middle of a program could be very disorienting. When she was confident it would not fly or slide off, she turned it on. external cameras presented her with a pass-through feed of her surroundings, along with a virtual menu suspended in the air. The menu could be manipulated by hand gestures, or from voice command. She preferred to reach out and 'touch' a virtual option to select it, even if she could not actually feel anything when she did. She loaded her usual martial arts training program, a solidly constructed simulated boasting interesting arenas, and a variety of opponents and fighting styles. She liked to fight against warriors who were stronger and faster than she was. She enjoyed the challenge, and in her opinion the only way to improve, was to face fighters capable of defeating her. She warmed up in front of a virtual mirror, the sensors in her armor and HUD giving the program enough input to effectively map her movements to a simulated reflection. She performed a series of stretches, followed by a basic martial arts routine that included punches, kicks, and blocks.

She was skilled at fighting even from a very young age, although she had no idea where she learned it from. When they got the VR HUD, she started training with it regularly, she was now rated at expert level in all categories. Ten minutes of warm up had her blood flowing, easing the pain in her muscles, and making her feel more loose and limber. She selected one of her favorite sparring partners, an evil looking tall Asian man with gray hair drawn up in two, tall spikes extending behind his head. He was shirtless, but wore a pair of odd wooden sandals on his feet. He was a perfectly villainous character, and she always liked to be the hero. Because she used this simulation often, her settings were saved and ready to go, no need to wade through menu options for a challenging fight.

She selected an outdoor stage resembling her current locale, and started the match. The old villain, who she called Jim, was taller than her by a head. Meaning that in addition to being faster and stronger than she was, he had a longer reach too. For a moment Jim did nothing more than watch her, his eyes following her in a creepy way that fit his evil persona, she drove a punch at his head, only to have it blocked by his arm. Then it was his turn. He landed a flurry of punches on her arms and torso, the hits showing on a small representation of her body in the corner of her vision. She was glad this fight was virtual, and the hits did not add to her pain. The fight went back and forth for a while. At first she was losing badly, but as time wore on she held her own against Jim.

She spent a little over two hours in the fighting program, facing off with several opponents before she was happy with the workout. Taking a break to rest from her exertion, she sat on a large rock and drank from the bottle in big gulps, feeling sweat trickle down her back beneath her armor. She loaded the data from their fight in the village, sending it to the VR system over the computer link. She assembled everything available on the crab robots. When the data finished compiling, she created a crab simulation and ran it, studying the simulation with its statistical overlay, she was amazed by how much information there was. It told her the tensile strength of the crab armor, how powerful a laser had to be to damage it. Most astonishingly, it showed how much force was required to physically puncture it, and what it took to rip off a manipulator arm. She could not envision what sort of monster was capable of such a feat, or how the data came to be in her armor.

The good news was that she now had a clear idea of what it took to destroy a crab, but that knowledge was tempered by the fact that their weapons were insufficient. Powerful weapons would have to be obtained fast. The technology site really had to come through for them. The place would have to hold advanced military stuff, that was the only way it could be better than what they already knew how to make.

She shut down and removed the VR HD, relishing the breeze on her sweaty face after so long beneath the device. She started the short trek to the cave for lunch, exercise always left her hungry. Whatever they found at the technology site would need to be big, powerful, and preferably pink.

Mark watched Kat leave the cave with her armor, nearly dumping the tray on the ground when she tipped it sideways to get it through the narrow mouth. He was a little surprised by how well she was taking the destruction of White Sheep. She had not cried or raged even once, not in his presence of least. *But then again,* he admitted to himself. *We've both seen so many people die, so many friends, that we're not as sad as we would have been when we were younger. And anyway, many of the villages are still alive as captives of the robots. We have a chance to rescue them later if the technology site works out, maybe even if it doesn't. I just wish I knew why the robots were taking people at all, what use are people to a robot?*

He filled a tray with the morning dishes, and started a cycle in the scrubber, thinking over what he would do for the day. First he had to shower, he was stewing in a good two days' worth of sweat and stink. He almost laughed at that, remembering a time when they would go days or weeks without a bath or clean clothes. Next up, there was the battle damage on the Truck to repair, and a new helmet for Kat to fabricate. He had come up with a few enhancements to her targeting and guidance systems, things he never got around to implementing since she was such a good shot already. He also wanted to design a feature to regulate energy flow, to prevent system failure in the event of a massive power surge, like the one that broke Kat's old crystal. But it could not be allowed to shut her power off completely, that would leave her defenseless in an emergency.

When the dishes were done he took a shower, put on clean clothes, and stuck the dirty ones into the scrubber. He walked out of the cave and to the Truck, then spent a moment looking for Kat. She was a short distance down the slope, exploring the area in her armor.

He pulled the nanomachine case out of its compartment, and set it on the ground near the Truck. Then opened a storage bay to retrieve the materials he knew were needed for the repairs, and for the new helmet. He grabbed electrical components and wire, along with alloy bars for helmet and shell. The super strong alloy that Kat's armor was made of, was light weight but incredibly tough and resistant to laser fire. To increase its strength even more for her armor, the nanomachines formed the alloy into nanotubes. The result was armor that could withstand high intensity lasers, tremendous heat, and take punishing physical blows without deforming. The outer layer of the Truck, beneath the solar cells, was made of the same alloy.

Once he had all of the necessary raw materials laid out, verifying it with a list from Sky, he opened the nanomachine case and slid the controlled from its sleeve. Interfacing with Sky, he loaded the current template for Kat's armor, isolating the helmet onscreen. He accessed the upgraded targeting routines, adding them to the default template and saving the file. Opening a new file, he reviewed the power control system, making changes that should fit his needs. When he thought it was ready, he saved it and asked for Sky's input.

"I want you to look at this new template I made for Kat's armor. It has to protect her power supply in the event of a major overload, like the one in White Sheep that destroyed her last crystal. Let me know if you think my changes will work."

"Initiating analysis." After a pause of a few seconds for Mark, but many hours of processing time for the AI, the verdict was in. "The upgraded armor template is satisfactory. By my estimation of statistical probability, the alterations will successfully perform their intended function. Only in an extreme case should physical failure be possible."

"Good, thanks Sky." He loaded the overload protection routine into the helmet template, again saving it to the default build. Then double checked that all of the upgrades he wanted were included, remembering the pink interior Kat wanted at the last second. He reviewed the configuration twice more to be absolutely sure it was correct. Better to be overly cautious now, than to realize he missed something critical when it was time to fight. Activating the swarm, he saw that it would take sixty-five minutes to complete the helmet.

He was worn down from the battle at White Sheep, both physically and mentally tired. Was it two days ago already? There was a large rock to sit on, one that was clear of moss and bird droppings, a rarity this close to trees. Lowering himself to the rock with a shaky arm, he sat quietly for a few minutes, thinking on what happened at the village, trying to imagine something more he could have done to help the people. Nothing presented itself, but that did not mitigate the guilt eating at him for escaping when so many could not. He had slept soundly and could think properly now, but he remained unable to explain Kat's frightening transformation. Maybe Sky could share a useful insight.

"Do you have any idea what happened to Kat at White Sheep?"

Sky was silent for several seconds, securing his memory banks for answers. "I can locate no non-fictional references in my database that might plausibly explain Kat's enhanced physical performance. The only partially applicable correlation I can make, is that under situations of great emotional distress, people have been known to accomplish seemingly impossible physical feats." Sky paused as if considering the validity of his next statement. "I have made one possibly irrelevant observation. It relates to the octagonal tattoo on Kat's right calf. The images of it that are stored in my memory, are inconsistent with its current appearance. The central dot in my archived images is black, the current dot on her leg is deep red. It is remotely possible, although through no mechanism with which I am familiar, that this change is in some obscure way related to the observed alternation in physical strength. It may be pertinent to point out that the red of the dot is consistent with the red of her power lights during the incident. I do not believe these two changes to be entirely coincidental. However, I am unable to reach a useful conclusion as to a possible correlation, or what the significance of the red coloration may be."

Mark was at a loss for an explanation, and Sky's revelation of Kat's changed tattoo did not help. Could Kat's tattoo somehow be more than a simple ink image? An if it was, then what could it possibly be? What could ink have to do with the nightmare scene in the village? The eye had been put on her leg before they met, whether given to her by her parents or someone else they had no idea. He asked her about it once, but she had no memory of getting it. If only they could use one of the medical scanners Sky had in his database. They could build a scanner using the swarm, but without a comprehensive medical database it was worthless. Perhaps there would be a working scanner at the technology site, or at least a medical database to use with one of their current scanners. Such a device would be valuable not only for them, but also for the people they encountered. How many more people could be helped with a medical scanner, could be saved if they knew how to treat an illness. But first the robots had to be stopped and their friends rescued, and for that they needed stronger weapons. He had to lay his hopes on the technology site, and proceed from there.

He lost himself in thought, his mind mulling over the question from every angle. When the swarm finished its work and drifted into its case, he was no closer to an answer. The new helmet was indistinguishable from the old one at a glance, colored the same purple as the rest of Kat's armor. The color came from the non-glass radar absorbent coating on the armor's exterior surface, which could be any hue dependent upon the pigment added to it. The coating absorbed some light as well as radar waves, making it harder to see in low light situations, or at any kind of distance in daylight. Beneath the stealth coating was a layer of thermal insulation, protecting Kat from both heat and cold, and also dampening her external thermal signature. He tucked the helmet under his arm, and set the swarm to fix the battle damage to the Truck. He rotated the helmet in his hands, it really was identical to the old one. Aside from the pink interior. He heard soft footsteps coming up the slope, turned to see Kat returning from her exploration. Her armor was in battle mode, minus the helmet, and its power lights were pink again.

Her eyes latched onto the helmet. "Is that my helmet? It looks different, did you change it?"

He looked between Kat and the helmet raising an eyebrow, how was she able to see a difference? Then a question occurred to him. "You lost your helmet in the battle at White Sheep. You don't remember what happened to it?"

Her head shook, eyes glued to the new helmet. "Last thing I know it was on my head, I'm a little hazy on the end of the battle. I remember that we were losing, that we could not defeat the robots. And I remember the crabs were dumping people into their baskets, that they took Tula, and we will rescue them. But I have no idea what happened at the end, or how we got away from the village to come here."

Mark struggled with how much he should tell her of the change she underwent. Would it upset her? But she ultimately deserved to know the truth. Maybe it would help prevent a recurrence. "I have something to tell you, and you're not going to like it." He took a deep breath and plowed on. "At the end of the fight you removed your helmet for some reason, I wasn't there so I don't know why. Then your power levels shot up really high, and when I found you, your armor was shining bright red. You were covered in blood, it was all over your armor, on your face, and in your hair. Your eyes were empty, and you were angrier than I ever saw you. You did impossible things, had incredible strength. It was like you were some kind of demon. You didn't recognize me. Your claws came out when I go close, and I thought you might kill me. It was absolutely terrifying, I thought I lost you. I don't ever want you to be demon Kat again, please promise me. No matter what happens in the future, even if I am hurt or killed. Please only be good Kat the hero, that's who you are. Alright?"

She stood there for a long time, her eyes unfocused and her brow deeply furrowed. "I don't remember that, it sounds very bad. I could never imagine hurting you. I will think about it, and I will try not to do it again. I promise." Her gaze lowered to the helmet, her curiosity returning. "You made me a new helmet?"

"Yes, I just finished it. I added several upgrades. Most important is a power regulation program to protect you from an overload. Plus I improved the targeting and guidance systems." He held it out to her by one of the blunted cat ears.

She eagerly snatched the helmet from his hand, shoving a VR HUD at him in exchange. "I love new stuff, and upgrades are always fun. I'm going to try it right now."

He hurried to grab the VR HUD before she dropped it, and watched her examine the new toy.

She flipped it upside down to peer inside, a wide smile spreading on her lips. "You made the inside pink like I asked." She shoved the helmet onto her head, her ears erect to slot into the top, and closed it under her chin. The pink lights came on as normal, not a trace of the darker red to be seen. She turned her head, getting a feel for the new optical system. "Wow, this is really cool, I can see much better than before and I can switch between viewing modes easier."

She paced off twenty feet, head bowed low to the ground. "I want to try the new targeting system." She stated enthusiastically. She bent over at the waist, plucking fist size rocks from the ground, and mounding them at her feet. She tapped a command into the wristpad, alternating the intensity of her lasers, and grabbed a hand full of the stones. Hurling a rock at full force, she let it fly for a second, and blasted it to bits in a single shot. She continued the impromptu target session for ten minutes, throwing rocks in different directions and at varying speeds. Near the end she threw two and three at once, never missing a single stone. Despite having witnessed Kat practice many times, it was hard not to be impressed by this casual display of superior skill.

When she had enough fun, she returned her armor to standby mode. The small interlocking plates slid sequentially into themselves, until each part was compact and unencumbering. She turned to him smiling happily, then ran up the slope to give him a firm hug. "Thanks a bunch Mark, this new targeting setup is awesome. I never have to worry about missing a robot again. Now all we have to do is go to that tech place and find a new weapons. Then we can save our friend and obliterate the crabs. After that we take the villagers home. I bet they bake a whole pink cake for each of us." She thought that over for a moment. "I'm sure you can have any color cake you want. But you really should choose pink, it's the tastiest."

He withheld comment on the concept that a cake's color was in any way directly related to how good it tasted. "Speaking of food, I think we should eat lunch. Then we can decide when to leave for the technology site."

Her vigorous nod at the mention of food, was all the encouragement he needed. Careful to avoid the busy swarm. He opened the refrigerator compartment for a hunk of previously roasted sheep, then grabbed a loaf of bread and utensils. They were down to the last two loaves of bread, he would have to bake more today or tomorrow, a simple matter of dumping ingredients into the cave, unable to resist verifying Sky's assertion regarding Kat's tattoo, and sure enough, the iris was red. How was that even possible? With no answer forthcoming he sat at the table, sliced the meat and bread for cold sandwiches, and handed the first plate to Kat.

"Thanks." She gobbled her lunch hungrily, needing the extra calories to recover from the battle. After the meal Kat cleaned the dishes and came back to the table, it was either that or sit on her sleeping mat in the limited space.

It was time for the business of determining their next move. "I have been thinking about what we should do now, and I believe we need to rest here for another day, to recover our strength and recharge our power crystals. Then we can head for the technology site."

Kat tilted her head back and to the side, staring at the cave root in thought. She stood, moving her arms and legs through their full range of motion, then nodded agreement. "I would rather we left right away, but I think you're right. I'm still pretty sore from the fight, I guess we will lose one more day to rest. But the day after tomorrow we have to get moving. I don't want Tula and our friends to be stuck with those robots one minute longer than they have to be. Who knows what the robots are doing to them, they may not even have food or water."

Kat was full of cheerful thoughts today. On the one hand, the robots would not have gone to the trouble of capturing people unless the intended to keep them alive. On the other, machines may not automatically think of biological needs, unless they were specifically programmed to address them, and then would provide no more than the minimum required for survival. He did not share that notion, no reason to upset Kat with it.

Sky vocalized an opinion. "I must, in this instance, agree with Kat. Haste in these circumstances is warranted. Not only for the continued health and survival of the villagers, but also for the inescapable fact that the longer we delay, the more difficult it may become to track the robots' movements."

"Um, thanks Sky."

Mark nodded along with Sky's points, his logic, as always, was sound. "We have a plan them. Tomorrow we rest all day, and I emphasize the word rest Kat." He shot her a stern look. She grinned at him innocently and nodded. "The first thing the following morning, we will leave for the technology site."

The day passed uneventfully. Kat spent her time playing games on her MGP, and otherwise resting conspicuously, which primarily involved laying on her sleeping mat with her back propped on a folded blanket. Mark sat at the table analyzing the crab data with Sky, determining exactly what it would take to destroy one, home powerful their weapons needed to be in order to penetrate the thick blue armor. In the evening they ate a quiet dinner of hot stew, and retired to their sleeping mats early.

They were awakened in the morning by a pre-determined alarm from Sky, rising long after dawn. They cleaned and dressed in fresh clothes, then ate breakfast as usual. Mark dedicated the day to working on possible upgrades to the Truck's sensor software. He was deeply worried about how the robots were able to come so close to White Sheep without being detected by the village sensor array or by Sky. That many machines on the move should have registered on scans more than five miles away, probably closer to ten. With Sky's help, he was able to develop software tweaks that would improve the precision of the sensors. Increasing the sensitivity of the detection algorithms, the system would now alert them to much smaller readings that before, things that it would presently ignore as background noise or sensor ghosts. Hopefully it would give them more warning of approaching robots, specifically the new stealth models. When he felt that they had pushed the algorithm as far as it would go, and that it all worked properly, he stood to leave.

"Kat, I'm going to install upgrades to the Truck's sensor software. If it works as it should, we will have more warning of a robot attack. I will be gone for maybe an hour. I want you to keep resting while I'm out, no strenuous exercising, okay? And that includes your martial arts stuff."

Kat glanced up from her MGP. "I'll lay here and play my game. I'm only relaxing today, see?" She pointed to her legs stretched out on the mat.

Accepting that Kat would behave for a while, he ducked under the low entrance to exit the cave. Outside he blinked rapidly in the much brighter daylight and went to the Truck. He opened a cab door, and was hit in the face by a blast of hot air from the enclosed space. He climbed in and opened the passenger door to let a breeze blow through, cool it off a bit. Switching on the Truck's computer, he entered configuration mode.

"Go ahead and upload the new software."

"Commencing code update now. I estimate that it will take twenty-five minutes for the update to install."

The main console display on the Truck's dashboard showed a progress bar and a countdown timer, ticking down from Sky's estimate. The computer that ran Sky's program possessed twelve processor cores, each capable of manipulating four simultaneous strings of data, a feature called super-weaving. Because of this extreme multitasking capability, Mark new that the updates were only using a tiny fraction of Sky's processing power. The AI could hold an intelligent conversation while performing multiple functions.

"Is there any way for us to physically upgrade our sensors? With larger ones maybe? Or push more power through them?"

"The Truck is already utilizing the highest quality sensors available in my database. I am aware of no process by which to physically enhance them. If you have any theories, you may postulate them for testing. For now however, I am fully confident that the alterations we have made to the software, will be sufficient to detect the stealth robots."

Sky's assurance aside, there had to be some way to effectively test the sensors, without actually running into stealth robots. A few minutes of thought presented him with a potential solution. "I want you to design a new drone for me. I need something we can use to test the sensor upgrades. It has to be small, have no heat or electrical emissions, and it must use our best stealth coating. I want it to be as invisible as we can make it. I want it to have all of the cameras and sensors and things that our other drone is equipped with, that way it can do all of the same things. Can you do all of that?"

"Processing, please wait." Sky was silent for several minutes, he was going all out on this one. "I have completed a design template that will meet your criteria, it is ready to be constructed by the nanomachine swarm."

Mark loaded the template on his HUD, reviewing the specifications with mounting enthusiasm. "Thank you Sky, this should work."

"You are welcome. There are ten minutes and sixteen seconds remaining until the sensor update is complete."

Mark left the cab and unlocked the storage compartment holding the nanomachines, removed the swarm case, opened it, and ran the startup diagnostic. He loaded the stealth drone design template into the controller, and went over the list of required materials. Once all of the raw materials were laid out, he started the build sequence.

A chime sounded from the Truck's cab. "The sensor updates have finished installing. I have run a general diagnostic on the system, the results indicate that they are functioning as intended."

"Good, now run an active test of the sensors please, use them to scan the area, tell me what they detect."

After a pause, Sky reported. "The sensors are presently operating at a significantly more precise level than before the update. I am able to detect small birds small mammals such as rodents, and a number of larger insects, all at a considerable distance. I currently detect no robots or large biologicals within sensor range."

The bit about robots must have been for his peace of mind, and Mark appreciated the consideration after the events of White Sheep. "Excellent, let's hope the sensors see the new drone. If they can, then we should have no trouble spotting the stealth robots at a functional distance."

Mark impatiently waited the additional twenty-two minutes for the drone to finish building, antsy to play with his new toy. When the chime sounded, he returned the leftover material and swarm case to their respective compartments on the Truck, then picked up the drone. It was lightweight and took the form of a thick disc a foot in diameter. There were five high-resolution cameras spared evenly along its outer edge, capable of a variety of optical filters including night vision, infrared, and ultraviolet. There were four inset utility ports interspersed with the cameras, allowing extensions like manipulator arms or cutting lasers to be attached as needed. The drone was a non-descript gray color that absorbed some light, its surface was smooth and free of ornamentation.

He opened an access plate on the bottom of the drone, and inserted the appropriate size of power crystal, then closed the plate and plugged it into the Truck to charge. The synthetic crystals charged quickly, and without generating an excess of waste heat, the one in the drone only required five minutes to fully charge.

"I want you to turn off all of our sensors. I will fly the drone away from us, and when I tell you to, turn on the sensors and try to find it okay?"

"Sensors, deactivated, you are free to proceed."

Mark piloted the drone using the Trucks' computer, trusting Sky to play nice and not peek. He flew it around the peak of a mountain five miles from them, to an altitude of over six thousand feet, leaving it to hover in place. "Alright, that should do it. She if you can find it."

Sky was silent, his power light blinking with activity during his search. "The only likely object I detect, is a tiny sensor ghost five point zero two miles north, and one point two-one miles in elevation. If that is the stealth drone, then I am barely able to detect it."

"You found it. I will move it slowly for a while, then faster. If you can, track it at all speeds, determine how hard it is to follow." Mark started the drone creeping forward keeping it to twenty-five miles per hour at first. He gradually accelerated to one hundred. After tracking it for six minutes, Sky reported. "It is slightly easier to track at faster velocities, than it is at slower ones. I lose contact with the drone entirely at a distance of five point six-three miles. The drone is difficult to track, perhaps impossible for us prior to the sensor updates, but I am able to detect and follow it. This exercise has allowed me the opportunity to further calibrate the sensor software. He tested the drone for another twenty minutes, more because it was fun to fly the thing, than from any need to evaluate the sensors. "I think we should be okay now, I expect us to detect the robots long before they come close to the Truck."

"I concur with that assessment Mark, we will not be caught by surprise or ambushed by the robots again."

Mark landed the drone and picked it up. "This should prove useful for spying on the robots. I expect them to have the same trouble detecting it that you do. If we're lucky, more. Now that we have a way to spot the stealth robots and watch them from a distance, we only need a new weapon to destroy them with." He placed the stealth drone in the remote launch bay with the old drone. If the new drone worked out as expected, he would convert the old one to a stealth drone. Closing the Truck, he walked to the cave. There were more preparations to be done for an early departure.

CHAPTER 8

B ecause he had insisted on packing most of their things the day before, with the exception of breakfast, their sleeping mats and blankets, and the scrubber, there was little left to do in the morning. They were awake before dawn, rested and mostly recovered from their ordeal at White Sheep. They ate a cave temperature meal of bread and fruit, cleaned their plates, and had the last of their things loaded into the Truck as the sun rose. They were driving north from the cave as the sun's first golden rays touched them on the right. As was their custom, Mark was on driving duty, navigating with the aid of a map on his HUD provided by Sky.

It would take them most of the day to reach the technology site, depending on the terrain they encountered. And that was if nothing unexpected transpired along the way, like running into more robots. For an hour Kat passed the time watching the scenery roll by, but she got bored and turned on her MGP for entertainment, filling the cab with primitive projectile bangs.

They talked every so often, but for the most part he was preoccupied by the robot problem. What might be at the technology site that would destroy the crabs? He wondered what kind of weapon could be carried by them, or mounted to the Truck like the laser turrets, but still be capable of penetrating the crab's armor? According to his analysis with Sky, they needed a laser eleven percent more powerful than the wall turrets at White Sheep, in order to melt crab armor. A concussive or explosive weapon such as Kat's missiles, would have to be three times more potent than what she was currently using. They did not have anything that strong, and what they could build would be prohibitively large. He preferred not to use explosives, there was too great a chance that something could go wrong. They could go off by accident, or damage things they were not intended to hit. And he did not like the idea of Kat running around carrying that much dangerous material waiting to explode, it was too big a risk. No, lasers were safer and more precise. Perhaps he could make a projectile that could drill into a crab, and melt it from the inside. He quietly dictated notes to his HUD while he drove, he could discuss them with Sky later, not that he had come up with any really good ideas yet. His preference never wavered from a new laser, they had plenty of crystals that could handle the extra power draw. The problem was in finding the schematics to build one. With their current library of designs, a laser strong enough to destroy a crab, would melt its own circuits before coming close to melting crab armor. The view changed gradually as the sun rose in the sky. Their route taking them steadily uphill, with larger mountains looming to the north and west.

The plant life was greener and more lush, small plants and leafy bushes rolling by under the bumper guard, and trees nearly dense enough to be called a forest. The dirt sprouted a loose carpet of short grass and wider leafed plants, holding the soil in place on the gently sloping foothills. The day was bright and warm without being overly hot. Small, fluffy white clouds floated lazily in the pale blue sky.

He was feeling hungry at midday, and thought it was a good time to stop for lunch. He spotted a copse of large, leafy trees ahead, and drove over to them to part the Truck. Kat , who was engrossed in her game, sat up to look around.

"Time for lunch?" She echoed his thoughts.

He smiled, Kat was always ready for two things without fail, fun and food, or both together when she could manage it. Which she frequently did. He turned off the Truck, the lights on panels and screens going out being the only visible change from when it was on. "Yes, time for lunch. Would you get the food out of the back?"

She hopped from the cab enthusiastically, bringing another smile to his lips. He lowered himself more slowly to the grass, using a handhold next to the door to moderate his descent. He gave in to the urge to stretch, loosening stiff muscles in his back and legs after hours of driving. In the time it took him to walk to the trees, Kat had already opened the box containing their lunch, and was sitting cross legged on the ground chewing on a sandwich. Perhaps not her first. He sat on the other side of the box, the sun's heat lessened by the shade of the trees, and selected a sandwich for himself. The meal was consumed quietly, while enjoying the day's calm. *I'm eating quietly at least,* he thought listening to Kat noisily scarfing her food.

"Remember to close your mouth while you chew."

"Mff." She mumbled around a mouthful of food. She did, however, obediently close her mouth looking a little abashed.

It was amusing how she could eat every meal as if it was the best thing she ever tasted, and at the same time like she was on the brink of starving to death. He was never able to think of a satisfactory explanation for Kat's eating habits, it was one of those personality quirks he had come to accept.

After they finished lunch, he stood and looked over the pleasant little glade they stopped in, watching the play of speckled light on the grass as the branches above swayed in the wind. "I'm going to walk for a while before we leave. Don't wander off to far, alright?"

She rose fluidly to her feet. "No problem, I will hang around by the trees. Shout when you want to go, and I'll run over."

She disappeared quickly behind the trees, off to do who knew what to muse herself. He closed the lunch box, and returned it to the Truck to be cleaned that night. They strolled in no particular direction from the Truck. There were many trees here, with even more on the tall mountains in their path, that could slow them quite a bite. The air was nearly calm, with only a soft breeze to rustle the leaves. The tread of his boots on the grass, and lively bird calls, were all that broke the silence. It was the kind of quiet that let sound carry great distances. The clatter of robots would be heard from miles off, stealth system or not. If only the whole world could be so peaceful, but such peace could never come unless the robots were eliminated. It was not that robots were inherently evil, but they were certainly slaves to their programming. According to Sky, in the old world people used robots to perform all sorts of jobs, their builders programming them to work with and help people, not kill them. *Maybe I would make a robot, a kind of anti-robot robot that would with us. I will have to put thought into that later, right now my priority has to be finding a weapon at the technology site.*

He made a wide turn in the grass to return to the Truck. Relaxing though this interlude was, they did not have time to waste standing in a field. He was striding fast when something exploded out of the bushes two feet in front of him, sending leaves flying. "Raah!" It roared in his face. He stumbled away from this unknown attacker, his arms pin wheeling as a heel caught on a rock, and he landed on his butt in another bush.

"Ach!" He shouted in pain when branches poked at him, his hand fumbling for the laser at his hip. His head shot up when laughter incongruously filled the air.

Kat, covered in leaves, stood bent over with hands on her knees in front of the bushes she had jumped out of. Her eyes were squeezed shut, and her chest heaved in mirth.

"Oh, ha, ha." He grumbled extricating himself from the bush with difficulty, its branches snapping under his weight. When he regained his feet, he brushed the foliage from his clothes. He waited for her laughter to fade, speaking when he thought she was ready to listen. "So how long were you waiting in that plant, to jump out at me like a lunatic?"

His annoyed tone was lost on her. "Since you walked away from the Truck?" She replied happily.

His heart was slowing to a more natural rate, only a couple of hundred beats per minute, giving him a chance to speak calmly. "Okay Kat, you got me, I was very surprised. Could you try not to do something like that again?"

She nodded, the smile never leaving her face. "Sure, I won't jump out of a bush like that again, any time soon."

He glared at her, exhaling noisily from his nose. Kat would always see the world differently than he did, and it was hard to stay mad at her. "Alright you little bush monster, let's go. We still have a long way to drive."

She gave him a funny look, a slight lowering of the brows that was there and gone in a second, but she said nothing as they returned to the Truck. Behind the wheel, he turned on the Truck for the drive, and resumed the journey to the technology site. They drove in silence for quite a while, Kat staring out of her window in deep thought, not even pulling out her MGP. He was ready, to ask her if something was wrong when she finally spoke.

"Mark?"

"Yes, Kat?"

"Um, what uh, what does a Bushmonster look like?"

Mark glanced at her. He wanted to feel surprise at the question, he really did, but somehow he almost expected it.

She misinterpreted his expression, apparently believing that he required clarification of her inquiry. "I mean, I've never heard of one before, so I want to know what they look like, how big they are, what they eat. Do they eat plants? Insects? Small animals maybe? Is a Bushmonster still a bush? Or a type of monster that looks like a bush? I want to know everything you can tell me about them."

Mark had to work to keep his face neutral, tried not t laugh at her questions. But she was so earnest, that he could not hold it in.

Her mouth curved into a confused frown. "What's so funny? I only want to know about Bushmonsters."

The whine in her voice had him laughing harder, nearly losing control of the Truck, a sharp pain developing in his side. She was becoming so upset that he choked down his laughter. When he could breathe properly, he explained what was so funny. "I'm sorry for laughing, but there is no such thing as a bush monster. I made it up when you jumped out of that bush to surprise me. You were a scary thing in a bush, hence bush monster."

"You're sure there are no Bushmonsters?" She asked sadly. When he nodded she went on. "I really wanted to see a Bushmonster, it sounded neat." She was really disappointed by his revelation.

He made a mental note to have Sky add a bush monster to one of the Kat's favorite games, that should cheer her up. She turned on her MGP. From the sound of it, she was venting her frustration by violently exterminating monsters.

An hour later she paused the game, and for a second he was afraid she would bring up bushes or monsters. "What we need is a BFL, with one of those we could destroy the crabs easily."

He waited a moment for an explanation, one was not forthcoming. "Okay Kat, what is a BFL?"

"It's the ultimate weapon that can kill anything in my game in a few shots. And some of these things are way tougher than the crabs."

"Does the game tell you how to build a BFL?" He inquired a touch facetiously, not in the mood for a useless idea from a fictional game.

"Not at all." She admitted. "You have to find it. But isn't that what we're doing? Looking for a super weapon to destroy a bigger bad guy? All we have to do is find something like a BFL, then we can destroy the crabs with it."

He considered that. She was making a strange sort of sense. They were in fact hunting for a better weapon, like the BFL in her game. The thought was growing on him. "Alright Kat, let's find your BFL."

She punched his shoulder, making it throb. "That's the spirit."

The pain did nothing to diminish his smile, he drove on to the technology site in renewed enthusiasm.

The sun dipped on the horizon, dimming the sky as evening set in. they were forced to stop farther from their destination than they anticipated, three horizontal miles from the technology site according to the sensors. The whole area was steeply mountainous, preventing the Truck from getting any closer. No matter how capable it was on most terrain, the Truck was not built to traverse a seventy-five degree grade. The slope before them, with its steep angle and dense population of trees, was entirely impassable. The mountain rose another three hundred vertical feet between the Truck and the center of the sensor reading. They would have to hike up the slope, through thick under foliage to reach their goal.

Mark examined a topographic holographic map. "Sky, do you detect robots or people here?"

"Scans presently indicate no danger, I detect no robots or intelligent biologicals."

The projection glowed brightly in the fading light, it was too late to continue. "We should sleep here for the night and go to the technology site in the morning."

"Sounds good to me."

He cooked a simple stew for dinner. Stew was his go to dish when he was feeling lazy, or did not have time to make something fancy. It was fast and easy, all he had to do was toss meat and vegetables into a pot of water and let it boil. When the dishes were clean, they put out folding cots with mats and blankets by the Truck.

By then it was dark, the only illumination coming from a small portable light sitting on Mark's cot. "We should both sleep now, I want to start early in the morning. That will maximize the daylight for us to search the technology site."

She nodded agreement, stripping off her armor and laying on her cot.

He was anxious of what tomorrow would bring, there had to be a good weapon here, he did not want to dwell on the alternative. The idea of truly abandoning the villagers to the robots, was too abhorrent to contemplate. He had accepted the necessity of running, mainly because he knew they were coming back to help later, no other possibility was worth considering. When he finally fell into an uneasy sleep, it was filled with dreams of large lasers and melted robots.

In the morning they ate breakfast, then packed a lunch and the tools and supplies they would need at the site. Once they had everything else stowed in the Truck and the security system turned on, they started up the hill.

The beacon on his HUD was a flame to his moth, he glanced at it routinely to keep them on the right track. Their path led them up a steep, tree dotted slope. It was frequently more of a climb than a hike. He found himself seeking footholds, and hauling his body along using tree limbs. He knew that Kat could have made it to the top in half the time it would take him, or simply fly up there, but she politely held back to match his slower pace. Soon he witnessed a small green lizard scurry away from them, its rapid movement catching his eye. He pointed it out to Kat, who smiled in delight. After that she watched for more animals, pointing to every one she could find. There were birds flitting among the branches, a few rodents, and a small deer that bounded off before they could get near it. Kat thought the game of animal spotting was tremendous fun, and was kind of sad when he told her they were almost to the site, she was not ready for the fun to end.

It had taken them more than an hour to crest the hill, and the sun was low in the sky. From their vantage atop the hill, they looked down a hundred feet into a bowl-shaped valley, hemmed in almost entirely by more hills. The lone break in the natural depression, was a narrow canyon between hills. Running along the valley floor and into the canyon, was a thing he saw only rarely, an intact road. Stretches of drivable road could be found most anywhere, the land was littered with them, but they were typically no longer than a mile or two in length, and were impossibly pitted with holes. From where Mark stood, this road appeared smooth and serviceable, and he could see a good two miles of it before it vanished around a bend in the canyon.

The road, unusual as it was, could not hold his interest for long. At the end of the road, centered in the flat, empty space below, stood a large, walled complexed of buildings a mile across. The wall was twenty feet tall, four feet thick, and in a remarkable state of repair for its age. The entire place, from walls to buildings, was drab and close to colorless, save for a smattering of darker green plants growing through cracks in roads and walkways. He was surprised by how preserved the compound appeared, he had never seen so many upright and unbroken old structures, not outside of a game or video.

"Sky, activate the stealth drone and fly it up here please." His heart thumped in his chest, his excitement over this unbelievable discovery mounting fast. This would be the first, and maybe only, chance he would have to see for himself the kind of places the old world people lived in. To touch their furniture and tools, to explore their rooms as they left them, unaltered by other hands since the Devastation. It was a dream comes true.

"Drone launched. It will arrive in two minutes and seven seconds."

A holographic display and controller materialized in front of Mark, showing views from the drone's five cameras, its forward view in the larger center display. The drone buzzed over them to the right, coming to a hovering stop at the tree line. His HUD radar was clear of red dots that would indicate danger.

"Are there any active security systems down there, Sky? Anti-aircraft lasers for example."

"There are no discernible defensive or weapon systems in operation. However, there are minimal power readings that could indicate active systems of unidentified functionality within the facility, most probably in standby or energy conservation mode. It is possible that these will be the first functional pre-Devastation systems we will encounter."

Mark shuddered at a renewed thrill of exhilaration, and put a hand to the drone control panel. "Time to have a look."

He was excited, but not so excited as to allow it to override his caution. His first move was to fly the drone higher, and out over the complex, stopping when it was centered above the buildings. He wanted an overview of the complex's layout, Sky recorded a basic street map. The second consideration was to see if anything below reacted to the drone. From the air it was clear that the complex had a very orderly layout. Judging by the precise placement of the buildings and streets, he surmised that the facility was constructed for a specific purpose. It did not have the feel of a village or town where people lived, those places were far more random and organic in design.

He descended slowly, bringing the drone lower to see if any dormant defenses came to life for a sneak attack. He brought it down to one hundred and ten feet above the ground, only seventy feet over the tallest rooftop.

All of the structures looked ready to fend off an assault, as if the place was expecting an enemy to arrive at any moment. The windows on every building, if indeed they were windows, were covered by heavy retractable shutters, unquestionably defensive armor plating. The doors were closed and almost certainly locked, and laser turrets were visible but inactive on several of the flat rooftops. The complex was simple and utilitarian, everything was painted gray, tan, or pale green. Even accepting that the pain had faded over the decades, it would have been boring when new. If it was up to him, he would have insisted on adding some color, red or blue trim maybe.

He digitally zoomed the camera in for a closer look, revealing indications that the place was attacked at some point in the past. There were scorch marks from lasers on walls, and small chunks missing from building facades and roads. There was a no way of knowing when the damage was done, it could be from the Devastation, or only a year ago. There were a handful of identical vehicles parked on the streets, rugged little trucks with open cargo beds. The roof of one wide building held a pair of small, broken aircraft of a type he did not recognize. From what he knew of the old world, from the lens of games and videos, he believed they were seeing a military facility, possibly an important one.

He wanted Sky to validate his impression. "What do you make of this place, Sky?"

"It is my determination based upon the style of vehicles and structures visible here, that this is a military facility. I surmise that it was abandoned after the devastation, and with significant haste. I am detecting several faint active energy sources, none of them register as defensive in nature. I anticipate that we will be safe entering the premises, but I recommend that you exercise caution in your exploration."

Mark grinned at Kat. "What do you think? Want to go down there and look around?"

She smiled back. "Try to stop me."

He tapped the red circle in a corner of the display, closing it to return control of the drone to Sky. "Let's go check it out. Sky, keep an eye on things from above with the drone, tell us if there's a problem."

"Certainly."

Their hike down the slope was faster than the trip up, but it was more harrowing. He was in near constant fear of falling, losing his footing twice on the descent, recovering both times by quickly grabbing hold of tree branches that rubbed his fingers raw. At the bottom it was a twenty minutes' walk to reach the front gate, where the road met the wall. The wide, metal double gate hung open, swaying lightly in the breeze to a small creak of old hinges. The locking mechanism was undamaged, as if the people inside had abandoned the facility without caring who might enter it later.

Setting foot within the wall, it was soon apparent that everything was in better condition than it looked on the drone video. The buildings were completely intact, somehow, incredibly, unharmed by the Devastation and the long passage of time. Perhaps it was protected by the valley in which it was sheltered, or was constructed in such a way as to survive the quakes. The scorch marks he saw from above were cosmetic, doing no real damage to the surfaces they marred. The small chunks missing from walls were shallow, revealing armor plating beneath a thin facade. The roads were clear of large debris, and even with plants growing through in places, were mostly smooth and drivable. He examined one of the small trucks. It was covered in heavy dust and the headlights were clouded with age, but even with flat, desiccated tires, it would take little more than a recharge to get it moving. With only two seats and that short, uncovered bed, it was probably intended to carry supplies around the complex, not for long hauls. If not for the layers of dust and dirt, and plants growing where they should not, the facility could almost still be in use.

Despite sensor scans showing no one to be present, he could not shake the feeling that someone might pop out of a door at any second, demanding to know why they were here. Yet as they walked the eerily quiet street, all was calm and still. No doors were flung open, no people came running, and no demands were made.

Sign plates adorned the fronts of the buildings, each bearing a concise yet descriptive label. He read them as they walked by, 'Infirmary', 'A Barracks', 'Mess Hall', and so on. Finally he saw what he was looking for, a sign plate bearing a jagged lightning bolt and the words 'Power Distribution'. The door to the building was sealed by an electronic lock. There was a keypad next to the lever style door handle, and a dim light shining red above the keys. He pulled on the handle, it did not budge.

"Can you unlock this door, Sky?"

"Attempting to break encryption now, please wait." Minutes passed in silence as Sky worked far longer than Mark would have expected for the powerful computer. He was on the verge of asking Sky if there was a problem when the light turned green, followed by a buzzing click from what sounded like a substantial lock.

"The encryption was more complex than anticipated, it did not conform to any known model." Offered Sky by way of explanation for the delay. "It should be easier to decrypt other systems in the compound, now that I have constructed a template for the encryption key."

Mark opened the door cautiously and peered into impenetrable gloom, the shutters effectively blocking light from outside. He felt the wall for a switch, remembering that people used them to turn on lights in the old world, flipping it did nothing but make a clicking sound. Either there was no power, or it no longer worked. He turned on the bright LED on the front of his HUD, providing them with plenty of light to see where they were going, Kat mimicked him with her own HUD. Before them was a hallway lined on either side with doors. He walked down the hall, his boots thudding on the hard floor, reading doors until he found one labeled 'Control Room'.

He tried the handle and found it unlocked. Opening the door, he stuck his head into the large room of buttons, dials, and monitor screens. Some of the equipment was functional, at least partially, with blinking lights and waving needles. He walked to a computer terminal with a solid amber power indicator, suggesting that it worked. He touched a button on a keyboard, bringing the screen to life from its long hibernation. The message it displayed was simple, and exactly what he expected, 'Base power in standby mode.'

"Sky, would you try to restore power to the facility?"

Lights on this console, and those around the room, began to flash, and more screens came on scrolling information. Much of the text was there and gone too fast for him to read, what he was able to make out was in unfamiliar terms. It looked to be a series of diagnostic reports relating to the power systems in the complex.

"This facility obtains its power from photovoltaic cells and wind turbines. There are several banks of cells and rows of turbines three point four miles from here. Their power generating capacity has degraded, reducing their efficiency by eighty-six percent. I am able to supply only fourteen percent of the facility's normal operational power at the time. That should provide sufficient power to access most of the systems we will encounter."

"Please activate what you can. Also, did you find a map of the place in the system?

"Affirmative. I have downloaded maps and schematics. I have learned that this was in fact a military base, specifically it is the EMF Invasion Command base. Details on what precisely that means, are not available at this terminal. Sensitive information must be obtained elsewhere."

"I want you to upload the map to our HUDs, the first place I want to go is the security building, or whatever they call the building that controls the door locks. I want to deactivate the security system, open the base to us."

The lights came on, the bulbs overhead flickering a moment and a few staying dark. "I have restored what power I can to the base, and your HUDs are now updated with the maps. I have highlighted the security center."

"Thanks, Sky."

Kat was peering at images on a panel. "Shall we keep exploring?" He asked to get her attention.

She lifted a hand with the thumb raised, and walked to the door.

The locked doors and shuttered windows may have effectively blocked the light, but they were not airtight. With the lights on he saw how dirty everything was. Every horizontal surface was coated in a heavy layer of gray dust, so thick that their footprints on the floor looked almost like they had trudged through freshly fallen snow on the way in. Using their dust snow tracks as a guide, they retraced their steps to the street. He checked the map on his HUD, which now included names for the buildings. Their current location was displayed with the customary green dot, and the security center with a red square.

He led them onto a smaller side street that cut across to the security center, reaching the designated building in only a few minutes. The sign plate on the building read 'Base Security Center.' The door was locked, but it took Sky only a moment to hack it. When the light went green, he opened the door and stepped inside.

Every surface was shrouded in dust, the same as the power building. The lights were on, or two thirds of them were, the rest had either ceased functioning from age or disuse, or the lower power supply automatically kept a predetermined number of them off. The air smelled old and stale, not with the stink of rot so common in the scrapwards, but with the scent of stagnation from great age and lack of circulation. The entry room was the size of most houses in the towns and villages they visited. Chairs stood in a neat row along one wall, a squat table arranged squarely in front of them. Cutting across the rear wall to separate the room into two unequal parts, was a wide counter beneath a transparent barrier. He walked to a door to the right of the counter, that Sky unlocked for them to pass. Here was a short hallway lined with doors, he read their labels until one stood out to him, 'Control Room.' This lock was more complex, including, as Sky was happy to inform them, a retinal scanner. Sky bypassed the scanner with an additional second of time.

When the light changed to green, the handle less door slid open, vanishing into the wall in a way he had never seen before. Mark walked inside, but Kat was enamored by the novel door, repeatedly pressing the button to open and close it with a repetitive swishing noise. The rectangular room was ringed in computer terminals and chairs. Many of the screens illuminated upon his entry, displaying various bits of unknown information and status reports, far more useful to those who once worked here than to him. Plastering the walls above the terminals were the largest video screens he had ever seen, most of them divided into dozens of smaller viewing segments. The majority of these segments showed video from around the base, a fair number were black save for the message "No signal." Another large screen showed a map of the base, doors and windows displayed almost exclusively in red. At the top a message scrolled by, 'Base locked down. All personal are ordered to evacuate.'

"Sky, we need to end this 'lockdown.' I want you to turn off all security systems and unlock the doors, so that we can explore freely. Can you do that?"

"I will do what I can, please wait."

While Sky was busy, he thought about what may have happened to the base. There was no question as to this being a pre-Devastation facility, organized military simply did not exist anymore, certainly not one capable of building a place like this. And it miraculously survived the Devastation intact. But for inscrutable reasons it was abandoned by those who manned it. Why would military people leave an armed and armored base, where they could readily defend themselves from robots and bandits? A base hidden in the mountains surrounded by farmable land. Where could they have gone that was better than this? Nowhere that he could think of, that was for sure. Examining the various screens, and status readouts revealed no answers, the old world remained resolutely impenetrable.

Kat was parked in front of one of the segmented screens, intensely studying its video feeds. Was she seeking something specific, or just anything that might be fun? He eyed the base map, there were several buildings that held promise for exploration. Next on his list was the infirmary, which he knew to be a kind of hospital, followed by the armory.

"Mark!" Exclaimed Kat a bit too energetically. Anything she thought was that interesting, usually meant trouble for him. "I found a kitchen on one of the screens, a big one. I want to go see if they have something good in there." She touched the desired segment to show him.

He was relieved that her discovery was so innocuous, though a kitchen could present its own problems. "Um, Kat. Any food you might find in there is not going to be edible after all these years. It would make you really sick." There was a good diplomatic answer for her, one that should be clear enough to work.

She frowned briefly, unconsciously pressing a palm to her stomach. "That's true, but there might be recipes we can use. I want to try the food they ate long ago. I bet it's really amazing, like stuff we never imagined."

He laughed, Kat said the funniest things. "And I suppose I'm the one who will cook it for you?"

She smiled, her head bobbing up and down. "Of course you will. You don't want me to cook it, do you?" The question was mostly rhetorical.

The red lights on the base map went green without warning, indicating that the doors and windows were now unlocked. The message above the map change too, it now read 'Normal Operation.' A synthetic feminine voice came from unseen speakers. "Emergency lockdown concluded, all personnel are to return to normal operations."

"I'd like to search the infirmary for a medical database next."

"Okay," she conceded. Kitchen second.

Following the hallway they came in through, they exited the security center, returning to a street transformed. The window shutters were gone, retracted in a clever way as if they were never there, save for a band of less faded paint banding each window. If it felt stranger walking these abandoned streets before, with the windows uncovered it was downright creepy. He felt an unwanted stranger intruding into the lives of those who once resided here, a sensation he never experienced in a scrapward. Everything in the buildings was intact and organized, room after abandoned room filled with furniture waiting to be used, screens and computer terminals to be viewed. Every so often they passed a truck parked besides a building, as if its driver had run inside on the errand to return any moment and drive on. But aside from the lonely echo of their footsteps on the road, and the shadows following in their wake, there was not the least specter of people to be found.

Using the map on his HUD, Mark picked his way along the short streets to the infirmary, a squat, two story building with a lot of windows. The wide front doors deposited them in a waiting room similar to that in the security building. Chairs lined the walls, a bookshelf on one side held severely aged magazines that might be worth a look later, and a blank screen was set into the rear wall. A low counter extended from the back wall, curving around to cover much of the space. An ancient signup sheet and pencil waited for visitors and patients, the writing no longer legible. Through an opening by the counter, a hallway led deeper into the building.

He knew a little of hospitals from the old media, and an infirmary was a small hospital. The best place to start his search for a database would be an examination room, and there were three 'Exam Rooms' in the hall. He entered the closest exam room, creatively labeled 'Exam Room 1.' Inside was a padded table, a desk, two chairs and several cabinets and shelves containing what he presumed was medical equipment. On the desk was a working computer terminal.

"Sky, please search this computer for a medical database."

"Accessing. Most of the data, including patient information, has been erased. However, it does contain a complete medical database. The database is extensive, it will take one minute, forty two seconds to achieve a full download. I recommend that you retrieve the medical scanner that was used in conjunction with this system." Sky projected a holographic image of the scanner into the air, rotating it slowly. The scanner was a slim rectangular device with a screen for its front surface, much like the swarm controller.

Mark rummaged in the cabinet and shelves, finding two of the scanners in a drawer. He shoved them into his travel bag.

"Download complete."

Kat, waiting patiently by the door during his search was anxious to move on. "Can we go to the kitchen now?"

He held up a finger, "Sky, does the database have all of the information we need to diagnose and treat medical problems?"

"Affirmative, In addition, it contains a comprehensive chemical breakdown of medications. We should be able to synthesize at least simple medications with the information provided here. We have schematics for many of the necessary tools."

"Excellent, we can help a lot of people with this." He looked at Kat, who was watching him with hands clasped in front of her. "Alright, we can go to the kitchen."

She jumped, punching a first in the air that nearly hit the ceiling. "Yes!" she grabbed his arm, pushing him in front of her and out of the infirmary. She walked swiftly down the street before he could locate the kitchen on the map, wasting not a moment in reaching her objective.

Their shadows were shortening as the sun neared its zenith overhead. Noon was upon them, and that meant lunch. It was convenient they were on the way to a kitchen. After Kat finished playing around, they could take a short break to eat before going to the armory. Kat was in such a hurry to reach the kitchen, that he was practically jogging to match her.

Like the infirmary, the mess hall was ringed with windows, at least around the dining area. It was a single story building with most of its interior volume dedicated to rows of long tables and benches. The space was well lit, more from the noon sun streaming through the many windows, than from the dimmer electric lights in the ceiling. A broad aisle ran between rows of tightly spaced tables, to a serving area at the back of the room. Plates, bowls, and utensils were in place, resting in holders on the metal counters and basin that once held food for hungry soldiers. Apart from the ever-present dust, the room was ready to serve a meal, he imagined opening the kitchen door to find cooks bustling around in preparation.

Kat examined everything eagerly, touching a hefting plates and utensils to experience how these people ate. She pushed open one of the two-way double doors on the wall, it creaked a groaned from long disuse, a little maintenance was in order. She immediately began opening cabinets and pulling out drawers, rushing to look in every nook and cranny. Cupboards and warm refrigeration units were flung open, items within gleefully examined in close scrutiny. Nothing escaped her notice, not the smallest utensil was neglected. She was smiling and having such a grand time, that he left her to the fun.

Mark spotted a computer terminal on one side of the room, most likely used to display recipes while the food was cooked. He sat on the backless stool parked in front of the terminal, tapping a dirty key to reveal a welcome screen and meal search menu. "Would you download the recipe database from this terminal, Sky?"

"Download complete. The recipes available are scaled for large numbers of people, and I do not anticipate military recipes to be particularly desirable."

"You're probably right, but I'm sure we can cook something that Kat will like."

He halfheartedly poked around the database while waiting for Kat to finish. Many of the ingredient names were completely foreign to him, things that were no longer available or did not exist anymore. He lost interest after a minute, the recipes might as well be written in another language for all he understood them. Maybe Sky could help with translations and substitute ingredients. He brought up the detailed base map on his HUD, hunting for a room or building name that would be worth visiting. The armory was the obvious first choice in locating a weapon, or a schematic for something stronger than what an ordinary soldier carried. None of the other names on the map stood out to him as promising, nothing that said test or research, which he knew were words related to new equipment. That left the command building, as their last chance, it being the most important structure in the base, any secrets were certain to be kept there. Curiously, the map showed a section of rooms in the command building that were unlabeled, not even numbered as many others were. Three possibly reasons for this popped into his head. The map was incomplete or the file corrupt. There was simply nothing in these rooms, and therefore no reason to name them. Or the area was classified, which could be exactly what he was looking for.

A more remote search option was the garage, where a vehicle with a big new weapon might be waiting. Beyond that there was nothing else worth checking. There were barracks, officer housing, administrative offices, a laundry, and a gymnasium.

A loud clatter brought his head around. Kat was amassing a large assortment of packages and containers of old foods, an armload of cans toppling from her hands. She arrayed them on a previously empty counter, their labels were faded, but he could still make them out readily enough. What she was doing was less clear than the labels, but it seemed harmless, so he left her to it. He proceeded to set out the food from his travel bag, a simple meal of bread and fruit.

When he looked at Kat again, he understood what her purpose with the old food packages was. To take pictures of the labels. She placed each items on an open spot of newly dusted table, and recorded an image of it with the photo receptor on her MGP. She likely hoped they could replicate all of the foods she was discovering. He watched in amusement as Kat methodically catalogued her finds.

When she was finally done, she walked over to him with a bounce in her step, and her tail in the air. "Did you see all of the foods they have? There was so much in here, more than I've ever seen. I know I can't eat any of it." She assured him hastily. "But look at all of those packages, aren't they incredible? There are pictures of the cooked food right on the boxes, cans, and bags. This is one of the absolute coolest things I ever found."

Her enthusiasm was infectious, bringing a smile to his face. "That is really something, it might be fun to take pictures of the food we make too."

She nodded vigorously. "Yes, you cook the food and I take the pictures." That was not a particularly fair division of labor, but at least it did not give him more to do. "Lunch is ready. We can eat, then go to the armory for weapons."

They ate, packed up, and returned to the street. The food packages were left on the counter, once more abandoned to stagnation, but no longer forgotten. He followed the map along the cracked roads to the armory, hearing a distant chirp of birds from behind the wall. The armory was larger than the mess hall, not unexpected given that this was a military base, weapons here were more important than food. The building was on the tall side for only one story, but a bit short to be two. Unlike the mess hall, the armory was windowless, and probably had reinforced walls to protect it from attack. Opening the front door revealed a small room with a second door at the far end. There was a window in the right wall, below which was a low opening four feet wide above a flat counter. The window was opaque, possibly from age, making it impossible to see what was on the other side. Tapping it, he decided the window was some type of plastic, and thick.

He swung open the far door, and stepped into a warehouse with a high ceiling. The floor was packed with rows of tall metal shelves higher than his head, the topmost shelves beyond the reach of his outstretched arms. But devastatingly, there were no weapons present, every shelf in sight was empty. When the base personnel evacuated, they had taken all of the weapons with them. He fought to keep the disappointment from showing too much, and quickly surveyed the room. It stubbornly remained weaponless.

"We should have a look around, see if there's anything left." He said tonelessly.

Kat looked as upset as he felt, but nodded and stalked off to see what was there.

He shuffled slowly to the back of the room, peering at each shelf he passed, listlessly trailing a finger on the dusty black metal. Arriving at the far wall, the room was no less empty than when he entered it. Getting an encouraging idea, he scanned the room visually for a computer than might contain schematics. There was one on this side of the entry window, and he strode to it with renewed purpose.

He kept the desperation from his voice. "Sky, check this computer for weapon schematics please. Or anything we can use, anything at all."

The response was immediate, and it was not good. "This computer has been systematically wiped of all pertinent data. Any information it once contained is irrevocably erased.

Disheartened, Mark continued his fruitless search of the armory. There were no other terminals, or anything at all beyond empty shelves. His best remaining hope was the command building, or more remotely the garage.

Kat rejoined him at the door, her tail low and twitching in irritation. "There are no weapons in this armory." She said viciously. "What good is an armory without arms? From now on it's an ory!"

He ignored the anger, but agreed with her sentiment. "I'd like to go to the command building next, there could be something good there."

She nodded and left, he followed her outside. She activated her wrist laser, and proceeded to burn the letters A R and M off of the sign plate. The building really was an ory to those who came after them. He laughed, glad to have a release for his mounting frustration over the empty warehouse. He ought to know by now that Kat always meant what she said, literally.

She laughed with him.

The command center, as it was listed on the map, was several buildings away, but since it was the tallest structure in the base. It was visible from the rechristened ory. He examined the building as they approached it. Aside from the extra height, it was much the same as the rest of the base. Rising from the roof was an array of antennas and satellite dishes. Reaching the building, he opened the front door and stepped inside. They found themselves in a large and surprisingly ornate lobby. Glossy wood moldings lined the walls where they met both floor and ceiling, and even under an obscuring layer of dust, the floor gleamed dully as if polished. Prominently displayed on the center of the floor, was a circle containing the letters EMF. The building's full title stood in tall black letters across the back wall, 'Earth Military Force Invasion command Center.' Below the words were a wooden desk and three chairs. Doors with shiny golden handles led off of the lobby to other rooms and areas, and a pair of what he was pretty sure were elevators were recessed into the right wall.

The words invasion command center so large before him, swelled new hope in Mark's ebbing emotional tide. It made the place sound very important, and that mean there really was something good here. He enlarged the internal building map on his HUD. There were four floors above ground, and two more below. Most of the room names were ordinary enough, break rooms, offices, meeting rooms. But in the second basement, the lowest point on the map, there was a whole section of rooms completely separated from the rest of the floor. The unlabeled rooms, the same ones he noticed earlier, occupied half of the floor. On closer inspection they were not entirely unnamed. The first room in the section, actually a hallway that was the only way in, bore a single word title of professor. Why would a bunch of rooms be labeled professor? He knew that a professor was a kind of teacher, but why would one be in a military base? Could the word be a code? Perhaps for the type of experimental equipment he was here for? Whatever this was, he was determined to begin his search there.

He asked Sky to project a holographic map of the second basement in front of them, and pointed the rooms out to Kat. "I want to go to these rooms first, okay?"

She shrugged in differently. "Fine by me." Then she perked up on seeing something more interesting. "I'm going to look for more old food containers in this break room, while you search for weapons." She poked a finger into the hologram, at a room across from the professor hall.

"All right, come on." He walked to a set of stairs near the elevator, and started down. He was intrigued by the concept of an elevator, curious about the experience, but not so much that he would trust an ancient enclosed box dangling from a decaying cable. At the second basement, the stairs emptied into a long hallway, that had to extend from one end of the building to the other. There was a single door on the right wall, at the midpoint of the passage. The sign plate held the word 'Professor' as the map stated. In large letters below that cryptic title, was a simple but encouraging message. 'Authorized personnel only.'

A tug of the handle told him this door was locked, but there was no keypad on which to enter a code. The door must use a different security lock than the rest of the base, and that lifted his expectations another notch.

"Would you open this door Sky?"

"This door, and in fact everything beyond it, is isolated from the main security system of the base. The encryption is more complex. Please wait."

Kat shifted her weight to one foot, resting a hand on her hip. "Do you think Sky can unlock the door?"

"Of course he can unlock the door." Replied Mark without hesitation. The AI never failed to subvert security systems.

There was a click from the lock. "Voice print authorization accepted, entry granted." Came the soft, feminine computer voice from the security building.

Mark stared at the door, unsure of what to think. "What was that?"

"I am uncertain. I broke the encryption, but I had not yet issued the command to disengage the lock. I can only surmise that my infiltration of the system, caused a glitch in the recognition routine."

Kat was less interested in why the door was open. "I'm off to look for food in that break room.

"Remember Kat, don't eat what you find in there," he said to her receding back.

She gave him a thumb up over her shoulder without slowing.

"She better not come back sick." He grumbles.

"On a positive note, if she contracts a case of food poisoning, it would present us with a prime opportunity to test the medical scanner."

"Thank you Sky, that's very helpful." Mark grunted, opening the door to a faint whoosh of escaping air. This section was also on its own air circulation system, completely isolated from the rest of the building. *These people really had a thing for door lined hallways.* Like almost every door he entered today, behind this one was a long hallway and lots of doors. The corridor was strangely clean, not a spec of the so far omnipresent dust marred the polished white floor, and every light in the ceiling worked. the first door he reached was labeled 'Genetics Laboratory.' His heart beat rapidly, thumping hard in his chest. This was it, the research and science labs he was counting on. They would find a new weapon after all. But he would hold off on calling Kat until he actually had it.

"I want you to search every computer and electronic device we find down here Sky. Download every bit of information you can, no matter how unimportant it might seem. Who knows what could prove useful."

"Understood. Search initiated."

He pushed into the genetics lab, banging the door on its stop in his haste. The room was crammed with computers and equipment. He saw large incubation chambers, microscopes, centrifuges, and other complicated machines he could not readily identify. He ran his fingers along the face of an incubator, feeling giddy at the touching the name 'AST71 Incubation Chamber' written on it in raised letters. He pulled the handle to open its door, and froze, staring at the machine in mute astonishment. There was a symbol on the chamber, one that he was unquestionably familiar with, an icon he had seen every day since he was a child. An oblong silver octagon with a black outline and a black dot in the center. It was identical to the silver eye tattoo on Kat's right calf.

What was Kat's tattoo doing on a device that no one had seen or touched in one hundred and fifty years? He looked at the lab more alertly, scouring every surface for anything linking this place to Kat. The eye was everywhere, painted on any device larger than a thermometer, and written beneath it in most instances, were the words 'Omega Project.'

"Are you seeing this Sky?" He blurted. "Am I imagining it? I don't get it, what is Kat's eye tattoo doing here? It's on everything. And what is this Omega Project? I have to know what's going on, what do the computers tell you?"

Sky constantly monitored their surroundings using any camera available, primarily through the HUD cameras. "I regret to inform you, that these computers have been wiped, in precisely the same manner as the computer in the armory. I suspect that it was done using the same algorithm. As to the correlation between this Omega Project emblem and Kat's tattoo, they are identical in design, and in color prior to the incident at White Sheep village. I can offer no explanation for this occurrence."

Mark swallowed the bile rising in his throat. Between his disappointment over the blank computers and the lightheaded shock from seeing the octagons, he was physically ill. Stay calm, he told himself. There were other rooms to be searched, computes to be scanned. He returned to the hallway, the lightness gone from his step, his hopes diminished.

Across from the Genetics Laboratory, was a room called 'Temporal Laboratory.' He stepped inside, initially thinking the wall was several feet thick. But there was large machine of unfathomable purpose flush against it within the room. The machine was dull white, its surface covered in display screens, none of them active. Occupying the center of the device, was a chamber six feet square and sealed behind a transparent barrier. Whatever it was designed to hold was missing, as empty as the computers were. The rest of the room held desks and wheeled chairs, atop the desks were computer terminals. These computers were also erased, Sky informed him, and he could discern no other clues in the room.

Uselessly searching every room, he reached the end of the hallway, capped by one final door. It bore a sign plate saying 'The Professor.' Did this mean that the professor was an actual person, not a code name? And this was where he worked? Mark opened the door to an office, as plain and undecorated as the rest of the base. The man who used this space believed in keeping an antiseptic environment. The desk did not even hold the usual pictures that were so prevalent in old videos, as if his personal life should not intrude on his work, or that such a life did not exist. In addition to the desk, there were two chairs and a metal box with drawers. At waist height on the wall behind the desk, was the Omega octagon, this one different than the others. The dot or iris in the center was pale green, instead of black. He could not take his eyes from it, was drawn to the dot almost hypnotically.

"This computer is empty. I am sorry Mark, but there is no information to be obtained here."

Scarcely hearing Sky's anticipated report, Mark shuffled around the desk blankly, reaching out to the iris without thought. It moved slightly at his touch, depressing like a hidden button. The iris lit up, glowing bright green like the beams from his laser, and a dull click issued from inside the wall. A door sized rectangle of wall slid away, leaving a yawning, impenetrable void in its place. The space was pitch black save for a small area dimly lit by light filtering in from the office. He stood at this unexpected precipice, staring blindly into the darkness, until multicolored pinpoints of light resolved themselves in his vision. Those dots shining from the depths of the room, were like the stars in the night sky, if stars came in red, green, and purple. He switched on his HUD light, brightening the room only enough to tell him the space was much larger than he originally believed. The wall was an amazing three feet thick, and this time it really was wall. The only explanation he could think of, was that this chamber was a reinforced bunker. If the people who built the base went to the trouble of making a hidden bunker, then whatever it was meant to protect, must be important.

Metal steps led down into the chamber, far down. He located a bank of switches on the wall inside the opening, and flipped them one by one, lights came on high above the chamber floor. A few lights no longer functioned, but enough were lit for him to see most of the huge space. The chamber was vast and rectangular, stretching out before him for a hundred yards with a floor twenty feet below where he stood. He could not make out the far end clearly in the dim light, but there was a large black object at the base of the stairs.

His eyes locked on the object as he descended the stairs, a boxy device standing ten feet in height, five in width, and six deep. A display screen was chest high on the side, with an angled keyboard protruding below it. A thick bundle of wires and hoses snaked away along the floor, supplying it with power and who knew what else. There was a small window on the front of the device, but it or the box's contents were too cloudy for him to see through.

He was transfixed by the mysterious device. Not only was this something utterly alien to him, but unlike the equipment in the rooms above, this thing was still working. He had not the faintest notion of what the machine did, but perhaps lulled into a false sense of safety by the peaceful emptiness of the base, he felt no fear as he tapped a key on the terminal. The screen came on and the machine beeped. Data scrolled up the display, and a bright amber light on top of the box started flashing.

"Reanimation sequence initiated, please stand clear of cryochamber." Said the now familiar electronic voice.

For several minutes he watched information flash by faster than he could read. He had no way of knowing what was happening, but this operational ancient technology was intensely fascinating. What was this black box? The voice called it a cryochamber, but he had only a general idea that it was something like a freezer. The device made a series of explosive clacking sounds, and a cloudy white vapor vented out with a hiss. The hissing subsided in moment, leaving behind a strange chemical smell he could not identify. The entire front of the box swung open, and more of the foggy vapor billowed outward. The hollow space inside was obscured by the fog, which flowed along the floor to swiftly dissipate.

Within the unknowable depths of the fog, illuminated by the flashing amber light, there was slow, shaky movement. Something large and dark was rising from the confines of the box. Mark breathed shallowly, his mind emptying with the first hints of fear that this may not have been such a good idea after all. A huge black hand reached out to him from the fog. Scared witless by this impossible apparition from the distant past, he did what any rational person would in this situation, screamed like a little girl.

CHAPTER 9

In the break room, Kat opened every cupboard, drawer, and cabinet, emptying their contents onto the counter or floor. Any items that interested her were placed on the table for closer scrutiny. The packages and containers here were smaller than those in the kitchen. Many of them were single use items for individual people, candy bars, drink cans or bottles, and microwave popcorn pouches. She did not know what microwave popcorn was exactly, but the people of the old world liked popcorn in the videos, so it was fun to actually hold a package of it. As she had in the kitchen, she put items one at a time on a clear spot of table, then recorded its image with her MGP. She badly wanted to know how the food tasted, but had learned a painful lesson years before, it was bad to try eating old food. When she was a lot younger, she found a bag of what was once cookies while on a scavenging trip. Because she was by herself and curious, she unwisely opened the bag and ate some of its contents. The image on the package was of tasty looking cookies, but what greeted her tongue was a lumpy gray powder that tasted terrible. Worse than the awful taste that left her coughing and heaving, was that she got horribly sick afterward, unable to eat at all without vomiting for a whole day.

She shook off the memory with a shudder. She might not be able to eat the old food, but she could look at pictures of it and imagine what it tasted like. Maybe it she was really lucky, Mark could cook some of it with the base recipe database, or at least something close. She was at it for twenty minutes, and was nearly finished documenting it all. She took pictures of the last few items, and with one final longing glance at her discoveries, she sighed and left the room.

She wondered if Mark had found the BFL yet. It was probably too much to expect him to find an octosub, but he did need to find a new weapon. If the weapon was a laser, the beam should be pink.

With those reasonable expectations firmly in mid, she crossed to the door Mark went through, opened it, and stepped into the spotless hallway beyond, she peeked into the first room on the left, wondering how far Mark was in his search, when a piercing scream cut through the placid calm of the corridor.

A spike of icy terror lanced down her spine. "Mark!" The scream tore from her throat. She launched forward, running with everything she had and more, rushing to where her HUD showed Mark to be.

"No, not again. I won't fail again!" She cried fiercely, clearing five feet with every bound, the nightmare of White Sheep burning in her mind. In seconds she had flown down the hallway, and was in an office hurdling a desk to stare into a massive chamber below. For a moment she was confused by the apparition that confronted her. A tall, dark figure with a bulbous, oversized head, was stepping out of a fog filled box. Small lights blinked on and off all over the misshapen head, and wires dangled from it into the mist. A single oval eye was centered on a face lacking all definition, it was without mouth or nose, those she recognized as such any way.

Then she saw Mark on the floor facing the strange monster, scrambling from it with hands and heels, and all doubt instantly dispelled. The thing took a lumbering step, advancing toward Mark with a grasping hand extended. Rage filled her, blinding her to all but the need to protect her family. She threw herself at the creature, leaping down the steps three at a time. She lashed out at the beast with vicious intensity, punches and kicks blurring into it with blinding speed. It stumbled backward off balance, unprepared for the strength of this tiny attacker. It caught foot on the box, reaching back with a large hand to steady itself. Then it mounted a defense, using its free arm to block some of her attacks. She pressed forward, hitting the monster anywhere she could, her hand tingling after a blow to its incredibly hard head. Shoving off of the box, it blocked her assault with both arms and both legs. The monster was fast, more so than any real opponent she had fought. But it could not match her speed, not even close.

She slammed the beast in the stomach with her shin, hearing it grunt in pain or surprise. It whipped an arm around in a solid backhand blow to her shoulder. The hit knocked her back several feet, her arm going numb at the point of contact. She charged at it with renewed fury. The thing made a loud, muffled sound, as if it was attempting to speak. It reached for her with a meaty black hand. She ducked under the outstretched arm, then leaped into the air with a shout, kicking at the rounded head with all her might. Her foot struck it right below its unblinking eye, and a loud crack split the air as the monstrous head was flung into the box. The headless beast fell hard in a stiff heap.

She turned from her formerly fearsome opponent, only to find Mark standing out of range of the fight, staring unafraid at the monster.

"Are you okay?" Her relief at seeing him unhurt was immeasurable.

"Oh I'm fine, thanks for asking." He told her absently, moving closer to the monster. "But he may not be doing so well. I think you nearly took his head off."

"Nearly?" She was puzzled, turning her head to look at the monster. Sure enough, underneath the oversized headgear she had aggressively removed, was an undeniably human head. The skin on his face and neck was deathly pale, as if he had not been exposed to sunlight for a long time. He was clean shaved, and his close-cropped hair was dark brown. He was, she thought idly, not bad looking.

Mark leaned over the man, all traces of fear forgotten. The man lay motionless, and she started to worry that she had accidentally killed the guy. He groaned, rolling onto his back and opening his eyes.

"Who?" He rasped faintly, then coughed roughly, spraying phlegm to the floor. Getting his legs under him, he pushed himself to a sitting position with effort. He groaned again, reaching for his head. He rubbed his neck, turning his head from side to side. "What hit me?" His voice was stronger, but sill stiff from lack of use.

Mark pointed at her. "That would be my friend here."

The man cast an annoyingly doubtful glance at her. "The little Grymal?"

Mark defended her. "Trust me, she's a lot stronger than she looks.

He shrugged dubiously, then hauled himself upright using the box for leverage. She was a little offended that he did not believe her capable of hurting him, but she felt guilty for hitting him so hard, and kept her mouth shut. She guessed him to be an inch or two over six feet in height, and weigh close to three hundred pounds, all of it muscle. He was easily the biggest human she had ever seen, and stronger even than Korta or Mallo.

He was dressed in black shirt and pants that clung to him like a second skin, thin gloves covered him hands, and socks his feet.

He leaned heavily on the box, clearly in a weakened state, despite his great strength. Whatever the box did, if he came out of it in this condition, she was in no hurry to try it herself.

He stared at them with a growing frown. "Who are you, and what are you doing here? You're not dressed like lab techs, and there's no way either of you are military."

"My name is Mark." He nodded sideways at her. "And this is Kat. We are scavengers and traders, and we came to this base to find powerful weapons. A village was destroyed by robots, and the people living there were taken. We need weapons to fight the robots and rescue our friends."

The man snapped fully upright, his eyes drilling into Mark, disturbed by what he heard. "Robots?" He demanded. "Has the invasion already started? They were supposed to wake me in time to prepare for the fight." He was becoming agitated, eyes darting in search of something he could not find. "There should be lab techs here to supervise my release from cryo-sleep, where are they?"

Mark spoke soothingly. "Please calm down. A lot has happened since you went to sleep." He hesitated, unsure of how to break the news to this man that his old life was gone. She did not envy Mark the task. "I have to tell you something, and you're not going to like it. The world you knew no longer exists. The Devastation, what you call the invasion I think, happened a hundred and fifty years ago."

The man's brow creased in anger. "That's not funny, why would you say that?"

"It's true." Confirmed Kat tactfully. "Your world broke."

Mark winced for some reason.

"No, you're lying. They told me I would make up before the invasion. He promised me I would help save the world, he promised me!" He raged at them, unable to accept the truth. Without warning, he dashed up the stairs on somewhat unsteady legs, vanishing into the office at the top.

"Come on, we better go after him, keep him from hurting himself." She jogged up the stairs. When she reached the hallway on the other side of the office, she was surprised to see it empty and the door swinging shut on the far end. The guy was moving faster than she expected in his condition, he must be running on adrenaline. She picked up her pace, determined to catch him quickly. Beyond the hall door his path was obvious, his socks leaving smeared footprints in the dust alongside the boot prints she and Mark had made. She vaulted the stairs after him, pausing on the ground floor to see which way he went. His footprints continued upward, his pounding steps echoing from above.

She updated Mark with the HUD. "He's going upstairs somewhere, I'm following him."

Keeping one eye on the dust prints, she sprinted the stairs past floors two and three, going up and up until there were no more stairs. On the fourth and highest floor, the trail moved on from the stairwell, the wide spacing of his steps informing her that his breakneck pace was not slowing. He knew this place, and had a specific destination in mind. She slowed to look around, not convinced it was entirely safe here. A sign on the wall in front of the elevators said, 'Command Level. All personnel are required to present identification. Use of deadly force authorized.'

There was a hallway and more doors, one was wide open and reinforced with armor plating, everything in this base was made to survive an attack. The room past the door was an office with a desk and chairs. She moved on without interest. Halfway down the hall was a shielded alcove, eleven feet wide and the same deep. There was a small desk toward the front, with an armored wall behind it. The wall had a narrow slot and a window in it, and an opening in the middle for people to pass. The setup looked to her like a guard station, designed to keep unwanted people from entering the room beyond. Past the wall was a large metal door, it was open and the dust prints led inside.

She eased forward cautiously, dipping her head into the room with a hand on the frame to haul herself back in a harry if needed. A voice she did not recognize was speaking, and it sounded drained of all feeling.

"....I have recorded this message for any EMF personnel who may one day return to this base looking for us. I thought we had won. The XRs were all but defeated, disordered and offering no credible threat. Transition was seconds from completion. But one of their command ships was still under their control, it fired at the central power relay satellite. How it affected transition we don't know, the techs think it was successful. The interaction of the XR laser and our transition energy, caused a chain reaction that was nothing short of cataclysmic. The earth has been enveloped in mass devastation. The quakes have not let up for days..."

Not understanding what the voice as saying, she looked at the big man. He was watching a message playing on a screen, his face a mask of intense focus. The screen showed a gray haired man in a military uniform, his expression profoundly sad, as if he fate of the world had rested on his shoulders, and he dropped it.

The message continued. "....Those of us who are left, have chosen to gather all of our weapons, and as many provisions as will fit in the transports, then make our way to the nearest shelters. The XRs are indiscriminately attacking anything that moves. We will protect the civilian population as best we can. That is the new mandate for the EMF, humanity must survive. If you are hearing this message, you can find us in sector Charlie sixty-two follow us there if you can, we will give aid to all who come. I wish you luck, I wish us all luck. Above all stay alive, help each other, we're all that's left. This is general John Samson of the EMF, goodbye." The old man saluted gravely, and the screen went dark.

Kat had never heard anyone sound so desolate, she felt immensely sorry for the old man whoever he was. What happened to make him so sad? Was it the Devastation, was that what he was talking about?

The big man slumped in the chair, elbows on the desk and head held in his hands. He shook as if racked by silent sobs, coming to terms with what he had learned, that his world had ceased to exist. She heard Mark in the corridor behind her, but her eyes were on the man. He was oblivious to everything, giving no reaction when she placed a hand on his holder in sympathy. Glancing over as Mark entered the room, she motioned for him to have a seat.

She waited patiently for the man to pull himself together, it was not every day you woke up to find your world gone. After a time his hands dropped to the console, and he stared at the wall ahead.

"It's true. Isn't it?" He said tonelessly, not really asking a question. "All of it, everything is gone, everyone. We lost the fight, the world was nearly destroyed. And I wasn't there. People counted on me, and I could not help them. How many died because of my absence, how many friends? All my hard work, everything I sacrificed to save the world, it was all for nothing." He drew a long shuddering breath, and lapsed into silence.

"What will you do now?"

His head turned to her, his gaze blank. "Do? What do you mean?"

"Exactly that, what are you planning to do? The world you knew may be gone, but you're still here. What is it you want to accomplish?" She spoke firmly.

"I don't know." He replied quietly. "I don't think it matters anymore, I don't think I matter."

She was having trouble making sense of his words. "What are you saying? You're here aren't you? Of course you matter."

He waved a hand dismissively, his words bitter. "You don't get it. Everything I did was to save the world from the XRs. I gave up all that I was, let them permanently change may body. I sacrificed my own future, my dreams, to become a weapon capable of destroying the XRs. Winning was everything. But it's all gone, the XRs won and we failed, I failed. There's nothing left for me to protect. I have no purpose, no reason to exist."

She had tried to go easy on him, the guy had received phenomenally bad news after all, but his boundless self pity was infuriating. How did he survive so long with an attitude like that? "Oh, come on already, what are you going to do, cry? You think you're the only one to lose friends? To lose family? You think that makes you special?" She shouted to penetrate his dejection.

He lurched to his feet, fists clenched, staring down at her menacingly.

"How dare you speak to me like that. Don't you get it? I failed them all. I was supposed to save them, and I failed. I lost everything." He shouted back at her, smashing a fist into the console, its little letter keys flying everywhere.

She was undaunted by the petulant outburst, and lashed at him just as hard. "You lost, what could you know of loss? You were not even there! How would you know what it's like to lose friends, to lose family? To see them killed right in front of you? To hold them in your arms, covered in their blood as they die. And to know, that there is nothing you can do to save them. Tell me mister big, tough soldier, what have you lost?" She shook with the release of pent up emotion, her voice was raw and tears streamed from her eyes.

Withering under the force of her reprimand, his shoulders drooped in defeat, and his hands hung open at his sides. He looked her directly in the eyes, really seeing her for the first time. "I'm sorry. Hearing that I missed the fight, learning the Earth was lost, was such a blow that I didn't stop to think about what your lives must be like in the ruins we left you. You're right, my world might be gone, but I was asleep when it happened. I never really lost anyone, not like you have. Your name is Kat?" He snapped rigidly upright at her nod, and gave her a stiff salute. "Commander Zachary Mason of the Earth Military Force, commanding officer of the Omega Corps." He released the salute, grinning lopsidedly. "Thanks for chewing my hide miss, I needed it."

"No problem soldier. And call me Kat, we're all friends now." She grinned back, wiping at her eyes.

"Sure thing Kat, and I'm Zack."

She turned to find Mark staring at her oddly, was it something she said? "You've already met Mark." She pointed to him anyway, and they exchanged greetings. "Plus there's our computer friend Sky."

Mark raised his left forearm, pulling down the sleeve to reveal Sky. "Greetings."

Zack was uncertain how to greet a computer. "Uh. Hi?"

Mark let his arm drop. "Zack, you mentioned something called the Omega Corps. What is it exactly?"

Zack started for the door, jerking his head at them to come with him. "Follow me back to the emergency bunker, that's the room with her cryo-chamber. I'll fill you in on the way, I'm pretty sure any security protocols have expired." He paused at the door, silently bidding farewell to his past, then nodded and strode out. "The Omega project was a program intended to create an enhanced fighting force, soldiers capable of combating whatever the XRs might sent against us. All of us who were in the program volunteered to be there, although I use the word loosely. What choice did we really have? Still, many of the candidates did not volunteer, and went back to their old posts. Those of us who stayed, were warned that the changes would be permanent. They started by subjecting us to painful genetic modifications, making us stronger and faster than normal humans. We need less sleep, eat less food, and have greater stamina. Bone augmentation was next, our bones were encased in an alloy lattice to make them almost unbreakable. That was not a fun process." He rubbed an arm in sympathetic memory. "We were implanted with microchips that let us interface with our gear. We were trained extensively to use experimental weapons and power armor. After all of that, only a hundred and three of us completed the program."

He fell silent at the door to the Professor's office, glowering at the sign plate. He spoke again only when they had descended the stairs into the bunker. "The Professor told me that I was chosen to receive one last enhancement, one that would help to 'save the world.' He told me that of all the Omegas, I showed the most potential. He said I would be able to move beyond my limits when the need was great, or something like that. It sounded like a bunch of fantasy nonsense to me, but the man was a genius, so I figured why not? He gave me that final genetic manipulation, and placed me in cryo-sleep. He told me it was necessary for the change to work, and promised I would be revived when it was time for me to help save the work. "He put a hand lightly on the cryo-box and closed his eyes." The invasion was only fifteen days away." He said softly. "Somehow fifteen days became one hundred fifty years. Must have got the decimal wrong." His laugh was devoid of humor.

Pulling himself away from the treacherous machine with a visible force of will, he continued. "That," he gestured to a long armored vehicle at the back of the room. "Is an Omega XJ32 mobile command center."

The XJ32 was something akin to a large RV, which she knew of from watching old videos. It was ten feet wide between its armored wheel wells, which extended past its central mass. The wheels were at least three feet tall, and were wide and knobby to drive anywhere. Two large laser turrets were mounted to the roof, with two smaller turrets on the front compartment. The vehicle was fourteen feet tall and thirty-two feet long, and was a dark grayish color.

Zack walked to the dormant vehicle with authority, a man who acted decisively, and expected to be taken seriously. Most of the wobble was gone from his stride, the exertion from running the stairs helping his recovery from the long nap. He stopped at a door in the side of the XJ32, and tapped a code into the keypad located there. A low hum came from the vehicle as it smoothly powered up, and the lock clicked. He opened the door, climbing into the vehicle and motioning for them to do the same. The interior was designed like the base, except that everything was more tightly packed together. The cabinets, counters and floor were all in shades of gray, knobs and handler were utilitarian in shape and dull silver in color. It was all very functional, and boring, only the various indicator lights showed any life. Was this how all military stuff was? If so, she could imagine a lot of soldiers going crazy from monotony and boredom.

"You two make yourselves at home." He pointed at a table and bench seats near the door. "I'm going to shower and change. I have been asleep for a century and a half after all." Smiling at his own joke, he turned and peeled off the gloves and shirt, tossing them on a seat on his way to the rear.

Kat snapped a question at him, her voice raised in surprise. "Where did you get that tattoo?"

He looked over his shoulder at the silver octagon standing out against her pale skin, shrugged indifferently. "It's the Omega Project symbol, all of us who completed the program got it. The professor said it was important, but I think it was just part of the PR campaign."

She spun on her heel so that her back was to him, then reached down to touch the tattoo on her calf. "I have the same tattoo." She glanced from his shoulder to her calf and frowned. That's strange, I thought my iris was black like his, was it always red?

"That's not possible." His eyes widened in shock, more surprised by the matching marks than she was. "Only those of us who completed the training and modifications received the tattoo. There's no way you were part of the project. But if not, the how could anyone from this far in the future have seen the Omega eye?"

Her brows drew together in thought, her mind working feverishly to dredge up an explanation. "I don't know where I got it, or why. I found Mark when we were both little, and I already had it then. I have almost no memories from before meeting Mark. I honestly had no idea what it was until you told me, neither of us has seen it anywhere else."

Zack was bewildered by her tattoo, no longer paying them the slightest attention. This might not have been the best time to add another shock to his heavy load. He started muttering to himself as he moved to the back of the cabin, entering a small room to his left. "It doesn't make any sense. She can't be part of the program, she's from a different time." His voice cut off when the door closed.

She looked at Mark, raising her eyebrows in question. He shook his head, understanding Zack's behavior no better than she did. She sat on the bench with Mark to stare after Zack for a minute, rubbing her calf absently. "Do you think I could be a highly trained super soldier?"

"You were only four of five years old when we met, I really don't think someone trained you as an infant to be a soldier. And how could you be part of a program that ended with the Devastation? There's no such thing as time travel, outside of a game."

His rationale made sense, but she was so enamored with the idea that she could be some kind of superhero, that she would not be dissuaded so easily. "But I have the tattoo, and Zack said only Omega people got it." Then something occurred to her. "They put him to sleep in that cry box thing all those years, maybe they did the same to me."

It took him a minute to come up with a response, but when he did, it was an annoyingly good one. "Not everyone who worked here would have died in the Devastation. One of them could have put the tattoo on themselves or their children, and over the decades it was passed down as a family tradition. Or someone may have found an object with the eye on it like this truck." He patted the seat where the eye was sewn into it.

"And liking it, used the eye as a decorative mark. Or a loony created an Omega cult where all the members and their kids were tattooed in a wonky religions ceremony." Zack finished Mark's line of thought. He stood nearby in fresh gray pants and shirt, having listened to the end of their conversation.

"You see Kat? There are a lot more plausible explanations for your tattoo than thinking you were altered as a baby and put into cryo-sleep. The tattoo is only a coincidence, it doesn't mean you're a super soldier."

"You guys are no fun." She said in mock irritation, then sighed wistfully. "It would have been nice to be a super soldier."

Zack started at her for a moment, then shook his head. "And regardless of any wild theories, all of the Omegas, including the women, were big like I am. You 'e too short, and way to thin, to be one." He entered a command on the front of a boxy device next to the table. "Is anyone else hungry? This is a cryo-chef, it can make just about any food you can think of. It has a storage compartment full of powdered food that's cryo-frozen to keep it super cold, way below freezing. And it takes very little space for a lot of food. I'm told that the food will stay good for a thousand years at that temperature. I select what I want from the menu here, and the cryo-chef turns the powers into real food. Don't ask me how, I didn't invent the thing, but it does work. When the timer hits zero the food is ready to eat, open this door to get it." He pointed out the features as he described them.

Kat was in front of the cryo-chef in an instant, pressing icons and exploring menus. "This is the most fantastic machine ever invented. It shows you a picture of each food, like we were going to do, and it gives you a description of it." She was overwhelmed by the endless number of choices in the magic food box, she wanted to try everything at once.

"There are too many things to choose from, would you pick something good Zack?"

"Sure, how about pizza?"

They started at him blankly, neither having any idea what pizza was, or if it was good.

"Okay then, one pepperoni pizza coming up." Zack entered the selection into the cryo-chef. A faint mechanical buzzing came from inside the box, much like the swarm.

Mark heard the sound as well. "It uses nanomachines to synthesize the texture and shape of the original food out of the powders, doesn't it?"

Zack scratched his head, this was definitely not his specially. "It does use nanomachines somehow. Anyway, it will be twenty minutes for the pizza to be ready, you can see the remaining time on the screen here." He tapped the display where numbers were indeed counting down over an image of the food, a large round thing covered in red spots. "We don't have to worry about running out of food, the system contains a large supply of powders. When it runs low more can be added by putting plants and animals into the desecator for powderization. The system breaks the organics down into basic proteins and sugars and things."

She silently watched the cryo-chef, pulling her gaze from it only when a thought came to her. "You have food, do you have games and videos too?"

He considered the question. "I was told the computer was loaded with some entertainment selections, but I honestly don't know what's in there. I never had a reason to check."

She looked for a terminal, barely restraining herself from conducting an active search. "Can I look at them?"

Opening this mouth to reply, Zack was interrupted by an electronic chime. "The pizza is ready, what do you say we eat first, then you can mess around with the computer."

She was torn between equally compelling urges, her desire to eat the unknown food, and the draw of finding new games to play. The noisy rumbling of her stomach settled the internal debate. "Food first."

Mark laughed, earning himself a grin.

Zack opened the door on the cryo-chef, unleashing the most singularly amazing scent she had ever experienced, a sort of sharp, spicy aroma tinged with copper that was difficult to describe, she inhaled deeply through the nose, delighting in this new smell. "That's wonderful. What are those little red circles?"

"Those are called pepperoni, slices of spicy sausage. And this, is a pizza." Zack set the pizza in the middle of the table, took a knife out of a drawer, and started cutting it. "You can put a lot of different toppings on a pizza, meats and vegetables, but pepperoni is the most popular." He picked up a wedge of pizza and bit off the pointy end, demonstrating for his guests the proper was to eat it.

She copied him eagerly, biting a large mouthful from her wedge of pizza. Chewing on the gooey cheese and soft bread, the spicy taste of hot pepperoni exploding in her mouth. It was indescribable, unlike anything she had every eaten, she never new flavors like this existed. She rapidly devoured wedge after wedge, finishing off half of the pizza in no time at all. She paused when she noticed Zack staring at her open mouthed, and lowered her hand from reaching for the last wedge.

"Oh, did you want another piece?" She asked politely.

Nodding mutely, Zack quickly snatched the wedge, yanking his hand back as if he feared losing it.

Mark finished his pizza without a word, a smile on his face.

"That, was super awesome Zack, we don't have food like that around here. Is all of your old food this good.?"

Zack chewed on the pizza and swallowed, staring at her strangely. Was there sauce on her chin?

"That all depends on your tastes. Some things you'll like, some you might hate." He put the dishes into a machine she presumed was a scrubber, and wiped the table with a cloth and a spray bottle of blue liquid. The spray smelled funny, stinging her nose.

She was dubious about hating the food, how could anyone hate food? "Is it alright if we sleep here for tonight? It's getting late, and it would take hours for us to hike back to the Truck."

"No problem. The XJ32 has beds for up to seven people to sleep inside. I'll take the big bed in the front. The benches we're sitting on convert to beds, you two can use those."

"That's great, thanks. Can I check your computer for games and videos now?"

"Go ahead, there's one right there." He pointed behind her to a terminal she missed in the quick search.

"Thanks." She rushed to the small desk and sat on the pull out seat. The computer lit up right away, bothered not at all by the passage of so many decades between uses. She looked to see what Mark and Zack were doing. Zack showed Mark how to fold the benches flat, and removed a pair of blankets from a cabinet, then they sat to talk. She ignored them, far too absorbed in digging into the computer to listen to what was being said. It was several hours before she drifted to sleep in the seat.

The harsh buzzing of a digital alarm was almost deafening within the narrow confines of his bunk space. he slapped a button to silence the alarm without thought, swinging his legs over the edge of the stiff, framed-in mattress, he sat up and stifled a groan, every muscle in his body aching. Why am I sore? Did I train too hard yesterday? He was disoriented and confused, not at all certain what was going on. He was in an XJ32, but could not remember why.

He looked down the length of the cabin, laying unbelieving eyes on two youths in civilian dress. What were a couple of civilians doing sleeping in command vehicle, and on the eve of the invasion? This was no time for some uppity official to bring his kids in for a private tour. He was deciding how best to handle the situation, when the events of the previous day came rushing back to him. For a moment the failure and despair threatened to crush him, but the memory of his embarrassing breakdown strengthened him. *I am an Omega, one of the finest soldiers the Earth has ever produced, and a soldier must be in control of his emotions.* Besides, he suspected his young guests had experienced worse than he could imagine, and they were holding it together fine.

Still, the girl's question was a good one, and not an easy thing to answer. What would he do now? The mission had long ago ended in what he had to characterize as abject failure, everyone and everything he trained so hard to protect was gone, even Anne. What was the point of being a soldier, when there was no military, no country, maybe not even an organized local government? There was not a single soldier for him to regroup with. Was there a need in this time for an ancient military relic like him? Could he still help save the world, even after the apocalypse?

Maybe these two kids could lead him to an answer, they knew this world and its problems. The boy was clearly intelligent, the kind to think things through and plan ahead. He was the solid base of their team, quiet and reserved a good balance to his friend. Kat was harder to pin down. She was friendly and outgoing, and genuinely fascinated by everything. But while on the surface she came across as flighty, a person did not become that good a fighter without hard work and dedication to training. She was far stronger than she looked, his aching neck was testament to that. *Strong or not, she never would have beat me if I hadn't just come out of cryo. One of these days I'll get a rematch.*

I think I will travel with hem for a while, if they'll have me. They talked about fighting robots, that has to mean XRs. If I stick with them, I should be able to break XRs after all. I may have missed the invasion by a year or two, but there are still XRs to waste. Right this moment I should make breakfast, have a hot meal waiting when they wake up.

He passed Kat on the way to the cryo-chef, she had fallen asleep at the computer, her cheek pressed to the keyboard and a blanket draped over her back. With the timer counting down on breakfast, he sought a place to sit. The boy was awake and watching him, the beeping when he programmed the meal was enough to wake the kid, must be a light sleeper.

"Mark, was it?" He spoke softly so as not to bother Kat. They boy nodded. "I have breakfast coming, should we wake Kat.?"

Mark's smile suggested that Zack had told a good joke. "No need, she will wake when she smells the food."

Zack was skeptical, but left it go. The kid knew her better than he did. "Do you know what you're going to do now?"

"We have to go back to White Sheep, that's the ruined village we told you about, and try to figure out where the robots went. The robots captured a lot of the people from White Sheep, dumped them into cages and hauled them away. We are going to find and rescue our friends. We couldn't damage the crabs with the weapons we had, they were not strong enough. But after examining the database in this vehicle, I found the schematics I need to build stronger lasers for the Truck, one's capable of destroying the crabs."

He spoke with conviction, and Zack believed he could do it. This kid was smart, making new weapons based on schematics from the XJ32's computer was not something he could have done. Nor could he have broken the encryption to get those plans. But there were other things he was good at. "I was trained and augmented to fight XRs, and you plan to track some down. Since I have no long-term plans, for now I would like to come with you, if that's okay?"

"I have no objection to that, we are on our way to fight, and you have powerful weapons and specialized training. I say you're welcome to join us, and Kat will almost certainly invite you along any way."

The chime of the cryo-chef signaled that breakfast was ready. Zack converted the beds back into benches, and put cups for the juice on the table. He opened the cryo-chef, removing a tray of sticky doughnuts and a pitcher of juice. The sweet aroma of steaming doughnuts filled the cabin, starting his mouth watering. He placed both on the table, and poured himself a glass of juice.

The cup was not yet to his lips, when Kat was up and walking to table with a drowsy grin on hers. "Those smell ready good, what are they?"

"These are glazed doughnuts, the most common type of doughnut. They're a popular breakfast food where I come from. The liquid is orange juice." He did not bother to describe oranges, surely there were still oranges.

He was not done explaining when Kat snatched a doughnut from the plate, and bit of huge chunk out of it. "Oh." She exclaimed in delight. "They're tasty little round cakes. What a fun idea."

Her reaction was amusing, it was so odd to watch a teenager trying such an everyday thing as doughnuts for the first time. If he stayed with them, it would be interesting to see how his world looked through their eyes. Even after watching Kat inhale the pizza last night, he was surprised when she ate seven doughnuts, to his three and Marks' two. *How is there so much room in her stomach? She couldn't' weigh more than one twenty,* he thought incredulously.

He loaded the empty dishes into the scrubber. "What will you do today?"

"As I said earlier, we have to start by going back to White Sheep village, try to track where the robots went, and follow them." Mark did not sound enamored by their prospects.

Kat nodded her agreement.

"It will take us two or three days to reach the village, and I want to start upgrading our weapons on the way. I expect to be ready to fight the crabs when we find them."

Zack needed clarification. "You've mentioned crabs several times now, I'm guessing they are robots of some kind?" He waited for a confirming nod before continuing. "We had only limited information on XR types before the invasion, and nothing about any crabs. Would you transfer all your data on them to my computer?"

Mark was ahead of him. "When I downloaded your database, I also uploaded ours. Sky formatted everything to work with your file types. I thought it was only fair to trade data."

"Thanks, I'll look it over later. I think we should set off on the clue finding trip to that village of yours right away. I will drive you to your vehicle in the XJ32, and we can all go together." He expected Kat to be happy he was going with them, or at least that his cryo-chef was. After all, another combatant, armed to the teeth, could only aid their cause. But instead, she looked confused.

"I think it's great you want to come with us, and I was going to ask if you would. But how can you drive this big truck anywhere? We have to be forty feet underground, and the only door is way too small for it to fit through."

Zack burst into laughter, realizing how absurd his words must have sounded to them. Without his knowledge of this bunker, they had to think he lost his mind. He held up a hand for patience so he could explain. "Sorry I laughed, I should have told you. There's a tunnel right in front of the XJ32 that leads to the surface, it's one of several emergency exits from the base. It lets out three miles from here. Come on, I'll show you."

Opening the side door, he led them to the wall five feet in front of the XJ32. The exit was so large and well concealed, that it was indistinguishable from the chamber walls. He rapped his knuckles on the metal surface. "This is the tunnel door."

Kat looked from him to the wall, her silence conveying disbelief. "This is commander Zachary Mason, authorization Zeta, one, three, six, bravo. Open the exit door." He stated clearly for the base computer.

"Voice print and authorization confirmed." Said the synthetic voice of the base computer. An amber warning light flashed high on the wall, and an alarm sounded, pulsing harshly. "Exit tunnel door retracting, please stand clear."

A large section of what looked like wall pushed into the chamber two feet, forcing them to take a step back. It slid slowly open parallel to the wall, accompanied by the low clanking of large meshing gears. Five minutes later the door stopped, and the flashing light and alarm switched off. They now stood before a large, dark void, only slightly illuminated by light from the bunker. This was his first time using the tunnel, did the engineers not install lights?

Kat was awed. "Now that's a big door."

"Shall we go?" Zack turned to the XJ32, this time opening one of the doors on the front, and climbing into the spacious cab. There were four swivel chairs mounted to the floor, all of them much bigger than a normal sized person needed, having been designed for use by an Omega in full power armor.

"Go ahead and take a seat." He adjusted the driver's seat to hold him snugly.

Kat claimed the seat to his right, and Mark the one behind her.

Zack tapped an authorization code into a keypad and pressed his thumb to the reader, then turned on the vehicle. The power on diagnostics ran in seconds, the results displaying on the main screen. All systems were operational, no errors reported. Switching on the headlights, he put the XJ32 in drive and eased it into the tunnel, proceeding nice and slow. The glare of the headlights pushed back the darkness, revealing an arched passage twenty-five feet high and thirty-five wide. Two XJ32s could pass each other in the space, although they could lose paint in the attempt. The otherwise plain surface of the tunnel's concrete walls was broken by the steel ribs of support beams every ten feet.

The tunnel was initially straight, and so far as he could tell level, stretching away from the base under forty feet of protective dirt and rock. He feathered the accelerator pedal, crawling forward at a snail's pace of five miles-per-hour. The headlights clearly illuminated the unfamiliar path two or three hundred feet ahead, and he did not want to risk damaging the XJ32 by diving so fast he smashed into a wall on an unseen curve, or hitting a pile of rubble from a tunnel collapse.

The thrum of the XJ32's electric motors vibrated back to them from the walls, joining the basketball thump of knobby tires on the floor. A mile out the tunnel sloped noticeably upward and began to curve, the gradual change designed for rapid egress during an emergency evacuation. Long minutes later the floor leveled off, and they reached the exit. Zack hopped down from the cab and gave his authorization again, thankfully the system was working on this end and the door swung slowly open. Otherwise, he would have had to risk blasting his way out, possibly causing a cave in. He returned to his seat to wait for the door to fully lift out of the way. When the warning light stopped flashing, he drove onto the mountain slope. Stopping on the grass and shrubs, he got out and ordered the door to close. His two passengers joint him, watching the exit swing shut in fascination.

"It looks just like the side of the hill, grass and all." Observed Kat when it was closed.

Mark was on the same page. "That is impressive. It must have taken a lot of work to make."

Zack examined the ersatz hill, trying to see it from their perspective. Such constructs were not that uncommon in his time. "I guess it is well done. I couldn't tell you how long it took the engineers to build through." He turned from the door, looking over the mountainside. There was a large green vehicle not too far off, it was unlike anything he was familiar with. "Is that your truck over there?"

Kat followed the direction of his gaze, spying the vehicle a mile from where they stood. "Yes, that's it. Hey, your secret entrance was really close. It would have saved us a lot of time finding you, if we knew it was here. But we couldn't open it anyway, so I guess it doesn't matter."

"What do you say we return you to it?" He reentered the XJ32, putting it in gear when the passenger door closed. "I have the coordinates to White Sheep village from Sky, but I will follow you there. When you want to stop for food or sleep let me know, and I will stop with you. Sky should have my standard comm frequency."

Mark and Kat got out when he parked next to their strange truck. Whatever the truck started life as, it was heavily modified since. Mark hurried to open a compartment built into the side out the vehicle, and took something small out. He walked to Zack's door holding up the device, he reached through the open window to take it.

"We call these HUDs. We use them to talk to each other, and to display maps and things." Mark touched the HUD he was wearing, and showed Zack how it clipped to his ear. Once on, the device was calibrated to his voice print.

"Thanks." He moved his head to see how it felt, light and hardly noticeable.

"I want to drive for a few hours before we stop for lunch at noon. Your XJ32 looks like it can handle the same terrain the Truck can, so I'll move at a quick pace. If you have any trouble keeping up, tell me on the HUD and I will slow down."

"Agreed, let's roll out." He said mimicking one of this favorite old cartoons.

Mark left without reaction. *I wonder if any of the shows I watch still exist,* he thought sadly.

He trailed the smaller truck swiftly down the mountain, a bit surprised by how fast the custom vehicle moved. The uneven ground did not pose a problem for the odd truck. If the thing was constructed from any vehicle in his time, it was not one he knew, or was too modified to be recognizable. If anything, he suspected that it was put together out of spare parts and scrap, expanded and altered as the need arose. Judging by now well it moved on the mountainside, whoever did the work knew what they were doing.

He had gone on several training exercises near the base in the weeks leading up to the invasion, and the terrain here one hundred and fifty years later was unexpectedly familiar. Somehow he expected the passage of so much time, to have a more profound impact on the area, like time travelers in movies. But his was reality, where mountains usually stayed the same after a century. The wind through the window, and the gentle rocking of the XJ32 over the rugged ground, lulled him into a relaxed state until his mid wondered. The calamity described by general Samson and his new friends must have been terrible, physically altering the planet on a global scale, and decimating the population. How much of the world would be recognize, and how much was totally gone? Are all of the cities gone? All traces of civilization wiped away like Noah's flood? *It's something I will have to see for myself.*

At twelve o'clock Mark's voice came over the comm. "We're going to stop for lunch now. Kat requests that you please make more of your old food for us."

He had no problem with being put in charge of lunch. Truth be told, he was a little afraid of eating food from this world, would it make him sick? "I have the perfect thing."

He parked to the left of their truck, so that the side door to the XK32's cabin faced the smaller vehicle. He walked into the main cabin, opened the side door for his new friends, and programmed the cryo-chef to prepare peanut butter, strawberry jam, and a half a loaf of sliced white bread. He was fairly certain neither Kat not Mark had tried peanut butter, and American kids should all try it. Not that there was an America anymore.

He was putting a pitcher of water on the table, when Kat bounded into the cabin. "What new old food are you making for us?"

"It's called peanut butter and jelly sandwiches, or PB and J for short. We used to eat them all the time, parents fed them to their kids, mine did anyway. And kids usually loved them."

Mark knocked politely on the door frame before stepping inside, and sat at the table.

Kat checked the cryo-chef timer, anxious to know how long she would have to wait. "Lunch will be ready in fifteen minutes. It's peanut butter and jelly sandwiches." She informed Mark as if she was an expert.

Mark addressed a question to Zack. "What is a pee nut?"

"Peanuts are not actually nuts, they're related to beans. And we used to grind them into a cream, like butter. We ate them whole too, mostly roasted and sprinkled with salt."

"Mark, can we make a cryo-chef for the Truck?"

"We have the schematics for it, and the recipe database, so it can be done. But we would have to convert part of our current food storage to a cryo-freezer for the powers. Then we would need to build the desecater device to powderize food. It would take a white to plan and do all of that."

Kat was undeterred. "We can have one soon then?"

Mark sighed resignedly. "I could probably have one ready in a few weeks."

"I can't wait."

Amused by the exchange, Zack waited for them to finish before speaking. "Trying to get rid of me so soon?"

Kat waved a hand in negation. "No, you're welcome to come with us for as long as you want. I just don't want to bother you every time I want to eat food from the distant past."

What am I a museum exhibit? "Do you think the XRs will leave a trail for us to follow?"

"Before the attack on White Sheep I would have said yes unequivocally. The robots we normally encounter evidence a low level of intelligence, attacking people without thought, and would not be expected to hide their trails. But the robots that attacked the village were organized, and the assault was premeditated. The answer to your question, is that I don't know. Even should they try to cover their tracks, it would be difficult to hide the trail of so many metal feet."

"What concerns me, it that it's been days since the attack, the XRs could be far away from your village by now." He regretted the words the moment they left his lips, it was insensitive of him .

"Yes." Said Mark quietly.

They lapsed into silence, Zack considering whether he should apologize. The cryo-chef chimed, giving him an escape. "Who wants lunch?" He asked it lightly, hoping to lighten the mood. He opened a cabinet for plates and cups. When he turned to place them on the table, he knew he had screwed up again. Kat was stuffing a heaping spoonful of peanut butter into her mouth. "No Kat, wait!" The warning came too late, the spoon left her mouth empty.

She looked at him without comprehension, then jumped to her feet in boggle eyed alarm, hands flying to her mouth, her throat convulsing hard in a desperate bid to swallow with a mouth glued shut. Low muffled sounds came from her sealed lips, futile attempts to shout in distress.

"What's wrong?" Shouted Mark, rushing to her side.

Biting back a laugh at her dilemma, Zack acted quickly, catching her hands to stop her from hurting herself. Her strength was shocking, far greater than her size suggested, it was all he could do to hold on without her breaking free. He shouted to get her attention. "Kat! Calm down, you're fine. Take your time, all you have to do is eat slowly."

She looked him in the eyes and stopped struggling, breathing hard through the nose and glaring accusingly at him. She heeded his advice, her jaw moving slowly as she ate the peanut butter, until her mouth was clear. "You should have warned me!"

He felt guilty, but it was hard to keep a straight face all the same. "You don't want to eat that much peanut butter in one bite, or it's like glue in your mouth. You eat a little at a time, or spread it on bread or crackers. Here, watch me do it." He demonstrated by making a proper sandwich, maybe slightly thin on the peanut butter.

She skeptically watched him eat the sandwich, not trusting there was no trick, making one for herself only after she observed no ill effects. She ate cautiously at first, picking up the pace upon finding she really did like it. "Alright, peanut butter is good. Next time I will wait to see how I'm supposed to eat something, before I shove it into my mouth."

It was his turn to be skeptical, but said nothing.

As usual, after overcoming her trepidation, Kat ate more than he and Mark combined. When the food was gone, he loaded the dishes into the scrubber. "We should get moving again. It will take us another two days to reach this village of yours, and the XRs are getting further away by the hour."

"Why do you call the robots XRs?"

He should have anticipated the question, he used the old acronyms without thought, and there was no way people now would know them. "That's what we called them in my time. They are XRs or Xeno Robots, because they're robots from beyond Earth."

Kat did not seem to fully understand, but she nodded.

Mark rose from the table. "You're right about the need to move fast. We will stop again at sundown for dinner and sleep, then start out first thing tomorrow." He left the cabin.

"Thanks, for lunch." Kat gave a last look at the cryo-chef, and followed Mark outside.

Zack buckled into the driver's chair and turned on the XJ32 to pace the smaller truck as it departed. If nothing else, staying with these two would never be boring. To pass the time on the drive, he used the terminal next to his seat to access the data Mark gave him concerning the XRs. He spent the long hours of the day learning what he could about the machines. After all, the better he knew the enemy, the easier it would be to defeat them.

CHAPTER 10

louds had pushed in during the night, heavy, dark clouds that covered the sky to cast the land in dingy gray twilight. The world outside the cab was blurred by rain and wind, washing everything into a muted monochrome that felt an external manifestation of Mark's inner melancholy.

Kat rode beside him in deathly silence, speaking only when required, if then, the barest handful of words since the previous evening. She hardly noticed the breakfast Zack provided form his cryo-chef, eating only one of the fluffy little cakes called blueberry muffins. In truth he could not find it within himself to comment on her behavior, he was in no better condition. He ruminated on what awaited them in White Sheep, circling in an endless loop to the most horrible things he could imagine, no matter how hard he tried to hope for better. Maybe a few of the villagers found a way to escape capture or slaughter, perhaps finding a hole to hide in to evade the machines, and were even now waiting for them in the ruin. He dared not voice such hopes, for fear they would be snatched away on the drear wind.

The village wall was visible now, a misshapen, abbreviated mass of broken brick. Only small lengths of shortened wall remained erect, and those were pitted and blackened by laser fire. Mark parked close to the wall and turned off the Truck, staring blankly through the windshield. The only sound within the close confines of the cab, was the mournful rapping of steady rain on its roof. Each hollow tap drilled an accusation of cowardice into his troubled mind, demanding to know how he could abandon these people to save himself. The tension pushed in on him oppressively, building until he spoke into the quiet of their isolation.

"Sky, can you detect anything alive? I don't care how faint the reading is, I have to know there are survivors."

There was a long pause before Sky answered, far longer than could be necessary for the AI to formulate a conclusion. That alone told Mark everything. "I detect no activity or thermal signatures of any kind in or around the village. There are no biologicals present. I am sorry."

"Zack, we don't see anything out there, we're going into the village now." He said over the comm.

"I understand, I'll be right behind you if I'm needed."

He opened the door, fighting with it as a gust of wind tried to keep it closed. The sound of rainfall on the ground was pervasive, muffling all but the loudest noises. Even the passenger door closing was hushed, adding to the gravity of the moment. He walked with Kat towards the village, his footfalls sinking a little into the saturated dirt beneath what remained of the crushed grass. The closer they got, the more apparent the devastation became. Even through the hazy veil of rain, he could see that most, if not all, of the buildings had fallen. The robots were thorough in their deconstruction, as efficient as only an unfeeling, uncaring artificial mind could be.

Both he and Kat wore hooded raincoats to keep them dry, but they would scarcely have noticed the chilling rain without them. He spotted an opening in the wall, a spot less clogged with shattered brick that may have been the location of the main gate. They sloshed through the downpour, trudging slowly into the ruin under leaden weights, to a place that in another lifetime might have been home.

Zack stayed a respectful distance behind them, keeping thoughtfully silent to give them time and space to mourn their loss. He understood that this was something they must face, or forever be haunted by the specter of what transpired here.

Mark forced himself to look at the village, fought the urge to close his eyes and flee. Struggled with the rationalizations in his mind, telling him it was better to keep hope alive, than to confirm a terrible truth. Devastation surrounded him, infusing him with despair as thick as the sickly, charred smell that coated the back of his throat. Homes were smashed to rubble, mounds of snapped timber and crumbled brick. Fences and sheds trampled to splintered kindling under metal feet. Roads kept proudly clear and full of healthy traffic, were rutted and packed with debris. A formerly pleasant home lay flattened, walls crushed and roof resting nearby, spine broken and forlorn in the dark mud. Recognizable bits of wood from tables and chairs littered the ground, never to host another meal. A device that was a cloth loom, sat in a crumpled heap against the remnants of a wall. Torn flower petals he knew from someone's happy garden were strewn in their path, next to a lump of wood he realized was a basinet.

His knees shook, every muscle in his legs numb. It took all of his strength to put one foot in front of the other, to continue on his path of hurt and sorrow to what used to be the village square. Hoping in almost crazed futility that the shelter was intact, that even a few of their friends had survived, and Sky's sensors had somehow missed them. Kat's face was a frozen, featureless mask, eyes staring resolutely ahead. As if she believed she could deny the reality of her surroundings, that what she did not see, could not therefore be real. Mark steeled himself to examine every broken building, to identify each splintered object he passed.

Setting foot in the village square felt indescribably wrong. This was a place of happiness and joy, crowded mere days before with people dancing and laughing in celebration. He had been with them, shared in their food and song, seen their vigor and merriment. But it was gone, crushed like an insect underfoot. Only something as cold and artificial as a machine, could have defiled a place of warmth so efficiently and completely. The platform was obliterated, its splintered fragments littering the square. The ground, once carpeted with welcoming grass, was a muddy brown mess. There were ominous spots of dark reddish mud that he did not want to identify, or approach. There were limits to his resolve.

And there before him was the centerpiece of his fears, shattering his carefully crafted armor of justification and self delusion, revealed in all its horrific clarity. The village emergency shelter, a bunker of last resort safety and protection, a place thought securely hidden from all threats under ten feet of earth. Its entrance had been secreted beneath the base of an uninviting storage shed, the kind of structure no one would look twice at. The shed was gone, the shelter excavated and exposed. All that was left of the haven, was a ragged hole slowly filing with rainwater. Its earthen covering was heaped nearby, the solid brick and timber roof thrown haphazardly aside and shattered. He felt utterly lost, not a single person was spared, every last one of his friends was either dead, or possibly worse, captives of the mindless mechanical monsters responsible for this evil. He was unable to think, unable to act. He collapsed to his knees in the mud at the precipice, staring sightlessly into the murky brown abyss.

The world turned while his mind was locked in frozen misery, minutes or hours passing unnoticed. When he finally came back to himself, he was on his knees in the mud, his butt resting on his heels. The rain pelted him unheeded, rolling down his back in cold rivulets. Kat stood at his side, her hand placed firmly on his shoulder, a pillar of support in the bleakness. She started resolutely, almost defiantly at the ruins. As if knowing what now was to be done, despite the apparent hopelessness of the situation.

"Are you back with me?" She asked gently.

He nodded numbly.

"Good, then it's time." She spoke with such unquestioning certainty, such fire on conviction, that his crushing sorrow was swept away. He knew again what he must do.

"Yes," he said rising to his feet with her help. "It is time. Time to find our friends and rescue them, and it is definitely time to kill robots."

He clasped her hand and nodded, she looked into his eyes and nodded back, sharing the kind of deep understanding that only close friends and family can experience.

He turned to Zack. "We're finished here. As you heard, we are going after our friends, and we will save them. What about you? Will you go your own way? I wouldn't blame you if you did, not after seeing what the robots did here, knowing what we will face."

Zack nodded in approval. "Count me in. I'm a soldier, my mission was to save the Earth from an XR invasion. I may have missed my war, but I can help win yours.

"Great!" Kat's shout startled him. "Let's bust some bots."

Smiling, he looked at Zack. "Sounds good to me."

"Then we should dry off, and figure out our next move."

They walked away from the dark hole of the past, the future was what mattered.

Dried and warm within the confines of the XJ32 cabin, they sat at the table eating a hot meal of hearty soup, discussing their options. Zack watched the live video feed from Mark's ingenious stealth drone, the image clearer now that the rain had let up. "Our priority has to be tracking the XR raiding party. From what I'm seeing out there, it's not going to be easy. With the rain and all."

He looked at his young friends. He had to admit they were really starting to impress him. They had to be somewhere in their late teens, hardly more than children, yet they were possessed of amazing fortitude. What they went through in that village, was enough to break many of the people he had known, including trained soldiers. But these kids not only pulled themselves together after a crippling tragedy, they chose to do something about it. Had chosen in fact to take the harder path, to rescue their friends from an enemy that had already soundly defeated them. Where did that kind of resolve come from? Was it a product of living in this broken world? Or was it an innate quality possessed by these two survivors? The girl was the biggest surprise to him. She seemed so oblivious and carefree most of the time. Yet when the chips were down, she knew what to say, and more importantly what to do. That ability to keep her mind clear and focused when it counted, would be a great asset when it came time to flight. The pair worked well together, their long years of surviving in a harsh environment, let them function as a better team than many trained military units he had known. How would that dynamic change with a new team member? They would learn soon.

Zack returned to the challenge at hand. "As we saw from the attack on White Sheep village, the XRs are organized. Someone, or something is coordinating and planning their actions. They completely surrounded the target before launching their assault, and that required a considerable investment of time to prepare and execute. They would have deployed far in advance, and communicated with each other to maintain their formations."

Mark thought it over. "So if we follow every pathway from the village, we should eventually find the one that the robots used to take the villagers away."

Kat saw a flaw in his reasoning. "What if they took a different path to leave, than they did to arrive? How do we know which path to follow?"

"Good question. The answer is that we won't know which path they left on, until we find them. That leaves us two choices as I see it, neither of them very positive. We can follow one path and hope for the best, or split up and try both paths."

"It's also possible the XRs took more than two paths, or only one."

"Wait!" Shouted Kat. "I have an idea. We damaged or destroyed a lot of robots, but there are no broken bots out there."

Zack shrugged, not getting her point. "They must have taken the scrap with them, to recycle them into new XRs."

"Exactly, you have all those busted and damaged robots, walking or being carried along, leaving a trail of bits, pieces, and lubricants for us to follow." She concluded smugly.

Mark slapped the table. "You're amazing Kat, of course there will be a trail of scrap. There is no way they could collect or even notice every little nut and bolt. I should have thought of that myself. Sky, have the drone search for metallic scrap, sweep around the village starting at a distance of five miles."

"Search parameters set and engaged. It will be twenty minutes and thirty one seconds for the drone to complete a circuit of the village."

While he was waiting, Zack loaded the dirty dishes into the scrubber and wiped down the table. He returned to his seat to watch the drone's progress with his companions, Kat had surprised him again with that insight about the XR scrap, finding a solution to their problem when he and the obviously intelligent Mark could not. He made a mental note that Kat was not to be underestimated.

The cleaned dishes were put away before Sky issued a positive report. "The drone has located the probable route of egress taken by the robots. Their scrap trail is readily identifiable, and leads to the southeast. "Sky displayed a red arrow on the projected map.

Mark was raring to go. "If there are no objections, I want to go after the robots right away."

"I'm with you."

Kat stood. "Let's get moving."

Mark shrugged on his green raincoat and made for the door, followed closely by Kat in pink. She gave Zack a thumb up and leaped into the drizzle, shoving the door shut behind them.

Zack buckled into the driver's seat and turned on the drive system. When their truck started to pull away, he drove after it, keeping an eye on the muddy ground.

The afternoon sun shone warm and bright, helping to dry the last remnants of moisture from the recent storm. The rain left the bushes and trees a healthy photosynthetic green, and the air smelling fresh. It was two days since they left the shattered vestige of White Sheep, not so much tracking as following in the wake of the robots. The path left by the machine army was laughably obvious, a wide swath of trampled flora visible from a mile distant. Either they did not care if anyone came after them, or they had not considered the possibility that they could, or would, be tracked. The robots had traveled in an unwavering line to the south-east, tramping over hills or trees without care for the difficulty of the terrain. There was no indication that any robots had strayed from the main group. If they were lucky, this meant that when they caught the robots, the villagers would all be present.

They were driving as quickly as they reasonably could, Mark pushing the Truck hard, but not so fast that he risked a time-consuming crash, one that could delay them hours for repairs. They stopped only for the time it took them to eat or sleep, and slept for no more than six hours per night. He and Kat took turns driving and sleeping in the day, and Zack claimed that his omeganess made him need only six hours of sleep. The big question now, was how fast the robots were going. He knew that the normal bipedal robots were capable of twenty miles-per-hour over smooth ground. But the crabs could move substantially faster, and there was no guarantee that these bipedal robots were not upgraded to keep up. He thought it likely, after weighing the variables, that they were all moving around twenty. The crabs would logically stay with their slower escorts. This was not a certainly, and if they separated the crabs might be twice as far away. He was confident that the robots were programmed rationally, and the weaponless crabs would not leave their armed and more versatile anthropomorphic counterparts behind.

Mark had a drone flying ahead of them as they drove, keeping one in the air non-stop, swapping them out to recharge when one was low on power. He was determined to spot the robots before running into them, thereby giving them time to plan in advance rather than rushing in unprepared.

He spent much of the drive working with Sky on upgrading their weapon and defensive systems, both for the Truck and for Kat's armor. They used the database from Zack's XJ32 to find schematics that could be modified for their purpose. When they stopped for sleep, he would start the swarm building or altering their equipment. The output intensity of the Truck's laser turrets was higher, as was that of Kat's wrist lasers. And he doubled the number of crystals in Truck and armor, extending their use, even under the heavier draw.

When time allowed, Mark reviewed the schematics and specifications for Zack's armor. The armor was constructed from a high density allow he had never seen before, something called titamant. The alloy was extremely durable, stronger even than the stuff they used for Kat's armor, and it was not excessively heavy for that strength. It was not light, however, and would not be practical for Kat's armor. Some of Zack's supply might be used to strengthen a few of the Truck's armored body panels, with his permission, the rest had to be reserved for repairs for the Omega armor. Zack's weapon was an oversize hand laser capable of launching explosives. It contained three high-capacity power crystals, and could be slowly charged in the field from Zack's armor, but it would take a prolonged firefight to drain it. The joints of Zack's armor utilized servo motors to enhance the wearer's strength and speed. And it had a jump system much like Kat's flight pack, that propelled it high into the air briefly, or allowed him to run fast for short bursts. The overall design of the Omega armor was brutish and utilitarian compared with Kat's, but despite the size and bulk of the suit, it was surprisingly sleek and appealing in form.

While he was scrolling through the data on Zack's armor, Kat paused her MGP, which she played with increasing distraction as the hunt wore on. "Do you think we're going to catch them? I mean, we've been chasing the robots for days, and have not seen a single bot. only a bunch of flattened plants."

"We're driving faster than most of them should be able to walk, so we're definitely closing on them. We have to be patient. Remember, the robots have been traveling days longer than we have. It may take a little time, but we will outrun them. Or they will stop and we will catch them then."

"I still don't understand why the robots would take people. The only thing they ever do is attack people, or other robots. What could have happened to change them, and why now?"

"I have no theories, but I have been wondering the same thing. Maybe Zack knows something." He opened a comm chanel to the XJ32. "Zack, we were talking about the robots, how strange they are acting. We've never known them to take captives, or to display anything resembling organized behavior. They have only acted violently. Were they different in your time?"

"I was frozen in that cryo-chamber before the XRs arrived on Earth, and we had limited intel on them. Most people only knew that they were coming, that they wanted to destroy us, and that they wanted to take something from us. I was not told exactly what they wanted to take, I don't know if anyone knew. We knew some of the basic XR types, infiltrators, tanks, and HCs, but there were no detailed profiles or schematics. We were pretty much in the dark. The fact that the XRs are kidnapping people for an unknown, but likely nefarious purpose, is troubling."

"Such conjecture is futile. Until such time as we locate the robots and ascertain first hand precisely what their objectives are, we have no way to deduce them. I recommend that we abandon idle speculation, and focus our efforts and energy on overtaking the robots to emancipate the villagers."

"While I agree with you in theory Sky, you need to understand that we flawed biologicals thrive on conjecture and speculation, it keeps us from getting bored or losing our minds. Now, please display a map of the area, and overlay the path of the robots on it. I want to see if we can determine where they are going." The requested map displayed to his right.

"If the robots continue in an undeviating line as they have thus far, they will have reached the coast by now traveling at estimated minimum velocity."

A red line was drawn on the map to indicate the expected course, advancing from White Sheep village to the ocean.

"They're headed for the water plant." Said Kat.

"Looks that way."

Zack was lost. "What is this water plant?"

"The water plant is a water reclamation and desalinization facility, run by a group calling themselves Hydros. They sell and distribute water to anyone who can trade for it."

"Who are these Hydros, and why are they controlling the water supply? Everything I've seen looks green enough, is there a shortage of water I don't know about?"

Sky cheerfully launched into a detailed explanation. "The water plant is operated and controlled by a militaristic group of biologicals called Hydros, led by a Grymal known only as X. The Hydros wear black and red uniforms and are organized in a manner similar to an army complete with ranks. As to the water situation, there is regular rain, providing sufficient water to hydrate local plants and for small groups of people to survive on. Streams and lakes help as well. But for larger settlements with significant farming operations, or flocks of livestock, more water is required. The need for the supplemental water is not great, but it is enough to keep the Hydros in business. They are not excessively greedy, supplying water for any reasonable trade, and they operate pipes that pump water to larger nearby farms and villages. In exchange for this service, they receive food and other supplies from the settlements."

Zack pinpointed a problem with the Hydros' operation. "And what happens when someone who needs water can't afford to pay for it?"

"Then they go thirsty." Said Kat factually. "Sometimes people are attacked by bandits in front of the plant, and the Hydros only watch. If no one claims the bodies, the Hydros dump them into the ocean."

Zack was appalled. "No one helps them?"

"What can they do? Bandits have weapons, and most people don't even have working lasers. And no one will fight the Hydros, who else would run the water plant?"

Zack was not giving up so easily, his sense of justice oddly skewed. "There are enough people to fight these Hydros, to band together and do what's right for everyone or are the people of this time all cowards?"

Kat was not amused by the unjust accusation. "And how will you convince people to band together? To risk their lives, and the lives of their families, for people they don't know? For people would not do the same for them. Were the people in your world better, or braver? Didn't you listen to what I said at your base? What gives you the right to call people cowards, when you have no idea what their lives are like?"

There was a pause from Zack, and an apology. "You're right, I have no business judging people I don't know. And people in my time were not morally superior, not even close. Many ignored the suffering of others, unless it impacted them directly. Now, do you think these Hydros could be working with the XRs?"

The question sucked the breath from Mark's lungs, his first instinct was to deny it outright. "I've never seen robots work with anyone, all they do is destroy. And anyway, I don't think the Hydros would willingly help robots eliminate such a big source of supplies."

"I can understand that, but what if they were being forced to work for the XRs?"

"I suppose that is possible." Mark allowed. "But the question is why?" Zack paused again. "I don't' have an answer to that, but it may not be a coincidence that the XRs are heading in that direction."

"I hope you're wrong." Said Mark fervently.

CHAPTER 11

The sun had long since dipped below the horizon when they stopped for the night. Weary and worn from another day long drive, they ate a quick meal from the cryo-chef, and retired to their beds for an abbreviated slumber. An alarm was set to the wake them in six hours, getting them up before dawn. Mark and Kat slept on fold down bunks mounted to the inner wall of the Truck. The bunks were small, and not the most comfortable things to sleep on, and were therefore used infrequently. Few words were exchanged as they slid onto their bunks in exhaustion, and soon Kat heard Mark's breathing fall into the slow, steady rhythm of sleep. She pulled a small crystal cylinder out of her pocket, turning her treasure over in her hand. *We sure have come a long way since you saved me, and we've been through so much together. All of the things I've seen, good and bad, I wouldn't trade them for anything. What would have happened to me if I hadn't found you that day in the forest? If had given up and let it all end?* She put the crystal away and drifted gently to sleep.

"C o o o ld." Said the girl through chattering teeth. She hugged herself for warmth, huddling in the comparative comfort of her box. It was always cold in her hiding place, a cramped, cave like space with a dirt floor and rotting wood for a roof. The simple jumpsuit she wore was ragged and stained, the once pink and purple cloth had become a dingy, splotched brownish color. It frayed at the edges, the cuffs at her ankles and wrists separating into individual threads, and holes wearing in the knees from crawling through the narrow opening that led outside. Her shoulder length black and purple hair was tangled badly, encrusted with greasy dirt, and flaked with dried blood where she banged her head two days ago. Her tail was a muddy bedraggled mess trailing limply behind her, and itching fiercely.

The world outside her hiding place was covered in a thick blanket of snow The icy air froze her nose and fingers in seconds if she stuck them out. She could bring the snow into her hiding place to melt for water when she was thirsty, but food was another matter. The very first thing she could remember in her whole life, was waking up here in her box. The box was dry and soft and kind of warm after she sat in it for a while. When she woke in her box there was food in it with her, a bunch of sweet, tasty bars wrapped in sleeves. But they were so good that she ate them all up without thinking, and now she had no food at all. She was so hungry she thought she would die.

She had to find food, but she was afraid to go outside, bad things could be out there. All she could see from the opening was snow, and smashed buildings, and lots of trees, it was scary. She had no idea where she was or she got here. She did not even know her own name, in fact she could not remember anything at all from before waking up in her box. That seemed strange to her, she was sure most people should know their own name, right? *Why can't I remember? Why was I left here all alone? Why are there no other people anywhere?* She was full of difficult questions, and it was too hard to think clearly. She was cold, and confused, and terribly hungry.

It was three days since she finished the last food bar, three whole days with nothing to eat. Her stomach felt like a huge, empty hole in her middle. She had to go look for food today. If she waited any longer she was sure to die. Gathering her courage, fueled greatly by hunger, she crawled through the small opening to the scary outside. She paused just inside, letting her eyes adjust to the glare of snow brightened sunlight, and listened for the sound of danger. She was not clear on what danger sounded like, but was sure she would know it when she heard it. She scrabbled into the icy snow, her arms flailing in the loose pack to keep her balance. She trudged awkwardly along, looking cautiously at anything and everything in sight her legs sinking to the knee with each numbing step.

Her surroundings shared a haunting sameness under the cover of snow. The decayed and broken structures were indistinct shapes, dark shadows hiding their interiors where some of them were still standing. A building close by had an open doorway, the entrance black and scary against a backdrop of pure white. But she knew that her best chance of finding food would be inside, away from the biting cold. She hiked slowly to the doorway and peeked in. The interior was black after the blinding snow, it was impossible to see more than a rough outline of a room. She stepped into the house, feeling instant relief from the snow on her legs. She rubbed feeling into her numb shins and feet, the room gradually resolving itself to her eyes. The empty rectangle stank of rot and poop, wrinkling her nose in disgust. There were little black pellets all over the floor, and it looked rotten and old. Water dripped steadily from above, and paint curled in long gray strips from the walls.

Taking small, measured steps across the decaying floor, she cringed at every creak of her light footfalls. When nothing rushed out to get her, curiosity began to overcome her fear. One room was fall of cabinets and a couple of rusted metal boxes big enough for her to hide in. she opened all the doors and examined very space she could reach, but there was nothing to eat. She searched room after room in the house, but as the minutes increased, her hopes dwindled.

When the final room was searched, and found foodless, she returned to the front room and sighed dejectedly. All that work and she still had no food. What if there was nothing to eat in the whole town? It was way too cold to go anywhere else. She plopped onto the floor in defeat, not knowing what to do next.

There was a loud crack, for a second the world went crazy and her stomach was in her chest. Then her back slammed painfully into a hard surface. Dim light filtered on her from the floor above, and she understood what happened. Before she could berate herself too badly for being stupid, a pained squeaking came from nearby. A large rat was impaled on a splinter of wood from the broken floor. She picked up the injured animal by its hairless tail for a better look, and the mean little creature twisted around to bite her hand. Angry, she swung the rodent hard at the concrete floor. There was a sickening crunch, and then silence.

She started to feel bad about killing the poor rat, tears welling in her eyes. Then she smelled the fresh blood and hunger took over, her mouth watered and her stomach grumbled. The dead rat was warm in her hand, and the blood smelled really, really good. She tore into the animal ravenously, quickly devouring the fresh meat. When she was done, she methodically picked the bones clean, determined not to waste even a little of the precious food.

She tossed away the white and pink bones, sat back on her heels, and belched contentedly. It felt good to have a full tummy again. A faint skittering in the darkness had her smiling, she found a food supply, and would back tomorrow for her next meal.

Ready to return to her hiding place for a nap, she felt her way around the edge of the unlit basement, looking for a way out. She eventually stumbled into stairs leading upward. The door at the top was jammed, blocked by something that would not let it open. She did not remember seeing the door when she explored the house. She kicked the old wood until there was a hole she could squeeze through. It turned out that the door led straight outside, and was nailed shut under a board.

She trudged through the freezing snow, hurrying to her hiding place before she got too cold. At the entrance she cleaned the blood from her face and hands in the snow, shivering hard when she was done. She crawled inside, brushed herself off, and climbed into her box. Once she was comfortably settled in, she pulled her treasure from a pocket on the jumpsuit. She found her treasure in that same pocket when she first woke. It was a crystal cylinder as long as her hand, a pretty translucent green, and it was the most beautiful thing she ever saw. It had to be very important, why else would it have been given to her? One day she would figure out what it was, and that would lead her to her family, she knew it would. Placing her treasure back in its pocket, she curled up tightly in the box and slept.

For the next several weeks she spent her days happily exploring the ruined town that was the breadth of her world, in between hunting the rats and bugs that were her food. There were days when she found nothing at all of interest. But on good days, she would discover something fun or useful, she liked those days best. She brought her prizes to her hiding place, where she could take the time to look them over, making a game of trying to figure out what they were. Then she sorted them by size, color, and shape. She built a large collection of tools like hammers and wrenches. Unmatching dishes, knives, and cooking utensils. And other less readily identifiable objects. But her really favoritest thing, was a small bedraggled pink horse.

She spent endless hours with pinky, sometimes passing whole days in play, making him dance or run across the dirt floor. She talked to pinky all the time, even though he was not a big talker himself. They had parties and went on adventures together, like the time pinky helped her slay a dragon that threatened their home. Pinky was her bestest any only friend. She searched diligently for more friends to play with, but there did not seem to be any. She was more cautious inside the decaying structures, walking lightly and staying close to walls. She did not want to fall through another floor and be hurt again. When she wanted food she carried a hammer to hit rats with, so they did not bite her.

As weeks stretched into months, she got more and more lonely. At first she was sure that whoever left her here would come back later for her. After all, they had left her in the warm box with food and her pretty treasure. But it was slowly becoming clear that no one was coming for her.

Where were all the people? Were there any people left in the whole world? She wondered one day while staring out of a shattered window at the empty, broken town. *I don't wanna be alone no more*, she thought crying herself to sleep that night. Day after increasingly dreary day she withdrew further into herself, no longer exploring the town or playing with her prizes, or her friend. Trying not to feel anything at all. She left her hole less frequently, and then only for food and water. Some days she could not even rouse herself to ease her hunger, an empty stomach bothering her less than the deeper pit of loneliness. Her thoughts turned inward, she started to understand that there was something wrong with her, that she was unwanted or unloved. What if they abandoned her because she was defective, and no one could stand the sight of her? Maybe because she had ears and a tail like a cat, that was not normal, was it?

More time passed, and with it the weather changed, slowly growing warmer. The snow was gone now, replaced by rain and mud, and the bugs and rats wandered the town freely. She was no longer physically cold, but the heating of the world did nothing to warm her increasingly cold thoughts.

She had to be a bad person, she must have done something so horrible, that she needed to be left all alone in this broken place, to prevent her from harming anyone ever again. She was really bad, she had to be, that was why the birds and little animals ran away if she got too close. They knew she was bad, and did not want to be near her. *What did I do? What was so wrong that I had to be sent away?* She thought huddling in her box one night, not caring that she was sore and itchy all over. Not caring that she was starving. Not even certain she wanted to wake in the morning.

"All I want's a friend. I promise I won't be bad no more, just please let me have a friend." She whispered weakly as a dreamless sleep overcame here.

She awoke in darkness, how many hours she slept was uncertain. She stood in her box, groggily wondering what brought her awake. Then she heard it, a strange chirping followed by a loud bang. In moments there were more chirps and crashes, a lot of them. Were there huge birds out there breaking things?

She crawled from her hole, her confusion only heightening in the open air. There were bright red flashes in the forest, the lights coming from the same direction as the sounds.

She was so entranced by the strange spectacle, that it overrode her caution, and she walked toward the lights unable to tear her eyes from them. She had never before ventured beyond the edge of the little town that was all she knew, but she did not so much as slow her advance as she left it behind. The lights were far ahead of her and she was weak with hunger, but she moved onward without pause. By the time the light and sounds stopped, the sky was brightening with the rising of the sun. The lights and sounds had gone, but on she walked. Driven by a need deeper than hunger or fatigue, a compulsion she could not have identified had she considered it. Dawn was lightening the cloudless sky, and the usual birds chirped merrily to celebrate a fresh day. In the light of morning, she could see smoke rising above the trees ahead of her, and she went right for it. She did not want to miss whatever she might find.

Hours later her legs burned in protest from overuse and insufficient food, making her steps less stable, but no less determined. There was a sniffling from the trees to her right, and she made quietly for the noise, wondering almost desperately what it came from. Then she passed a tree and saw it, the most wonderful sight she thought she would ever lay eyes on. It was a person, a real live person, there were still people in the world. Leaning slumped against a tree ten feet ahead of her, was a small, green haired boy of about her same age. He looked away from her, staring toward the smoke and crying.

Immense joy surged in her at not being totally alone in the world, while at the same time an icy tendril of fear curled around her spine. She was terrified that he would run when he noticed her, like all the little animals did. Tiptoeing as quietly as she could, she stalked glacially closer to the boy. She wanted a better look at him, to absorb every detail. She wondered what happened to make him cry, it was not right for him to have to be so sad. She wished with all her being to go to him, to do something to comfort him and make it alright. But she feared he would run away in disgust, and leave her all alone again.

She watched him silently for a long time, frozen with indecision and fear. Her body betrayed her, her tummy grumbled noisily to give her away. She dropped to hands and knees scared. Startled, the boy stood and spun to see what the noise was. His cheek was bruised, and dried blood crusted his face where it had run down from a wound on his head. The skin around his eyes was red and puffy from crying. She ached to comfort him, but dared not move.

He stared at her out of bleary, bloodshot eyes. Mucus ran freely from his reddened nose, and he sniffled loudly. He was still the most beautiful sight in all the world. She watched him, unmoving save for the slight, uncontrollable twitching of her tail and ears. She waited painfully for him to react, fully expecting him to flee in terror and repulsion, and wanting to watch him for every last second until he disappeared forever.

Instead, wiping his gloopy nose on a sleeve, he smiled uncertainly at her. "Good cat." His voice squeaked. He raised his hands palms up reassuringly. "S' okay, I won't hurt you. Good cat."

"Me?" She croaked hoarsely, not believing her ears, certain she was dreaming, that her mind was playing a cruel trick on her. "Me good cat?" She asked, tentatively straightening up. If this was a dream, let her never wake.

The boy nodded, that glorious smile never leaving his face. "Yes, you silly. Cats good, I like cats." He spoke the words without understanding the profound impact they had on the scruffy girl.

Smiling at him now, warmth blossoming in her chest, she asked. "Is your family near?"

His own smile fading, he looked toward the smoke. "No." He said quietly. "I'm all alone now."

She had to make him smile again, needed it the way plants needed rain. "Me too, I'm all alone."

He looked at her, his eyes boring into her as if reaching a critical decision. "My name's Mark, what's yours'

Not wanting to look stupid, she said the first thing that popped into her mind. "Kat, my name's Kat."

His smile returned, warning her to the core. "That's great."

Her tummy growled again, and she grinned sheepishly.

He dug something from his pocked and held it out to her. "You want food. Kat?"

Se stretched out an arm hesitantly, still worried that this was all a dream, and it would all vanish at a touch. He nodded encouragingly, and she took the food from his hand. biting into the soft lump, she smiled and chomped it down rapidly. "That was tasty, it's sweet and chewy like the food bars from my box. Thanks lots." She was proud of herself for remembering her manners, even though she did not know where she learned them.

"You're welcome, Kat." He fixed her with that serious stare, making her worry again. "Um, since you're alone, and I'm alone, you want to be friends? We could stay together so we won't be alone, be like a family."

Her throat tightened, she could barely breath. Tears ran down her dirty cheeks, leaving tracks in the grime.

Not understanding her reaction to his offer, he rushed to apologize. "I'm sorry, I didn't mean to make you cry. I just thought it would be nice to be friends."

A semi hysterical giggle tore from her and she lunged at him, nearly knocking him to the ground as she wrapped her arms around him in a tight hug. She did not want to let him go, still not quite believing this was real. "Yes!" She whispered with all her heart. She found it, what she had so desperately wanted through her empty months in the broken town. The one thing she had not dared to wish for in the miserable depths of her lonely heart. It was hers now, she had found a family.

Gray predawn light filtered lazily though the windows of the Truck, easing her into the waking world. She sat up on the bunk, and swung her feet to the floor. *We'll reach the water plant and the ocean today*, she thought stretching out the night's kinks. She put on her boots, smiled, and left the Truck, filled with warmth from her pleasant dream, her most cherished memory.

Mark's bunk was empty, he was already up and making breakfast, and had let her sleep a little longer. *He was like that, always knowing what needed to be done, and always knowing what to say to make everything alright*, she thought fondly. Outside, she breathed in the cool morning air, and looked for Mark. She found him sitting with Zack and eating breakfast.

"Morning Kat, we'll arrive at this water plant in a few hours, and If we're lucky the XRs will be nearby."

She nodded at him.

Mark handed her a plate of food. "Eat up Kat, today we get our friends back."

Her smile widened, he always knew the best thing to say.

CHAPTER 12

Sunlight sparkled and flashed in Zack's viewfinder, reflecting off of every glossy surface I the metal and concrete expanse of the Water Plant, hitting his eyes with renewed intensity at each shift of his digital binoculars. He had to concede that it was a genuinely impressive facility, by far larger than he anticipated. It was big enough in truth, to have been constructed before the invasion, and likely was. The people of this time almost certainly did not have the knowledge or expertise required for a project on this scale, and they would have no need to process so much water, not with the severely reduced population and obliterated infrastructure. There were many facilities of this size in his time, not only water reclamation plants, but also solar arrays, wind farms, and any number of manufacturing complexes. The plant had to be a mile and a half wide, and a mile deep. There were buildings inside as much as seven stories tall. Streets sectioned the complex, wide enough for two big trucks to pass each other side by side. The storage tanks alone contained the water to supply a large city for a week, and he estimated the desalinization pools were sufficient to keep up with that demand.

Huge pipes ten feet tall extended from the plant in several directions, disappearing into the ground after a quarter mile. These pipes, he was informed, were for the Hydros to pump water to nearby villages who traded with them. How was all of this powered?"

The plant was unexpectedly well defended for a civilian installation. There was a twenty foot high concrete wall around the immediate perimeter, and a hundred feet outside of that was a chainlink fence topped with concertina wire. There were large gates in the fence and wall lining up with streets inside the plant. Each gate was guarded by a pair of armed men wearing black uniforms accented in red. More black clad men patrolled the fence line, some of them on foot, others riding small, armed all-terrain vehicles with four seats and thick roll bars. Mounted to the top of the wide wall, were laser turrets spaced at strategic intervals.

The largest entrance was centered along the front face of the plant, surrounded by eight guards and a laser turret on the wall on either side.

Outside of this entrance was a massive tank of water manned by Hydros. A long line of people with empty containers waiting to be filled, stretched away from the tank a half mile. Most of them clustered in small armed groups, transporting their containers on wagons or carts.

The main gate opened outward, and a large tanker truck rolled out escorted by four of the ATVs loaded with Hydros. The convoy drove away from the plant heading northward for a delivery. The scope of this operation was far beyond anything he had imagined, he had expected a world filled with tiny settlements and tribal people, like the movies promised him. He should have guessed that civilization was not so easy to eradicate, it was actually comforting.

Extending for over a mile from the fence, was a flat, dry expanse of dirt and gravel clear of all plants, and broken only by the paved roads. There was no way for anyone to sneak up on the plant, if the sentries were awake. Whoever designed the defenses down there knew what they were doing, or maybe this was the result of hard experience.

On the way to the plant was a small hill a bit over two miles out, behind which they parked the trucks to keep them from being seen by the Hydros. Unless, that is, the Hydros sent a patrol over. He, Kat, and Mark were laying on their stomachs atop the hill, hidden amongst the leaves of bushes and trees, surveying the plant.

Frustratingly, the XR trail had disappeared five miles back, where it intersected with a road leading to the plant. There was no more trace of them all the way here, not one nut or bolt. Even worse, there was nothing to indicate the XRs were anywhere in the area, or that they ever had been. There were no XRs, no trail, and the Hydros went about their business as if ever thing was normal. By all appearances the XRs simply vanished into thin air, maybe he should add magic tricks to their list of new abilities.

"I don't see a single blasted thing to tell me the XRs were ever anywhere near the place. Are your sensors getting anything?"

Mark exhaled sharply, an indication of his annoyance. "With all of these people moving around, and all the metal and machinery in there, I couldn't find a robot unless it stood on the wall and waved at me. And even then, only if I was looking at the right part of the wall when it did."

Kat glanced at the display. "Can robots wave? I'd like to see that."

Zack was never quite sure if Kat was serious when she said things like that, but decided silence was the best response. "With the XRs no longer leaving bread crumbs for us to follow, our only option is to pick them up on our sensors, or if we're really lucky spot their trail or the XRs themselves."

"I'm going to have the stealth drone fly a grid-based search pattern around the Plant. I will have it start at a distance of three miles, and move outward from there. That should be far enough from the plant that the Hydros won't spot it. If the robots are moving away from the plant, we should be able to locate their trail. At the very least, when they leave the road and start trampling plants again. Of course if it turns out they are hiding in there somewhere," he waved a hand at the water plant. "Then there won't be trail at all."

"Or they could have gone out over the ocean, or under it if they're waterproof."

"Way to dampen our spirits." Said Kat dryly.

"I'm going to start the search." Mark crawled back from the top of the hill, returning to his truck.

Zack watched him go for a moment, before putting his face in the binocular again. In the viewfinder the entire facility seemed extremely well maintained, almost unnaturally so. It looked practically new from what he could tell at this distance, better cared for than a similar complex would have been in his time. How were these Hydros able to repair everything that broke? Where did the replacement parts come from? Systems inevitably failed with age and use, and parts had to come from somewhere. There was something not quite right with this place, and he wanted to know what it was.

He heard Mark scrabbling up the hill behind him.

"I programmed the search pattern and launched the drone, it will take a few hours to complete. The farther out it flies, the more ground it will have to cover, and the longer it will take. Sky will alert us if the drone finds the robots, and we can catch the live feed." Mark settled into the bushes, his hair snagging on twigs.

"Have you noticed how the plant is a little too perfect? It could have been built a year ago."

Mark peered at Sky's projected images with renewed interest. "I never thought about it. But now that you mention it, the plant does look too clean and orderly. The Hydros don't strike me as the obsessive cleaning type. And the only way they could maintain the machines, is with the use of nanomachines. There is no possibility of having a stockpile of replacement parts that could last this long."

"Could they be using some kind of maintenance robots, may be XRs, to clean and repair it?"

Shock was plain on Mark's face, that was something he had not considered. "No one sane would try to use robots for anything, the only robots we encounter try to kill us." He hesitated, an idea forming in his mind. "I suppose they could have small cleaning and repair robots, but the Hydros would have to hide the things. No one likes robots."

Kad disagreed. "I like robots, they're fun to destroy. And sometimes they come in nifty shapes and do funny things."

"Like I said, no one sane."

Holding the binoculars to his eyes, Zack panned across the area to continue his recon. A group of people with a horse drawn cart, were moving toward the water plant on one of the roads. The cart was filled with wooden crates of food, and empty barrels. The men, armed only with simple knives and clubs, looked worn and tired. It must have been a long walk to get here, and they were in need of a good rest. He was panning away from the weary travelers, when movement a few dozen yards from them caught his eyes.

Shifting the lenses to center on the motion, there was another group emerging from a stand of trees, where they had lain in wait. This new group was a dozen men in non-descript brown clothing and light body armor. From the way they moved, all were in good physical condition. Cloth masks covered every face, and they were armed with lasers, knives, and axes. This was no trading party peacefully seeking water, they were more like highwaymen out of an old western, all that was missing were horses. One of them drove a four seater off road vehicle.

The man at the reins of the horse cart must have heard the bandits, because he suddenly urged the horse to go faster, snapping the reins hard. The men of his escort ran in a failing attempt to match the cart. The ATV group, seeing their prey flee, revealed their intentions by opening fire in the direction of the cart. They were too far off yet for accuracy, and their shots mostly missed, but that would not last.

Zack was not about to stand by and let something like this happen, not when it was in his power to stop it. He stood, all thoughts of hiding forgotten, and set the Omega armor case in front of him. He brought the case up here in the unlikely event he would need it, and was now glad of his foresight. He punched his code into the keypad on the case, and pressed his thumb to the reader. The case came to life, expanding upward in front of him into a roughly human shape, clattering metallically as it moved. He stepped into the open back of the armor, slotting his feet into the metal boots. When he was inside, the armor closed around him, sealing his body in with a mechanical ratcheting. Fully cocooned from the outside world, he was blind and deaf for a second until the audio and visual systems engaged. Pale blue lights illuminated in strips along the dark gray armor's surface, lending it a sort of ghostly quality. The heavy armor doubled his already substantial bulk, adding four inches to his height.

The armor was remarkably sleek in appearance, not at all blocky and utilitarian like typical military power armor. The mid-section, around his abdomen, was scalloped in layers, allowing him to bend and twist freely at the waist. The shoulders, hips, and knees were enlarged by strength and speed enhancing servo-motors. The multi-purpose Omega weapon was clipped to his thigh, a combination laser and explosive ordnance launcher. The front of the helmet framed a wide silver faceplate.

He glanced over the power up diagnostic readouts, everything was in the green, further testing would have to be done in the field. He looked at his companions. Kat was decked out in fanciful purple and pink power armor with exaggerated cat ears, and an alloy clad tail. It was smooth, stylized, and feminine, unlike anything he had seen outside a big budget movies. He felt like a tank in comparison. "I'm going to help those people."

"Obviously." Kat launched skyward.

"Show off." He grumbled power dashing at full speed after her. His armor's jump system could propel him forward, boosting each stride to a power armor record of twenty miles-per-hour for short bursts. Because she was flying so much faster than he could run, Kat would arrive at the fight before him. Examining the numbers on his visor HUD, he estimated that it would take him a good thirty seconds to close within firing range of the bandits, but his weapon was already in this hand, he would give these people all the help he could.

The cart took a laser hit, a streamer of smoke trailing from a charred burn on the side. One of the escorts was down, lying on the ground unmoving.

"Come on, move." Zack urged his armor, pumping his legs hard. This whole situation was surreal to him, he never expected to be doing these sort of things. Here he was, fighting off masked bandits to protect townsfolk on their way to the watering hole. There was nothing in his training to prepare him for this. He was supposed to be fighting XRs, or enemy soldiers, not playing cowboys and bandits with men in cloth masks.

Laser fire rained from the clear sky as Kat shot by overhead, pink laser fire. The unexpected attack paused the bandits' assault on the cart, to redirect their attention to this new antagonist. Kat landed in a crouch a short distance from the bandits, putting them between her and Zack, a classic pincer attack. He approved of the tactic, wondering where she learned it. The bandits fired at her, having difficulty landing hits on her compact crouched form, but showing discipline and accuracy that spoke to training.

Kat returned fire with incredible accuracy, displaying a level of skill that put his to shame. She destroyed their lasers one after another, without hurting the bandits beyond a burnt hand. Melting the final enemy laser, she charged into the bandits, punching and kicking them with more speed than he had ever seen, even from the fastest Omega. Three bandits were out of the fight by the time he arrived. He put away the Omega weapon and entered the fray, quickly downing an enemy with a measured blow to the back of the man's head. The collapse of a companion drew the attention of other bandits, shifting their focus from Kat to him. Four of the closer bandits came at him, hacking with axes and slashing with knives. Knowing that ordinary hand weapons could not so much as scratch his armor, he ignored the blades to concentrate on downing the men without killing them. His training as an Omega had been to save humanity and the world, he had no desire to kill people. But that did not mean he was opposed to roughing up a few dirt bags every now and again.

Deflecting a blow from an axe blade with his forearm, he punched lazily at the bandit. Surprisingly, the man dodged his punch to land a kick on his thigh. Grunting at the unexpected hit, he took a step back to reevaluate this opponent. After a moment of trading blows, it was clear that these men were trained in military style hand-to-hand combat, brutal and effective if not pretty. Between that and knowing how to shoot, these men were no simple bandits. They displayed a competent level of skill and fought as a team, not just a bunch of individuals in a brawl. They were not bad in his estimation, but they were no Omegas. Using his genetically and mechanically enhanced strength and speed, he brushed aside a knife thrust, and gabbed a bandit by the shirt. He hurled the man into one of his buddies, and both men hit the travel had.

When the next bandit charged in blindly, he pivoted on his hip to kick the man's torso, toppling him with a crack that implied at least one broken rib. He stared at the fourth man with hands on his oversize hips, watching the guy back away nervously. Obvious fear shown in the bandit's eyes at facing an enormous, armor-clad warrior alone, but neither did he want to flee like a coward and leave his companions to their fate. An admirable sentiment, even if it was from a criminal. Taking advantage of the bandit's indecision he charged in, easily knocking the man's attack aside to deliver a blow to his head. The man collapsed limply.

He tried to find another opponent, the first four barely counting as a warmup, but all the rest were out of commission. Kat stood watching him helmetless, her gaze evaluating. Much to his disappointment the fight was over, she had only left him four guys.

She smiled at him, impressed. "Well, mister giant soldier guy, it looks like you really can fight."

Removing his own helmet, he smiled back. "Well, miss flying Ninja girl, you're not bad yourself." He counted the downed bandits. "You could have left me one or two more."

"Sorry, it was so much fun, they were all down before I knew it. I don't think these guys will cause more trouble anytime soon. We should leave them here to bake in the sun, while we check on the cart people, see if they need more help." Without waiting for a response, she flew off again.

Smiling crookedly, he jogged to the bandit ATV. Figuring out the basic controls, he drove after her. He reached the cart slightly before Mark pulled up in his truck, and Kat was already tending to the man who was shot. His injury was only a minor graze to the shoulder, it would heal in days. None of the other men had visible injuries, though most were winded and panting from their flight from the bandits.

Up close he could tell that the cart had taken only slight cosmetic damage, the shallow scorching on the wooden slats no longer smoked, the beam had not penetrated the boards. The cart driver, a sinewy little fox Grymal, held the reins to his sturdy horse tightly, watching the newcomers warily. The four men of the escort, including the wounded man, were average humans. They had the healthy muscular appearance of men who toiled daily at physical labor, and who got enough to eat without being fat. They wore simple brown and tan clothing and boots.

One of the men, who was older than his companions with hair more gray than brown, stepped forward protectively. He looked at the three of them in turn and probably because he was the largest, addressed Zack as if he was the leader. "I am called Alex, and my friends and I hail from a small farm two days from this place. You have our thanks for driving off the thieves." Alex hesitated a moment, as if afraid his next words might offend his clearly powerful benefactors. "But we have little to offer you in payment for your aid, and what we do possess is needed in trade to the Hydros for water."

Zack stared at the man in momentary confusion, what was this talk of payment and needing what they had for trade? Then it dawned on him, the guy was afraid they wanted the farmer's goods like the bandits did, but this was no extortion ring. "Relax guy, we did'nt save you for a reward. We are well supplied, and don't need anything from you. We saw that you were in trouble, and we were in a position to help, that's all."

Upon hearing that he was truly safe, Alex smiled warmly and extended an arm in greeting. Zack clasped the proffered arm and return the smile

"Then your help is welcome indeed." Alex introduced his men, who looked relieved, and greetings were exchanged or all around. When the polite chatter died down, Zack said, "you and your men should head to the water plant and get in line. The three of us will catch up with you later. We have business to finish the bandits."

"As you say, we should get our water while there is light in the day." Alex and his friends left them for the water line, and Zack turned to the bandits. "Now let's see if these punks have anything to tell us."

"Sounds good." Said Mark

Kat joined him in the ATV, always on the Prowl for new fun, and he drove to the bandits with Mark trailing in his truck.

Blades were scattered over the gravel where they fell, not yet reclaimed by the bloodied and bruised bandits. The weapons may be harmless to his or Kat's armor, but would be a threat to future victims. "Kat, give me a hand rounding up the weapons and gear, would you?"

"Sure."

It did not take them long to police the gear, and when they were finished, they had a small mound of weapons, armor, and even boots. The boots were Kat's unique contribution, and he thought it was a nice touch. Many of the bandits were regaining consciousness, moaning and cursing in pain. Some of them were slowly hobbling away barefoot across the hot gravel, cutting their feet on the jagged rocks.

Zack watched the low-speed escape. "Did you notice anything strange about these guys?"

Kat thought it over, her head tilting to one side, hands resting on her hips. "For one thing, they were pretty good fighters compared to most people I've fought. And they dress better too, all in the same clothes and armor. And it looks new."

"That's it exactly. They were well trained and worked together as a unit, dressed like one too." He looked to Mark. " Do you know of any military type group that would have the resources and knowledge to train and equip troops like this?"

Mark's head shook. "I don't know anyone who is training and out fitting their people as an army, except for the Hydros and I've never heard of such highly organized banditry."

"I'm with you, these petty thug types tend to be stupid and disorganized. There's something fishy about these guys. Why go to all the trouble of organizing people, to steal food from farmers?" He went to the nearest bandit, lifting the man off of his feet with one hand. "Alright dirt bag, who are you morons, and why did you attack these people?"

The idiot sneered smugly. "You will regret messing with us, you have no idea who you're dealing with."

A strange reaction from a thief, the man was not scared at all, he was way too confident. But Zack had a plan. "Why don't you enlighten me then?"

"I'll tell you nothing."

That was the answer he expected. He covertly removed a small device from a compartment at his waist, and carefully planted it on the bandit with a fake slap to the arm, fake but hard. He grunted in only partially mock disgust, and tossed the bandit. "Get lost, loser."

Dirt bag joined the last of his groaning friends in painfully shambling away.

"Why did you let him go? They might attack more people." Kat was more curious than upset.

He watched bandits leave, waiting until they were out of earshot to answer. "I implanted moron with a micro tracker while I pretended to interrogate him. His movement will be monitored and logged by my computer, and in a day or so he'll lead us to their lair." He started loading bandit gear into the ATV.

Kat grinned

Mark approved. "That's quick thinking. It should be much more effective than trying to force them to answer questions."

"Shall we see how our new friends are coming with their water?"

"Lead the way." Zack remounted the ATV, and followed behind Mark and Kat to the plant. They stopped short of the line of people waiting for water, and got out to watch the process.

Each group of customers brought their own containers for the water, and varied in number from four to fifteen people. There was no standard for the type or size of containers. Most had barrels or tanks loaded in the back of a cart or wagon. One group brought a huge tank with wheels mounted to it, pulled by a team of bulls. If people had cows, then there should be hamburgers, although he had yet to see anything resembling a fast food joint. When a group reached the front of the line, they presented whatever they brought in payment. The Hydro accepted the goods, food, clothing, and tools every time, regardless of quantity or quality. As Mark said, the Hydros were not that greedy, or picky. The goods were transferred to a large truck by the Hydros, and with payment taken, they pumped water into the provided containers. Depending on the payment a container might not be filled to the top, though not far from it. The customers would then depart with their water, and the cycle would begin anew. Everything was run with the smooth efficiency of long practice.

Seeing that it would be a while before Alex's group had their turn at the tap, Mark suggested they eat lunch. Mark insisted on preparing a meal with actual food from their stores, and despite his misgivings, Zack was determined to eat it, out of curtsey if nothing else. He returned his armor to storage configuration, and dumped the more than four hundred pound case into the back seat of the ATV. *I think I'll keep this thing, with a few upgrades it will be really useful, not to mention fun.*

Mark and Kat had a table on the gravel, with an electric cooktop and a frying pan on it. Mark was browning slices of meat, which Kat placed on bread with cheese, not every slice making it to the bread. The food smelled good, and Zack there and then resolved never to ask what kind of meat people in this time served him, there was a good chance he would be happier not knowing. They ate the grilled, melted cheese sandwiches, while observing the water filling station. It was probably a bad tactical move to sit in the open in front of what could be an enemy fortification, but it was a little late to hide now, after the show they put on with the bandits. An hour later the table and dishes were packed away, and Alex's group was having their turn at the pump. The filling went fluidly, and soon they were leaving.

Alex led his people to them. "Hello friends, we will be returning to our farm now. We want to put distance between us and the water plant before nightfall." His eyes flicked to the ambush site. "Thank you again for your help."

"Do you need an escort to the farm, or will you be okay on your own?"

Alex looked openly to where the bandits attacked his group, they had slunk into a hole somewhere. "I believe we will have no further problems. But thank you for the offer."

On impulse, Zack plunked the bandit loot into Alex's cart, overriding the man's protests. "Good luck to you and your farm." Zack held out an arm.

Alex clasped it. "And to you." Formalities complete, they moved south across the gravel.

Zack leaned on the ATV, watching Alex's group until they were out of sight. "We should head to the XJ32, and wait for your drone to find the XRs."

"Okay." Said Kat cheerfully, hopping into their truck.

Mark hauled himself after her, and they set off.

He followed them in the ATV as they circled the hill to the XJ32. Once there, he examined the ATV and XJ32, making a mental list of what he would do to the little vehicle. After a brief deliberation, he settled on armor plating, a more powerful engine, a heavy laser turret between the back seats, a rack for his armor case, two, smaller forward mounted lasers, a high output EMP, and a winch. There might be more additions to come, but this would do for now. Since most of the time he would be driving the XJ32, a hitch would be added to it to tow the ATV. He took one of the nanomachine swarms out of the cabin, and scanned the ATV with the controller to obtain a base schematic, then entered his desired upgrades into the build program. Consulting the controller for what he needed, he pulled the materials out of storage, thankfully the tech guys had thought to stock the vehicle. He started the upgrade routine, which would take four and half hours to complete. If he used the swarm often, and he suspected he would, he would have to source more material to replenish his stores. Maybe from one of those scrap places he heard of.

It was midafternoon, and would be time for dinner in another three hours. He entered the XJ32, and programmed the cryo-chef to have a meal ready at dinner time. Leaving the cabin, he wandered over to see what the others were doing. They were out of their truck. Kat sat on a stump playing something on her game machine, her face tight with concentration. Mark lounged on the ground with his back to a tree, staring intently at a holographic display projected in front of him.

"Anything yet?"

Mark glanced up, his eyes giving nothing away. "Nothing robot related. Only road, dirt, and travelers. The drone finished searching the northern grid, but found nothing on any scan frequencies. It's halfway through a search of the western grid, which is where we came from. In three hours it will start on the southern grid, if it finds nothing there, I will send it to the eastern grid, out over the ocean."

I set the cryo-chef to make dinner in three hours. When the Drone picks up the trail, we can get moving after we eat."

"I see you decided to keep the vehicle you took from the bandits. It should be fun."

"I figured it would be useful." He hedged. "I have a swarm upgrading it with weapons and armor. I'll call it the Bear, it's tough and ready to go anywhere."

"Bear huh? I like it, but you know Kat will want to play around with it."

He laughed. "I'll let her drive it sometime."

"Ha!" came a triumphant shout from Kat. "That will teach you to mess with a ninja, you ugly mutant fly creature."

"An ugly what now?"

" I find it's generally preferable not to ask." Replied Mark evenly. "Care to join me?" He gestured at the display with his head.

Zack lowered himself to the sun warmed grass.

They watched the incoming data from the drone stream across the display, images from its five cameras were shown in different wave lengths, alongside more technical information from the sensors. They passed hours looking for anything that would lead them to the XRs, until a chime sounded on his wrist unit.

Zack stood. "Food's ready."

Mark nodded and touched the projection to turn it off, before pushing off of the tree to stand. They started for the XJ32, and when they were next to the Kat he said, "okay ninja, it's time to stop fighting flies and eat dinner."

Rising to her feet and saving the game in one practiced mention, she asked. "What are we having."

"Something called chili, it's meat and beans in a spicy sauce." Inside the XJ32 Zack opened the cryo-chef and removed three steaming bowls, one twice the size of the other two. He put them on the table with spoons.

Kat frowned at the steam. "If it's chilly, why is it hot?"

"It's spelled C H I L I, and I don't know why, so don't ask."

Kat dug into her food energetically, shoveling it in faster than he thought she could chew. He and Mark ate at a more rational piece, having no reason to rush.

Upon finishing the last spoonful of chili, Kat dropped the spoon into her bowl belching loudly. "The food was great again, thank you Zack, and thank you mister cryo-chef."

Mark smiled around a mouthful of chili,

Zack blinked at her. "You don't need to thank the cryo-chef, it's only a machine."

Kat frowned reproachfully. "It would be rude not to thank mister cryo-chef, he prepared our dinner. And computers having feeling too, ask Sky."

By now Mark was shaking with suppressed laughter, and studiously examining his beans.

Zack could not tell if she was putting him on, and Mark offered no guidance, so he opted not to ask.

Sky however, possibly taking offense, chose to address the issue. "While I am gratified that you acknowledge my ability to experience emotional stimuli, it is my preference that you not compare an advanced artificial intelligence such as myself, to a kitchen appliance."

"Okay, if you say so." She replied amiably.

Zack collected the empty bowls and put them into the scrubber.

Mark reactivated the holographic display, projecting it onto the newly cleaned tabletop, and checked the progress made while they ate. "The drone has moved to the southern grid. It looks like the western grid is clear. The only movement the drone has picked up so far, is from people coming to or leaving the water plant. If the robots passed through here by land, south is the only direction they could have gone. If they did, we should pick up their trail soon."

"How soon?" Kat wanted to know.

"An hour, maybe as long as two."

"Good. Then we can smash them."

"I'm going to check on the upgrades to the Bear. You two should get ready to leave as well."

"We're all set to go the moment we have a direction. I'll be monitoring the drone's progress if you need me."

Heading outside, Zack walked to the rear of the XJ32 where the swarm was hard at work. He picked up the controller, the status display was ticking down the last fifteen minutes on the upgrades. Looking over the nearly completed ATV, he was pleased by the result of the changes. The little vehicle looked rugged and powerful, and as a soldier he appreciated the value of a strong first impression. If a potential enemy believed he was stronger than they were, it made them less likely to pick a fight, and more inclined to listen to what he had to say.

The hitch on the XJ32 was finished, it must have been high in the build queue. He circled wide around the Bear to reach the hitch, so as not to interrupt the swarm. He pulled at the hitch with all of his strength, even stepped on it. It was solid, certainly strong enough to tow the Bear without a problem, probably Mark's truck if the need arose.

The nanomachines completed their program and made an orderly return to their case, silencing their ubiquitous buzzing. Latching the case shut, he returned it and the leftover materials, to their proper storage compartments in the XJ32.

It would be a little longer yet until the drone found the XRs, making this a good time to try out his new toy. "To be sure it's working right." He told himself unconvincingly. Climbing into the driver's seat, he turned on the power, checked the gauges and readouts, then tested the various systems. He set the lasers and EMP to their lowest levels, and with everything in working order, he put the ATV into gear and drove off. He spotted Kat by their truck, and headed to her on impulse. "I'm taking the bear here for a test drive, want to come along?"

"Sure." She vaulted into the empty front seat, hardly budging the suspension.

He floored the accelerator, spraying a fan of dirt and rocks behind them. Spinning the Bear around, he pointed it toward an open stretch of ground, and tried to see how fast it could get safely there. For the next ten minutes he put the Bear through its paces. He drove it for all it was worth, climbing a steep incline, jumping a small rise, and pounding the suspension on rocks. Kat laughed, shouting encouragement from her seat. When he had a solid feel for the Bear's driving capabilities, he moved on to the weapon testing. Selecting a number of larger rocks in the near distance as targets, he fired all three lasers and the EMP at them. Checking the targeting software and honing the weapons alignment.

Everything was good, all systems working properly and efficiently. Remembering his words to Mark, he got out. "Do you want to drive it back?" He had a brief flash to worry, there was no drivers ed anymore. She did have experience driving their truck though, so it should be alright.

"Yes." She shifted to his seat without leaving the vehicle.

His butt just reached the passenger's seat, when Kat launched the Bear hard. It felt like the tires hardly touched the ground as she jumped them over every bump and dip she could hit. By the time they skidded to a stop at the XJ32. She was laughing almost hysterically, and breathing hard with the exertion of keeping the Bear upright.

"That was radical Zack, thanks." She got out between breaths.

He unlocked his fingers from their death grip on the seat and frame. "Sure, no problem." He told her while inwardly vowing to never repeat the experience. *I'll have to check for busted suspension components, and add a thicker roll bar.* Striding toward them purposefully, Mark looked like his pet just died. He stared at them silently.

"What's wrong?" Kat's voice was heavy with concern.

"I found the robots. They are sixty miles south of us and moving at seventeen miles-per-hour."

"That's good news. We can go destroy them now."

Mark shook his head. "The robots are headed in the same direction Alex and his people went. I think they're going to attack his farm, like they did White Sheep."

"No, they're not!" Kat said with venom.

"How do you know?"

"Because we will destroy them first."

CHAPTER 13

Darkness cloaked the world as the two large vehicles raced at dangerous speed through the night. The ocean, miles to their left, was an indistinct, sparkling expanse in the starlight. They drove hard over uneven and unknown terrain, trusting the sensors to map the topography, once again following in the trampled wake of the robot legion. They chased after the robots in grim determination, but unlike before, this time they knew exactly where the vile machines were.

On Mark's HUD was a red square indicating the robots' position and vector, and a distance counter flicked slowly but surely down, listing an ETA to contact. Unless there was a change in relative velocity, they would catch the robots in under an hour. An hour did not sound that long, until he considered the fact that they had no idea how far they were from Alex's farm. There was no way he would let what happened at White Sheep befall anyone else. These robots would never again be allowed to hurt people, not if he could stop them.

The Truck's front window was illuminated in the pale, ghostly green of an infrared night vision display mode. Night vision was what made this mad dash in the dark possible. Without it they would have crashed any number of times by now, they came close as it was. At the speed they were going, hitting a large rock or an unseen hole would put the Truck out of commission for repairs, possibly for several hours. A delay like that could have tragic consequences for the people on that farm.

Sky focused the Truck's sensors primarily on the ground ahead of them, plotting a reasonably safe course for them to take at their reckless velocity. From the driver's seat, Mark kept a close eye on both the route projection, and on the green tinted landscape whizzing by outside the windshield. He was on the lookout for obstacles that Sky and the sensors may have missed.

Two hours earlier they had each swallowed something Zack called an energy pill. According to Zack, the pills would help keep them awake and alert for four hours. Four hours, only two hours from now, that should be enough time to for the battle to end, one way or the other.

In the seat to his right Kat was a green phantom in the eerie light, concentrating on the displays with the kind of narrowly focused intensity, that she normally reserved for playing a particularly difficult part in a game. He stifled a feeling of hollow uneasiness. He did not want to see a repeat of what happened to her at White Sheep. Whatever emotional or technological overload caused her frightening transformation, would hopefully be absent from this encounter. They were far better equipped and prepared, no longer would they be dominated. In all their years of fighting robots, they had never been so indecorously outnumbered, never faced a situation in which they could not even run from a stronger foe. One thing that troubled him deeply, was what he did not see in the drone video feed. There were no people in the crab's cages, every last one, as confirmed by sensors, was totally empty. What had the robots done with the villagers? Other than the water plant, there was nowhere for the crabs to have deposited their cargo.

Could the Hydros really be working with the robots, or for them? None of it made any sense, the robots never displayed organized behavior in the past, had never shown any indication of thought or desire. What could have changed them, and why? He shook his head to clear his jumbled thoughts, it was all so confusing, perhaps answers would be forthcoming, after the robots were destroyed.

"Sky, watch for stray robots please. We're getting close to the main group, and they may have left some to guard the rear. If you see any, blast them."

Mark's impatience and anxiety increased with each passing minute. His heart raced and his palms were slick with sweat. He wanted to pay the robots back for White Sheep, destroy ten of them for every person they hurt, and repay them for his own humiliation in being forced to flee. But after their last encounter, he was not certain they could prevail against the robots' superior numbers, even with the upgraded weapons. He kept these concerns to himself, because he knew that Kat would not be deterred from destroying every last robot, and he honestly had no desire to convince her otherwise. He wiped his moist hands one at a time on his pants, and concentrated on driving.

Zack's voice over the comm system broke into his thoughts. "It won't be much longer before we reach the XRs, I think it's time to discuss tactics."

"Did you have something in mind?" Asked Kat.

"Here's what I was thinking, let me know how it sounds. Mark should drive your truck, while Sky pilots the XJ32 remotely. The two heavy hitters can concentrate on eliminating the crabs with their laser turrets. And Kat and I will get out to take on the infiltrators in our armor."

Mark turned it over in his mind. "Yes, that should work, with four points of attack we can destroy the robots a lot faster. The two trucks ram up the center of the robot army, separated by a hundred feet or so, blasting the crabs and running over the smaller robots. Kat can fly to the right side of them, and you drive the Bear to the left. We surround them and destroy dozens before they can organize a counterattack.

"Then we destroy every last one of them, not a single robot will survive, not even parts." Kat's hands clenched into fists.

Considering the fight ahead of them, Mark was interested in the numbers. "Do we have an estimate of how many robots there are?"

"My count, compiled from visual and sensor data, is one hundred crabs, and four hundred of the anthropomorphic or infiltrator robots. Given the logical nature of algorithmic thinking, precisely even numbers are to be expected. However, these numbers should not be taken as a definitive count. There could be up to twenty robots more or less in each group. In addition, I have detected an anomaly."

"What kind of anomaly."

"Sensors indicate the presence of a small ground vehicle, not dissimilar to those driven by the Hydros. It is occupied by four biologicals."

"What do you mean biologicals? Asked Kat dangerously.

"Unless my readings are in error, two of the occupants are human, and two are Grymals."

Kat slammed a fist into the doorframe with a bang. "Those filthy Hydros, they are working with the robots. I didn't want to believe it, I did not think people could have anything to do with the horror that was done to our friends. I want those Hydros alive, I want to talk to them."

Mark spoke diplomatically, sharing her sentiment, but willing to give the Hydros a chance to explain themselves. "I think we all have questions for them. And before you overreact, we should listen to what they, have to say. They may have been forced to be here."

"Fine, we talk nicely at first, but they had better have a *really* good excuse." Her tone strongly suggested that such an excuse did not exist. Maybe she was right.

"Sky, what are our current power levels? Will we have enough power to destroy all of the robots?"

"Our energy reserves are at ninety-eight percent of capacity, with the additional power crystal that you installed, we will be able to fight the robots continuously, for three times longer than we were capable of at White Sheep village. I cannot answer with absolute certainly, but from the data I have compiled, I am fully confident that our reserves are more than adequate to destroy the robots."

"And that takes into account the higher power drain from the upgraded lasers?"

"Yes, the increased consumption from the lasers was factored into my estimate."

"Alright, thanks Sky. How are your power levels Zack?"

"The XJ32 is an Omega command vehicle built by the EMF, it has a significantly larger power supply than your truck. It will still be fighting at full output, long after your vehicle has run out of juice." Replied Zack with more than a touch of smugness.

"That's good to know."

There was nothing more for them to do but wait. He had done all that he could think of to prepare for the upcoming battle. A week and a half had passed since the robots attacked the village. A few short days that went by quickly, and yet felt like a lifetime of self-recrimination since that terrible night. The last time they faced the robots, they were forced to run, to leave people they loved to an unknown fate. He hated the necessity of it, the cold cruelty of saving his own life in exchange for theirs. But Kat mattered more to him than anything, he would choose to save her every time, even if it killed him. When they fought the robots this time it would be different, because this time they were far stronger, and it would be the machines that were caught unprepared.

"We have closed to within one point six miles of the rear of the robot formation. It will take us an additional five minutes and eight seconds to overtake them." Reported Sky.

"Kat, Zack. It's time for us to split up. The two of you head around to your attack positions on the sides of the army. Zack on the left, you on the right. Sky, you and I ram up the center with the trucks." He concisely restated the plan to be sure everyone had it.

The trucks stopped only for the time required for Zack and Kat to get out, and for Zack to unhitch the Bear. In less than a minute, they were underway again.

"You know what to do, good luck and stay safe."

"Don't worry about me, the robots couldn't hit me if they tried."

"How about you hope they don't hit you by accident then?"

"Yeah, yeah. I'm still going to destroy twice as many as you will, mister giant soldier man." Boasted Kat.

"Maybe, maybe not. Little flying kitten."

"If the two of you are done comparing the size of your lasers, try to focus on the battle." Mark smiled despite the admonition. "Sky, move the XJ32 into attack position on my left." He veered to the right. He used the HUD radar to be sure the vehicles were in line to split the robot army into three equal groups. "Sky, our primary targets are the crabs, focus the heavy laser turrets on them. All other weapons are to fire on the smaller robots as they come into range, or smash them on the bumper guards."

"Understood, combat parameters engaged. Attack will commence in forty three seconds."

Mark switched on the weapon systems, red crosshairs appearing on his HUD screen. Wherever he moved his head the crosshairs followed, staying centered in his view. They glowed green when a target was locked on. The firing controls for the Truck's weapons were located within easy reach on steering wheel. The crosshairs could also be manipulated by a small analog joystick on the left side of the steering wheel, but it was less accurate than using the HUD.

"Thirty seconds to firing range."

His breathing grew ragged, and his heartrate accelerated. His hands were cold and damp, shaking slightly as he wiped them off again.

"Twenty seconds."

Anxious thoughts swirled unbidden in his mind. What if he was wrong, and the upgrade were not enough to destroy the crabs? Was he dooming Kat to an unwinnable battle? Would they be able to escape if things went wrong?

"Ten seconds."

Mark swallowed hard on a dry throat, he could see them now, a gigantic undulating blanket of death atop the night shrouded landscape. He was paralyzed, the helpless fear from the night of White Sheep's destruction returning to him in force, holding him in the icy grip of frozen panic. Could he really go through this again? What would he do if they failed, and another town was destroyed?

Sky's voice broke through his fear like a knife severing invisible bonds. "Engaging enemy." Stated the AI opening fire on the robots. Brilliant beams of blue light streaked across the space separating the XJ32 from the robots, exploding in a shower of sparks and shrapnel as the first robot was destroyed.

"Let's do it!" He shouted over the comm., Kat and Zack shouting back their enthusiastic agreement. The fight was on.

He opened fire, giving every robot entering the crosshairs a pulse from the lasers, as he rapidly tapped the button. His thumb twitched on the button, firing as fast as he could find a target, dropping robot after broken robot to the earth. Heads and arms vanished and glowing holes appeared in armored torsos.

The first crab lumbered heavily into view on long, multi-jointed legs, the towering monster coming directly at the truck. It was oblivious to any consideration of danger, or desire for self-preservation. Targeting the crab's carapace where it hung between four pairs of legs, Mark triggered a two-second burst from a heavy laser turret. The laser bored a hole through the machine, emerging from its back in a spray of molten alloy. The crab's momentum carried it onward to angle forward to the ground, burrowing its leading edge three feet into the dirt, and tossing clumps of grass into the air.

"Yeah!" He roared exultantly, hurting his throat. "Guys, the crabs are going down. I blasted a hole right through one, we can do this!" He yelled over the comm.

"That's great. Now let's send every last one of its buddies after it."

"Right, every one." He muttered hunting for another crab.

Flying wide of the robot army along its right side, Kat was picking off robots one by one with her wrist lasers. When she heard Mark's victorious message about the crabs shouted in her ears, her confidence in their eventual success was boosted. She swooped in low, landing in the middle of a group of robots. She immediately tore at them with her claws, shredding alloy like paper. Robots fell headless to the ground, some nearly cut in half with jagged claw marks through their smoking torsos. Robots further away were holed by bursts from her lasers, as she alternated shots with slashes. She clipped a robot on the shoulder with a laser blast, causing it to spin while firing rapidly, damaging its own companions before it too was destroyed. A robot, arm severed at the elbow and weapon missing, charged at her. The lost arm was held in the robot's functional hand like a club. Before it could bring the makeshift weapon to bear, she spun at it to deliver a punishing kick to its chestplate. The kick caved in its armor, and sent it crashing into another pair of robots, all three hit the ground in a tangled heap of twisted limbs.

She barely spared a second to be sure they would not rise again, and saw two more robots level hand lasers at her. With a thrust from her armor enhanced legs, she leaped toward them twisting in the air to land on her hands. Using the built up momentum, she kicked the robots from their feet. Pushing off from her back, she flipped onto her feet to blast the robots point blank with her lasers. She swiveled to decapitate one more.

The robots were not complacent for her rampage, maintaining an endless barrage of red energy bolts. The majority of their shots missed her outright, and because she was surrounded by so many robots, they inadvertently, if uncaringly, hit other robots. The air slowly filled with smoke from the firefight, scorched metal, electrical shorts, and brush fires each contributing their particular tang to the thickening haze. This was when the air filtration system on her helmet became indispensable, it would be hard to fight effectively with eyes blurred by tears, and hacking through burning lungs.

She caught a flash of movement in her peripheral vision to the right, light glinting off of a laser being pointed at her. She jumped high, flipping smoothly over its mechanical head. She casually slashed into its electronic brain. Sparks erupted from the gashes, and it crumpled noisily as she landed facing away from it to find a new target.

By now she had destroyed enough robots to create a lawn of scrap metal around her. She switched to blasting the approaching robots with her forearm lasers, while they closed on her mindlessly in a circle. Bot after bot fell, the ones pushing in from behind forced to clamber over their inactive compatriots, doing so with neither grace nor coordination.

Flinging her arms wide, she spun in place blasting the encroaching bots without pause. A circular mound of scorched parts rose around her like an inflating tube. She laughed, "Die, die, all of you die!" She shouted at them.

After a minute of twirling her fun came to an end, when the robots stopped climbing the death mound to get at her. *Why did they stop attacking me?* Then she had the answer, as two of the crabs loomed over her through the smoke. "Huh, I guess you forgot I can fly." She launched straight up, slipping deftly past the crabs grasping hands and sought more humanoid robots to break.

On the left flank of the XR strike force, Zack stood firing two handed at the infiltrator. In his right hand his powerful Omega weapon made short work of the human size machines slowly and stupidly closing on him. Every hit scored on an XR melted alloy and circuits, leaving the pitiless machines broken or disabled. In his left hand he held a laser appropriated from a downed infiltrator, that he used to similar if less dramatic effect. With an improvised barrier of slagged XRs providing cover, he fired into a group of infiltrators bearing down on him from the left, picking each target and firing with trained efficiency. When those XRs were out of the fight, he scanned his tactical radar for more. Using his armor's physical augmentation, he dashed at a small squad of infiltrators twenty feet away.

Crashing shoulder first into the XRs as if they were bowling pins and he the ball, he crushed two of them instantly, and drove his first through the chestplate of a third. Not giving them time to react to his attack, he yanked his armored hand fee of the XR and picked it up, swinging it to smash two more. With a sweeping kick, he knocked the final XR from its feet and crushed its head with a mighty stomp of a titamant-clad foot.

He dashed right, strafing XRs with the lasers. They got off only a few shots at him before being destroyed. Its head was nudged a tick forward by a hit from behind. With so many enemies shooting at him, it was impossible to evade every incoming beam, which is what the armor was for. With a boost from his jump pack, he leaped high into the air backward, moving in the general direction he thought the blast came from. He twisted his body mid jump to face his target, blasting a likely pair of infiltrators, and landing feet from their inert forms. His acrobatics may not be as flashy as what Kat or Anne could pull off, but they get the job done.

More beams hit the ground at his feet, searing the grass. He rolled to throw of their aim, and simultaneously to reorient himself for an attack. They missed him again, leaving plenty of time for him to methodically take them out. That done, he glanced at his faceplate HUD to find another squad of infiltrators. He found twenty infiltrators a dozen yards left, and power dashed in their direction, weaving thumping foot falls over the debris laden battlefield. He downed three before reaching the intended targets. Smoke was filling the air, obscuring XRs in a curtain of nebulous haze. He saw the first two infiltrators visually, the rest of the squad could only be found on his radar display located by their movement and electronic signatures. Dropping into a crouch to make himself harder to hit, he fired on the XRs as they prepared to shoot him. The front row of XRs dropped fast under his double handed attack, but the XRs behind those were harder to strike in the concealing smoke. He traded shots with the infiltrators, the XRs managing to score several hits. It was not long until he scrapped the last of them.

"I'll be buffing scorch marks out of my armor for hours." He muttered at the blackened alloy.

A light tap on his shoulder reminded him to pay attention to the fight. Rolling away from the impact direction, he checked the radar and turned to take out the closest XR. He continued his attack on all nearby infiltrators, until there were no more in range.

According to has radar, the only XRs left in this sector were crabs, the nearest infiltrators were a hundred yards away. He power-dashed to the Bear and got in, then made for the next large concentration of infiltrators. Stragglers could be mopped up later. If Mark and Kat were making such quick work of their XRs, the enemy strike force would be annihilated within the hour, probably only in minutes.

With the more powerful laser turrets, the once practically indestructible crabs were virtually helpless. So long as he kept the truck beyond the reach of their manipulator arms, there was little they could do to attack him. Every so often a crab would pick up a large rock, or a piece of scrap like one of the broken robots, and lob it at the Truck. But their aim was poor, and he could generally swerve out of the way, or blast the improvised projectile in flight. When a crab did hit the Truck, it caused no more than scratches in the armor plating. The rocks around here were too small for real damage.

He ignored the smaller humanoid robots for the most part, their hand lasers were too weak to be a threat, and his job was to destroy crabs. If one of the smaller robots did come close to the Truck, he shot them with the front mounted lasers, or ran over those dumb enough to stand in his path.

That the robots were void of self-preservation programming was abundantly clear. No matter how many of them he smashed or blasted, more robots lined up behind their broken buddies for their turn at eternity. He triggered off another extended laser blast into a crab, watching it collapse to the dirt before speeding to find the next one. Puncturing a hole anywhere on a crab's body, was effective in disabling them, suggesting a lack of redundant systems. Two robots in his path clanked noisily on the impact bars protecting the front at the Truck, disappearing beneath it in a flash. Firing on more humanoid robots along the way, he closed on a crab to fill it with a laser burst.

Experimenting on the crabs by varying laser intensity and duration, Sky determined that a one point three second full power burst from the roof turrets, was sufficient to destroy one. He set the turrets to a one point four second burst, to be sure of kill. After all, it was better to waste a little energy on overkill, than to have an enemy he thought dead, attack him by surprise later. Sky assured him that they had plenty of energy for the fight, but he waited until each crab filled the windshield before firing at it. He did not know how long the fight would last, and he definitely would not leave the job unfinished. Not a single robot would be left functional to attack Alex's farm.

He triggered a burst at his current target, the crab managed to raise a manipulator arm into the path of the beam. But the ineffective shield was no help, the laser melted through the less armored limb, and drilled into the carapace. The crab shuddered and collapsed.

The battle clock in the bottom right corner of his HUD, showed that the fight had gone on for ten minutes. He was not sure that he believed that number, it felt like a lot longer. In those minutes he had destroyed twenty eight crabs, and twenty of the smaller robots. At this rate they would finish the last crab in under twenty more minutes.

Looking at his HUD for another crab, displayed as larger red dots, he saw the Hydro ATV moving rapidly from the battlefield, fleeing right between the Truck and the XJ32. Ignoring the crabs for now, he gave chase at full speed.

Bouncing dangerously ever the scrap filled terrain, the Hydros made a desperate bid to save themselves. The unmodified ATV was pitifully overmatched by the Truck, and Mark took advantage of that difference to close the distance between them. Hitting a rock or robot he could not see, the little vehicle tipped and nearly overturned then slammed back onto all four tires, the front right rebounding harshly.

When the Truck was thirty yards from the Hydros, Mark called to them on the external speakers, his amplified voice cutting through the noise of combat. "Stop now, or I will fire on you." Their only response was to veer sharply right, nearly rolling the ATV again. "This is your last warning, stop now or be destroyed."

He counted silently to ten, but the Hydros stubbornly failed to stop, or even to slow. Aiming carefully, he fired on the left rear wheel of the ATV, shattering the metal rim. Rubber tore off in chunks and the empty hub slammed into the ground ground. The sudden drag on one side sent it into a twisting aerial flip. The rollbar smashed into the dirt with a crash of tortured metal, and the machine slid over the ground bleeding off inertia and gouging a rough, narrow trench into the earth. It finally came to a screeching halt heard through the window of the Truck, and lay belly up on the grass. It was unlikely that the Hydros would be going anywhere soon. If any were conscious, they would have to run or hobble away on foot. He turned the truck back to the battle.

"Kat, Zack. I disabled the Hydros' ATV when they tried to run, and possibly the Hydros along with it. After we finish off the robots, we can have a nice long chat with them."

"Got it." Replied Zack

"Looking forward to it," snarled Kat.

Locating a crab on his HUD, he saw that the only crabs remaining, were at the front of the robot army. Most of them were at the rear when the fighting started, but he and Sky had destroyed the majority of them. The few crabs still active, were dispersed randomly farther forward among the throng, what was left of it. There were far fewer of the human size robots as well, perhaps only two thirds of them were moving. Zack and Kat had been busy.

Firing freely but picking his targets, Mark blasted as many of the smaller robots as he could, while maneuvering the truck through the scrap to kill crabs. When close to one he triggered a laser burst, and the crab slumped unceremoniously. The HUD radar showed only ten more active crabs, no nine as Sky got another one. It took the two trucks a short time to finish off the remaining crabs, then they helped clear out the last humanoid robots.

When the sensors registered no functional robots on the field, he contacted Kat and Zack. "Okay guys that's all of them, meet me behind the robots." He inhaled a deep shuddering breath, and waited for the adrenaline to leave his system. He really preferred to leave this sort of thing to Kat, she enjoyed thrills.

Being able to fly, Kat was naturally the first to arrive at the rendezvous site. He found her standing on clear ground when he arrived in the Truck, waiting impatiently with arms folded and tail ticking side to side. Zack came next, the Bear bouncing over robot parts and fresh divots in the dirt. Lastly, the XJ32 plowed through the junk to stop by the truck.

"First thing's first," began Mark. "Is anyone hurt?"

"Not me." Said Zack.

Kat raised a thumb. "I'm good."

Mark nodded in relief. "The blue dot on your HUD map, is where I left the Hydros' vehicle after I busted it. They may have tried to run, but I don't think they are in any condition to go very far. Now that we're finished with the robots, it's time we have a chat with them."

"Yes." Agreed Kat too eagerly.

"Sky, unless Zack objects, I want you to take the XJ32 and search for any robots that are still functional. If you happen to find any, destroy them." He said looking at Zack.

"Go ahead, Sky."

"Initiating search and destroyed protocol." Sky piloted the XJ32 back into the scrap strewn battlefield.

"Sky has a search and destroyed protocol?" Inquired Kat.

"Not that I know of, but it sounded good." If Sky was making things up because he liked the sound of them, then the AI was spending too much time with people. Not that Mark was complaining, he really did like the phrase.

Kat climbed into the passenger seat of the Truck, Mark got in and drove to the site of the Hydros' overturned ATV. Zack followed in the Bear.

Its three mostly intact wheels in the air, the Hydros' ATV lay bent and broken on its hood and roll bar. A trail of blood drops let away from the wreck, at the end of which was a man crawling slowly along the ground on hands and knees. A Grymal wearing the black and red uniform of a Hydro, sat stumped against the ATV, apparently unconscious. The other two Hydros were not in sight, but a quick glance at his HUD revealed them to be nearby and moving slowly from the crash.

Mark dropped down from the cab, and walked to the crawling man. Anger rose with the bile in his throat, the thought that these men could accompany the robots to hurt people made him physically ill. How could they do it, what kind of people were these? He examined the man's injuries dispassionately, holding no sympathy for him. The blood drops came from a wound on his thigh, a crude bandage was wrapped around it with cloth taken from his shirt. The Hydro ignored him, choosing to concentrate on his glacially ineffective attempt to escape.

Striding past him without hesitation, Kat stormed right to the injured man and kicked him in the side, knocking him flat on his back and eliciting a pained shout. Mark was not alone in having rage to vent. "Now Hydro," she spat with venom. "You will tell me exactly what you are doing here. And it better be good."

The Hydro groaned, holding his side where she kicked him. "Name, Jack Smith, rank sergeant. That's all I can tell you." He growled through clenched teeth.

Unsatisfied with the response and fighting to keep her anger in check, Kat took direct action. She grabbed the man by his throat and dragged him to the ATV with one hand, her tail lashing the air. He pried at her fingers in futility, trying to dislodge her iron death grip. She slammed him into the vehicle hard enough to make Mark cringe, in spite of his loathing.

"Why are you with the robots?" she shouted menacingly extending the claws on her free arm.

"If you want to keep all your parts attached, I suggest you tell the lady what she wants to know." Zack stepped heavily into the Hydro's line of sight.

The man's eyes goggled, shifting between Kat's claws and Zack's imposing armored form. "I'll tell you." He crooked in Kat's tightening grip.

Kat released the Hydro to slide limply to the dirt. "Then talk, Hydro." The word was fast becoming a curse on her lips.

"It was orders." He started weakly. "We were ordered to assist the XR with collection operations."

"Collection operations?" Zack demanded.

"That's what they call it when XRs go to a place and take all the people."

"Why do the robots want people? What are they doing with them?" Kat was on the ragged edge of control, he could see it in the way her tail was virtually motionless. She was poised to strike.

"I don't know, I promise I don't." He spoke rapidly as it his life depended on it, and with Kat in this mood, it might. "The XRs came to the water plant months ago, they had cages full of people and a huge army. There were too many for us to fight, but they didn't attack us right away. These XRs have a leader, a kind of fancy robot calling itself P5. This thing is scary smart, and it looks and sounds more like a person.

P5 demanded to talk to X, and she went out alone. She was out there for less than an hour. When she came back, X ordered us to do what P5 wanted or we would be killed. The XRs took over the plant, they were everywhere, rebuilding the plant to suit their purpose. They forced us to help built massive dropships, that they herded the prisoners onto. The ships fly inland, I have no idea where. The ships are controlled by computer, and us Hydros are not allowed onboard. Any Hydros who refuse to do what P5 says are put into cells with the other prisoners."

"If there are so many XRs in the water plant, why didn't we see any when we were there?"

"They hide inside. They have an underground facility to use, and many of them were in this collection force. I don't think they want people to know they're there."

"How long are people kept prisoner at the water plant, before the robots fly them away.?"

Jake shrugged painfully. "It could be a couple of days, or a few weeks. The XRs move people when they're ready to."

"I think we've learned what we can from this guy, we should see if Sky gleaned anything from scanning robot memory cores."

That was all the prompting Sky required. "I have successfully scanned twenty-three intact memory cores. Unfortunately, these robots are nothing more than drones with minimal instruction sets. None of them contain advanced or useful information. The only data I was able to retrieve beyond programming for basic functionality, was their current directive. They are tasked with proceeding to a nearby settlement of organics, no data other than grid coordinates provided, and initiating collection operations. This means the capture of every person in the area. There is nothing further to be learned from them."

"We need to think this through. What do we know so far? We know that the robots are capturing people for an unknown reason, and then flying them somewhere."

Kat scowled at the Hydro. "We know the Hydros work for them."

"We know the XRs are holding the prisoners at the water plant for a while before moving them."

"What we don't know." Said Mark. "What we need to learn, is where the robots are taking people and why."

"It seems to me that we know our next step. We have to go back to the water plant, rescue those we can, then capture this P5 XR, and force answers out of it.

Kat nodded. "And we wipe out every robot in the place."

Jake spoke, reminding them he was there. Not, perhaps, his wisest decision ever. "Most of us hate the XRs, and what they are doing to people. I have to warn you, the XRs are building stronger weapons and XRs. They've been working on something big, really big. I don't know what it is, but it can't be good. Be careful, and for what it's worth, good luck."

Kat looked coldly at the man. "I promise you this *Hydro*. We will get rid of the robots, but what happens to your friends is their choice."

Jake dropped his gaze. "I understand."

"Sky, please bring the XJ32 back to us."

"What should we do with them?" Zack jerked a thumb at the Hydros by the ATV.

"Leave them here, they won't make it back to the water plant for days in their condition. By then we will have the place shut down."

They walked to the Truck and Bear. When Sky pulled up with the XJ32, Zack hitched the Bear to it.

Mark looked at the brightening sky, they had stayed awake the whole night. "The sun will rise in an hour or so. We should sleep and let our crystals recharge for a few hours, then head to the Water Plant. And I want the nanomachines to repair the trucks and your armor, then replenish our supplies from the scrap. The robots should be broken down, turned into something good."

"I agree, we need to rest and repair, be at full strength for our assault on the enemy fortification."

Kat yawned, the energy pills were wearing off.

The trucks were parked in the middle of the battle site, to give the nanomachines easy access to the scrap. Mark and Zack took out their nanomachine swarms, setting them to gather materials and repair the battle damage. Sky, not requiring rest, was left to supervise the process while they ate a brief meal and retired to their bunks.

CHAPTER 14

Dark had fallen before they arrived at the water plant, a welcome concealment for their approach. They had driven through the remainder of the day since waking, a less dangerous, if no less anxious, journey. The sun was six hours below the horizon. They slept only for five hours prior to setting out that morning, but took turns sleeping during the drive. Mark and Kat easily switched seats to sleep in the cab, while Zack was forced to relinquish control of the XJ32 to the AI again. He would rather do the driving himself, not entirely trusting computers, but recognized the necessity of rest before a fight. Lunch and dinner were simple and quick affairs. Zack had the cryo-chef prepare food, and when it was ready, they stopped just long enough for it to be transferred through open windows.

They were laying in the bushes on top of the hill, looking down into the plant for more reconnaissance. Zack could not help thinking that this was a really convenient spot to observe the plant from. It was the only place for miles, where they could watch the plant unnoticed. If he was in charge of security for the Water Plant, the first thing he would have done was flatten the hill. Leaving it here was tactically unsound.

Laying on the bare dirt, Zack stared at the target through the night vision mode of his visor. He and Kat were armored up in anticipation of their impending infiltration. Trade for water was over for the day, the gate closed, and the only Hydros to be seen, were on patrol or guard duty at the wall lasers.

A few small groups of people were camped at the edge of the cleared area, parked near each other for safety. They had either come too late for water that day, or did not want to travel in the dark.

The plant itself looked much the same as it did in daylight, only darker and more colorless. From what he could tell, there was no activity of note anywhere, and practically none within the perimeter wall of the compound. In the short time they were here, he had not seen a single XR in or around the plant. Something about that felt wrong to him, but he dismissed it. The Hydro told them that XRs were hidden inside buildings, so he should not be surprised by the lack of visual confirmation. He could not altogether rule out the possibility that the man lied to them, that there were not XRs here at all. He could think of no reason for the Hydro to lie, but he wanted to be absolutely sure of an XR presence here, before attacking a potentially innocent target.

"Have either of you seen an XR yet?"

"Not one."

"I have nothing from the sensors on the stealth drone." Replied Mark.

"Keep your eyes open. I want to know the XRs are in there, before we go charging in lasers flashing."

Kat grunted noncommittally.

"We need a plan of attack, any ideas?"

Kat had one. "We drive to the front gate, and blast our way in with the trucks. They won't know what hit them."

Unsurprised by Kat's well reasoned plan, Mark intervened. "We don't know what kind of weapons the Hydros have. Those laser turrets on the wall may be able to seriously damage the trucks, or you armor. And more importantly, we don't know where the prisoners are being held. If we rush in and blast everything, those people could be hurt. We don't want to hurt anyone, even the Hydros."

"Not even when they fight for the robots?"

"Not even then, remember what that Hydro said, most of them don't want to help the robots, they are being forced to. Try to hit them with low intensity stun shots, okay?"

"Fine, I will try not to hurt them, too much." She said reluctantly. "But if we can't shoot our way in, how do we get inside?"

Zack had studied the water plant during the discussion, and now had what he thought was a workable strategy. "I've got an idea. The best point of entry, is the south-east corner by the ocean. From what I can tell, that is where the defenses are softest." He pointed to the pertinent spot on the holographic display. "The perimeter patrols are infrequent there, and they have only one turret on the wall for a hundred yards. I've seen no activity inside the base close to that corner either."

"We have a place to enter from, the question now becomes how we will do it. There's no gate there, we won't be able to drive the trucks inside. Not that they would be all that maneuverable on the narrower streets."

Zack nodded. "That's right. I think we should leave them outside. As you said, they may not be much help in there. Mark stays with the trucks and monitor the situation with your drone and the sensors. Kat and I will slip in covertly for the rescue, while you support us with external intel."

"But if anything goes wrong, you two will be stuck in there. What am I supposed to do if there's trouble?"

"If there is an emergency, you can go with Kat's original plan. Drive through the front gate, create a commotion so we can escape. Actually, that's not a bad idea. We may want to create a distraction when it's time to attack anyway. The XJ32 has heavy armor, it should take only minor damage in a frontal assault on the gate."

Kat was ready to start. "When do you think we should go?"

"I want to attack while it's dark, and we hopefully have the element..."

The thrum of what could only be large antigrav engines cut him off, and all eyes went to the plant. While they were deliberating, the roof of the biggest building in the plant had retracted unnoticed. A ship rose out of the hidden hanger, one he recognized from his pre-invasion briefings as an XR dropship. The Hydro had told them the truth, XRs were here. The dropship was an unimaginative boxy rectangular shape, and out massed both trucks combined. An escort of four wedge shaped XFs emerged to surround the pale gray ship, leaving no doubt in his mind of what controlled the vessel. He watched the ship fly over them bearing west, wondering how many frightened people were aboard, and where the XRs were taking them. The three looked on in troubled silence as the ship faded from sight, none of them willing to voice the dread they felt at the fate of its unwilling passengers.

Zack was prodded by urgency. "Kat, we will circle around the plant out of sight, then dash to the wall. Are you ready?"

"Do it."

The quarter hour it took them to run along the perimeter of the cleared area surrounding the plant, felt many times longer to Kat. She followed close behind Zack while he looked for a place to stop, matching his pace and movements, in the belief that his military training meant he knew what he was doing.

Zack crouched by a tree fifty yards from the shore to survey the plant. "When I say go, we're going to dash to the wall, and jump to the top." He told her as she crouched next to him. "What I need you to do, is when we're close enough, you stun the Hydro at the laser turret in front of us. You're a better shot than I am, and we have to down him on the first try, then pray that no one notices."

She gave him a thumb up. "No problem." His compliment on her shooting skill felt good, coming as it did from a genuine super soldier.

They heard the hum of an electric engine and crunch of gravel preceding the appearance of a patrol ATV. The four-man vehicle drove almost to the beach on its circuit, then turned wide to go back the way it came.

The ATV was barely out of side when Zack said. "Go!"

Zack leapt to his feet and sprinted all out for the wall. Caught off guard, she was a second behind him, but pulled even in only a few strides. She glanced to the left and right for movement, but all was still. Then after a quick hop to clear the chainlink fence, she glued her eyes on the wall, watching for people or robots that might give them away.

The only Hydro on the wall that she could see, was the man at the laser turret. He faced away from them, staring out over the ocean instead of watching for intruders as he should. Her right laser was preset to its highest stun intensity, and she raised it to aim at the Hydro. He would be in range in another second or two. His eyes must have caught their movement, his head snapped right to look in their direction. His hands flew to the turret controls, but Kat was faster, hitting him in the head to drop from sight.

She locked eyes on the turret, waiting anxiously to see if anyone noticed the fallen sentry, or if another Hydro was hidden up there. Ten seconds later they leaped to the wall top unhindered, landing softly by the unconscious Hydro. She sliced into the turret with her claws to disable it, and listened for shouts or alarms. The night was silent save for a distant metallic clanking that ended shortly.

Kat examined their surroundings in detail, taking the stealth ninja mission seriously. The wall top was ten feet wide and constructed from large gray bricks. There was a four foot high defensive barrier on either side of the wall, over which the turret leaned to fire down on attackers.

Inside the wall, the facility still appeared well maintained up close, even in the uniform green tint of night vision. The structures were an industrial mix of concrete and painted steel. The plant was built more for function than form, its workings hard and exposed, not intended for fun or comfort. Turning off her night vision for a quick look, she saw only pale colors in mostly blue and gray hues, some more faded than others. Although there were lights along the streets and alleys, only one in four was currently illuminated. Peering straight down from the wall, she saw no one around. The Hydros were unconcerned that anyone would attack them, and security was very lax.

"What now?" She pitched her voice low, even with her external speaker off.

"Our best chance of finding your friends is to infiltrate the hanger that dropship came out of. If the Hydro was telling the truth, the XRs are filling the dropships with people here. And the people are probably being held in or near that building."

"Makes sense."

"Remember, we have to be quiet. The last thing we want is to alert the whole place to our presence."

She nodded, gesturing wordlessly to the street below with a wave of a hand, certain that his big, heavy armor was a lot nosier than her's. If anyone was going to be heard, it was him. Zack dropped easily to the street, more quietly than she imagined, and she landed softly beside him. She was slightly behind him as he moved, letting him choose their path and speed. They were not fumbling blindly in an unmapped maze, Mark was feeding constant updates to their HUDs, using map and sensor data obtained by the drone flying overhead. The map included an overlay that showed the locations of Hydros, power sources, and other information Mark thought they should know. It also displayed their decreasing distance to the hanger building. Listening to their comm chatter, Mark was aware of their destination, and updated their map accordingly. The drone data simplified their undetected trek through the plant, and they easily avoided the Hydros. She hoped there would be robots to fight when they reached the hanger, otherwise this was going to be one boring rescue. And she might not get her pink cake, if the villagers thought it was too easy for her.

Wending their way slowly from building, to storage tank, to building, they stayed in the shadows whenever possible. Dashing from one point of concealment to the next, pausing only to see if the path was clear. There were few Hydros to be seen, and those mainly from a long distance with their backs turned. This was partially due to using Marks data to evade them, but also from how few of them were actually around. It looked like they would reach the hanger without being spotted. She was becoming uneasy, they had yet to see a single robot. The Hydro they interrogated told them that the robots were forcing them to work, but how could the robots force them to do anything, if there were no robots to do the forcing? Holding these doubts in, she followed Zack silently to the next shadow, his thudding mechanical footfalls far louder than a stealth ninja should be.

The sixty plus foot tall hangar loomed enormously over the shorter buildings around it. They were close now, another minute and they would arrive at the target. She was increasingly anxious, were her friends inside, was Tula? Did the robots already fly them away? Were they still alive? Her mind raced with questions, forming a hard lump over her heart. She cleared her mind with effort. She had to stay in control, stray thoughts or inattention could get someone hurt or killed.

The hangar was directly in front of them, huge and metal and ugly. Up close it was truly massive, seeming to stretch on for a mile in either direction. It was by far the largest structure she had ever seen in person, intact or otherwise. The sheer magnitude of the edifice before her, only served to heighten her unease.

"How do we get in?"

"The sensors detect a computerized security system in control of the building. It will have to be bypassed or forced open with weapons fire. I do not recommend blasting it open, unless you want the entire plant to know we are here."

Mark had a solution. "If you are close to one of the doors, Sky can hack the system remotely through Kat's armor."

Making sure no one was watching, they ran to the closest hangar door. The door rested in a darkened recess, with no Hydros nearby and no security measures visible beyond the lock. It was perfect for their purpose.

She stood facing outward, watching for Hydros and robots. Seconds later the lock disengaged with a click.

Zack opened the door slowly to peer inside, then waved her through and closed it behind them. She found herself in a short, brightly lit hallway with a single door at the far end.

Switching off night vision, she walked to the far door. "I wonder what's in there. I hope they built something cool, like a giant flapping pterodactyl robot with huge claws and laser eyes. It could even be pink." Realizing that Zack was no longer with her, she stopped to see what was wrong.

Zack stood motionless, his silver faceplate inscrutable. "What did you say?"

"The robots built those giant crabs, so I thought it would be fun to fight something cool." She told him earnestly. When he continued to stare at her mutely, she said. "I guess it doesn't have to be pink. What color would you like?"

"Were you dropped on your head a lot as a child?" He asked her for some reason.

"Not that I remember, why?"

His helmeted head shook. "Never mind, it's not important."

"You need to be careful in there. The drone's sensors are not able to penetrate the building, the interior is a blank. If they are intentionally shielding it, who knows what the robots are hiding in there. And Kat? I for one hope there are no giant pterodactyls waiting for you." Mark's voice in her ears was distorted by static.

"You're no fun." She muttered to herself.

Reaching the end of the hallway, she cracked open the door to peek inside. There was only darkness. Opening it wider, she reactivated her night vision, but it revealed snowy static. "There must be some kind of jamming in there, I can't see a thing."

"Then there are two choices here." Began Zack. "We turn around and leave, saving ourselves at the cost of leaving your friends to the XRs. Or we charge blindly in and spring this not so subtle trap."

She flung open the door without hesitation, and strode boldly through. She was forced to abandon Tula once already, it would not happen again. She heard Zack thump after her, and spun sharply at a heavy metallic clang behind them, just in time to see a thick panel slide across the door they entered through. "It really is a trap."

The last sound Mark heard on the comm, before the signal cut off, was a loud crash. "Kat, can you hear me?" His answer was static. "Zack, please respond." Silence.

Then everything happened at once. Distant klaxons sounded in the Plant, and every light in the facility blazed to life. Hydros and robots flooded out of buildings to surround the hangar. Scattered among the normal robots he was familiar with, were larger more heavily armed robots of a style he had never seen. A small army of robots and Hydros on ATVs raced toward the hill. They knew he was here, and they were coming for him.

"Looks like this was a trap, we have to fight our way into the plant to help them."

He ran down the hill to the Truck, he would be relatively safe inside. Dirt erupted around him, as robots sprang from the soil to completely encircle him. The trap was planned thoroughly.

"I'm out of the fight Sky, they are about to capture me. Transfer a fully copy of yourself to the Truck and the XJ32. It will be up to you to free us."

"I can control the vehicles remotely."

"Not if they jam your signal, it has to be direct control. Do it."

"Understood. I will require four minutes and nine seconds to complete the transfer, I will be offline for the duration. I cannot reliably predict a timeframe for when I can facilitate a rescue."

"Do it Sky, and good luck." He was surprisingly calm given the circumstances. He completely believed in his friends, they would find a way to win.

"And to you Mark commending transfer now."

A Hydro ATV braked to a stop feet from where he stood, and two Hydros got out. They searched his pockets, took his laser, and tied his hands behind his back.

"Get in." Said one of them shoving him harshly at the ATV. He hoped Kat and Zack were having better luck with the situation that he was.

After the door sealed behind Zack, amber lights high on the walls started flashing, accompanied by the blare of alarms. The lights did little to cut through the darkness, actually worsening the problem with the electronic jamming in place, he was essentially blind and deaf. Anything could be approaching them from the dark, and he would not know until it was too late.

Tapping Kat on the shoulder to get her attention, he guided here a short distance from the doorway, praying the enemy was as hindered as they were, with no ability to counter the jamming. Unsure that he could do more at this point, he crouched low to see what would happen.

The wait was short, as moments later the alarms stopped, and the hangar floor where he and Kat crouched was lit up, letting him see much of the lower half of the room. Most of the hangar's interior was a single open chamber, sized to hold an XR dropship with room to spare. The lights were only on one side of the metal cavern, the far end of the room and its retractable ceiling were still cloaked in shadow, impenetrable without the visual enhancements the jamming disabled. It was not the room's vast dimensions of bare alloy walls that concerned him just then, it was what currently shared the floor space. At a glance he estimated there to be one hundred fully armed heavy combat XRs. It was his first time seeing an HC in person, and now he crouched in front of a hundred of them, all with lasers drawn and pointed at him.

HCs were roughly human in overall shape, with two squarish arms and legs, an ovoid head and blocky torso. But they were significantly larger than infiltrators, and their bodies were covered in thicker armor plating. They carried laser rifles, rather than the smaller hand lasers standard on infiltrators. They were also armed with a rectangular box of mini rockets mounted on one shoulder. Although the HCs were incapable of speech, made no demands, did not so much as move, the message they conveyed was nonetheless clear. You are our prisoners, move and you die.

The standoff ended when the alarms stopped, and a female voice shouted to them from a catwalk mid-way up the left wall. "The Hydros welcome you to our humble home." The speaker was a cat Grymal who bore a striking resemblance to Kat, except that she had a red streak in her black hair as opposed to Kat's purple one. She wore a suit of black armor with red power lights that ended in a skirt at mid-thigh. Her shin high boots stood atop two-inch soles, and the hilt of a sword rose above her shoulder. It was the kind of get up he expected to see at a science fiction convention.

Standing next to the cosplaying Grymal was an XR, but not any ordinary XR, this one was completely foreign to him. It was larger than an infiltrator, but not so big as an HC. And this XR looked far more human than its clearly artificial counterpart. Its limbs and torso were rounded and sculpted almost organically, as if to give the impression of flesh and muscle on bone. More disturbingly, the machine's face was human shaped and disconcertingly articulate. It left him sort of queasy.

The Grymal spoke. "I'm X, leader of the Hydro army. My, um, associate here is P5, a representative of the XRs. "Her voice was annoyingly chipper, like this was all amusing to her. And bizarrely, she had what he was sure was a New York accent.

P5 inclined its head in acknowledgement.

"The XRs have come here under new management. They have a little project they're working on, and they've been collecting people for it. Naturally I can't tell you what the project is, that would spoil the surprise. If you live long enough to see it. But don't worry, the XRs won't be taking you for collection, they've got other plans for you. That means you especially, sister."

"I am not your sister!" Shouted Kat indignantly.

X giggled. "We'll see about that kitten."

P5 raised a metal hand. "That is enough X, we have no time for this witless babble. We must commence the testing. And you." It pointed down at them ominously. "Will advance, or you will surely die." Its voice was oddly gentle, almost grandfatherly. A peculiar choice for a bunch of homicidal alien robots.

Zack wanted to know what this was, something about P5 and the words it used were familiar. "What do you mean advance? What is it you want from us?"

The machine affected a sorrowful expression, "I do what I must. HCs, attack."

The XRs fired their laser rifles at the two of them, dozens of deadly energy beams crisscrossing the chamber to find their intended targets. Beams sizzled into the wall where he had stood, before power jumping at the XRs to his right. Several HCs tumbled to the floor hard, born down by his seven hundred pound mass crashing into them. Slamming his first into an HC, he spared a glance at Kat. She had taken flight and was blasting XRs with abandon. His last sight of her, was when she landed in the middle of a cluster of HCs. He shot two more HCs, prior to kicking a third with such force that it flew destructively into the two behind it.

The XRs closed on him to the point where his laser was more of a liability than an asset, taking too long to aim and fire. Clipping the Omega weapon to his thigh, he switched to hand-to-hand combat. He tore the head from an HC, hurling it into the head of another, shattering both to scrap. An HC grabbed his leg, he reached down to snap off the offending hand. At the same time, another HC fired a valley of rockets that passed through the location his body was just occupying. The rockets exploded into the HCs crowding behind him, cracking armor plating and wrenching apart robotic joints. He lifted the grabby HC by its shortened arm, and swung it destructively into the rocket firing HC.

Lasers zinged by him incessantly, sometimes hitting him, but damaging his armor only superficially. Enemy shots continually connected with other HCs, damaging and destroying each other almost faster than he could. Following directives was omnipresent to the machine mind, and collateral damage patently irrelevant. He snagged two HCs and smashed them together like cymbals letting their broken bodies topple.

As the minutes accumulated his breathing came harder, if there were many more XRs laying in wait after these, he could be in real trouble. Even with all of his genetic modifications, he only had so much stamina to fight all out with, particularly after yesterday's battle. Fortunately, the HC force before him was thinning. Now that there was space between himself and the HCs, he unclipped his weapon and opened fire.

While an HC in front of him occupied his attention, he was struck from behind by a rocket barrage, knocking him face first to the floor. Putting his palms on the ground, he pushed up, only to have a heavy weight bear him down again. He saw Kat slashing a pair of XRs that were about to attack him, then dance away leaving him weighted down by her scrap.

By the time he reached over his shoulder to yank off the HC, and roll to his feet, the fight was over. Kat was jumping and slashing her way through the remaining handful of XRs, an impressive ballet of violence. While he admired her handy work, a severely damaged HC latched onto his leg with a mangled hand. He bent over to casually finish it off, and the last thing he saw before his vision went black, was the HC's entire compliment of rockets launching point blank at his helmeted head.

Cutting the head from the last standing robot with her claws, Kat paused to catch her breath and survey the room for moving bots. An explosion whipped her around laser at the ready. Astonishingly, Zack was flying backward in the air trailing smoke with a robot clinging to his ankle. Ignoring the cold wash of worry that hit her, she sprinted to Zack, slashed the robot's head and ripped its hand from his leg. Tossing the junk aside, she knelt by Zack's head, checking his helmet for damage. To her instant relief, it was only pitted and scored, with a small crack in the faceplate. His armor was not indestructible after all, that was good to know.

"Can you hear me Zack?" She wiped at the scorched faceplate with an armor clad hand, roughly scraping off some of the black. "Come on, wake up. This is no time for a nap." She tapped the faceplate, his lack of response starting to upset her. She gripped his shoulders and shook him forcefully.

"Alright already, mister big, tough soldier. You're not going to let a little explosion in the face keep you down, are you?" She shouted at him.

Zack groaned, lifting a hand to his head that clanked loudly on his helmet. "You can stop shouting, I'm awake."

She helped him up, a smile spreading on her face.

"Ugh, remind me never to stop rockets with my head."

She slapped his back. "I'll do that."

"Are you okay?"

She looked at the broken robots. Now that she knew Zack was alright, she was disappointed that there were no more robots. "Yeah, I'm good, but we broke all their toys."

"This will be the last time they invite us over to play."

A sharp metallic clacking filled the silence of the hangar, drawing her gaze to the catwalk, where P5 was clapping. "Well done young ones. Your abilities are indeed impressive. However, what you are now is sadly insufficient. You must push past what you believe to be your limits, you must advance if you are to fulfill your ultimate purpose. Prepare yourselves, for now the real test begins."

X clapped her hands together excitedly. "Oh, that was really dramatic mister P5, I like it." She pressed a button on a control panel.

An ominous, high-pitched whine emanated from the shadowy wall at the back of the chamber, and scattered lights blinked on up and down the wall, shining in various colors. There was a shifting, the whole surface seemed to move as large electric motors whirred. A singularly enormous bulk took form out of the dim light. The thing reared up on two massive legs to a height of more than forty feet. The fingers of two gigantic hands, were the size of Zack's armored legs. With its bulbous shoulders and long arms, it could have been a monumental demonic gorilla. A pair of angry red eyes stared down at them balefully, and its mouth yawned open to loose a deafening roar that shook the chamber.

"Kat, fly!" Zack shouted at her.

Without hesitation she jumped, trusting his judgment. A wide laser beam from one of two shoulder mounted turrets, cut through the space she had stood a second ago. The laser left, a trail of molten metal across the floor, as if it was made to chop up whole buildings. She upped her wrist lasers to maximum output and fired on the monster, but her shots had no visible effect on it. The ape loosed a constant stream of deadly energy, while she weaved a random evasive pattern around the hanger.

On the floor Zack ran to the robot's truck size legs, blasting it with beams and pelting it with explosives. His weapons hurt it no more than her's did.

The titan swung a mighty arm at her contemptuously, as she might at an annoying fly, its hand slamming into the wall with a thunderous clang. It stomped its feet to crush Zack, but the soldier jumped and rolled out of the way, retaliating by shooting the ape's feet.

Continuing to dodge red bars of energy from the shoulder lasers, that magically never came close to the villainous catwalk, she returned fire on them. Like everything on the huge machine, the turrets were thickly armored and impervious to her attacks. It swatted at her again, coming alarmingly close to hitting her. She needed to come up with something soon, or it might squish her.

An arm came to her from the right, she dipped low, looping around it to come up behind the ape. "Zack, I need a distraction."

"On it." He immediately took a few shots at the ape's head.

The robot responded by reaching down to slap away the irritant, giving her a momentary opening. She used the time to land on the left shoulder next to the turret. She slashed at it viciously with her claws, feeling strong resistance as she tore chunks out of the armor plating. The turret turned in an attempt to target her, but she moved with it and kept slashing. Seconds later she cut into wires and circuits. The turret stuttered and sparked, then went still. Jumping off of the shoulder, she jetted up to the land on the right shoulder. She started slashing the second turret, but this time the monster was ready for her. It slapped at her heavily with the open palm of its left hand. She rolled off of the shoulder as the colossal hand crashed down, flattening the turret into a smoking pancake to save her the effort.

Her agility allowed her to turn feet down in the air, and, using her flightpack to reduce velocity, land gently on the floor. Not missing a beat, she took flight again. "No more mega lasers. Any ideas how to stop this thing?"

"Uh, not as such, no."

Reality was really closing in now. They had been blasting the ape for a while, but were simply not doing it significant damage. If something did not change, it could wear them down, maybe kill them.

Even without the laser turrets, the ape was a formidable foe, those long arms and legs were dangerous. They were big, heavy, and much too fast for their size. Dodging a swipe of an arm, she fired at its eyes hoping they were its only optical sensors. Again the ape was well designed, the eyes were protected despite looking vulnerable. The transparent material covering them proved a match for her lasers.

The sight of Zack scaling the robot's leg like a branchless tree, caught her attention for a careless moment of amusement, a distraction of a second, that nearly proved fatal. Her inattention gave the robot an opening to swat at her unseen. The back of a metal finger connected painfully with her left leg, slapping her to the floor like a wounded insect.

"Kat!" Shouted Zack from above.

Her head snapped up to see Zack drop from the robot's leg and run at her. He made it three strides, when massive fingers closed around him into a huge fist. The robot straightened, holding the prize up for inspection. Metal groaned and crackled as the robot clamped down on Zack, slowly crushing him.

"Hold." Commanded P5. The groaning stopped, but the pressure did not relent, suggesting a temporary reprieve. "It would seem little Kat, that our game has come to an end."

Irritated at the strange robot, she glared up at P5, and nearly collapsed in fear. What confronted her was more terrifying than anything she had ever known. Standing in front of the vile machine, hands held behind him and a laser pressed to his skull, was Mark.

"You are injured, your big friend is about to die, and your companion here is at my mercy. Go ahead young man, say farewell to your friend." P5 nudged Mark with the laser.

"It will be alright Kat. No matter what happens to me, remember who you are, good Kat, the hero of your story. Don't let rage control you, or pain overwhelm you. I don't want you to be demon Kat again. Always fight for good." Mark smiled warmly at her.

"That was eloquently spoken, and I apologize for this. But as I said, this is the end."

With a brilliant flash of blood red light, her world crumpled to the floor at P5's inhuman feet. She stared numbly at Mark's motionless body, a great empty void forming inside her. "No." She whispered. "It can't be."

"You have lost your dearest friend. How does that make you feel? Do you feel desperation, a deep need for more power to avenge him? Latch onto that need, draw it in and cultivate it. Pull it to your core and harness it. You must advance, the life of you other friend depends on it." Slowly, almost hypnotically, P5 extended a cold metal hand to the giant.

The robot again tightened its mighty fist, filling the hangar with a sound reminiscent of an aluminum can being crushed.

Time slowed to a standstill for Kat. She felt an indescribable anger toward the evil machine. Her family was gone, had been ripped from her by this robot, this monstrous artificial thing was responsible for everything. For all the things that had befallen them in the last week. For the attack on White Sheep, the deaths of her friends, the killing of Mika. And now it had killed her family right in front of her, the person who mattered more than anything, more than her own life. He was gone, Mark was gone, but he would not go alone. She wanted death, would be death. She desired nothing more than to tear the vile robot and its pet Grymal apart, slowly. She would make them pay, force them to feel every bit of the suffering they inflicted on others. Her vision clouded with red staring at the odious pair, her calf burning. Without Mark her life held no meaning, what became of her now was not important, so long as she got her revenge. She again looked at Mark, his face calm and peaceful.

"Don't let rage control you." Mark's voice whispered from a great distance. "I don't want you to be demon Kat again." His voice was stronger, penetrating her all encompassing hate. She strained to hear him, desperate for the smallest contact. Then she heard them, the first words he spoke to her. The words that meant everything, that saved her from a pit of self loathing and despair. "Good Kat." Said Mark clearly.

Her vision cleared, the red fog of rage and hate vanishing. She was good, she would not give in to the temptation of anger, would not let it take over. She would be a hero to make Mark proud. She looked to Zack, his silver faceplate shattering in the inexorable grip the ape's powerful hand, a million bits of glitter spraying out from his helmet. She would not lose another friend this day, the monster was going down.

An unimaginable surge of strength infused her, a great flood of pressure released from deep within. The normally dull pink lights of her armor flared to a dazzling vibrancy. It felt as though she had no limits, like nothing was beyond her reach.

The pain in her leg was forgotten, her body filled with new strength. Activating her flightpack, she flew to the huge machine.

Extending her claws, amazingly now edged with pink lasers, she slashed into the ape's thick fingers, her claws passing through without resistance. The broken digits released their captive, unwillingly dropping him from the robot's deadly grasp. She landed nimbly beneath Zack, catching him in her outstretched arms, while the last sparkling fragments of faceplate slowly rained on them. Carrying Zack to the far end of the room as if he weighed nothing, she laid him gently against the wall.

Time returned to normal for her as Zack spoke. "Kat?" His voice was weak.

"You can rest now Zack, everything will be fine. If you'll excuse me for a minute," she gazed at the monster lumbering toward them, rattling the robot scrap on the floor. "I have something to take care of."

She again flew, speeding at the ape. She easily evaded its slow, clumsy attempt to swat her, outmaneuvering its ponderous, clutching grasp. Somehow, in the last few minutes, the ape had ceased to be a threat to her. Swooping low, she slashed the back of one knee, severing hydraulic lines and actuators in a spray of fluid and sparks. The behemoth stumbled, landing heavily on the bad knee with a force that shook the hanger. The robot reached out with its good hand to arrest its fall, ringing the hanger like a gong.

While the mammoth machine was busy trying to stay upright, she landed on the shoulder above the supporting hand, and rapidly slashed two handed through the huge motor housed there. No longer able to support its own enormous weight with the shredded shoulder, it crashed face first to the floor. The impact of so many tons of mass on the hard surface was tremendous, indenting the metal several inches under the unimaginable weight of a building size torso. The near wall of the hanger bowed inward, drawn in by the distorted floor. The robot struggled to gain purchase on the smooth surface with its damaged hand, sliding across it like ice.

She did not give it a chance to recover, leaping onto the back of its hulking alloy torso. Defenseless, the robot could do nothing to prevent her from slashing it with both sets of claws, cutting into a neck wider than she was tall. Electrical sparks and lubricants sprayed from the deepening wound, igniting small fires. Then the head separated from its robotic body, falling to the floor with a resounding crash. She stepped off from the robot's back, staring into glowing red eyes the size of dinner plates, watching the evil light fade.

"You have done well this day." Said P5 sounding, of all things, pleased. "But you will face yet more formidable challenges. I wonder, can you remain successful? I will see you again, sooner perhaps, than you might expect." It gestured to Mark sprawled at its feet. "Oh, and do be sure to collect your young friend here." I would hate for him to be left behind. P5 exited through a door in the wall, green cape billowing behind it.

"That was lot of fun to watch. See you later sister." Said X energetically before following, P5. The door slid closed automatically, securing the villains' escape.

Gaze locked on Mark, she asked, "Are you alright?"

Zack heaved himself to his feet with a pained grunt. "I'll be fine Kat, go to him."

The lights on her armor faded to their normal pale color, along with the feeling of power. She retracted her helmet and hesitated, feeling empty now that the fight ended. Drawing a shaky breath, she flew to the catwalk where X and P5 had stood, and stared at the closed door. Bracing herself, she looked down at Mark. He was so peaceful laying there, he could almost be sleeping. Why did this have to happen? It was wrong, all wrong. What was she supposed to do without him?

She removed her gloves, and reached down to touch his face, then froze. There was warm wind on her fingers, he was breathing, Mark was alive. P5 had only stunned him, he really was asleep. She fell to her knees on the catwalk, strength abandoning her and tears streaming from her eyes. She hugged Mark hard to her armored chest, rocking him back and forth, "You're alive." She whispered. "Thank you, thank you."

Mark moaned, wriggling in her arms. "Kat." He said groggily. "You're crushing me."

She giggled and loosened her grip, but continued to hold him for a long time. She was whole again. Finally she released him and stared into his eyes smiling.

"It's okay Kat." He brushed tears from her cheek with an affectionate swipe of a thumb. She leaned her face into his hand. "I'm not going anywhere."

She nodded unable to speak, her eyes never leaving him as he stood to look over the rail.

"If you're ready, we should go down and help Zack explore the place." He pointed to where the super soldier was descending some stairs in the back corner.

Scooping Mark into her arms, she floated them down to land by the stairs, letting him go reluctantly. Together they followed Zack. They came to a long hallway, part of the underground facility the Hydro spoke of.

Zack forced open a sturdy locked door with armor powered strength, then stared inside. "It's okay everyone, we're friends. Mark, Kat, come have a look at this." He waved them over.

She walked to the door, taking Zack's place when he stepped aside. Not sure of what to expect, she was ecstatic to see a large cell positively crammed full of people. This was to be a rescue after all. Most of the people were sitting or lying on shelves bolted to the wall, a few stood on the stark, cold floor. They were dirty and forlorn, but also cautiously curious about these strange visitors.

A drawn out, high pitched squeak rose from the depths of the cell. A dark feathered blur ran at her, jumping to hold her tightly around the neck. "Kat it's you, you came for us. We were so scared since the robots attacked home and brought us here. But you're here, you can." Cried Riss.

"It's okay now Riss, you can go home. You can all go home." She hugged the sobbing girl, patting her back between the wings, and feeling a little better herself. Some of her friends, at least, were alive and could go home. "Mark, Zack. Let's open these doors and take everyone outside." She set Riss down.

"The interference is gone." Mark informed them. "Sky says things are under control out there."

Kat searched every face in the crowd as the cell doors were opened and people funneled out. Most of the people from White Sheep village were present, but also many who she did know. The robots had taken people from more than one unfortunate settlement. To her surprise there really were Hydros mixed in with the captives, marked out by their red and black uniforms, rumpled and dirty from their time in confinement. When she was certain that no one was left in the cells, entering each one to verify its emptiness, she ascended the stairs to the hangar seeking Tula. She spotted a familiar woman from White Sheep, a baby cradled in her arms.

"Malaka, have you seen Tula." The baby was cute.

Her pretty face haggard from the ordeal, Malaka shook her head sadly. "I'm sorry Kat, they took her an hour ago. She was with the group who left on the last ship. She's gone to wherever the robots send people. I know Mika died in the attack, but no one knows what happened to Korta or Raag, they were not brought here with the rest of us. I think some people may have escaped, and I hope Korta and Raag were among them." Malaka patted her arm in reassurance.

"Kat." Said Mark walking over. "I'm going outside, I need to have the swarms build vehicles to take everyone home in. There's a rugged bunch from a nearby mine here, and they agreed to stick around a while to keep an eye on the Hydros, make sure they behave themselves. There are also Hydros who refused to help the robots, the captives seem to trust them, so they can be left to run the plant." He smiled in amusement. "Zack is telling Hydros outside, that if they misbehave, Kat the giant slayer will come back and punish them." He headed to the door still smiling.

She trailed him, shaking her head in chagrin. "I hope the villagers don't start calling me that."

Riss, her sister Raven in tow, ran to her, catching her right at the hangar door. "Kat, Kat. Did you really cut the head off that humongous robot? The whole building shook real bad when you were fighting it, so bad we all fell down and thought it was an earthquake. And it was super loud with all the banging and stuff. I thought the building was getting smashed on top of us. You're so amazing Kat, no one's ever going to mess with you." She spoke almost as fast as Tula.

The XJ32 was parked not far from the door, its turrets tracking Hydros threateningly as they walked past carrying broken robot parts. It had to be intimidating for the Hydros, none of whom held a weapon.

Zack was talking loudly to a group of Hydros. He was Kind of like a broken robot himself in that half crushed armor. She recognized the four Hydros he was addressing, they were part of the bandit group that attacked Alex. She let anger show on her face as she stopped next to Zack.

"....Well, make sure that not a single Hydro attacks anyone else. Because if you don't, the giant slayer here." He hooked a thumb at her. "Will see that you join the giant. Am I clear?"

There was a mumble of wide-eyed assent.

"I said, AM I CLEAR?!" He bellowed.

"Yes sir!" They shouted in unison.

"Then get your lazy butts to work cleaning up this mess."

The hydros practically tripped over each other in their haste to flee from her.

She laughed softly when they were gone. "See that you join the giant?"

Zack scratched his cheek through the jagged hole where his faceplate used to be. "Yeah well, it sounded good, and you saw how scared they were. These guys are terrified of you. After what you did to that robot in there, I can understand why." His smile faded. "Listen Kat, I'm real sorry about what happened in there. I screwed up big, got myself captured. I was trained better than that, I should never have put you in that position. I nearly got us both killed, because I didn't think before I acted."

That was hardly something to be worked up over, especially given her own track record. Time to put his mind at ease. "Hey, don't worry. I screw up all the time. We're all alive and everything worked out, so learn from the mistake and move forward." She held out a hand.

He shook it. "You got it."

The street flooded with warm golden light. She looked east to see Riss haloed like an angel in the rising sun. "Let's take these people home."

EPILOGUE

The afternoon sun shone hot and bright on the two trucks, driving westward, destination far off and uncertain. Mark and Kat spent several pleasant days with their friends in White Sheep village before setting out with Zack, a sojourn to recharge spirits as much as batteries, and eat a pink cake or two. While there, the village was rebuilt and reimagined with the nanomachine swarms. The new buildings, and far more fortified wall around a much larger village, were constructed from the robot scrap left behind at the water plant, and the collection squad battle site. Virtually every robot part was retrieved and loaded into wide trucks built from the self same scrap, and hauled to the ruins of White Sheep behind the villagers. Every building was made of robot alloy, and equipped with solar panels and power crystals. New wall turrets were installed, patterned on the upgraded specifications from the XJ32. If crabs came again, White Sheep would be ready for them.

In addition to big cargo trucks for the scrap, Mark constructed long passenger vehicles Zack called busses, to carry people to their homes. Thankfully, most of the people of White Sheep were safe, and relatively unharmed. But there were villagers unaccounted for, including Korta, Raag, and Mallo.

Among the captives released from the water plant, were people from other villages, farms, a mine, and smaller settlements. These people were provided transportation and provisions to return to their homes, or to go wherever it was they wished. Many of their homes were decimated by the collection squads, their people flown away in dropships. A fair number of miners along with a few others, elected to stay at the water plant to help keep the Hydros in check. The Hydros for their part, were utterly pacified, disinclined to cause further trouble after the battle they lost to Sky and the trucks. They would stay in line, at least for a while. Besides, many of them resisted the robots, or outright refused to work for them.

Their little, three vehicle convoy had departed White Sheep two days ago, heading in the general direction the dropship had taken, a direct pursuit course being limited by the terrain. They would find where it went, and their friends would be rescued, no matter how long it took.

Before leaving the village, Mark had, as he always did, said exactly the right thing. "Let's bring Tula home."

THE END

Don't miss out!

Visit the website below and you can sign up to receive emails whenever Aaron Bennett publishes a new book. There's no charge and no obligation.

https://books2read.com/r/B-A-NXUU-VSOAC

BOOKS 2 READ

Connecting independent readers to independent writers.

www.ingramcontent.com/pod-product-compliance
Lightning Source LLC
Chambersburg PA
CBHW060406260626
47160CB00006B/2452